Ravek Hunter

For Mrs. Wife and my two boys,

Table of Contents

First Edition, November 2025

ISBN:

978-1-948782-26-5 (Hardcover)

978-1-948782-25-8 (paperback),

978-1-948782-24-1 (eBook)

Fantasy Novels by Ravek Hunter

The Broken Pithos Saga

Red Wizard of Atlantis #1

The Fallen #2

Shadows of Lyonesse #3

The Imaziɣen Druid #4

Beasts of Courth #5

Ys: Legend #6

Related Novels

Saving Eridu

If you enjoy reading books by this author, please remember to leave a review at your favorite bookseller!

To learn more about the backstory, mythology, and character development in these stories or to view world maps visit us at:

www.RavekHunter.com!

Ages of the Golden Aspen

From ancient days, humanity recorded their affairs in time framed within the linear concept of Past, Present, Future, and the singular egocentric certainty of a world central only to themselves. It was and is the Age of Man. Yet, it is not this Age that the story of Mother Earth begins. In fact, the Age of Man is where the story ends. So, we travel back far beyond the known scale of time to Ages past when the world would look strangely alien to modern eyes. It was a world with shifting land masses, oceans which rose and fell hundreds of feet congruent with ice ages that expanded as far as the 40th parallel from the north or retracted to reveal a lush landscape beneath the ice of Antarctica in the south. According to those who would catalog this time, it was the Age of the Golden Aspen. Four Ages of the Golden Aspen, to be precise, that spanned nearly four-hundred thousand years before an extinction level event known as the Cataclysm would herald the arrival of the Age of Man. Echoes of those lost peoples, their stories, and their civilizations would filter into the legends, mythology, and oral traditions of modern humans. Sadly, the credence of such tales would diminish over time until they were nothing more than curiosities in history books. Yet, what if they were true? What if the Four Ages of the Golden Aspen might have been? What stories, yarns or tales might be told of mighty civilizations, magic, mystery, and high adventure where heroes of destiny strove for lofty ideals, power, wealth, and love? Thus, the ancient chroniclers began their labor, committing words of their day to clay tablets, chiseled stone, reed and vellum, the hereto unknown accounts of peoples that called their world Plethwih.

The Chroniclers of Time

IT IS NOTABLE THAT the four Ages of the Golden Aspen and the time periods they individually spanned, are interpretations by an enigmatic group of the Sylvan race called the Watchers, a highly secretive order of druids. These chroniclers of time have become the accepted authority on the history of Plethwih by all the races through the Ages including those who ruled uncontested thousands of years before the first Sylvan civilization burst forth upon the Emerald Isle. Curiously, the rise of the Sylvan race and the first day of Sylvan Year (SY) 0 of their calendar correspond precisely with the beginning of the Third Age of the Golden Aspen. It is further recorded that the Watchers claimed that date as the inception of their organization as well. So, it is remarkable that through their extraordinary efforts of research, relationships with the more ancient races of Plethwih, and a peculiar connection to Spiritual Nature, that the Watchers should be so highly revered. In light of this, and with no other conflicting source by which to contest the veracity of the Watchers chronicles, they shall be considered the true and accurate record of the history of Plethwih. *

One might also ask why the Watchers identified all four Ages with a 'Golden Aspen' rather than a tree of any other species such as Spruce, Oak, or Willow unique to each Age. And why four and not two, five, or ten? The Sylvan offer no explanation. For them, the concept is unambiguous. There is one instance on record recited in the court of the Atlantean Emperor by a Watcher who wondered, *"The history of Plethwih is long. Why would one assume there were not Ages named to honor other varieties of venerated trees?"* This enigmatic reply persists as the subject of debate among priests, nobles, poets, and scholars as either a clue to a wealth of unknown history or a perplexing jest. As to this, one might suggest asking the Dverger Dwarfs whose rage has not lessened one fleck since the day they became the subject of what most consider the greatest Sylvan hoax of all time – the insinuation that the Dvergr are a creation of the Tuatha De. Although, it should be pointed out that the Sylvan historically show rare inclination toward roguish humor.

A word about calendars. Although every kingdom, humanoid race, and religious congregation have a form of calendar unique to their own history, agriculture, politics, and notable events - nearly all have adopted the Sylvan Year - if not the precise structure of weeks and months. This is remarkable considering the reclusive nature of Sylvan society and in no small part due to the exhaustive efforts of the Atlanteans who had the foresight to not only influence how developing nations recorded time, but to also engineer a form of common communication between all peoples everywhere. Both of which have proved instrumental in furthering trade and fostering peace between regional powers. More on that later.

A word about Spiritual Nature. From the start all Sylvan peoples, including the Watchers, held an unwavering reverence for a kind of divinity that inhabited Plethwih (Mother Earth) and everything that grew or rose within her embrace. Thus, mountains, stones, trees, plants, water, wind, and animal life are all considered parts of the greater 'being' called Spiritual Nature that has existed from the earliest days. The Watchers claimed the unique aptitude to 'see' the history of Plethwih via communion with Spiritual Nature; however, through what means ritual, arcane or otherwise is a deeply held secret of their order.

Finally, for reasons unknown to any except the Watchers, no specific date or event marks the start of the First Age of the Golden Aspen. The earliest reference to the First Age principally remarks on the emergence of an enigmatic people who called themselves Tuatha De and their initial efforts to shape the future of Plethwih. Thus begins the abstract of the chronicles encompassing the Four Ages of the Golden Aspen.

* In later times, when human chroniclers became the only extant source of historical documentation, the 'Ages' were classified, cataloged, and ordered based on different contexts of a wide-ranging understanding, interpretation, and religious philosophies of highly divergent cultures. However, one lasting source of note regards the combined third and fourth Ages of the Golden Aspen as the 'Thurian Age' and the first several thousand years of the Age of Man as the 'Hyborian Age' of which much has been written by noble sources.

The First Age of the Golden Aspen

THE FIRST AGE OF THE Golden Aspen began some 350,000 years before present time. A people of unknown origin calling themselves Tuatha De, swept out of the frozen north across the mountain range east of what would become the Sea of Dragons, south along the coast and into the heavily forested territory inhabited by pre-evolution tribes of ape-like Wild People. The Tuatha De were the first intelligent species to inhabit Plethwih, and their foray south was not for the usual purpose of plundering the resources gathered by others. This, the limited intellect of the Wild People might have understood. What they could not understand was that the Tuatha De came for slaves to build their cities on the southern edge of the Great Glacier. The squat, thick-limbed, stout frame of the Wild People could be well adapted to such work. Or so they believed.

The Tuatha De struck with orbs of fire thrown from bare hands, bolts of lightning called from the sky, and waves of thunderous force that could fell trees as easily as their hairy leather hide-clad prey. Yet seldom did the Tuatha De's demonstration of God-like powers cause injury or death to their quarry for that was not the purpose. Rather, their intent was to intimidate the apish brutes into cowed submission, round them up, and lash them together with silvery cords not even their primal strength could break.

Entire tribes were herded north to the valley under the shadow of the Great Glacier. The Wild People were a strong species with the fortitude to survive the rigors of this cold climate, but they were taken beyond the farthest migration of the mammoths they hunted, where even their extreme resilience would be sorely tested. Most accepted the enforced servitude. Their spirits were broken and they had no understanding of what these terrible 'Gods' wanted of them or how they might have displeased them. So early in their evolution, the Wild People communicated mainly with grunts and gestures with only a rudimentary concept of Gods and spirits manifested in the solitary custom of burial rituals. The strongest rose as their leaders, fire was a recent discovery, and slavery was a notion unknown in their burgeoning culture.

While the Tuatha De compelled many thousands of Wild People into forced labor during the First Age, tens of thousands more either evaded capture or were lucky enough never to encounter the Tuatha De in the first place. These 'free' Wild People developed complex language, art, and religion. It was common practice to record their way of life on cave walls and stone blocks - mostly depicting animals and hunting. Yet, scenes with strange-looking beings were also prevalent. Scenes surely inspired by the Tuatha De and the creatures they created.

The Tuatha De set the enslaved Wild People to the building of their first city utilizing massive blueish-grey stone cut from the leading ice flows of the Great Glacier. Once taught how to use the basic tools to extract the stone, they excelled at the task and, of course, dragging the heavy stone over the ice and snow was well within their physical adaptation. But the Wild People were keenly skittish when it came to the display of simple magic the Tuatha De would employ to shape the stones or apply the shimmering iridescent sheen that made them glow. Often these demonstrations caused a spontaneous panic among the hundreds of primitive workers that sent them fleeing across the icy tundra. Sometimes it would take days for the Tuatha De to round up and organize the scattered Wild People into work groups again. Worse still, when it came to the actual construction of complex structures, the Tuatha De found that even the most industrious of the primitive folk fell far short.

The Tuatha De were at an impasse - they would either accept the Wild Peoples physical and intellectual limitations or apply their godlike powers to improve the situation. Never a people to stand against progress, the Tuatha De embarked on an agenda whereby they would enhance the strength and fortitude of the enslaved Wild People beyond what they could have achieved naturally. They considered the physical alterations something of an artform that produced blasphemous modifications such as longer limbs, greater size, wings, or tentacles. Each alteration designed to perform a specific task with greater proficiently. Ultimately, the Tuatha De settled on a handful of variations and soon, powerfully built giants strode the glaciers transporting the building blocks of their earliest cities more efficiently than ever. The Tuatha De were pleased with their creations and gave them a name: Fomorians. Still, the modified Wild Peoples physical prowess alone did not alleviate the ancient fears of mysticism engrained deep within their consciousness, nor did it improve their ability to reason, or problem solve any better than before.

As it happened, a new humanoid species emerged from the warmer climate of the south. They were slight of build with dark sun-touched skin of various tones and a wandering spirit that compelled their migrations. The first humans rose upon the lush savannahs of Plethwih and with them came the Second Age of the Golden Aspen.

The Second Age of the Golden Aspen

IT WAS A TIME MARKED by great migrations of the first human populations throughout modern North Africa, Europe, the Levant, Asia and over the land bridge into North and South America. The less populous clans of Wild People (Neanderthal) slowly disappeared. Most through assimilation and breeding with humans, some through conflict, and the smallest numbers retreating deep into The Wilds to live reclusive, isolated lives. Language, burial rituals, and the first concept of a greater power manifested as spirits or Gods as the immortal embodiment of the sun, moon, earth, fire, and natural phenomenon that was so mysterious to folk at the time. And although humanity shared many common threads of early cultural development, the further apart they spread the more distinct and unique they became. This too resulted in a disparity of advancement as tribes north and east of the Levant were among the first to move beyond hunter/gatherer societies with the discovery of agriculture and irrigation. Permanent and semi-permanent settlements soon followed.

The Second Age would experience longer periods of Glacial and Interglacial cycles as the climate grew colder or warmer every hundred thousand years or so, forcing further migrations over time.

And what of the Tuatha De? They were immediately fascinated with the lean, graceful humans who so readily adapted to almost any environment they chose to inhabit. As they did with the Wild People, many humans were taken as slaves to serve in whatever capacity the Tuatha De required. And just like the Wild People, humans were subject to physical alterations and experimentation.

The Watchers suggest that this practice was indiscriminate as the Tuatha De regarded the Wild People, Humans, and beasts of fin, fur, and feather that roamed Plethwih with equal indifference - their fundamental goal simply to modify species to the tasks meant to be performed with the greatest efficiency. Their creations were many, and in the span of the Second Age creatures of the wildest imagination would labor for the pleasure of the Tuatha De. It wasn't until the Third Age that the Watchers cataloged with detailed descriptions several volumes of the Tuatha De's arcane handiwork; however, the Watchers conceded that what managed to record was likely only a small fraction of the whole. Some of the more well-known creatures included small canine humanoids designed for the brutal work of mining; they were given the name 'Kobolds'; another small humanoid with mostly human features specializing in extraction of precious gems from rock would later be known as the 'Kabouter.' Then there were the leanly muscled pig-faced brutes known as 'Orks' designed to keep order in the mining camps and quarries, and great reptiles with bat-like wings trailing sinuous tails capable of transporting heavy loads by flight were identified as the earliest dragons. And of course, the Fomorian and Cyclopean giant mutations from the first slaves taken from the Wild People. Thousands of species were created by the Tuatha De. Some were numerous, while others were unique. The preceding represents only a sampling of those who survived into the Third Age. With this powerful labor force, the Tuatha De built four gleaming cities in their vale: Falias, Gorias, Murias, and Finias, where they lived in undreamed-of comfort and luxury.

Fortunately for the natural inhabitants of Plethwih, the Tuatha De rarely travelled beyond the Vale of Glaciers they called home. Thus, they almost never encountered tribes of humans or human settlements unless they were collecting more slaves. With this exception, the vast majority of humans were unaware that the Tuatha De existed.

The Second Age of the Golden Aspen lasted nearly 300,000 years. At its close, humans inhabited nearly every corner of Plethwih. It was the dawn of civilization. Cities of mudbrick, wood, and stone rose next to irrigated crops. Complex language and writing were in use, and religion blossomed with ritual and tradition. Not all people looked the same anymore and many clustered together for protection and community. In the modern geography of Europe pale-skinned folk with blond, red and light brown hair dwelt in tribes that warred with each other for resources and worshipped pantheons of Gods. In Africa tribes of black-skinned people of many tones ranged vast savannahs following the endless herds of antelope and wildebeests, or farmed fertile lands along great rivers. Further east the 'black-headed people' became masters of irrigation. In Asia populations with dark hair, slanted eyes, and yellow-hued skin carved out lives in strict societies, and in the Americas tribes of ruddy-skinned hunters followed the buffalo across the plains or cleared jungles to build temples of stone. And there were innumerable smaller societies besides.

There also existed an island-continent of immense size that stretched from the northern glaciers to the moderate climate of the savannahs. It was lush with trees and foliage, especially in the northern parts, with a mountain range that ran the length of the western edge of the island like a giant's spine. It would be called The Emerald Isle for its thickly forested coastlines that reflected a vibrant green radiance like a sparkling gem. In the thickest densest tangle of said wood where nature was at its purest and unspoiled, a slight light-skinned people with pointed ears and wide almond-shaped eyes walked through the veil and into Plethwih for the first time. They were a people born of nature and magic with lives that spanned centuries. Sylvan was the name that represented their varied population of elves, centaurs, pixies, sprites and more. They needed a new home, and the isolated forests of The Emerald Isle would suit them just fine. With the Sylvan came the Watchers, and the Third Age of the Golden Aspen.

The Third Age of the Golden Aspen: *SY 0*

THE FIRST DAY OF THE first year (SY 0) of the Sylvan Calendar began to record time with the dawning of the new Age. The quiet reclusive Sylvan were not for some time first noticed by the Tuatha De. Nor were there any Human or Wild Folk inhabiting The Emerald Isle to cast their curious gaze upon the newest arrivals to Plethwih. Not so for the Sylvan Watchers. Their seamless blend with nature allowed them to observe the peoples of Plethwih undetected. It was just as well. Otherwise, the gentle Sylvan might have been drawn into a cataclysm beyond their comprehension.

By Sylvan Year (SY) 2113, the Tuatha De were fractured and divided. Two major groups were at odds with many smaller groups falling somewhere in between. Their disagreement centered around the conduct of their own people with the largest faction led by a man called Dhroghan and woman named Laghfrin. These two claimed stewardship over Plethwih, protecting its natural inhabitants rather than enslaving or corrupting their natural forms into grotesque objects of grueling service to unsympathetic masters. While the other major faction despised the lowly beings of Plethwih demanding their right to subjugate and use as they pleased the inferior life forms, arguing that it was, in fact, the reason the Tuatha De chose Plethwih as their home in the first place. Eochu Bres, the cruel leader of the dissenting faction, compelled his followers to combine their magic to create a powerful artifact – the Radiant Crown - that Bres hoped would give his faction an advantage over the others.

The Watchers carefully scrutinized the Tuatha De, noting with no small curiosity how they appeared almost physically identical to the Humans that populated much of Plethwih. Only the faint aura of one color or another that most times bounded the frames of the Tuatha De and their strange shimmering robes caused them to stand apart. This carnal similarity would incite heated debate among the most enlightened Sylvan Scholars and powerful Arcanists for centuries to come.

There were children among the Tuatha De as well. Children born from the pure blood of Tuatha De parents as at that time no Tuatha De would consider copulation with an inferior species. In time, the Watchers would consider the children of the Tuatha De among the greatest tragedies of what was to come.

Centuries passed. No resolution, mediation, or accord could be reached between the factions. This puzzled the Watchers. The scant two millennia they had observed the Tuatha De in addition to the ancient knowledge passed on to them by the mysterious spirits of nature, revealed a subtle transformation over time in the Tuatha De that they had not noticed in themselves. So faint and cunning was the change, it was almost insidious in the imperceptible artfulness of the alteration that the entire Tuatha De population, counted over a thousand at the time, should be infected so uniformly. Yet, even as the Watchers became aware of the slow pestilence, they made the shocking connection to its source. And it was impossible to explain, for just as the Tuatha De corrupted the mind and body of their Human slaves, their own immortal magic worked against them by transferring, in turn, a piece of Humanity. It was the most savage and feral survival instinct Humanity possessed - Human Nature. The Tuatha De unknowingly infused themselves through arcane transference that which they believed set them apart from the lower cast, yet was that which tore them asunder. And they knew not why.

As throughout much of history, it began with a spark. From where or whom it came none could say. Suddenly, the Tuatha De, previously ignorant to the concept of war, were full upon it in a conflict of immortals who used their terrible creations against each other to devastate their rivals' cities instigating a catastrophic loss of life, both mortal and immortal, that raged across the whole of Plethwih. It was a conflict of feral savagery fueled by revenge, hatred, bitter loss that up until that time was unknown and unfelt. Incited by desperate fury, Eochu Bres joined with the surviving Tuatha De of his faction and drew arcane energy wild and unconstrained through the Radiant Crown that taxed its immeasurable power beyond capacity. And when they sought to release their wrath upon their enemies, an implosion rent the earth in a devastating collapse of negative force that shook the planet, tearing time and space, cleaving a rift in the heart of Plethwih that opened a portal to the Infernal Planes.

Eochu Bres and his followers were obliterated, along with a preponderance of the opposing Tuatha De. What they left behind, at a cost incalculable, would be later termed *The Breaking*. Perhaps incalculable to the Tuatha De. The Watchers knew precisely: barely half a hundred Tuatha De survived. Of these, the greatest in both power and moral distinction was Dhroghan and Laghfrin. Through the arcane efforts of these few Tuatha De was the rift to the Infernal Planes sealed beneath a crystalline barrier impervious to the gnashing maws and rending claws of unadulterated evil. Still, seven Greater Demon Lords - Tephras, Aesmadaeva, Mamon, Ornias, Alu-Abad, Yalal, and the worst of them - Ba'lzbl, plus thirteen unnamed lesser fiends simply known as Chaos Demons, slipped through the rift before it was closed.

The Sea of Glass, as the barrier would be known, was a temporary resolution to a problem with no permanent solution. And yet, despite all they bore upon their shoulders, the Tuatha De found the strength to banish what remained of the terrible creatures they created before *The Breaking* to a frozen land north of the Sea of Dragons they called Fomoire. In this harsh climate only the strong and clever survived. Many thousands died forever unknown and uncatalogued by the Watchers. And many hundreds survived or escaped beneath the distracted noses of the Tuatha De who did their best to track down and destroy any that dared to escape whilst Plethwih was ravaged by the scourge of demons.

As yet unseen and unknown, the Watchers recorded numerous contrived creatures of the Tuatha De that found their way to freedom in The Wilds. The Orks proliferated in the south, dragons, chimera, and other ferocious beasts of flight flew off to distant lands, trolls and goblins leveraged their stealthy talents to skulk away unseen, and many other species terrible and mundane somehow fell below the vigilant guard of the Tuatha De, but not the Watchers.

Consequently, only thirty-two years after *The Breaking* did the Dvergr Dwarfs emerge upon the surface of their island home of Tirnan Yog. The Sylvan date of SY 2145 marks the first Forge Year (FY) on the Dverger Calendar. The stout, broad shouldered Dwarfs lived below the ground tending the volcanic forces that grumbled far under their isle and reaped the rewards of gems and ore mined as a labor of love and compulsion as much as the material gain of wealth and prosperity.

Eochu Bres left one other thing behind – the Radiant Crown – sundered into four pieces. Dhroghan knew that if *The Breaking* could not destroy it, then nothing could. Instead, the Tuatha De used their powers to construct four mystical towers in obscure places far apart from one another, and a fourth of the Radiant Crown was placed in each one. Once this was done, the towers were sealed and protected for all time.

Thirteen hundred years passed as the Watchers stood witness to the plight of an immortal race resigned to bear the weight of their ancestors' sins upon their shoulders. This might have been the providence of the mighty Tuatha De chained by their own choosing to protect a world they nearly destroyed themselves - until an unexpected event occurred that surprised even the diligent Watchers. It was an advent that would profoundly shape the future of Plethwih and bring an end to the Third Age of the Golden Aspen after only thirty-five hundred years.

The Fourth Age of the Golden Aspen: *SY3487*

THE FIRST ANCESTORS of the Atlanteans came unto Plethwih. The Watchers record this momentous occasion thus:

It was from the stars they came, out of the vast darkness of the Primeval Cosmos, plunging from the sky in a great wingless beast consumed by smoke and fire. It fell with a thunderous crash upon the earth, plowing a long black rift across the open plain before it shuddered to a stop with an impressive display of sparks and lightning. The shining silver shell of the massive creature lay shattered and smoking where it came to rest, yet from its broken maw hundreds of odd-looking figures crawled through the acrid haze to stumble disoriented onto the lush green grass of a new world.

The Sylvan Watchers witnessed the arrival of the newcomers from the quiet repose of the forest. They scrutinized these strange bi-pedal aliens with blue-tinted skin, elongated skulls, and large almond-shaped eyes who came uninvited to their tranquil isle that up until that day lay isolated and protected from intrusion by the vast expanse of the Primal Sea. The Watchers observed how the survivors worked as a collective to remove the shiny scales of their battered host piece by piece to make shelters or cover the bodies of their dead. Unlike the Sylvan, these folk buried rather than burned the dearly departed, and they mourned their passing rather than celebrated their passage to the afterlife.

When that was done, they brought red glowing crystals that shone bright even in daylight from the metallic frame of the silver beast's remains. The crystals they handled with great care and reverence, depositing them in caverns deep in the earth near an inlet on the coast. Whether to hide or protect them the Watchers did not know. It was there too that they built the first structures with stones.

These were a people with no hope of return or rescue, determined to survive and resolute in their struggle to make a place for themselves. A permanent place that would bring irrevocable change to the Isle, to the land, to nature, to a way of life that existed long before their abrupt arrival.

The prophecies spoke of events such as these that would herald the beginning of the Fourth Age of the Golden Aspen, the Age when the winds from the north would bring an icy chill even in the summer and end the elves isolation from the rest of the world forever.

Still, the Sylvan Watchers watched with pragmatic detachment.

In time, the Sylvan learned that the unusual, blue-tinted people called themselves the followers of Atlan, the one who was the first to rise above the others offering leadership and hope for a new future. They would name the spine of the isle in his honor and build a shining city on the sea that would become known as the City of Atlantis.

And they thrived.

Recorded in the Fourth Age of the Golden Aspen
by Watcher CrellianRafkarSil of Avalon

It is a matter of some debate among the Sylvan Watchers the precise cause that triggered the beginning of the Fourth Age as more than one significant event commenced at that time. There was the arrival of the Atlanteans, an otherworldly people, and the start of a climactic change, later classified as the Younger Dryas (YD), that affected the whole of Plethwih. Most Watchers believed that since it was the 'Nature Spirits' that gave life to Plethwih and determined when the Ages began and ended, that it must be the Younger Dryas. Others speculated that the sudden instigation of the Younger Dryas was simply Plethwih's reaction to the Atlanteans arrival. While an even smaller division of Watchers believed the turning of a new Age had nothing to do with either one or the other.

Whatever the catalyst, the Fourth Age had arrived. Within the first few decades the glaciers rapidly advanced as far as the 50th parallel in some places, and temperatures dropped across the globe compelling human migration to follow the herds to warmer regions. In this Age, agriculture would take root, settlements would rise to civilizations, trade and commerce would bridge the divide between far-flung cultures. It would be an Age of scholarly pursuits, poetry, art, and literature of the highest form. And magic. But this awakening would not take place until after the first thousand years of this Age, as seven Greater Demons and thirteen Demons of Chaos were loose in Plethwih bent on the subjugation of all living things. In these years, pandemonium reigned freely across all lands.

Yet, even in these tumultuous times great strides were made by those cultures powerful enough to resist the diabolic influence of the Demons. While early humans quickly found themselves under the brutal lash of fiendish masters, the Atlanteans, Sylvan and Dvergr were largely unaffected. Less than five centuries into the Fourth Age did the great City of Atlantis appear on the southeastern shores of the Emerald Isle. It was an urban beauty from the start, built upon rings of land separated by wide channels of water encircling a mountainous island capped by a gleaming Temple dedicated to Pontus, God of the Seas. Atlantis was the jewel of the burgeoning Atlantean Empire rivaling the fantastical cities of the Tuatha De and even the natural beauty of the Sylvan capital, Avalon. A century later, the Dvergr Dwarfs constructed the foundations of Aquilon, on the southern edge of the Sylvan Forest in Atlantean territory and Andlang a few leagues further north on the eastern coast of the Sylvan Kingdom. The Dwarfs placed a massive sculpture of white marble in the center of each of the cities displaying the proud likeness of an Atlantean, Sylvan Elf and Dvergr Dwarf standing together in friendship. It was a stunning work of art and a powerful statement of concord between their peoples and by means of an elaborate celebration, the Dvergr formally gifted Aquilon to the Atlanteans and Andlang to the Sylvan. The year was SY4000, henceforth commemorated as the 'Year of Unity'.

The Dvergr Dwarfs, even in those early days, would never have been mistaken for a compassionate people and so it must be considered a sign of desperate times that their reclusive nature gave way to pragmatic wisdom. For they knew that the only path to survival was by aligning with the Sylvan and Atlanteans if they had any chance of purging the demons loose upon the earth. It was the beginning of a coalition that would soon grow to include the still powerful Tuatha De and the primitive, yet numerous Human populations gathered from the furthest reaches of Plethwih.

This Age would prove as tumultuous as any other. The demons who succeeded in crossing the barrier between the Infernal Planes and Plethwih before it was sealed arrived in physical forms described by the Watchers as vulgar, unnatural, grotesque. The Chaos Demons stood roughly the height of a tall Human man with ruddy leather-like skin, lean muscular frames, sharp claws completing disproportionate large hands and feet, with a long spike-tipped tail and red-glowing eyes under a thick brow crowned by twisted horns organically suited for impaling their adversary. There were thirteen, and they all appeared identical.

The same could not be said for the Demon Lords. Each was unique from another in both appearance and the horrors they could inflict upon the living. A Demon Lord's very presence wrought terror in those that gazed upon them. They were physically enormous – at least five times the height of a human man – each commanding a horde of nightmarish half-human, half-demon fiends compelled to aid them in battle. To make matters worse, the Demon Lords possessed powerful psionic aptitude; mental powers with the capacity to dominate or destroy another creature's mind.

So hideous was their visage that the Watchers dared describe only one in part thus: *"Its body was red like the crimson of human blood, bestowed with a muscular, humanoid physic that bore no clothing at all, and it towered over every living thing casting a shadow to rival the tallest trees ever known. From its maw great mandibles clacked mercilessly over row upon row of teeth longer than the longest broadsword, its eyes glowed blood red with a black pupil split in the center like those of a snake, and long pointed horns protruded from the top of its head to complete the perfect nightmare."* Which of the seven Greater Demon Lords this one represented is unknown.

For nearly two thousand years the demons were free to cause whatever havoc they pleased upon Plethwih. Humans suffered the brunt of the demons wickedness as thousands succumbed to their wrath or pleasure. Humanity may have disappeared forever had not the demons been so distracted with fighting amongst themselves vying for power. In time, such diversions would be their undoing.

While the demons waged war upon each other, the Sylvan, Dvergr, Atlanteans, Humans and Tuatha De formed a coalition so named the

'Alliance of the Free Peoples of Plethwih' for the purpose of opposing the demons and purging their evil presence in every land. They chose the man named Dhroghan, immortal hero of the Tuatha De, to lead them. Under his leadership, the alliance quietly gathered resources, trained warriors, mentored capable Humans in the use of magic, and diligently studied every detail about the demons and their minions that might reveal vulnerabilities, if any existed. By SY4048, nearly five decades after the "Year of Unity", the Allied Peoples of Plethwih were ready, and so began the Demon Wars or, as the Humans would term the decades that followed, 'The Generation of Sorrow'.

It started on the northern plains of the continent west of the Emerald Isle. Dhroghan combined the forces of Atlantis with the wiry ruddy-skinned Hisat'sinom tribes of humanity led by their War Chief Tekweneee'n, 'the Great Owl Who Watches.' The natives looked with wonder at the Atlantean warriors exhibiting elongated skulls, blue-tinted skin clad in translucent Aurinium armor that fit like a carapace over their tall, lean figures. To the Hisat'sinom, the Atlanteans looked like ants. Thus, the tribal folk of the plains would always refer to the Atlanteans as the *Anu Sinom*, or 'Ant People.'

Dhroghan led the first assault on a Chaos Demon laired deep within the Sacred Mountains, but the fiend was not alone. Packs of distorted shape-shifting humanoids fathered and corrupted by the demon swarmed from subterranean burrows to defend the fiend, fighting savagely with mindless disregard for their own lives. For seven days the battle raged through canyon and cavern, and each day Dhroghan slaughtered the Chaos Demon. Yet, with every morning dawn the fiend emerged again from a darkened hollow to fight on. Finally, the Tuatha De withdrew his forces to the grassy steppes to reconsider his strategy. Forty days passed. While the warriors ate piki, smoked tobacco and hunted small game with their dogs, Dhroghan and the tribal shamans spent their days in the Sacred Kiva communing with Kachinas of the spirit world. When he came out of the Hisat'sinom temple, Dhroghan knew what must be done, and on the next full moon Dagda-Dana Laghfrin, the Tuatha De Wizard Queen of Falias, arrived with a score of powerful Tuatha De Mages in tow.

Laghfrin conjured a dark cloud over the Sacred Mountains to blind the Chaos Demon to their activities on the steppes as she assembled her mages and the Hisat'sinom shamans in the construction of a powerful artifact from consecrated clay which they placed into a man-sized pottery jar imbued with spirit magic. This, she gave over to Phalaeh, Dhroghan's sister, who was a powerful Tuatha De sorceress. She inscribed enchanted symbols upon the vessel that would make it unbreakable. When it was done, the beautifully engraved jar stood gleaming in the sunlight. The Sacred Pithos was complete. Dhroghan bade Laghfrin lift her dark cloud as he gathered the Atlantean and Hisat'sinom warriors once again and swept into the Sacred Mountains. This time he went forth in the company of Laghfrin, Phalaeh, the Tuatha De Mages, and a magical pithos designed for one purpose.

As expected, hordes of contorted humanoids shapeshifting from animal forms riddled with mange and vile disease erupted from holes and hollows seeking blood to assuage their hunger. The Chaos Demon drove them fearlessly to confront Dhroghan and found itself confined within a transparent arcane bubble conjured by the adept sorcery of Laghfrin and her Tuatha De. Dhroghan knew they could not kill the demon, nor could they banish it back to the Infernal Plains while the rift was sealed by the Sea of Glass. All that was left was to confine it forever in an inescapable prison. Phalaeh brought forth the pithos, and into it Laghfrin and the Tuatha De Mages forced the Chaos Demon's essence inside. But there was more. The spirit magic within the shimmering confinement of the pithos stripped carnal flesh from the shrieking Chaos Demon separating its physical anatomy from the indestructible essence deep within so that it would atrophy over time to no more than a shade of what it once was.

From the tribal plains of the Hisat'sinom, Dhroghan trekked south with the Atlanteans and Tuatha De Mages into the jungles where the Jaguar King, Tuocelotl, reigned over a vast empire of pyramid cities connected by a complex network of roads paved with stone. In this dark rainforest two more Chaos Demons were confined to the pithos. From there, the Atlanteans returned home via ship while the Tuatha De used magical means to cross the Primal Sea and join the Chief of the Grass People, Amgar N'rrbi Suub, leader of the ebon tribes. Six clans of Sylvan Centaurs arrived from the Emerald Isle about the same time, and through their collective efforts, the number of captured Chaos Demons grew to six. Dhroghan then led the Tuatha De to the far east where they assisted the Yellow Thearch, Huangdi, with bringing several tyrannical city-states along the 'Mother River' under his rule through conquest and diplomacy. With the help of this burgeoning Dynasty, four more Chaos Demons lost their freedom. Turning south, Dhroghan and the Tuatha De hastened to the coastal city of Dvaraka in the Kingdom of Meluḫḫa. The King, Rega Durai, called upon the tribes of the valley to join the Tuatha De in their hunt which soon delivered two more Chaos Demons to the dreaded pithos. Only one fiend remained of the thirteen. Dhroghan soon discovered it was terrorizing the lands southwest of the Sea of Dragons and with the support of several northern barbarian clans, Laghfrin forced the last Chaos Demon into the pithos.

In SY4055, on a farmstead outside the seaside village of Ys, Dhroghan assembled the Alliance of the Free Peoples of Plethwih for the purpose of devising a plan to confine the Greater Demon Lords within Phalaeh's pithos. Although there was only seven Demon Lords to contend with, their power far outmatched that of the Chaos Demons, and they also controlled hordes of fiends bred over centuries of insatiable rapine coition with human populations.

Emperor Zamfer of House Atlan brought hundreds of Atlantean Marines and scores of Wizards; many from the Yellow Hall of the Imperial Enclave of Wizards, who specialized in psionics. The Sylvan Elf High-King RalnapianCalithIlon arrived with contingents of Elven Archers and Sword Masters, potent Arcanists, calvaries of Centaurs, and a forest of animated trees they called Treants. Brak Iron-Teeth, Lord of the Dvergr, led ranks of Heavy Infantry and Pike from Tirnan Yog. Queen Laghfrin represented the Tuatha De. And then there was the charismatic Human, Anlawd Dormont, the recently installed ruler of the unified clans from across the lands that would later become the Western Kingdoms. These pale brawny barbarians numbered in the thousands and constituted the bulk of the Alliance's fighting force.

It was decided that rather than chase down the Demon Lords wherever they might be in Plethwih, a select few Tuatha De led by Dhroghan would lure the Demons, one by one, to an open stretch of land one hundred leagues east of Ys where Laghfrin and the Alliance would be waiting with the pithos. It was a daring plan that took thirty-three years and cost thousands of lives before the last Demon Lord was finally trapped within the pithos. At the location of the last battle, row upon row of monoliths stretching over a league were placed to honor the dead and forever commemorate their sacrifice. Dhroghan declared it a sacred place and called it Carnac. So ended the Demon Wars.

The next several hundred years marked a period of peace across Plethwih. With the rise of the Western Kingdoms, Ys grew from a small village to a prosperous trade port. Anlawd Dormont, a devout worshiper of the Sun Goddess Sunna, and the barbarian clans so devoted built Yorwick and proclaimed him king. His descendants would go on to establish the Kingdom of Lyonesse. Other clans broke off to settle city-states, each ruled by their own king. Several of these independent cities with populations that revered Eriu, Goddess of the Land and Fertility, formed a loose confederacy in her name. Westward into the Primal Sea, many of the seafaring barbarians erected the first Vikja settlements on a large island near the Dvergr home of Tirnan Yog and would soon form a strong trade alliance.

The rise of the Eastern Kingdoms followed similarly with several smaller cities governed by a king or council. And in the south between The Wilds and the Great Sea, the logging Kingdom of Courth rose to prominence as many of the roving tribes on the Plains of Tarre crossed the Bodin River and settled in the lush valleys in the shadow of the Spine of Cel. The powerful theocratic city-states established by these folk would form a federation to be known as the League of Free Peoples in Rasna ruled by an Over-King. Other tribes migrated west where they cultivated the land and founded Provigi, the first city in Tarre.

Although the druids had been a murky presence associated mainly as tribal shamans, they became a prominent influence once Humans began to build cities. Shamans who settled in the cities established temples devoted to a single deity and served the populace as priests. However, most of the shamans preferred to maintain their devotion to many deities and spirits, and so remained connected to nature. They built enclaves in remote places away from population centers yet continued to serve rural settlements as healers and leaders of faith. These were the first organized druids with their own rules, laws, hierarchies, and a calendar characterized by the natural passing of seasons called an Oak Year (OY). To the frustration of many monarchs, the druids placed their loyalties in faith rather than kingdoms and after a few disastrous attempts to subjugate the druids, the monarchs grudgingly learned to tolerate their autonomy.

In other parts of Plethwih, tribes of Grass People on the fringes of the Ibhr Rrbi cultivated agriculture and built the cities that would become the kingdoms of the Mouillians and the Capsians while others sought to preserve their ancestral traditions and formed the Imaziyen tribes. All around the Great Sea civilizations were rising from the dust. Seafaring merchants and wagon traders traveled far and wide and with them came new ideas, innovations, tradecraft. The city-states of Hellas grew out of the migrations of the Enchele and Thraix tribes, the Sicans began as settlers from Hellas and later absorbed migrations from the Grass People and the tribal folk from the Plaines of Tarre. The city-states of Kur-Gal rose along the Idigna and Buranuna Rivers from hunter-gatherer tribes that mastered agriculture through irrigation. The Hisat'sinom clung tightly to their traditions and continued following the vast herds across the lush plains on the continent west of the Emerald Isle just as the Huangdi Dynasty and the Meluhha Valley Kingdom far to the east slowly expanded their influence over the tribes, villages, and settlements in their respective regions.

For nearly five-hundred years after the Demon Wars Plethwih enjoyed global peace. Yet, as would happen throughout the history of Humanity, greed and lust for power would eventually beget a never-ending cycle of conflict and violence. By SY4480, House Dormont founded the Kingdom of Lyonesse and began to exert territorial claims further away from its new capital of Yorwick. At first, the various cities, villages, and townships east of Lough Greely were eager to join a kingdom dedicated to the worship of Sunna as they were. All except the fiercely independent city-state of Cambria whose population largely revered Sunna yet included nearly as many worshipers of Eriu and Lunna. After inciting insurrection within the walls of Cambrian by citizens devoted to the Sun Goddess, Lyonesse marched on the beleaguered city and within a fortnight it fell. The city-states of Eriu quaked with fear that Lyonesse might continue its conquests westward, but the anticipated invasion was forestalled when a delegation of Tuatha De arrived in Teamhrach with a magical stone they called *Lia-fal* – Stone of Destiny. It was upon this stone in SY4487 that Dhroghan was coroneted as the first High-King of Eriu uniting the confederacy as a strong deterrent to Lyonesse's aggression. Once again, peace and prosperity ruled the Western Kingdoms as they learned to get along and trade with each other. Dhroghan abdicated the throne after one year and the Congress of Eriu comprised of all the kings of the member city-states chose a new ruler from among their own.

In this time the brother kings of a newly formed kingdom centered on the Aur River in the southeastern region of the Great Sea proclaimed their land would become two – Ta Mehu and Ta Shemau. Each ruled by one of the brothers. The twin kingdoms instituted a new calendar titled the Year of the Land or Ta-rnpt (TR) in SY4621. Further west, hundreds of Grass People migrated to a cluster of isles off the Mouillian Coast. They discovered the isles were inhabited by the descendants of Sylvan Centaurs who aided the Grass People and the Tuatha De trapping a Chaos Demon five hundred years previous, but they never quite made it back to the Emerald Isle. These were the Isles of Gades, ruled by a Sylvan Nymph Queen, and despite the natural Sylvan reluctance to mingle with humans, the immigrants were welcomed.

Peace in the Western Kingdoms was shattered again by an unexpected source: the druids. Initially the people of the Western Kingdoms believed the Druids of Eriu, Sunna and Lunna were at odds with each other. This was especially strange since the druids revered all three Goddesses giving preference to one or another only during rituals at certain times of the year. The druids had done more than anyone to blur the lines between the deities so there would be no repeat of conflict among worshipers of different deities as happened in the early days of Lyonesse. Only the priests remained exclusively loyal to Sunna, Lunna or Eriu, but they were tolerant of the others and as confused as anyone about hostilities between the druids. What the royalty, nobles, priests, and druids either did not realize or refused to see, was that the long peace that brought prosperity to the

Western Kingdoms also left out a huge swath of the populations. With their cries drown out in the exuberance of parties, balls, and celebrations so frequent in affluent society, those who went without turned to an obscure cult-like sect of druids called the Atiod-Bherto. For centuries they were shunned and hidden. Every kingdom declared them outlaws and banned their heinous rituals. The Atiod-Bherto worshiped the 'Horned-One,' practiced human sacrifice on their recumbent stone altars, and promised dark powers to those who joined them. The centuries of peace had swelled their ranks with desperate followers willing to do anything to relieve their impoverished situation. By SY4854 the Atiod-Bherto had grown powerful and confident. They came out of the shadows with their masses and made war upon the druids of Sunna, Lunna and Eriu. The war would last over one-hundred years, cost tens of thousands of lives and bring the Western Kingdoms to their knees. The druids referred to the hostilities as the *Oak War* considering that the oak was their symbol of nature and life, but the struggle was not limited to the druids. Death and suffering would permeate every level of society throughout the Western Kingdoms and set the stage for a conflict that would end one of the most prominent royal lineages in Plethwih.

While war raged between the druids, another long held dispute erupted into violence on the far side of the Great Sea. In SY4935, descendants of the brother kings who ruled TaMehu and Ta Shemau were at odds over trade and shipping rights. In a surprise action, Ta Mehu swept into Ta Shemau with thousands of shock troops and hundreds of war chariots that devastated the northern half of the kingdom. The city of Tjenu was the first to fall after feeble resistance and a month later Naqada submitted. It appeared Ta Shemau was teetering on the verge of defeat. Full of confidence, the ruler of Ta Mehu pushed his weary forces to take Waset, but they were met in the grasslands outside the city walls by the well-rested armies of TaShemau and their allies from the Kingdom of Kerma. The battle lasted three days and resulted in TaMehu forced to retreat to their stronghold in Naqada where they were surrounded and besieged for over a year. During that time Ta Shemau liberated Tjenu and fortified its northern border preventing Ta Mehu from sending troops to break out their forces trapped in Naqada. When the starving troops finally surrendered, they were given no quarter. Thousands of TaMehu soldiers were executed, and their heads were placed on poles lining the border between the kingdoms with their bloody vacant gaze facing northward. Several more years of skirmishes followed, gaining nothing for either side until a peace treaty ended the *War of the Brothers* in SY4957.

A decade later, the *Oak War* ended in the Western Kingdoms. The Atiod-Bherto was defeated and what remained of their cult was driven back into the shadows. While the end of hostilities and violence was a relief, a century of destruction left a devastated infrastructure, crops abandoned, and livelihoods in tatters that brought the Kingdom of Lyonesse to the brink of collapse. Lyonesse had borne the brunt of the ruin in the wake of the *Oak War*, but the people and the other kingdoms offered little sympathy. Blame for the war was set squarely at the feet of House Dormont in Yorwick and there was no shortage of resentment. In the decades that followed, the people tried to rebuild their lives, but the disparity between the misery of the commonfolk and the nobles of House Dormont, in addition to the unyielding high taxes inevitably brought the kingdom to a breaking point.

In SY5159, the Duke of House Monmouth led a revolt of the citizenry of Lyon's Gate against the tyranny of the King and House Dormont which quickly grew into a Civil War. Small skirmishes fanned the flames as the noble houses allied with one side or the other. In a move that enraged the King, the Priesthood of Sunna abstained from supporting House Dormont and to no one's surprise the druids followed suit. But the real shock to the whole of the Western Kingdoms came when the Temple Knights, who were certain to support the King, withdrew from Yorwick and declared their order neutral. One great battle determined the outcome of the war and fate of Lyonesse. It took place on the expansive flatlands one hundred leagues west of the Thayre River, southwest of Yorwick. The army fielded by the King and House Dormont far outmatched that of the Duke of House Monmouth whose forces included far fewer professional soldiers and less than half as much heavy cavalry. The outcome seemed assured until, at the last minute, the Temple Knights withdrew their neutrality and joined the Duke. Still, the outcome was far from certain. The battle raged back and forth across the field for hours until the King lost confidence and attempted to flee back to Yorwick. A mob of common citizens intercepted his retreat and tore the King to pieces. His fate was no different for every member of House Dormont, effectively ending the lineage forever. Their bodies were buried in unmarked graves in the fields of the last battle along with countless soldiers, knights, and citizens who lost their lives for the cause of hope. After the Duke of House Monmouth was coroneted as the new King and the capital was moved from Yorwick to Lyon's Gate, a monolith was erected at the center point of the battlefield proclaiming that place to be forever known as *The Dormonts*.

After the Demon Wars, the Sylvan and Atlanteans kept mostly to the Emerald Isle. Behind the scenes, the Atlanteans were monitoring the Human kingdoms. Unbeknownst to all but a few nobles, High Priests and Arch Druids, the Emperor's Court in the City of Atlantis was extremely concerned with the volatile nature of Humanity. How the Atlanteans could influence peace and prosperity in all lands was often a subject for debate. Every year, the emperor gathered representatives from many lands around Plethwih, especially those at odds with one another, to encourage peace through trade and cooperation. These conferences usually ended with promises of good will that were short-lived or quickly forgotten. It was during one such conference that a young child of one of the Atlantean nobles made a simple observation commenting to her mother, "How do the Humans talk to each other with so many languages?" The emperor happened to overhear the girl's remark, triggering an epiphany that would change the world.

For some time, Atlantean Emissaries were a common sight in the Kingdom of Kur-Gal, and particularly the city-state of Eridu. Something big was happening. Shortly after the Battle of the Dormonts, the Atlantean presence exploded in Eridu as day after day flying ships arrived shuttling Atlanteans back and forth from the Emerald Isle. It was soon apparent to anyone in Eridu that the Atlanteans were building an enormous tower utilizing a huge labor force of native folk calling themselves Sag-gig-ga working alongside scores of Atlantean Wizards whom they referred to as the *Anunnaki*.

The tower was completed in SY5172. It was an impressive structure constructed with white marble stone unknown in Kur-Gal. Wide at the base, the tower tapered as it rose skyward, each section separated by a terrace, with the spaces in between quilted with numerous broad balconies adorned with hanging gardens and lush foliage. Instead of a sharp point at its zenith, it featured a flat landing, upon which figures could be seen moving about from time to time and served as a dock for Atlantean flying ships. The most evident purpose of the tower was as a residence built exclusively for the Atlanteans and their guests. Perhaps it was intended as a long-term domicile from which to continue their building projects. Lately, the Priest-Ruler of Eridu had requested their assistance constructing a massive Temple-Pyramid he termed a Ziggurat. It would be used for rituals and ceremonies to honor the Gods and the first of its kind in Kur-Gal. The Ziggurat was completed before the end of the year. Like the Atlantean tower, it had a flat top, but rather than another dock for flying ships, there was a massive red crystal shaped like a four-sided pyramid slowly rotating in place.

From the day the red crystal was placed atop the Ziggurat, there was a low hum that arose from the Atlantean Tower reverberating through earth, air, ocean and all things on Plethwih until it could be heard by every ear capable of understanding language. As the hum subsided a miracle occurred wherein every language spoken could suddenly be understood by any who deigned to listen. The Atlanteans calculated that if all peoples on Plethwih could communicate with each other without misunderstandings, disambiguation, or misinterpretation, then trade would flourish, societies of all races and nationalities could connect more easily with each other offering a chance for peace in every land. The Watchers regarded this gift, this *Tower of Tongues,* as an endowment to humanity that would carry significance far into the future. All do to the innocent observation of a child.

As far back as SY4800, the Watchers were aware that the Atlanteans were discreetly building very unusual structures in cities throughout the world. Most often they were tall towers or multi-story edifices atop a hill or mountain and in every case matched the local architecture so not to appear incongruent to the casual eye. But stick out they did, as the common feature to all was a red-glowing orichalcum crystal that slowly rotated at the apex of each one. Such a sight might have been distressing to native folk unaccustomed to oddities perceived as supernatural, especially when the structures were built and occupied by an even stranger race of lean humanoids with blue-tinted skin and elongated skulls. Except that the Atlanteans were far too clever and spared no effort to gain the good-will of kings, chiefs, priests, and shamans to achieve acceptance by the resident culture. And where they could not, the Atlanteans avoided those societies altogether preferring to build in isolation rather than risk hostilities. This particular point could not have been demonstrated more tragically than in SY5175 when a small group of Atlantean explorers disappeared several hundred leagues south of the Huaxia Empire.

The loss of the Atlantean explorers revealed a jarring discovery to both the Atlanteans sent to locate their missing compatriots, and the Watchers whose curious gaze followed their progress. In an unexplored land of dense jungles and vast bug-infested swamps an unknown civilization rose in isolation at some point in the distant past. Centuries at a minimum if not millennia, as a network of hundreds of roads and canals crisscrossed a kingdom of sprawling cities with stone towers, rambling neighborhoods, swarming marketplaces, gabled palaces, and squat temples attached to massive pyramids draped with thick vines that towered above it all. Nearly all of it partially submerged in the brackish water of the swamps. Most startling, however, was not the strange architecture, nor the span of time that this civilization went unnoticed even by the Watchers, but the astonishing inhabitants of the swampy cities. They were a race uniquely evolved to thrive in that seemingly inhospitable place. Many cultures on Plethwih made vague references to creatures such as these in their mythology and legends. Ancient religious tablets stored within dusty backrooms of temples in Kur-gal called them Mus-lu; the Meluhha peoples named them Nagas; and the Huaxia believed in the Xian. All described a similar bi-pedal humanoid race with greenish scales for skin, clawed hands and feet, a long tail, and the head of lizard or snake. With the incredible discovery of their civilization, the Atlanteans would name them Reptilians and the Watchers aptly described them as a race of Lizard-Folk.

The Atlanteans approached the Reptilians as they approached all cultures they met for the first time – with cautious friendship. Thus, they arrived in a flying ship crewed by one hundred Atlantean Marines, and a handful of wizards and priests led by a trio of diplomats with a train of advisors. They landed in the spacious courtyard of a palatial structure believed to be the governing center of the city and immediately found themselves surrounded by hundreds of Reptilian warriors bearing tortoise shell armor and long serrated double-edged swords. A delegation of Reptilians displaying headdresses adorned with colorful plumes soon appeared, followed by six robed figures holding tall polls each adorned with the severed head of one of the missing Atlantean explorers.

Shaken and enraged, the Atlantean diplomats demanded an explanation and through the magic of the recent Tower of Tongues construct, the Reptilians understood that which they could not before. Equally enraged, the Reptilian High-Priest condemned the Atlanteans as heathen trespassers who dared desecrate the sanctum of their hallowed shrine. Confused by the accusation, the Atlanteans hesitated and turned their backs to the High Priest while they discussed their response amongst themselves. Infuriated by the perceived disrespect, the Reptilian High Priest released a low hiss and the hundreds in the courtyard swarmed the Atlantean Sky Ship. From afar, the Watchers witnessed the horrors of unrestrained slaughter alongside the flash and fury of arcane butchery by fire, force, and lightning that claimed lives a score at a time. Through luck or divine intervention, the burning Sky Ship lifted into the clouds leaving the courtyard littered with dead and the hatred of those left among the living. In only a few spare minutes the Atlanteans suffered the loss of more than half their number but gained a dozen Reptilian captives that would ultimately provide invaluable information about the Land of Mu, the various kingdoms therein, their Gods, and their people. Such knowledge would poove invaluable as only a few decades would pass before the Reptilians would venture out from their Shadowy Kingdoms and once again engender bloody conflict. However, as far as the Atlanteans were concerned, they showed little interest in further overtures of peace, nor would they ever set foot in the Land of Mu again. Even for vengeance.

The Watchers were under no such constraint, and they were determined to learn what they could from these odd amalgamations of something between monster and Human. There would be plenty of surprises along the way. The first of which was the discovery of another culture living quietly south of Mu on a forested peninsula. These diminutive folk were taller than the Gnomes from Kabouterhol north of Courth, their skin was dark if less so than the Imaziyen, otherwise they might have been mistaken for the Hauflin who live in Argyllshire between Lyonesse and Eriu. The Watchers named them Indo-Hauflin for their wild appearance and skittish behavior. They built compact huts in trees or vacant caverns and grew small gardens. From time to time, they would form hunting parties in search of small game or turtles and fish when near the coast. On the rare occasion when the Reptilians came out of the swamps to explore or hunt the southern woodlands, the Indo-Hauflin quietly melted into the environment unseen until the threat passed. There appeared to be no desire on the part of the Indo-Hauflin to seek trade or make war upon the Reptilians. For that matter, the Watchers were never quite sure if the Reptilians were even aware of the Indo-Hauflins existence and if the latter were true, the Watchers were of the opinion that it was sound testament to the small humanoids survival.

For nearly fourteen hundred years the demons were sealed within a pithos guarded by Metis - the Goddess of Wisdom worshiped in Hellas – formerly known as the Tuatha De Phalaeh. She had a daughter, Anesidora, by an unnamed human. The child displayed an entrancing beauty that compelled Metis's Tuatha De lover Kronos and other Tuatha De 'Gods' to bestow favor and gifts upon the girl that conferred extraordinary abilities nearly equal to that of a pure Tuatha De. Since *the Breaking*, no Tuatha De could bear 'pure-blooded' children and instead chose to mate with humans producing a part Tuatha De, part Human hybrid with some small magical talent, without benefit of immortality. A distinction had to be made and thus the few remaining pure Tuatha De would be known as Tuatha De Blood, whereas their progeny simply Tuatha De. Anesidora was something in-between and from the perspective of humanity considered a Demi-God.

From the start, the Watchers were gravely concerned. Anesidora's extraordinary gifts came with the extraordinary side-effect of magnifying certain human characteristics that as she grew to adulthood became impossible to suppress. It was her rebellious nature and insatiable curiosity that drove Akakios, an elderly human TaHiera Fire-Bringer of Kronos, to believe he was in love with a Goddess. Through dreams and visions,

Anesidora convinced Akakios that she was held prisoner in an ancient Temple of Metis at the summit of the Othrys Mountains. The old priest could not ignore his heart, nor her desperate plea. In SY5379 Akakios melted the magical seal on the pithos as only a Fire-Bringer of Kronos could do. He was convinced Anesidora was trapped inside. Instead, the shattered pithos liberated the essences of seven Greater Demon Lords and thirteen Chaos Demons released upon Plethwih, all for the trivial curiosity of a Demi-Goddess ignorant of the terrible dangers trapped inside.

One-hundred years passed before the Watchers learned about the first possession following the broken pithos. It was not surprising that so much time had passed considering that the demons were stripped of their corporeal bodies when forced into the pithos and thus emerged incorporeal thirteen-hundred years later in a much-weakened state. So, in SY5489, when a Demon Lord took possession of the formidable En of Eridu in Kur-Gal, those who were aware that the demons were among them again, braced for what they knew would come. Within a year the En was dispossessed, but the Demon Lord was unlikely destroyed and instead released from the body to find another. In that same year came word of a powerful wizard suddenly gone mad before he was killed in his tower somewhere in The Wilds, and then came stories about a crazed knight slain in a duel outside of Teamhrach in Eriu. Either or both could have been instances of possessions by a Chaos Demon. The common thread between them was what occurred after the death of a demon's host: a smokey orb blacker than night rose from the corpse before swiftly speeding away. Anyone unlucky enough to gaze upon the vile orb reported sickness and terror far beyond anything they ever experienced in their lives. Both events included these specific details.

In SY5491, the elegantly beautiful city of Ys was brutally swamped by an unnatural storm driven by nefarious magic linked to their tragic princess, Ahes. Although her body was never found, many expressed that her mannerisms took on an extreme nature in the months prior to the deluge. A year later there were rumors of a great battle in the Valley of Leprechauns that pitted the legendary brothers Myrllin and Wodanaz against the healer-turned-witch Aja, and on the Isle of Gades the 'Child of Gold' Alseid, daughter of Queen Lysithea and her consort Senjit, captured a Chaos Demon in a magical bubble of the child's making. SY5490 turned out to be a busy year for the demons. By the end of the Summer, Count Djago of Cambria sparked another Civil War in Lyonesse that ended in a second battle on The Dormonts. Myrllin and Wodanaz assisted the King of the Dvergr to dispatch a mythological creature known as the Three-Faced Man, after which they pursued a Pheonix that rose from the hot magma of the volcano on Tirnan Yog. Another tale told of the Gold Dragon, Senjit, who barely survived a battle with the Ancient Black Dragon Belthagore; and yet another described how the Cyclops Giant Kumida was killed in battle on Etna by the first Druid of the Imaziyen tribes. All presumed to be demons. Plethwih was once again in chaos. This time, the Tuatha De wouldn't be leading armies to defeat the demons. Rather, the responsibility would rest upon the heroic effort of a few individuals and their peers. And there was no pithos to which the demons could be imprisoned. By happenstance or fate, the Wizard Myrllin chanced upon a discovery that promised to end the threat of demons for all time – the Ourea. The massive volcano that dominated the Atlan Mountain Range on the Emerald Isle was also a one-way portal into the Infernal Planes. And once Myrllin learned the secret of trapping the demons in small bubbles from Senjit's daughter Alseid, he simply let fall their captured essence into the Ourea, sending them back to the home they hayed, with no fear of their return. Or so it was thought.

When the pithos was broken emancipating the demons, the magical seal between Plethwih and the Infernal Planes began to weaken. The signs were clear to all as the fracturing of the Glass Sea placed over the rift by the Tuatha De Blood was fraying like a withered bandage over a festering wound. A permanent solution was required to heal Plethwih and close the rift for good. To this end, legendary figures of Plethwih, and those who would become legends gathered to pursue the Prophesy of Crown and Blood through knowledge and quests with the aim of combing the Tuatha De's 'Radiant Crown' and the blood of the 'King that Never Was' with a mysterious 'Vessel' as their only hope to save Plethwih and all life that depended upon her embrace.

Salvation from the demons would only be a temporary reprieve from catastrophe. Only nine were aware of this truth, for Myrllin had awakened from his long sleep in SY5485 to speak his vision to this Assembly of Nine of which he was included. Formed in the dawning years of the City of Atlantis, the Assembly of Nine included nine of the most powerful, wizened, and influential persons on Plethwih to include: the Emperor of Atlantis, Dagda-Dana Laghfrin, the Sylvan High-King, the Dvergr Mountain King, a Human Arch-Druid, Wodanaz and Myrllin as permanent members, plus two Humans thought best to represent humanity as a whole. At the time these were the Yellow Thearch from Huaxia and the King of Lyonesse. Not all nine were present at this urgent meeting, but all nine would know every detail in short order.

Myrllin spoke of an unavoidable doom certain to occur in SY7500. An unstoppable cataclysmic event that would shake Plethwih to its foundations, obliterate a continent, alter climates, and bring life in all lands to the brink of extinction. It was a fate set into motion by nothing more than unkind chance, without mal intent or design, millions of years before Plethwih existed. Myrllin's Vision predicted the cataclysm in the form of a fiery rock, two-fold larger than the greatest city, that would crash down through the heavens and impact the Ourea sparking terrible eruptions along the Spine of Atlan to sunder and sink the Emerald Isle and the Great City below the waves forever. Smaller impacts would follow, raining serpents of fire that dotted the planet like stars on the belt of the Great Hunter in the sky. Massive waves in every sea would break upon the shores deluging the land for hundreds of leagues, washing away entire civilizations as if they never existed, and submerging forever the subcontinent of Mu. Then darkness would cover Plethwih. The forests would die, and so too the animals. For a time, the north would become colder and the south warmer. And when the skies shown blue and clear once more, nothing would be the same. Absent would be the Sylvan, Atlantean, Dvergr, Hauflin, Kabouter, Tuatha De Blood and all manner of creatures of fin, fur, and flight. Only Man and natural beasts would survive, thrust back to the earliest days of humanity as if by divine reset. Myrllin called it the "End of the Enlightened Times," but the Watchers knew better. With more clarity than any prophecy, dream, or vision could render, the Watchers saw a new Age looming in the future. An Age when humanity would rise and stumble, and rise again to dominate life and land. Knowing they would never live to see it; the Watchers designated the last Age on Plethwih as 'The Age of Man.'

Age of Demons: Prophesy

The darkest age of the Sylvan Chronicles are known by only a few. This lone volume, painstakingly recorded on platinum plates bound by a cover of petrified wood obtained from an ancient oak, is kept apart from the original volumes detailing the Ages of the Golden Aspen. The source of this dark chronicle, hitherto known as the Age of Demons: Prophesy, is a controversial figure of ancient times. An unnamed Sylvan Watcher, devoted of Niamh, in divine conference was granted the gift of prophesy. It was controversial in that the prophetic prescience, visions, and exultations thus expressed were delivered via a diatribe of ravings in the previously unknown *Werdom Enoch*, 'the language of Angels and Demons,' considered at the time jabbering madness. It was only due to the foresight of the Mad Watcher's favorite scribe, whom he slaughtered soon after his last utterances, that a record of his wild gibbering exist at all.

Separately in the scribe's personal journal, he described the Watcher's slow descent into insanity with each revelation, often accompanied by spasms of emotional extremes and eventual violent bloodshed. Centuries later, when came to light enough of the dialect of the *Werdom Enoch* to translate the scribe's blood-stained journal did the full measure of the prophesy reveal itself. The pages read with remarkable similarity to the form and cadence of a chronicle, and under first observation appeared thus, more so than a presage of future events. Until the final entry.

At the last, an unusual alteration occurred in the style of the writing that clearly projected a disturbing episode that would occur in an unspecified time and indeterminate Age. It was not until *The Breaking*, brought about by the Tuatha De Blood civil war, that such a time was revealed. So, it was decided by a conclave of the Elders among the Watchers that the Age of Demons: Prophesy, as it was known from that time forward, would be kept separate from the vault wherein the original Chronicles of Ages were safely stored for study and duplication. The few who were aware of the Prophesy were forbade to speak of it, no copies would be allowed extant, nor would any citation or reference allude to validate the works as fact. For all intents and purposes, the Prophesy of Demons was nothing more than idle fantasy.

Thus was written:

From a time primeval. Thousands of years before the dawn of the Age of Man, darkness reigned unchallenged, unprovoked. The land churned like molasses superheated and boiling under roiling winds more fire than air struggling through thick ash and haze of a newly formed sky, yet impatient to shape a fateful dome for life and light.

Life and light.

Life, sudden and uncontrived, took passage within rocks that plummeted through the searing atmosphere like so many thousands raining from an ever-diminishing celestial orbit. Of them, seven carried an essence of alien origin durable and enduring to such degree that they survived the impact into the primordial soup of an inhospitable world of dark elemental violence, where they sank deep below the molten waves.

What hope could there be for life under such extreme conditions? Incalculable heat and pressure stirred the pudding of what would one day be the highest mountains, hissing with rage, belching igneous eruptions in the throes of a world desperate to escape the cosmic womb. Yet, life inorganic and unknown to evolution or intelligent design somehow thrived. Seven drew strength from the nascent energy of turmoil and chaos over countless millennia until at long last, the earth began to cool, and iron-rich silicates formed a crust over the whole of it.

To the Seven that dwelt below, incubating in the stew of creation, the shift to terra firma was not immediately noticed. Slow to awareness, the danger of the land thickening around their molten lair was recognized too late. In a fury they sought to escape. So long were they trapped within the frozen nucleus of the comets that brought them to this world, weak and impotent, it had taken too long to regain a fraction of the strength they once boasted. Out of desperation, the Seven combined their powers in a final bid to break out. As one, they drew deeply from the energy generated by the immense pressures and heat at the very core of the planet. The power, so intoxicating to ones familiar with the allure, drew beyond their need, heedless of the practical restraint they once knew to wield it. They sought to be the Masters once more, lording over worlds, compelling lesser life forms to do their bidding, feeding their hunger for vile pleasures. These evil dreams induced the Seven to drink deep of the earth-energy to power their freedom until they could bear no more.

A terrible shudder shook the earth when the Seven released the energy they amassed. Unpracticed after epochs in time, the discharge was uncontrolled, hastened by unconstrained anticipation. Rather than breaking through the miles-deep crust that separated the Seven from their diabolical desires, a void of the smallest size came into existence for the smallest amount of time drawing the Seven into a new spatial dimension - a universe of their own making. Yet no less a prison for the immortal Seven. Arcane scholars and priests would eventually name this terrible dimension the Infernal Planes.

In time, the spark of a solar orb grew bright and illumed the world the Seven left behind. New life bloomed unfettered by their corruptive presence. It was savage, organic life in its primordial pre-sentience that instigated an impossibly conceived ascent to intellectual liberation destined to become humanity. A bipedal race murderous and cruel by necessity, kind and decent by nature, evolved alongside other peoples to dominate this world, this earth, home, - Plethwih.

Unbeknownst to the Seven, unknown to anyone, a lingering thread connects Plethwih to the Infernal Planes for all time. It is a thread no power can manipulate from where it joins the Infernal Planes, but there is an undetected flaw where it links with Plethwih. A flaw that can only be exploited by the release of unconstrained power and happenstance. Such shall be the case many thousands of years from this time, when a cataclysmic event shall tear a rift between the two worlds and form a gateway from which the Seven and Thirteen of their lessers will finally bring about their nightmarish fantasies on the mortal inhabitants of Plethwih. Until such time, a time that shall not be named, the Infernal Planes remains the only home for the Seven and their ilk, to await unknowing for their time to shape the future.

Ys (pronounced /ˈiːs/ EESS), is a mythical city on the coast of Brittany that was swallowed up by the ocean.

Prologue

"Wake'n visions are start'n up again."

Myrllin, slender of frame with shoulder-length jet hair, well-groomed mustaches and beard grown long from a swarthy complexion. His sunken black eyes, piercing and intense, stared out at the endless expanse of the Primeval Sea watching the sun set over the western horizon. The man at his side was taller, heavy of muscle, with long fair-hair falling from under a wide brimmed foppish hat. A hard sun-touched countenance with equally voluminous facial hair and pensive sky-blue eyes alight with a spark of cryptic humor, matched well his easy-going jocund disposition. The two men claimed to be twins. Myrllin was the eldest by a minute, so he boasted, yet so opposite in feature and dress that few could see familial resemblance. If it were more commonly known that their father was Drohgan, the legendary Tuatha De (of the) Blood, and their mother was once the Nymph Queen of Gades, perhaps their assertions would be more readily accepted. Neither cared either way what anyone thought, and few were alive who knew the truth.

Wodanaz glanced down at his brother and asked in a doleful voice, "Do they bring clarity to your dreams?"

"Some," Myrllin shrugged. Here too, the brothers stood in stark contrast as Myrllin spoke with the lilt and cadence of one native to Eriu whilst his brother's articulation employed a decidedly plaintive quality distinct to the Vikja. "Tha demons we been after are known to me now."

"How is this important?" impatience strained Wodanaz's tone. He was never much for tiresome details.

Myrllin sighed. "Seven Greater Demons, each a powerful Lord o' tha Infernal Planes, an' thirteen lesser demons o' chaos lately escaped tha Pithos wherein they were imprisoned by our father so many centuries agon. Tha Demon Lords I can identify now by their True Names."

Wodanaz responded with a grunt of disinterest.

Shaking his head, Myrllin surveyed the beauty of their island home under the fleeting orange and red glow of sunset. From the cliff-side balcony of the expansive manse built atop the highest peaks of Hy Brasil – a mist-shrouded island in the northern Primal Sea – he could smell the fresh salt air, hear the languid lapping of waves over the sandy beach far below, and feel the embrace of the thickly forested elevations under a bold sky fading in the twilight even as the brightest among the stars made their presence known. Here he found comfort. Here he could think in peace. Even standing next to his brother anxious to be off to a tavern where he so often entertained the common folk and caroused into the early morning hours.

"Tha visons came in the usual way; sit'n under a tree eat'n an apple, o' stroll'n a path in tha forest. They come upon me when I'm most relaxed, ya know." The cool evening sea breeze parted Myrllin's black robes and lifted his jet locks. He paused to enjoy the feel of it until the shifting rustle of boots warned him of his brother's increasing lack of patience. "As ye know, Senjit, tha Gold Dragon an' husband to Lysithea, tha Nymph Queen o' Gades, destroyed tha Black Dragon Belthagore in a terrible battle. In a vision I witnessed tha battle an' saw with clear eyes that tha Ancient Dragon was possessed by a Greater Demon. Tha demon was revealed ta me as Tephras. Lord o' Anger. Belthagore dispossessed tha demon when he died. What became of Tephras after is still unclear."

"So, we hunt for this demon, Tephras, next?" Wodanaz asked with a marked increase in his enthusiasm. His brother was always wildly eager to take on a demon, despite nearly meeting their end on more than one occasion to the powerful fiends.

"Let me tell ya tha rest," Myrllin held up a cautionary hand. "It seems only two o' tha Greater Demon Lords have been returned to tha Infernal Planes. One was tha Demon o' Greed, I now know as Mamon, that possessed Count Djago o' Cambria in Lyonesse. I dropped that one into tha Ourea myself. The other, an' apparently tha first to be banished, was tha Demon o' Sloth, Alu-Abad. Through some means o' faith an' magic, a

Kur-gal priest in Eridu ascertained tha demon's True Name an' through a ritual sent tha demon from this world."

"Well," Wodanaz gave a bitter laugh. "It seems humanity is capable of handling its own affairs from time to time."

"Quite so," Myrllin agreed, "an' all tha better for it consider'n tha visions pertain'n to tha remain'n demons runn'n riot all over Plethwih. However, I was surprised to discover that knowledge o' a Greater Demon's True Name by itself is not enough to banish it back to tha Infernal Planes."

His brother playfully elbowed Myrllin's shoulder nearly knocking him over. "You can't expect to be right about everything now, can you?"

Rubbing his shoulder, Myrllin glared up at Wodanaz and said, "I c'n expect many thin's."

Wodanaz grunted.

"In any event," Myrllin continued. "That leaves five Greater Demon Lords that must be dealt with. We spoke about Tephras, Demon o' Anger. Another is Aesmadaeva, Demon o' Lust, who my visions show a dangerous relationship with tha crown of Ys. Then there's the Demon o' Pride, Yalal. I've seen tha demon take'n an altered form drawn from its host to form a strange bond between man an' beast. I don't understand tha cause or the process, but it parallels prophesy espoused by priests in Hellas o' a creature they call Lukánthropos. This is tha beast tha rangers in Courth sealed in its cavern-lair deep in Tha Wilds. My sense o' tha vision is that it will not stay interned much longer, if it is still. Another Demon Lord, Ornias, has a similar circumstance o' transmogrification with tha one it possessed – a ruler from tha Easter Kingdoms. This Demon o' Envy is very powerful, provide'n its mortal host with near immortality among other strange an' unusual abilities. An' like Yalal, it can spread a weaker version o' itself to others that become like it, and themselves spread'n one to another like a plague. These spawn of Ornias call themselves Vampyr. An' tha last o' tha Demon Lord's is Ba'lzble, Demon o' Gluttony. Tha vision concern'n this one places it on tha isle of Aiaia, in tha western waters o' tha Great Sea There it possesses tha formidable Sorceress an' ruler of tha small island, Kirke. I see a terrible plot in tha make'n that uses humanity's avarice to destroy itself, although I've yet to discern tha details."

Myrllin peered side-eyed at Wodanaz thoughtfully thumping his fingers on the ornamented balustrade where he leaned. Only a sliver of light broke the horizon, a sea of stars peeked brightly from between the clouds, and the waning orb of the moon cast its wavering reflection on the placid sea. The wind picked up, as naturally transpired every night, bringing cooler air from the frozen tundra of the north where the Primal Sea stood frozen as if time itself refused to tic another cog in the wheel.

"These are dangerous times," Wodanaz wore a grave expression. "Every instance of the Demon Lords portends tragic consequences for the civilizations on Plethwih. Which do we prioritize? Or do we split up and take them on separately? Tell me, brother, what is the urgency of your visions?"

Myrllin took a deep breath. "None. Tha Demon Lords must be left to tha resources o' humanity an' tha other races of Plethwih ta resolve."

"But . . ."

Wodanaz's protest was cut short by Myrllin's lifted hand. "There's somethin' else."

"Speak it."

"Plethwih's die'n. Mother earth is die'n!" A shudder ran through Myrllin. "It's not just tha visions. I c'n feel it in my bones. I think tha druids are feel'n it too."

"What does that mean!" Wodanaz demanded, pounded his fist on the stone rail causing the entire balcony to vibrate. "Tell it straight for once, Myrllin!"

Myrllin was exasperated. The dreams and visions, as clear as they might seem at times, were only a glimpse into one possible future leaving much to his contemplation and interpretation. And the smallest alteration of course leading up to the events of a portent could change the outcome entirely. Almost none of it was within his control beyond the telling. "When tha Tautha De Blood resorted ta a powerful relic ta focus their combined powers in a last-ditch effort ta end their civil war, they inadvertently opened tha rift between Plethwih an' tha Infernal Planes in a cataclysmic event we know as tha Break'n. Fast came tha seven Greater Demon Lords an' thirteen Chaos Demons inta our world. In good time, tha survive'n Tuatha De Blood sealed tha rift with tha Sea o' Glass, an' no more demons came. Then with tha help of humanity, tha Sylvan, Atlantean, and Dvergr, all tha demons were imprisoned in a Pithos an' placed out o' mortal reach in tha Temple o' Metis. Yet, despite tha seal, tha link between tha worlds remained, if closed. An' now, over three-thousand years later, tha Pithos is broken an' tha demons are free ta' create havoc once again, though far weaker than before. Still, they grow stronger, an' the seal grows weaker. Plethwih c'n no hold tha magnitude of evil that corrupts now from both sides."

Wodanaz spread his hands wide in frustration, asking, "Then the resolution is explicit; we must rid Plethwih of the demons, and so the seal remains intact."

"That's tha heart o' tha quandary," Myrllin was loath to reveal the last part of his theory on the matter as it was based on fragments of obscure visions with little foundation. Although, in truth, it was the best he could adduce after significant contemplation. "Tha seal will not recover. Tha Sea o' Glass will shatter, an' tha sky cities will fall. O' that I am certain, whether tha demons are gone from Plethwih or no."

"You must have recourse," Wodanaz turned his steely blue-eyed gaze on Myrllin, lines of worry wrinkled his face evident even in the dim moonlight. "What's your plan?"

Myrllin's voice dropped to a whisper on the breeze, reluctant to voice the resolution so boldly, "We must recover tha Radiant Crown, an' use it ta heal Plethwih. There's no other way."

To his credit, Wodanaz nodded without question or complaint. He always accepted his brother's word with as much or more confidence than Myrllin himself. Wodanaz was the rock he could always lean upon, dependable, resolute, unwavering, regardless of the challenge or danger they faced. The thoughts prompted Myrllin to recall a dream concerning his brother that he would never voice. A sad dream wherein the brothers were separated forever. Myrllin would miss him desperately.

"Do you have confidence the peoples of Plethwih can handle the demons on their own?" a half smile twitched at the edge of Wodanaz's full lips.

Myrllin barked a laugh, "None whatsoever. I suppose we will have ta have a measure o' faith fer once."

"So, we must. For better or worse," Wodanaz chuckled.

There was a long space of silence between the two before Wodanaz asked the obvious question, "Where do we start?"

Myrllin shrugged, "Tha Tuatha De Blood, I think. We'll start with Dagda-Dana Laghfrin, tha Tuatha De Wizard Queen o' Falias. Maybe she c'n tell us somethin' o' tha Radiant Crown."

"Just so," Wodanaz agreed.

Sunset passed, and the breeze off the northern sea blew frigid. The two men turned from the balcony intent on a warm hearth, comfortable chair, and steamed wine as their voices retreated into the interior of the manse atop the mist-shrouded peaks of Hy-Brasil.

– – –

Ys was a fine city. Towering spires reached to the sky inspiring a grandiose impression of elegance and freedom from earth-bound constraints. Broad avenues stretching in long straight boulevards crisscrossed the city with winding lanes and lush public gardens that flowed around grey or white stone structures with soft curved angles easy on the eyes. Ys was crowded during the day with folk going about their business in common fashion as one might expect for the busiest port city in the Western Kingdoms. Yet, just as Ys drew trade from all parts of Plethwih, so did it draw the masses to the nightlife. Especially now that Princess Ahes was leading the trends of sensual and provocative fashion once considered daring if not blatantly fetish.

Naamah was in her natural element. In Ys, there was no shortage of willing partners to satiate her hunger. Better yet, there were no expectations or complications with those she mingled beyond the pleasure of the moment. She fit right in. And with the support of her current 'benefactor,' a man in the guise of a foreign noble, she needn't risk potential scrutiny or suspicion by contriving schemes to drain the wealth of her lovers to indulge her lavish expenses.

What did this foreign noble receive in return? Aside from occasional intimacies, he demanded little. A small task here and there. Trivial matters for the most part. But she knew he coveted something greater. Something she dare not ask, for she recognized a greater power beyond his façade, and woe unto the one who attracted his displeasure. So, in all the small 'favors' he asked of her, she accomplished each one without complaint and beyond his expectations.

So it was in her current task. She was to identify individuals with special talents and invite them to an exclusive dinner party where they would meet the foreign noble and consider a very lucrative proposition related to a terminal illness he was suffering from. Not only would these individuals have to possess the skills required for the foreign noble's undertaking, but also a good measure of empathy for his terminal condition. That meant Naamah would be mainly looking for travelers from beyond the territories of Ys. Not an easy task at all!

Day and night Naamah watched for new arrivals, distinguished potential matches, and assessed their behaviors, until finally, she found those individuals she believed would please her benefactor. Thus, to each she extended an invitation to the Agrabuta – the oldest standing manor house in Ys – now under the ownership of the foreign noble, Prince Zracul, Primogeniture of Vradesti.

Chapter 1 – A Fateful Meeting

What better gift of happenstance could fate indulge a demon, than possession of a royal princess's mind and body. And not just any princess, but the only heir to the aging king of the wealthy and powerful city of Ys, no less! The demon gazed through the princess's eyes admiring her naked form reflected by the dressing mirror within her private chambers. She was a beauty to behold. Only a few years into her reproductive years with a finely matured physique and porcelain face that would draw influential suiters from the edges of civilization. The feel of her skin was smooth and silky, fine blonde hair fell long down her slender back trailing wispy curls that tickled her finely sloped shoulders, her limbs were strong and athletic, and she displayed the full, round breasts of a youthful woman crowned by perky nipples the hue of a ripe peach.

The woman's mind belonged to the demon completely. Although she was extraordinarily intelligent, it wasn't much of a fight for dominance as she knew little of magic or psionics other than through fanciful stories from childhood. Her mind didn't matter anyway. The demon solely required her memories to provide reference for the information needed to impersonate her whims and personality. No one would ever notice the slow change in the princess's mannerisms or character until it was too late.

Fortune was with the demon in that regard as well. The princess had no siblings, her mother was long dead, and she held a contentious relationship with her overbearing father. Any oddity in her personality would be considered nothing more than the natural desire for independence typical of a woman her age. In truth, the demon cared little for what anyone thought. Who would dare challenge the princess? What was her name again? The creature quickly searched its host's mind. The satisfying echo of her internal scream still resonated from the final moment she lost control. No one came back from that. Ever. At least not mentally intact.

Ahes. Yes, that was it. Her name was Ahes.

In the thousand, thousand years of its existence, the demon never controlled so fair a prize. Ahes was perfect in every way. A beautiful young body ready to explore, resilient, and mindless. The demon would take full advantage in a city that offered every sensual, carnal, erotic temptation of flesh imaginable to the mortal mind, and introduce the unimagined, inconceivable to fill its unquenchable desire. For the creature was Aesmadaeva, Greater Demon of Lust that occupied the pulp and husk that was once Ahes.

"Your Highness? Did you want your bath drawn early this eve?"

The body of Ahes flinched, shifting her gaze quickly to the pretty chambermaid who entered so quietly. Or perhaps Aesmadaeva simply allowed itself to become too engrossed in the reflected image that would soon bring the endless pleasures it so coveted, that it did not detect her presence. Care must be taken in the future.

A wicked smile drew itself across Ahes's face. "Yes, Tipa, draw the bath. And remove your clothes as well. We are going to do things a little different tonight."

"I welcome you to our glamorous city, Prince Zracul. It is not often that we receive an emissary from the Eastern Kingdoms, and I'm quite certain you are the first noble from Vradesti welcomed at an Ysian court. Did I say the name of your land correctly?" King Gradlon sat straight-backed on his golden throne smiling broadly at his guests.

"Yes, Your Majesty, and we are honored that you granted us a moment of your precious time." Zracul stood ten paces from the king, with his brothers and sisters at his sides. They wore tailored suits and ruffled gowns deliberately chosen from the latest styles trending in Ys. Although, in truth, their attire reflected far more conservative cuts than the formal wear observed in the evening hours of this sleepless city.

The king waved away the compliment. "My trade advisor has informed me of your proposal. Should the numbers bear out, your realm will become the gateway to the east for the Western Kingdoms! By opening new trade routes to exotic destinations and facilitating the movement of goods both ways, the Eastern Kingdoms, led by Vradesti, will come out of the shadows and develop into a modern economy. Most importantly, your family, your realm, and your people will experience an unprecedented flow of wealth that even the most prosperous in the west will envy!"

Blood pounded in Zracul's temples, but he was careful not to show. This fool sitting on his gold throne under a vaulted ceiling that disappeared in the shadows surrounded by a massive chamber filled with priceless paintings, statuary, tapestries, and furniture all designed to show off the wealth of Ys was acting as if it was up to him to decide the fate of Vradesti. What would the stupid ass have to say if he knew Zracul didn't care a wit whether their kingdoms forged a trade agreement or not. The only reason Zracul agreed to his brothers plan to propose an accord between the two realms was because it provided pretext for their true designs in Ys. It gave Zracul immense satisfaction knowing that it would be by his hands that life would be squeezed from King Gradlon before he was done in Ys. Still, the man's condescending smile was infuriating.

Despite the rage he felt inside, Zracul smiled like an imbecile absorbing the wisdom of his betters and replied in a calm even tone, "I have no doubt that we will rely heavily on Your Majesty's advice and guidance once we have formalized a trade agreement."

The king slapped the armrest of his throne, enthusiastically barking a full-throated laugh. "I appreciate your humble nature, Prince Zracul, but I sense you are a skilled negotiator with a very specific agenda. I have a feeling we will become good friends in the years to come!"

Before Zracul had a chance to reply, a guard appeared from a side door and announced loudly to all within, "Her Royal Highness, Princess Ahes!"

The king turned toward the open door, as did every eye in the room. "Ah, my daughter interrupts us." The trepidation in his voice was a curious detail that Zracul did not miss.

The slow clop of heeled shoes echoed through the chamber as a young woman strode toward the throne. Zracul unexpectedly caught his breath. She was stunning. Quite possibly the most beautiful woman he had ever seen. Her long blonde hair framed a narrow face dominated by large intense brown eyes, red lips, and sun-touched cheeks. She wore a powder blue mantle cut high in the front to show off her long, lean legs behind the soft green gauzy material of the gown underneath. Every step was made with a deliberate unhurried grace with her unwavering gaze trained fully on her father without the hint of a glance toward anyone else in the room. It was like he was witnessing a scene through his scrying mirror of just the king and his daughter in an empty room, but Zracul knew the woman was very aware that everyone was watching her. She expected it.

"Good afternoon, father." The princess kissed King Gradlon lightly on the cheek, facing him with her slender bare back to Zracul and everyone else in a deliberate display of her lusty curves. "I'm sorry to interrupt, but I wanted to ask that you not send any more suitors to me today. I am very tired and would like to retire early tonight."

"Well, that would be a first," the king grumbled low under his breath so no one could hear. "At least you are dressed . . . somewhat appropriately today."

Zracul's keen ears picked up every word.

"I'll take that as your agreement?" She turned to walk away, but King Gradlon caught her hand. The look she gave him was pure loathing.

"One last introduction, my dear, and I will trouble you no more this evening." Without waiting for an answer, the king rose and roughly spun Ahes to face the room before releasing her hand. "It pleases me to introduce our guests from faraway Vradesti in the Eastern Kingdoms: the young Princesses Jaria and Daria, Prince Vadim, Prince Fain and the Primogeniture of Vradesti, Prince Zracul."

Princess Ahes did little to hide her wan smile over a bored expression as the nobles were introduced one at a time until her disinterested gaze fell upon Zracul. When their eyes met, everything else seemed to disappear. The king was still speaking - something about the trade mission - but Zracul was no longer listening. His focus was entirely upon the princess and she on him. It was like looking into a mirror in many ways. Something about her felt familiar, like an ancient kindred spirit, but deeper still. He *knew* her and yet she was a stranger. One thing he was absolutely certain about was the impious fire that ignited inside his breast. It was a savage, primal need to have her in a lascivious, physical sense that was powerful and undeniable. He knew lust. After the transformation that merged his consciousness with

Ornias, Greater Demon of Envy, the need to satisfy his lust was far greater than before. Jaria and Daria assuaged that need well enough that he rarely desired outside companionship. This was very different. Lust was hardly the word for it. Whatever this was, it was exponentially greater, and the strangest thing was that he knew without a single word ever passing between them, that Ahes felt the same way.

"Wouldn't you agree, Prince Zracul? Prince Zracul?"

Zracul's lecherous musings were abruptly interrupted by a sharp nudge from one of his brothers. Ignoring the question, he replied to the king with a question of his own without ever shifting his gaze away from the princess, "May I call upon your daughter, Your Majesty?"

The throne room was dead silent. Not waiting for her father's response, Ahes answered with a curt, "Yes."

"Uh, right. Yes, of course, Prince Zracul." King Gradlon stuttered in confusion as it dawned on him what Zracul was asking. "It would please me greatly."

"You will call upon me noon tomorrow, Prince Zracul." Ahes tone was commanding as she started back to the side door she entered earlier. Still, her bold stare lingered upon Zracul until it was impossible to continue walking without tearing her gaze away from his. She walked quickly then, with a seductive sway of curvy hips that all eyes followed, departing through the door that was firmly closed behind her by a waiting guard.

When she was gone, a crushing ache bloomed in Zracul's chest that heightened the pain of her absence. For a moment he thought his body was suffering a sudden and inopportune heart attack right there in front of King Gradlon. There was no reference for this sensation in Zracul's memories, but his combined consciousness with Ornias reasoned that it must be a corruption of the mortal emotion called love.

King Gradlon chuckled from his throne, drawing Zracul's attention away from the closed door. "I suppose a match between the heir of Ys and the heir of Vradesti would change the calculation of any trade agreement between our two kingdoms, best we have our people get to work on that right away. Wouldn't you agree, Prince Zracul?"

This time, Zracul managed a distracted nod before he and his entourage were ushered from the throne room harried by the delighted laughter of Gradlon, King of Ys.

It was the hour of noon. Prince Zracul sat somewhat impatiently in one of the many sitting rooms accorded for informal meetings at the palace. He wore long black breeches edged with silver threading, gallant soft boots turned down below the knee, a silk tunic embroidered with silver dragons on the sleeves with a ruffled scarf tucked inside the collars. His ermine lined cap and matching cloak hung dripping in a nearby closet from a sudden squall that managed to ambush his arrival at the palace. His sensitive hears could still hear the constant drip, drip, drop of the rain water forming a small puddle behind the closet door. Between that, and the subtle shifting of the bored servant standing against the wall, Prince Zracul was nearly at the limits of his tolerance for waiting on anything or anybody.

Finally, the door opened at the far end of the chamber and in strode Princess Ahes. Her depthless brown eyes bored into him with undisguised lust driving away all other distractions. Below those crafty eyes, Hellasian nose, and full red lips stretched in a conniving smile hung a necklace of small diamonds, hundreds of them, set in a dozen bands of silver that fell loosely over her bosom except for a single strand that trailed between her breasts and disappeared under the layers of an airy gown of sheer ocean blue and seafoam green silks tailored with such precision that only glimpses of her tempting figure were revealed as she walked. In an instant, Zracul's blood was boiling with desire.

"Why do you call yourself a 'Prince'?" Ahes stopped only a few steps inside the room and half turned as if to leave immediately if the meeting was not to her liking. "Your father and mother are dead, are they not?"

Slowly rising to his feet, Zracul took a hesitant step forward intent on greeting her in the traditional fashion of kissing her hand, but he stopped fast at the sharp raise of her eyebrow. They stood easily twenty feet apart, yet he could distinctly smell the fragrance of her perfume, lightly applied to her slender neck and wrists as the heady scent of lilac. Zracul carefully controlled his breathing as he drew himself up in a formal posture to address the princess's unexpected query.

"Good day, Your Highness," Zracul began with a bow. "The noon hour suits you well," he glanced up at a window set high near the vaulted ceiling which permitted a wide band of sunlight to cleave the chamber at a sharp angle between them.

"Have you come to discuss the weather?" She took a step back toward the door.

"Not just, Your Highness . . ."

"You may call me Ahes," she interrupted.

Zracul bowed once more, "Of course, Princess Ahes, I . . ."

"Just Ahes," she again interrupted taking another step toward the door through which she entered only a minute before. One more step and she would be through it.

Zracul smiled. If he had ever met his match, she stood before him now. "Ahes, it is the tradition of Vradesti nobles to honor their fathers by claiming their titles after a year of mourning. So, although the powers to rule Vradesti transferred at the time of my father's death, his title is deferred out of respect for his memory."

"Has not a year already passed?" she asked in a bland voice.

"It has, Your . . . Ahes, but since I have been abroad the matter has seemed trivial until I return to Vradesti for the formal transference of the title." Zracul stopped himself from moving toward her as he spoke. It was like holding a powerful magnetic stone from metal. He wanted to be close to her. He needed to touch her.

The Princess gazed at him cooly through the haze of sunlight. "So, you plan to court the Royal Princess of one of the greatest nations in the Western Kingdoms as the ruler of a foreign kingdom who still titles himself 'Prince' in the fashion of a child hanging on his dead father's coat tails?"

Zracul was taken aback by not only her directness as to his purpose, but her concern with titles, and station. His agents described her as impulsive, even reckless as far as her reputation was concerned, but never did he imagine the princess as petty. "If my intent is to court you, what title would you prefer?"

"What was your father's title?"

"Vojevoda of Vradesti," he replied. "The closest translation is a kind of Warlord or 'Comte' as known in YS, or 'Count' in Lyonesse."

"Comte?" she echoed with disdain. "How does a Comte come to rule a kingdom and name his sons princes? Who is your master?"

Anger flared wildly within Zracul's breast. "I have no master," he replied coldly. He noted a slight flinch at the edges of her lips that broke her stoney façade for just an instant, and in that instant, he knew she saw though him. Just as he saw through her. But what truly lay behind those beautiful eyes, he did not know.

His voice warmed when he continued, "The Eastern Kingdoms have less complex ranks of nobility than here in the west. We have Magnates who represent powerful, wealthy families with extensive landholdings, and a title similar to 'Baron' which is generally granted based on military or administrative service. As there is no word for 'King' in our language. Every monarch uses the hereditary title of their fathers. In the case of Vradesti, Vojevoda, or 'Comte,' or 'Count' is a title no less equivalent to any other monarch's title. His wife, the Vojevodina, would be similar to 'Comtess.'"

"Very well," Ahes huffed. "Let's stay with a foreign flavor Ysians will hold in high regard. Court me with the fashion of a title of Lyonesse as 'Count Zracul' or not at all. However, if I was to accept a proposal do not presume I would stoop to the designation 'Countess.' Any marriage contract would include the provision for titles of my choice that are viewed and accepted in the west equal to that of 'Queen' or better. If you accept my terms, you may see me again at midnight. I will be entertaining at The Black Door and perhaps we will discover if we are justly a compatible match for each other." She flashed him a wicked smile and disappeared through the doorway.

Zracul was alone in the chamber staring after her abrupt departure, except for the servant who was desperately trying to blend into the wall. This strange appointment with Ahes did not go at all as he planned. Bitter anger rose like a tempest within. He called for his coat and carriage. He decided it was best to return to the Agrabuta immediately where he could vent his rage in private.

– – –

Ahes pressed her back to the wall outside the meeting room panting for breath.

"Your Highness, are you unwell?" Tipa rushed to her side.

"That man is infuriating!" Ahes raged. "What does he take me for? A besotted daughter of a pig farmer or whatever stinking carcass passes for livestock in Vradesti? He presumes too much!"

"Will you still be going to The Black Door tonight?" Tipa asked.

"Of course I will, you idiot," Ahes answered sharply. "I have to have him!"

– – –

A chair crashed against the wall splintering it into a thousand small shards. At least four other chairs, a desk, and a cabinet lay in shattered ruin around the room.

"The arrogance of that woman!" Zracul shouted. "The brazen, shameless insolence of her! How could she be so blatant and audacious to speak to me thus?"

Zracul swung around to face his brother Fain calmly sitting in the last piece of intact furniture within the chamber. He eyed the chair and calculated how far he could throw it with his brother still sitting in it.

Fain, sensing the danger, slowly rose and thrust the chair forward scraping and clattering across the stone floor. "So, you don't plan to see her again?" he smiled with undisguised mirth.

"Of course I will, you idiot." He snatched up the recently vacated chair and sent it hurtling against the far wall. "I have to have her."

– – –

The Black Door. Truth be told, it was more of a dark eggplant purple to the discerning eye that reflected an ominous luminosity in the light of torch or lantern. The door stood insignificant against the curved wall of a short tower of perhaps two stories attached to a cluster of taller towers and buildings such that most passed it by without a second glance. In the center of the black door was a small irregular hole through which only certain persons owned a key that could be slid into the aperture to release the latch. That was the just first step for entry. Inside, a long, darkened, silent corridor illumed by a single torch ran straight and level to a second black door. Anyone of a mind to regard the walls closely in passing might notice a series of very narrow horizontal slots along the way. Looking into any one of them was subject to cause the mortal heart to skip a beat at the startling sight of glittering eyes peering back.

The second black door was fitted with a handle without a lock. Through it, a man wearing a hooded black robe sat upon a stone block tucked into a shallow alcove. He was known as the Gate Keeper. Little of his pale features were visible aside from his pallid hands and ashen face sunk deep within his cowl, further obscured by the wavering shadows oppressing the dim lantern hung from the ceiling in the center of the small room. His purpose here was simple. In trade for the key, he marked the bearer and any guests in their company with a glittering ash-like substance produced from a small kettle. He applied the modest smudge by running his thumb shortly over each forehead before gesturing toward a stone stairway with steps leading up and down. The surrendered key would be returned upon their departure.

Most made their way up the stairs to the tavern where a buffet of delicacies from around the world was served throughout the night paired with the finest vintages from as far away as Atlantis and Hellas. Entertainers of the highest aptitude played music, regaled the crowd with fantastic tales, and recited tragic verse that moistened every eye. It was rumored that even the enigmatic Wodanaz the Wanderer entertained in that great chamber from time to time. And what a great chamber it was. The tavern encompassed two stories. The second floor being mostly a wide balcony that formed a circle around the inner perimeter of the tower under a vaulted ceiling hidden in shadows. Here, patrons dined leisurely on couches or tables, or leaned on the balustrade watching those milling below.

Zracul recalled little more about the upstairs as he had visited the tavern but once. His interests always drew him to the downstairs. For a fact, he would have no consequence to frequent The Black Door at all if it were not for Ahes. Everyone fawned over her, doing whatever they thought would please her. It was like a second home where she could be herself without the stern-eyed judgments of her father's court. If they only knew.

The downstairs was like an informal ball every night. A large chamber as big as any in the palace was always thronged with young beautiful people from the upper crusts of society. There were frequent themes where the regulars would wear masks, gaudy costumes, or nothing at all. Food and drink were plentiful, and it seemed everyone's first objective was to imbibe whatever it took to lose their inhibitions. For the night would always end in groups or pairings writhing together within large alcoves along the walls open for all to see. Only Ahes had a private chamber.

At first, she would only allow him to watch. It made Zracul's blood boil with furious desire. He knew that's precisely what she wanted. To watch others please her or be pleasured by her would push him to the point of madness. And her stamina knew no limits as she exhausted one after another only to be replaced by one or more of her ardent admirers. Eventually, Zracul always fled; her mocking laughter echoing in his ears. On these nights he would satiate his lust for blood and passion on poor unfortunate souls he found on his flight back to the Agrabuta. It was not jealousy or envy that drove his passions. He cared little what she did with anyone else. Under normal circumstances he would have just taken her, but she was the king's daughter, and more than that, there was something about her that stimmed his aggression although he could not yet name what it was. Zracul would play her game for now, but when his time came, he was determined to arouse in her such yearnings to leave her panting and begging for more.

_._._

Ahes was pleased. Her plan to provoke Count Zracul to the brink of lusty rage was working better than she expected. For many nights had she kept him at arm's length while she trooped from one ignominious den of flesh to another, trailed by her entourage, where she bade him observe her perform lewd undertakings with and upon others. He always watched for long hours through staring eyes burning with furious desire before stalking off in a fury. She liked it when he watched, but she sensed a viscous danger in him that, while exciting, must be manipulated with great care. Ahes intuited Zracul was nearly at the point where he would be pushed no further. His zeal for her was flaming hot and she decided it was time to fan the flames into an inferno of passion and licentious abandon unlike any mortal coupling.

This she knew, or rather, the Greater Demon Aesmadaeva who claimed Ahes as its host knew with certainty, for the two were now one and the same. On a night two days prior, when Zracul's attention was distracted by her lurid routine, the demon carefully probed his mind with undetectable tendrils of psionic energy. What Aesmadaeva found was completely unexpected. The delicate tendrils slid away from a guarded mind hardened against stealthy intrusion. The demon considered prodding more forcefully, but it knew not how quick and adept was his mind. In any case, Zracul's supernatural nature was exposed if not exactly identified. The discovery caused no great concern, but more readily an erotic curiosity that filled the demon-possessed-Ahes with intense anticipation. She and Zracul would once again convene at The Black Door that night, and this time she would lavish every pleasure upon him he ever dreamed, and much, much more.

Chapter 2 – The Gathering

"Welcome to the Agrabuta!" A broad smile painted the sharply handsome features of their host.

The tall slender man with pale skin and long jet-black hair cut a striking figure as he stood straight-backed holding a glass of red wine aloft in a welcoming gesture. His evening attire consisted of a smartly tailored dinner jacket with long tails over tunic and trousers – all black – except for silver embroidery with the aspect of dragons that ran up the arms and around the turned-up collar. Anywhere else his choice of fashion might have appeared dated and archaic, but here in Ys, old was new and personal elegance was in vogue among the bodies of anybody that prowled the circuit of parties, afterparties, and balls. All, of course, by invitation only.

This was a man who knew the politics of social etiquette, the cabals of who to know, and the eloquent tongue of a seasoned diplomat. It was a persona he projected with easy perfection. What about the subtler aspects of this man called Zracul of the Eastern Kingdoms, Primogeniture of Vradesti? And there were other, outrageous names whispered only in dark places, never in polite company; 'Blood Prince' and 'Dragon of the East' seemed the most popular. Intimidating to most for sure and advantageous in the fluency of political gamesmanship.

Yet, none of that concerned Enguer at all. It was the prince's dark eyes reflecting the light from the fireplace that held his attention. Or was it a burning light from within? He had seen eyes like these before a while back. Stared into orbs consumed by hate, pain, and anger from as close as a handspan, before watching the light fade and die from the beast who bore them.

"I am Lord Zracul of Vradesti in the Eastern Kingdoms. It is my pleasure to have you all here in our humble home away from home." Zracul's smile never wavered as he shifted to sit rigidly in an over-stuffed chair before sinking into a more comfortable posture. He glanced up at the beautiful blonde-haired woman that strode gracefully to a position at the back of his chair. "Naamah has told me so much about each of you, but to my embarrassment, I do not believe you know each other. Would you do us the favor of introducing yourselves so that we may push past the awkward consequence of anonymity?" He gestured first to a dark-skinned man wearing layers of earth-toned robes decorated with colorful feathers, bones, and beads hanging from short leather thongs in a seemingly random pattern on his garments.

"I am called Khulani. I am Imaziyen; a warrior of my tribe and a druid of Ayur." His eyes scanned the others sitting nearby and settled on a blond fellow sporting a silver-fringed white cloak tossed over his shoulder to fall draping over the side of his chair.

Careless, Enguer thought to himself as he followed the druid's gaze. *A good assassin could use that cloak to strangle the pompous look right off the man's face.* He interrupted his own thoughts with an internal eyeroll. *Geez. I'm starting to sound like Reskalin!*

"Ayur is the Moon Goddess worshiped by my people," Khulani continued, his eyes still fully on the Temple Knight. "Same as Luna, except by a different name."

The blond man's cheeks flushed, but he simply replied with a polite nod.

"Fascinating!" Zracul clapped his hands together. "A real druid, right here in my home. You know, druids are mostly legends from folklore where I am from. Sadly, the tradition of druids is absent in the Eastern Kingdoms."

Khulani smiled, showing bright white teeth and a hint of red gums, "The druids have lived apart from the places where people gather since ancient days. Sometimes they are closer than one knows, yet farther away than one can reach."

"Isn't that extraordinary," Zracul marveled at the druid. "I pray the rest of you are as interesting as this one!" He shifted his gaze neatly to the pair of

Atlanteans sitting together on a green-paneled couch that seemed off-color in the room.

Nothing in this place looks like it belongs together, Enguer mused to himself.

"The Exceptional Ones. Children of Atlan, faithful of the Sea-God Pontus. From far across the Primal Sea, they come away from their shining city of Atlantis said to sparkle like a jewel on the Emerald Isle!" The prince paused to laugh at his own dramatic introduction. "Did I get that right?"

"Indeed," the Atlantean nodded with a smile. "My name is Qelel of House Mekali and this is my friend Havaciante of House Talika, but please feel free to call us by our short names, Qel and Havacian. We are intrigued by your invitation this evening."

Enguer was fascinated by Atlantean people. Their extraordinary appearance was at once jarring and a thing of beauty. Exhibiting sharp features and pointed ears, they might easily be confused for elves, except that Atlanteans were generally taller, with larger eyes and their most telling features – blue-tinted skin and elongated skulls.

Their host nearly jumped from his chair, he sat up so quickly. "Mekali? The Vignerons?"

Qel smiled proudly. "The same."

"The finest wine in all Plethwih! I am now ashamed of the swill I serve you." Zracul tilted his glass and with a deliberate motion to demonstrate a casual display of the dramatic, poured his wine onto the thick burgundy carpet. A servant rushed over just in time to catch the glass on his serving tray immediately after Zracul released it. "Open the cask of Mekali wine and replace everyone's glass," he commanded the servant.

The Atlanteans appeared shocked by what had just occurred. In fact, everyone did except for the beautiful blonde woman named Naamah. Her unwavering perpetual half-smile painted her exquisite features.

"The wine we have now is a very fine vintage," Qel stammered. "Please do not waste the plum from a highly respected Ysian vintner!"

Enguer knew enough about wine to know that the Atlantean spoke truly. The rare Ysian wine they drank tonight was considered top shelf among a short list that only those who tread the highest affluent circles could get their hands on, let alone afford.

"Nonsense!" Zracul countered. "Even a fool knows that there is no finer spirit than Mekali, unless you discover one that changes common metals to gold!"

Chuckles rippled through the room dispelling the contrived tension brought about by the drama with the wine. Enguer eased a bit as well. This man was a master at working the room. So far, the evening was turning out better than a play at the theatre.

"Now to our noble Temple Knight," Zracul settled back into his chair. "Would you please grace us with an introduction?" The smile on Zracul's face appeared to stretch wider than with the others, showing sharp teeth that reminded Enguer of a snarling wolf, and much like the banner bearing a white fang on a blood-red field that hung on the wall behind their host.

The tall knight rose to his feet. "I am Sir Perault Eckert of Stoddenferry Castle in Lyonesse. I would be pleased if all of you would simply address me as Sir Perault." He stood rigidly in his blue ruffled tunic and fitted breeches that did little to conceal his muscular well-proportioned figure. He was not armed, but he needn't be. Temple Knights were trained to be as deadly without a weapon as with one. The long white silver-fringed cloak trailing down his back bore the embroidered image of a golden Lyon in rampant pose that shimmered in the light like a living thing.

Zracul leaned forward as he accepted a new glass filled with a smooth burgundy liquid from his servant. "So, what brings you to Ys, Sir Perault? Convalescence after that unfortunate business on The Dormonts?"

Enguer stiffened. The Dormonts. The place was a vast tract of rolling hills and flats covered by a carpet of tall green grass and wildflowers in the heart of Lyonesse. It was also quite possibly the most blood-drenched land on Plethwih. The final battles of two civil wars were fought there. One, hundreds of years ago. The other, only a few months before. Led by Count Djago, the city of Cambria revolted against the realm and besieged Yorwick. The count was convinced that the king's brother, Duke Banfield Eldorath, ruler of Yorwick, was behind the assassination of his wife. As the rest of Lyonesse rallied to the king's banner and marched north, Count Djago did the unthinkable. He allied with tribes of giants and cyclopes from Fomoire who took over the siege of Yorwick, thus freeing the count's army to march south to meet the combined forces of the king. They met on The Dormonts, where Count Djago was defeated, and the giants were driven back into Fomoire. Enguer wasn't anywhere near Lyonesse at the time, but he had heard the stories. Of note, the most astonishing thing occurred after the revolt was squashed. The count's orphaned infant son, Pen Djago, was adopted by King Praetor Eldorath and Queen Penelope of Lyonesse, who were rumored to be unable to have children of their own. The boy's name was modified to Artur PenDjago Eldorath and in an instant became the heir to the throne of Lyonesse. A strange twist of irony that the count's son would effortlessly obtain what his father couldn't take by force and the spilled blood of thousands.

A grim smile devoid of humor appeared on Sir Perault's face. "By the grace of Sunna, I survived what many did not, and I stand here fully unspoiled except in my heart. And you, My Lord? Did you ever discover the whereabouts of the wicked sprite that sabotaged your saddle during the Tourneys?"

For the second time Zracul nearly leapt from his seat. "I thought I remembered your face! There was an itch in my brain causing such annoyance I was sure it would drive me mad. But you have solved the mystery!" He stood from his chair, raised his glass in salute, and to everyone's delight, spoke in verse.

"I met a boy barely a squire,
Who fought a war but did not tire,
He came to Ys draped in white,
For now he was a Temple Knight!
Here's to Sir Perault!"

The timing was perfect as everyone had just received a fresh glass of Mekali wine. Applause and laughter caused Sir Perault's face to redden with embarrassment, but it was all in good fun. Enguer was really enjoying himself. Lord Zracul, Prince of Vradesti, the so-called Blood Prince, was quite entertaining.

Enguer glanced over at Reskalin, and the sudden reminder of her appearance took his breath for a moment. She was more beautiful than he had ever seen her. Tonight, she laughed without a care, her eyes sparkling and joyful, her jet hair lifted above her shoulders with straggling tendrils curling down her pale neck in the latest Ysian style, and she wore a sapphire blue gown accented with actual sapphires around her neck and wrists. It was unsettling to see his lover in a dress at all, let alone a gown and all the rest. It wasn't very long ago when Reskalin was believed to be a man, growing up as a male in the guild where her father, by adoption, was the guild master. The infamous 'FatMan.' It was for her protection, so they said, and she filled the part to perfection. Even Enguer never saw through her disguise until she revealed her true nature several weeks after they first met. According to Reskalin, she was content to remain in the guise of a man for the rest of her life, until fate brought her and Enguer together. Somehow, they fell in love. It was very confusing for Enguer at first as he had never thought of a man in that way, and then Reskalin showed herself for who she was, and everything began to make sense for both of them. Sometime later, the FatMan revealed that the two of them played a part in a foretelling visited upon Myrllin in a vision. Why a legendary figure such as Myrllin would have visions about the likes of them, Enguer couldn't fathom, and no additional detail were forthcoming.

The Temple Knight made a half-bow to the room before he resumed his seat, taking a long sip of his wine.

"Such an interesting and entertaining group this is!" Zracul grinned broadly at all of them. "I believe Naamah chose well." He reached up and patted her hand, drawing a subtle smile from her thick red lips.

It was then Enguer noticed that the beautiful woman's eyes almost never left their subtle contemplation of Sir Perault, and when they did, those deep brown orbs surely snapped back to the knight inside a quick moment. What made the whole thing interesting was that Sir Perault was trading glances with her in the same manner, almost as if they were coy lovers hiding a tragic secret. Enguer would have laughed if he saw the same scene in a play.

There was a sudden sharp stab to his ribcage that he recognized as the point of Reskalin's elbow, and he realized Lord Zracul was speaking.

"Enguer? Are you well?" Zracul's intense eyes were full upon him. The whole room was looking at him.

"Sorry, Lord Zracul," Enguer recovered quickly saying, "Your clever rhyme made me think of my mother. She was a performer in the theatre of Courth, and often recited verse from her plays while at home. She died a few years ago." Reskalin's fingers twitched with subtle movements Enguer understood to mean, *Nice Recovery!*, in the guild's thieves cant.

Zracul nodded solemnly. "I am truly sorry to hear of your mother's passing. Was Courth your home?"

"It was," Enguer felt comfortable telling this man anything. "Well actually, we lived on a farm some distance from the city. My father was a ranger. He loved to spend his days in The Wilds hunting and fur trapping. After my mother died, he would take me with him. Thanks to his training and guidance, I am now a ranger as well. When he died, I decided to experience the world outside of Courth, so here I am."

"Your family name is Rand, yes? I recall reading something about a famed ranger named Gauren Rand from the Southern Kingdoms. Was he your father?" Zracul spoke to him as if they were the only ones in the room.

Enguer didn't mind. He had spoken of his father on many occasions to strangers curious about the legendary ranger from Courth. "Yes. I never realized how renowned his reputation was until after he died. It seems everywhere I go my name invokes his as well."

"So now you must endeavor to make a name for yourself!" Zracul raised his glass again in salute. The others in the room raised their glasses as well and murmured their agreement. "So, who is this beautiful woman at your side that mine eyes have been begging for an introduction?"

Reskalin quickly cut Enguer's reply, "My name is Reskalin. Enguer's lover and companion." She smiled sweetly as Enguer's cheeks bloomed red with embarrassment.

Zracul tilted his head back in a hearty laugh. "I'll wager everything in this ridiculously expensive manor house that you are more than that. Much more."

Reskalin effected a demure shrug and sipped at her wine to hide her sly smile. Enguer knew that last part was for him. She never tired of finding ways to remind him not to take himself too seriously, and he was talking far too much in a room full of strangers.

"Well now that we all know each other, I'll tell you a little about myself and why you are here." Zracul absently held up his glass and a servant moved swiftly to fill it.

"My family and I have traveled over a thousand leagues from our home in Vradesti, a small domain in the territory you call the Eastern Kingdoms. I am the eldest of brothers three and sisters twin, and Naamah here," he smiled up at her, "adopted daughter, but daughter still. Therefore, I am the first heir to our realm. Sadly, my father too, passed not long ago, and mother longer since. Thus, it falls to me to take responsibility for our kingdom far sooner than I might have expected, and now that the specified period of mourning has expired, I will be officially coronated upon my return."

"You cannot be coronated until after a period of mourning for your father?" Sir Perault sounded surprised at the idea. "If I may, how long is your kingdom's tradition that you can travel so far for so long?"

"One year is our tradition," Zracul chuckled. "And yes, it is a long time. But not so long that we can tarry in our affairs."

"You have my sympathies," Sir Perault offered with a nod. The others in the room quickly repeated the sentiment.

Zracul lifted his hands into the air, one holding a wine glass that was filled once more. "Thank you, my friends, but my father's death was no tragedy. He lived a long life filled with much happiness."

"Don't you worry that political rivals or enemies of your kingdom might take advantage of the king's death with all his heirs out of the country? Will you have a kingdom to return to?" Reskalin was as blunt as ever.

Enguer tensed hoping that she had not insulted their new friend.

"No," Zracul replied flatly. "None would dare."

A chill went up Enguer's spine. The look that flashed within Zracul's eyes was suddenly intense. And dangerous.

"We have capable stewards of the kingdom that have served our family for many years." The eyes softened, and his smile returned. "They are loyal. I am certain of it."

Zracul paused to stare into his wine glass. The room took on an awkward silence during the gap in conversation. Sir Perault shifted his eyes to the floor and then back to Naamah, Reskalin studied Zracul as if he were prey, Khulani sat quiet and contemplative, but it was the Atlanteans who seemed the most uncomfortable as their gazes swept from one face to another seeking a que that would somehow relieve the tension.

To Enguer's surprise, it was Naamah who finally rescued the moment. "My father is reluctant to speak of it himself, so I will say the words for him."

Gently, she placed her hand on his shoulder. He reached up and briefly squeezed it. "Some of you are already aware that my father is dying. It's the creeping disease. There is no cure – medicinal or magical - that will remedy his condition."

"How can that be?" Sir Perault shook his head in confusion. "You nearly won the Tourney not so long ago. Have you fallen ill since your arrival in the Western Kingdoms?"

'No, no," Zracul waved his hands for emphasis. "I became ill just after my father died. As my body fights this disease, I am sometimes filled with energy. Enough to compete in the Tourneys, for instance, before collapsing for days with exhaustion. As it spreads, there will be less and less of the former and exponentially more of the latter. Already I feel the strain of fatigue."

Naamah smiled down at her father. "Don't you worry a bit. There is lots of time for our assembled heroes to accomplish what you need before your days run short. Assuming they accept our hopeful pursuit."

"I don't understand," Khulani, who was sitting in silence since the introductions. He leaned forward in his chair. "You said there was no cure and that not even magic could sway the path of the creeping disease. Yet you speak with words of hope."

"There is hope," Naamah shifted with a smooth glide to the side of her father's chair showing off the full figure of her perfect form.

From the corner of his eye, Enguer could see Sir Perrault's gaze eagerly taking in every inch of her lithe curves revealed through her tight gown. He barely managed to stifle a chuckle with a cough and received the sharp end of Reskalin's elbow again, followed by a dark look.

Naamah did not appear to notice the antics as she continued, "My father's younger brothers, my uncles, are accomplished scholars and philosophers highly respected throughout the Eastern Kingdoms. Some time ago, they happened upon an ancient tome with the faded symbol of a sphere on the cover. Within its dusty pages there were precise instructions on how to control an artifact of great power. Unfortunately, there was no artifact paired with it, so they assumed it was either lost to history or a hoax. Eventually, they shelved the tome and focused their attention on other matters. Years passed and the tome was all but forgotten when Vadim and Fane came across the identical image of the sphere from the cover of the tome. It was carved into the ruin of a wall along with several symbols that appeared to be writing. They found it deep inside Ta-Shemau while exploring the ruins of a long-dead temple. Not even the locals could say to what god the temple was built. As fortune would have it, they came across a hermit priest living alone in the hills not far away. He too, was unable to shed any light on the origin of the temple itself, but he did recognize the sphere symbol and recalled a story from his childhood about it."

The servant keeping everyone's glass filled with Mekali wine must have been as enthralled by Naamah's tale as everyone else in the room as she sloshed a small wave of the crimson liquid over the lip of the crystal flute held by Havacian.

"It's fine, it's fine," Havacian laughed as the servant desperately wiped at the small stains on his robes. "It's not the first time I've bathed in Mekali and likely not the last!"

Qel joined in the laughter as did the others. Of course, the Atlantean was gracious and unperturbed by the minor incident, but the unmistakable terror in the servant's eyes after a stern glare from Zracul gave Enguer pause.

"Shim, go take a rest. You need a break." Naamah's words were sweet and kindly as she addressed the servant. "Have Mitsa take your place for the evening."

Shim sobbed, and nearly ran from the room.

"It's really nothing," Havacian held a troubled look on his face. "See? I have many stains on these robes and each one tells a story."

"Thank you for your consideration, Havacian." Zracul slumped his shoulders in mock despair. "We only recently moved into the Agrabuta with little time to assemble a proper staff. We hoped no one would notice."

Qel was the first to reply, "I'm sure she will improve with experience. We find humans to be a fickle . . ." His sentence trailed off as his cheeks reddened. "I apologize. That sounded terrible."

Zracul barked a hearty laugh. “Even in the Eastern Kingdoms we know of the Atlanteans. The whole world knows about Atlanteans. Some cultures revere your people as gods walking among men! Whom else can be crooned as, ‘The Enlightened Ones’ by the likes of kings and queens, proclaimed ‘Anunnaki’ from the vaulted ziggurats in Kur-gal, ‘Children of the Gods’ so often whispered by enigmatic priests in the dark temple corridors of Ta-Mehu and Ta-Shemau, and there are many, many more. You are young yet with much to learn about the world and your places in it. Have no fear, in a few years we will all tremble to sit so near.”

Zracul’s laughter echoed around the chamber isolating the shrinking Atlanteans who clearly wanted nothing more than to disappear within the folds of their chairs. All the while, Enguer traded glances with Reskalin. They could not have paid for better entertainment.

“Enough, enough. All this over a little spilled wine.” Naamah finally cut in. “Stop annoying our Atlantean friends for your own amusement, father. Remember, we are asking them to save your life!”

“My apologies,” Zracul wiped away tears of mirth from his eyes. “Sometimes I get caught up in the moment. Please continue dear.”

Naamah cleared her throat. “So, this hermit priest recounted a story about the sphere as a holy instrument of the gods. An artifact imbued with such power that no one God could claim it as their own. At times it was used by one God or another to raise the dead, lift mountains, or part the oceans. The sphere was attributed as the source of the Aur River and the giver of life. Disease, infertility, disfigurement, and madness were all vanquished by its restorative powers. In the end, the legend tells a final tale of the sphere in possession of an unnamed God, who, jealous of its power conjured a serpent from mist who swallowed the sphere whole and flew away beyond the horizon. The stories and legends of the sphere died with the temple. Or so we thought.” Naamah paused to take a long drought of wine. The room maintained the awe of silence. No one spoke or even stirred.

“Vadim and Fane now had a second connection to the sphere and a better understanding of its powers should the legend be true. Yet, still no sphere or any direction where to find it. For years the pair traveled from one place to another following whispers of ancient spheres that led to nothing.

Well, sometimes the occasional bit of ancient treasure or a magical bauble if they were lucky. Just no spheres. It wasn't until their father, the king, passed that they were forced to spend a few weeks at home while his body was prepared for burial and the public ceremonies were observed, that they had a real breakthrough. Vadim and Fane are scholars at their core and as scholars would do, they spent most of their time in the royal library. There, Fane discovered a vague reference to an antiquated city that perished in the mist hundreds, maybe thousands of years ago. Further study turned up clues, and with a little more information from various sources, they finally had a name: Kiltullagh. With the name they soon had a location, and it couldn't have been more obvious. Kiltullagh, or the ruins of what remained of the once proud and powerful city was situated within the obscure tangle of dense forest on the northern shore of the Lake of Mists!"

Gasps of surprise burst from every throat followed by chuckles for the irony of it all. Just when Enguer thought the evening had reached its peak, something would send it higher with a hammer blow like that from forge of a Dvergr Dwarf.

"The Ruins of Kiltullagh!" Naamah chortled. "The answer was in the Royal Library of Vradesti, where my father and uncles grew up, played, and called home the whole time! The ruins are not far from where we sit tonight!"

Naamah paused a moment and raised her hand to stay any questions. Her features grew serious and thoughtful as she navigated the emotions of the room from triumph to guarded caution. "Vadim and Fane discovered something else while searching for the location of the ruins. There were references to a fearsome guardian protecting the sphere. An otherworldly creature that stalks the memory of Kiltullagh hungry and forgotten. Maybe it's the serpent of mists that swallowed the sphere, if the story is true, or something else entirely. This is no expedition for scholars to undertake. It's impossible to know what horrors await until those brave enough to take the journey, face the dangers, and recover that which we seek for the life of my father. Of course, the first step is for this fine group of heroes to undertake the hunt. What say you all?"

A heavy silence settled over the room. No one breathed or batted an eye. The tension weighed upon every shoulder for a decision that could well become their death sentence. Enguer looked deep into Reskalin's brown eyes searching for a clue. He knew that if either of them agreed to go, the other would follow.

"I will go," Sir Perault spoke barely above a whisper, his eyes squarely on Naamah who nodded and smiled her acceptance.

"As will I," Khulani's tone was solemn and absolute.

"We will go as well," Havacian replied in a hoarse declaration.

"If we are to be gods, I think we must go." Qel agreed with a smile.

Naamah's gaze turned to Enguer and Reskalin, both still locked in each other's scrutiny. Finally, Reskalin gave a slight nod unlikely to be noticed by any except Enguer. He waited a second longer before slowly turning his head to meet Naamah's gaze.

"It looks like we're all in." Enguer hardly recognized his own voice.

A loud bong suddenly assaulted his ears sending jarring vibrations through his body. Blood rushed to his head and his heart pounded wildly in his chest from the abrupt shock of the sound. It was hardly any comfort that everyone in the room reacted the same way. Except Naamah and Zracul, both calm as a placid river in springtime while amused smiles flickered on their faces.

"We dine!" Zracul stood from his chair and escorted Naamah through a set of double doors opened by a pair of servants. Beyond, bright candlelight illuminated a table crowded with overflowing platters and goblets filled with more wine.

The delicious range of scents prompted a growl from Enguer's gut as, he too, rose to escort Reskalin into the dining room like a princess on the arm of a pauper. Inevitably, tomorrow they would be themselves again, but for tonight, they 'dined.'

Chapter 3 – The Sprinter

"Is this the right mooring?" Havacian dubiously eyed the midsized double-masted ship bobbing at the dock.

Qel smiled inwardly as his eyes scanned the pier, but their companions were nowhere in sight. "We are early. I'm sure our new friends will be along shortly."

"Do you think the boat will be large enough for all of us?" For a Wizard of the Blue Hall specializing in elemental water arcana, Havacian never reacted well to voyages that required a waterborne vessel.

Several burly dockhands carrying sacks, baskets, crates, and small barrels of supplies brushed by the Atlanteans, stepping nimbly onto the swaying ramp to the ship already swarming with sailors busily preparing for departure. The deck of the shallow boat was pulled up between two rows of benches on each side of the vessel to reveal a void where the dockhands stored the provisions for the journey ahead. Assuming the calm weather and the winds held steady, it would be a ten-day voyage up the aptly named River of Mists and into the Lake of Mists where they would presumably locate the ancient ruins of Kiltullagh. Overseeing the stacking and packing stood a grizzled old sailor with long sun-bleached hair and a strikingly athletic tanned physic that defied the age chiseled on his face. From time to time, he bellowed an order sprinkled with curses and insults at one sailor or another who appeared to take more humor than offense at the terse commands.

"Let's ask the captain," Qel motioned toward the old sailor. "I'm sure he will set your mind at ease."

The pair made their way down a short flight of steps to a landing closer to the water where the gangplank bridged the gap to the ship. Having noticed their approach, the captain moved to the ship side of the short walkway and awaited their arrival, curiously eyeballing the Atlanteans the entire way.

"Captain Rusee?" Qel called loudly when they reached the gangplank.

The old fellow ambled over and bowed his head in respect. "I was not aware that we would be transporting 'Enlightened Ones' on this voyage. My ship has no cabin to accommodate such esteemed passengers. Please accept my apologies."

Qel smiled warmly, or so he hoped. In truth, he assumed a cabin, and was disappointed the ship offered none, but there was no point in complaining about it. "We will be just fine sleeping on the deck with everyone else, captain. Please call me Qel, and this is my friend Havacian. We will be joined by four others soon. Will your vessel have adequate room for all of us?"

"But of course! The *Sprinter* can hold up to fifty, including the crew, without slowing her down!" the captain beamed proudly. "She is built for speed to avoid coastal pirates and raiders, and she boasts a deep enough hull to carry a respectable cargo."

"Should we anticipate pirates or raiders?" Havacian sounded nervous.

The captain shrugged, "Hard to say. If we do, my men can hold their own. And with a pair of Atlanteans on board, I doubt anyone would have the nerve to take us on. Anyway, come aboard! Make yourself comfortable at the bow or stern, and if you wouldn't mind, please keep clear of the walkway down the center of the ship so my men can do their work."

Qel quickly crossed the gangplank onto the *Sprinter* closely followed by Havacian. The two-dozen or so sailors onboard openly goggled at the Atlanteans until Captain Rusee spurred them back to work with orders shouted between strings of vulgar curses that made Qel blush.

Within the hour Enguer and Reskalin arrived wearing black leather armor that looked almost like an exoskeleton formed over their bodies allowing them to move so fluidly they might not have been wearing anything at all. Each wore a curved blade at their hip, but Enguer clearly favored the fine bow over his shoulder and Reskalin bristled with at least a dozen daggers.

Dangerous lovers, Qel thought, noting the way they looked at one another and sat so close.

Soon after, a sudden flapping of wings accompanied by the sharp warning cry of a large seabird landing on the deck drew everyone's attention. Just before its wide webbed feet touched the wooden planks, the creature abruptly transformed into the human form of the druid Khulani. Initially startled, several of the sailors cried out in shock, yet were soon hooting with laughter and delight at witnessing the dramatic arrival of a real druid. Havacian was less amused, as he nearly fell overboard backpedaling out of the bird's flight path. Qel flashed him a smile, drawing a dark look in response. *This was starting off to be quite an adventure!*

Another hour passed with no sign of Sir Perault. The boat was fully loaded, the sailors stood at their stations ready to row them out of the harbor, and a very agitated Captain Rusee paced at the edge of the dock muttering under his breath. Finally, a young boy ran up and handed the captain a note.

Moments later, the captain crumpled the paper and stormed back onto the ship. "Cast off! Let's get underway," he growled.

"Has the Temple Knight changed his mind?" The smooth deep tone of the Imaziyen Druid bore no anger or accusation.

"All I know is he will not be coming." The aggravation in Captain Rusee's response was far more telling. "Perhaps he could not be bothered to rouse himself earlier to let me know. We could have been well along the coast by now! One thing for sure is that we must be clear of the Bay of Morgen by nightfall."

The Bay of Morgen. Qel heard tales of the infamous Bay of Morgen from the sailors who brought he and Havacian from Andlang two weeks earlier. The Morgen, and Marimorgan, were a half-fish half-humanoid people living under the waves in a coral city called, 'The Rock Garden.' They were said to be man-eaters who coveted steel, iron, bronze tools, and weapons which could not be forged in their underwater lairs. According to the stories, the morgens eyes were very sensitive to sunlight, such that ships could generally pass safely through the bay during the day without fear of assault. It was during the night, or under dark overcast stormy skies dimming the radiance of the sun, that the morgen were most dangerous.

Countless sailors had been pulled from the decks of ships never to be seen again, and in some cases the ship itself disappeared beneath the waves with every soul onboard. Only fools dared to traverse the bay after dark. Qel didn't know how long it would take the *Sprinter* to ply its way to the mouth of the River of Mists, but his eyes were not deceived by the effort of the captain to hide his nervous agitation.

The morning passed by swiftly. The companions spoke idly between themselves while the sailors bent their backs over the oars to the beat of a drum keeping the fluid sweeps in sync with one another. None of them bothered to speculate as to why Sir Perault failed to join them, at least not out loud. It bothered Qel more than a little considering the knight was the first to volunteer in his eagerness to impress Naamah. He thought back to the night before. There was ample wine, the food was delicious, and the conversation light with humorous tales and anecdotes mostly provided by their host, Prince Zracul. The funny thing was, Qel barely remembered how the evening ended. He was sure they all departed at the same time with fond farewells and endless toasts to a successful journey, but he couldn't specifically recall Sir Perault leaving with them.

"Does anyone remember Sir Perault departing the Agrabuta after dinner last night?" Qel addressed the group.

"That came out of the blue." Havacian was looking at him quizzically.

Qel felt a little embarrassed. "I was just thinking that maybe he stayed longer or left early, and I didn't notice."

Enguer and Reskalin looked at each other and shook their heads uncertainly, but the druid, Khulani, paused in thought for a moment before he spoke. "Yes. I remember that Naamah asked if he would like to see some of the art brought from Vradesti to decorate their home. Sir Perault eagerly accepted the invitation and the two strode from the room arm-in-arm, wine glasses in hand. I was thinking that, I too, would have liked to see this art, but the way they acted gave me the impression that they were planning other . . . activities . . . besides art."

"Ah, well, perhaps that's it then," Qel shrugged. "My father is fond of saying that too much wine and a beautiful woman often results in a late morning, bad headache, and a broken heart."

The others nodded and chuckled.

"We can check in on him when we return to Ys," offered Havacian. "I'm sure he's fine."

By midday, any other ships travelling north disappeared in the vastness of the Primal Sea as the *Sprinter* stayed close to the coastline. The shore had grown rocky and dangerous, devoid of the smallest patch of beach with the forest growing right down to the edge of the water. Sharp rocks pierced the surface off the starboard side of the ship as well, yet the drum beat continued at the same pace, never slowing.

"Over there somewhere is the Rock Garden," Captain Rusee pointed west over the port bow. His tone was ominous. "The Morgen know we are here, and given our speed and heading, they likely know we will still be in the bay after dark, if barely. What remains to be seen is if they will follow us into the River of Mists. If they do . . ." The captain left the rest unsaid as he strode away.

Reskalin stood and stretched her arms into the air. "Looks like we may be tested sooner than anticipated. I can't say that I'm disappointed. It would be best for us to have some idea of each other's skills before we get to Kiltullagh."

Qel agreed, but from a different perspective. "Learning to trust each other and work as a team should be our top priority. Let us discuss how we can use our individual gifts in a way that will keep us all alive until we return to Ys."

Enguer, Havacian and Khulani all voiced their agreement. Only Reskalin remained silently staring. At first, Qel feared she was angry for contradicting her, but as their eyes met, he found no anger in them. Only respect.

Hours later, Sunna began her final retreat beyond the horizon, relinquishing the sky to her beloved sister, Luna, to reign for a time. With the fading light, the drumming slowed to a quarter as the rocks and shallows would be harder to navigate by starlight. The nervous sailors complied, if reluctantly, knowing that it would take that much longer to reach the river. Twenty-four heavily muscled men covered with tattoos sat in pairs on two rows of six benches holding fast to their oars. They wore a bit of leather armor, carried narrow curved swords in scabbards on their backs, and long daggers on their belts. To meet one in a dark alley at night would have sent the bravest soul running in fright, yet as the last rays of the sun evaporated from the sky, the worry on their faces made them appear more fearful than ominous.

"Easy boys," the captain spoke hoarsely. "Stay with the rhythm."

Every eye darted everywhere at once, searching the water, jumping at every slap against the hull. Enguer stood near the bow holding a knocked arrow in place on his bow. Reskalin crouched next to him with a black-bladed dagger in each hand. Khulani had transformed into an owl and circled the ship in wide arcs – his eyes, the owl's eyes, would be their early warning system if they were attacked. Qel stood with Havacian at the center of the ship on each side of the main mast waiting to do . . . something.

Except for the slow beat of the drum and the smooth lap of the oars breaking the water, all was quiet. If not for the tension that clouded the air, it might have been a pleasant evening. A shallow, cold wind blew from the north. According to the captain, it was a breeze that would favor their travel as soon as they made the turn onto the River of Mists. Earlier, Captain Rusee believed the estuary was less than a league away. They couldn't see it in the dusky light at the time, nor would they in the dark until they were nearly on top of it. The captain also expressed his doubts, once again, that the estuary would cause the Morgen to turn away.

The shore was at least 100 yards away, but it might have been a million. The rocks that sprang from the water around them like malevolent shadows grew taller and more frequent the closer they hugged the coastline. Without the forward motion of the ship keeping them on course, the rocks would surely tear a drifting vessel apart.

Twenty minutes passed and all was quiet, when a sudden thump against the hull pushed the port side up high and back down again. Several sailors shouted with fear, one released a high-pitched shriek, Enguer unintentionally loosed an arrow into the water followed by a curse, and Qel found himself clutching the mast for dear life.

"We hit a rock," the captain growled. "All is well, no damage. Rhys, was that you screeching like a deflowered tavern maid again?"

A long silence preceded a sullen "no" from one of the sailors in the dark. Several others chuckled with a much-needed release of tension as everyone relaxed. It didn't last long. An urgent hoot from above returned the sailors to silence. The crew warily drew their blades preparing for what would come, when a voice, beautiful and perfect, gradually rose in song that carried over the waves from somewhere ahead.

O' sailors rest your heads to sleep,
Against my breast to slumber deep,
Cradled in my arms so tight,
Protected through the endless night!
The sea beckons softly in your dreams,
The cold in your bones not what it seems,
Sleep O' sailors never to awaken,
Once your life the sea has taken!

Qel was infatuated by the haunting voice that sang lyrical perfection so pure that it made his heart ache for more. He felt a sudden desperate need to seek out this poet of the gods and shower her with adulations on the chance she might sing again! A form shifted in the darkness on the other side of the mast he grasped so tight, and a face resolved to his vision. Havacian! Eyes wide and wet with tears, Havacian must have been moved by the song as well! He was about to tell Havacian to join him. They would seek out the enchanting voice together, when there was a loud splash, then another, and another.

Twisting left, Qel's eyes located the source. There were men in the water swimming hard toward a boulder rising barely above the waves sixty feet from the ship. On that boulder sat a vision of unrestrained beauty. Her hair was wet, falling long down the front of her naked torso, big blue eyes glittered over sumptuous lips pressed together as she hummed, and her skin was milky smooth and radiant in the moonlight. Qel felt lusty stirrings and the pull of desire at the sight of so sensuous a maiden.

Another commotion of splashes announced more sailors diving into the water. They all swam like desperate men, sometimes struggling with each other to get ahead, and other times suddenly disappearing below the calm surf. Qel's eyes were drawn to Captain Rusee bellowing at his crew to stay on the ship. His face was flushed and red, and the veins in his neck swelled near to popping from the effort, but his orders fell on deaf ears attuned only to the song of the enthralling Sirine.

A spray of salty brine off the side of the Sprinter alerted Qel that he was standing at the port-side rail of the ship. He didn't remember walking there. What matter? The woman sitting on a rock in the sea sang with such divinity that he was sure he could walk upon the surface of the bay to reach her before all the others. He was going to try. He could use his magic to try.

Qel was a Wizard of the Red Hall, born with the talent to evoke elemental fire, and trained to control it by the Masters at the Imperial Wizards Enclave in the City of Atlantis. Yet, he was still a novice in his craft, which was the overall purpose for his and Havacian's travel to YS. They were on a 'Journey of Discovery' – a five-year expedition to experience the world and hone their skills outside the shelter of the Enclave – before returning to the college to decide upon their vocation. Some returned. Many did not. Already Qel and Havacian had cheated death more times than he would have ever imagined, and they were not even halfway through the first year of their Journey.

Flames sparked to life over the palms of Qel's hands as he concentrated on transferring the energy from the heat through his body and below his feet. The fire conjured through his magic did not harm him as it was essentially an extension of energy drawn from the orichalcum crystal that hung from a leather thong around his neck. It was essentially a conduit meant to enhance the power from the orichalcum crystals at the apex of Atlantean towers spread across the whole of Plethwih. Even a day north of Ys, the red glow from the Atlantean tower in the city faintly illuminated the night sky.

Qel slowly rose into the air, the tips of his leather travel boots sliding a half second on the deck before fully slipping the bounds of earthly contact. He rose until he was clear of the ship's rail and drifted forward to follow the flashing white foam of the wakes left by the half a dozen or so sailors still swimming franticly toward the beautiful woman sitting on the rock.

Barely past the edge of the ship, Qel's progress came to a jarring stop. Someone had taken hold of his leg. He glanced around to see the anxious face of Havacian staring up at him. His mouth worked, shouting words Qel could not hear over the sound of the song. He could only assume that Havacian was upset that he was leaving him behind.

"Use your magic to walk across the water!" Qel shouted above the song. "You are a Blue Wizard! And I have seen you do it before!"

Havacian's expression contorted in confusion, then he yelled something incomprehensible in return. Qel shrugged and shook his leg. Havacian held fast. He shook his leg harder, shouting at Havacian to let him go, but his friend doggedly held on. Qel was getting upset. He would have to force Havacian to release him. A quick look back at the swimming sailors revealed that only three remained and they were getting close to the rock where sat the divine vocalist. Her eyes locked with his, and Qel knew without a doubt that it was him she desired above the others. He had to hurry lest one of the sailors claim her first!

As Qel's gaze swept back toward Havacian, his attention was arrested by the bellowing captain. His eyes were wide with alarm as he frantically pointed to the water. Almost amused, Qel assumed the captain thought he was going to fall overboard. Then a sharp snap cracked near Qel's right ear and a shocking pain wracked his body as something wrapped itself tightly around his neck. Qel barely held the concentration of his spell as his body was jerked into a horizontal position with his head pulled by the neck by some sort of coil or rope coming from the water and Havacian holding tightly to his leg.

Song filled his ears louder than ever. The coil strangled his breath as it tugged him into a painful contortion with his head lower than his feet. From his awkward position Qel saw one last sailor in the water only a stroke or two away from the rock. Someone was screaming. It sounded like Havacian, but Qel could not be sure with the song so loud in his head. Black spots blotted his vision from lack of oxygen. He clutched at his throat and felt a wet sticky slime-covered cord he had no strength to break. As Qel's head lulled back at the edge of consciousness, he glimpsed a pale torso with broad shoulders and muscular arms adorned by glittering bands of gold and silver. The figure bobbed in the water holding fast to the other end of the lasso that was looped tightly around his neck. The creature's head bore long dark hair braided with silver strands, numerous loops pierced its long-pointed ears, and it had a wide face with large black eyes that could almost be human. Its smile, however, betrayed a maw filled with long needle-like teeth that sent a chill through Qel's spine. And then he was falling through darkness.

—·—·—

A loud crack rent the air just behind Khulani's tail feathers. The jarring sound was followed by a small tempest of air produced by the vicious snap of the whip held by a Morgen floating easily on the waves next to the ship. In his current owl form, a hit from such a vicious weapon would likely shatter several bones and send him plummeting. Khulani couldn't risk the danger. He angled sharply toward the deck of the *Sprinter* and transformed into his human form as fluid and graceful as a light breeze through the leafy boughs of an ancient Oak. Grace and style was the last thing on Khulani's mind, however, as he quickly surveyed the state of his comrades and the ship's crew. It was a scene of chaos. Men, seemingly driven by madness, had jumped into the sea, furiously swimming toward an unclad woman sitting on a rock that peaked just above the surface. She was full figured and beautiful with long hair decorated with brightly colored coral, pearls, and strings of silver. Her voice was at once alluring and hypnotic, so much so that Khulani felt that if he listened too long, he would be drawn deeply into its mystical notes, and to her, just like the others. Yet, it was his lucid mind, honed to a sharp focus by years of training in the druid enclave of Nabta, that he resisted the siren's song and saw with clear eyes that below her waist was not the shapely legs of a fetching humanoid, but the long scaley fish tail outline of a Marimorgen.

Until recently, Khulani was ignorant of this creature. It was only after his arrival in Ys that he overheard sailors talking about the dangers of the Morgen and the Marimorgen. And knowing that the path of their journey would take them right through the Bay of Morgens, Khulani had prepared for just such an encounter.

One sailor was only a few feet away from the Marimorgen still singing on the rock. The other sailors who followed him into the water were no longer visible, having been pulled below the waves by hungry Morgen. In the seconds that it took for Khulani to mutter the words that would release a spell upon her, his divided attention kept an account of the events taking place all around him. Captain Rusee bellowed orders to the men who remained on deck, Enguer and Reskalin fought side-by-side loosing arrows and thrown daggers at the Morgens who surfaced long enough to strike with their whips. One such attack pulled a sailor off the deck of the *Sprinter*. He flailed in the water screaming for but a moment before he disappeared below the surface where his last position was marked by a red stain agitated by bubbles and crimson foam. Another whip lashed out and coiled itself around Qel's neck. It would have pulled him off the deck, but for Havacian holding fast to his friend's leg causing a kind of tug-a-war between the tall Atlantean and the powerfully built Morgen below. In this heightened state of awareness, Khulani was acutely cognizant of the cold breeze that swept over his shaven head, the taste of salty air on his tongue, the subtle smack of waves against the hull, and a myriad of other sensations that his brain compartmentalized and stowed away while maintaining a calm focus to release the spell he so conjured.

All went silent. The singing, the waves, the captain's bellows, the war cries, the shrieks of pain and death. All of it. Still, the motion continued unabated, leaving confusion on both sides. It was like a soundless nightmare where the absolute silence served to heighten the fear and instill panic. With no song to lure the sailors to their peril, the Morgen lost their confidence. Whips loosened releasing their prey even as iridescent blue and green tails slapped the surface before fleeing to the safety of the murky depths far below. The Marimorgen, vexed and outraged at the loss of her song, stared hotly at Khulani, snatched up the disoriented sailor clinging to the rock where she sat, and slowly ripped open his chest starting at the collarbones. The sailor's mouth stretched wide in a shriek of agony that none would ever hear before sagging like a ragdoll in the Marimorgen's sharp-nailed grasp. She turned a triumphant hate-filled glare on Khulani one final time, and then plunged beneath the waves dragging the lifeless corpse of the sailor with her.

Khulani dropped the spell, and the onrush of sound returned so sudden that it was nearly overwhelming.

"Is everyone ok?" Khulani's deep smooth tone was the least jarring of all.

Reskalin and Enguer indicated with a nod that they were fine, although their faces and arms showed long cuts from the barbed tips of the Morgens whips. Havacian had pulled Qel back on deck where he coughed and sputtered desperately trying to regain his strangled breath.

Khulani moved quickly to his side and spoke a few words that instantly returned Qel's breathing to normal. "A little rest and he will be fine."

A grateful expression replaced concern on Havacian's face. "Thank you, druid. It seems you have saved us all today."

The shuffling of boots from behind drew Khulani's attention away from the Atlanteans. In the moonlight he could see the pained faces of the surviving sailors. All of them bore injuries to one degree or another that needed tending.

"Form a line," Khulani called out, "and bring the ones with urgent need to me first."

As the crew took their turns gaining whatever measure of healing and restoration Khulani could offer, Captain Rusee wasted no time getting the *Sprinter* underway under the power of his most able sailors. They lost eight of their crew in the battle, by Khulani's count, and although they could still continue their journey, every life now held more value than before. Not just for finding their way to the ruins of Kiltullagh, but for the return to Ys. Of course, Khulani could fly away at any time and abandon the Atlanteans, the couple from Arre, and the crew of the *Sprinter* to their own fate, but his honor would never allow that. Nor would he bring shame upon his circle and the gods they served. For good or ill, his fate was tied to these strangers he travelled with. So, it is. So, it shall be. As the shaman of his tribe always said - the spirits would guide him.

Chapter 4 – Love or Seduction

Perault awakened bleary eyed with a head pounding like a war drum after a long night of endless wine. He tried to raise a hand to his temple, but his limbs were restrained. The room was dark. No light entered through window or under a doorway to give him any hint as to where he might be. It was cold, he wore not a strip of clothing, and bound spread eagle on a board or table with his head slightly elevated above his feet. The stench of urine hung in the stale air. *What time was it?* he wondered. The night was a blur of drinking, and . . . pleasure. He recalled vague images of Naamah, naked and beautiful, performing unspeakable acts of erotic indulgences pervaded by carnal amusements that gratified his desires over and over more fully than he thought a body capable. The memories alone, hazy as they might be, were enough to instigate fresh provocation in his exhausted body.

As if summoned by his desires, hinges creaked, and Naamah's unadorned perfect form was dimly silhouetted in the doorway. She walked forward slowly, leaving the door open so that sparse light revealed a small room devoid of any furniture other than the plank whereupon Perault lay.

The clean scent of fresh lilac tantalized his senses when she came close, instantly clearing his head of the fog that shrouded his brain. Naamah slid soft hands down his chest and abdomen, and lower. He needed no encouragement, but her touch somehow heightened his arousal to unprecedented levels he never dreamed possible. Then, with languid proficiency, she smoothly straddled his prone form with exact calculation. Perault tried to speak, but her lips closed over his as the tips of her full pale breasts swayed over him, barely stirring the hairs on his chest. Everything was forgotten. Nothing else mattered. He lived in the pleasure of the moment.

Hours, days, weeks gone by. How much time, Perault could not be sure. There were rare moments of lucidity when he lay in the darkness strapped on the inclined table as he always was. Sometimes the bonds held his limbs tight against the plank, while other times links of chain fastened to eyebolts allowed for some small freedom of movement. In either condition he lay flexing the muscles in his arms, legs, and torso, straining against the shackles as he worked through the exercises learned as an initiate of the Temple Knights to keep his sinews conditioned and ready. Even so, he knew any attempt to break the bonds would be futile.

These periods, alone in darkness, gave him time to think. He wondered at the passage of time, the fates of the others who dined beside him at Zracul's table, when his beautiful tormentor might return again. Naamah. It was impossible to think clearly in her presence. She was never clothed except for those tall-heeled sandals that clacked loudly on the stone floor with each delicate step. To gaze upon her naked figure instantly filled him with mad desires. Every word she spoke, every touch, flash of her blue eyes, even the incidental brush of her long golden hair was seductive. And no matter how exhausted or drained his body might be, it responded to her every time with peak performance.

Sometimes she brought food, water, or wine, and fed him from her own hand. Other times she brought instruments of pain. Always, their unions lasted for what seemed like hours until her unquenchable thirst for every last drop of fluid Perault could produce was finally drained leaving him limp and sagging in his chains. These were his lowest moments when he screamed, begging for her return.

Eventually shame would set in, crashing over him like an avalanche of frozen spikes and needles. Alone in the dark, he felt shame for the carnal acts of flesh. He felt shame for his uncontrollable lust and constant yearning for her touch. He felt shame, most intense, for betraying the woman to whom he was betrothed; Lady Melisende Brigham. Thoughts of her brought tears and sorrow, climaxing with great sobs that wracked his body, before he finally slept a dreamless slumber, until awakened once more by the creak of yonder door.

Time past unknown. He dreamed. Sometimes uncertain in which realm occurred reality. Perault was in such a state when pleasant giggles and laughter of young women stirred him to wakefulness. They were happy sounds that provoked memories of fresh-scented ladies in elegant gowns strolling together through flowery parks or dancing in circles at a summer festival. These fanciful images were quickly despoiled by the odious stench of his own filth that muddied his inner thighs and leisurely sluiced down the angled board dripping into a widening clump on the floor.

Once again came the playful laughter. Perault turned his gaze toward the door where he spied two sinfully beautiful faces peeking into his chamber. Jaria and Daria. The door closed suddenly and they were gone. Perault lay alone and miserable in the sticky awful powerless to do anything about it when the door opened again as Jaria and Daria boldly strode in. They wore sheer white night gowns that hugged their lithe curves and perky breasts as soft dark curls fell over bare pale shoulders, and one's sharp features with cruel angular brows seemed almost a twin to the other. They came bearing large buckets. With one they splashed a cold cascade of water over Perault's body, the shock of it caused him to cry out, and he shivered violently from the chill.

"Aww. Is he cold?" One asked the other.

Perault could not distinguish between the two which was named Jaria and which was Daria.

"I think he is, sister!" The other laughed. "Let's clean him, so we can warm him up properly."

The pair produced dripping sponges from the second bucket and proceeded to casually wash every intimate inch of his body with a liberal drenching of lukewarm water. It was a humiliating experience for the noble Temple Knight, but gradually his teeth ceased to chatter, and the stench in the room faded away as the last of the awful trickled down the drain in the floor. Satisfied with their work, the women put away their sponges and stood side by side gazing lustily over Perault's naked physique.

"He is very well proportioned," one of the women observed.

"I agree, sister," the other replied. "He has strong arms and hands. But how can we feel his touch bound as they are?"

"How true!" the woman replied. "Why sister, I do believe we must remove the unsightly impediments to our pleasures."

"But a moment!" the other sister spoke with wide innocent eyes. "If his arms are free to touch and stroke as we please, wont he also contemplate a more dangerous feat?"

The first sister crooked her neck in a dramatic pose of thought. "You may be right, sister! We should extract a sincere promise from Sir Knight that he will not harm, abuse, hold for ransom, or make any attempt whatsoever at escape while he is paroled from those foul shackles."

"Yes, sister, that should do it," the other nodded her agreement vigorously. "But wait! Shouldn't we include the ones that hold his feet as well? Surely it is more desirous for a man to have proper use of his legs to achieve appropriate thrust in his exertions?"

"Quite so!" The first sister agreed enthusiastically. "What a tragic oversight that might have been! Shall we ask him now for his promise? I am eager to test his endurance!"

"Let's!" agreed the other sister.

The twins turned to stare down at Perault. He stared back dubiously. He was incredulous at the banter he witnessed between the two of them. More so, because of the innocent expectation that since he was a Temple Knight, he might keep any promise he was coerced to acquiesce.

Finally, the first sister spoke, "Sir Knight, do you agree not to harm, abuse, hold for ransom, or make any attempt whatsoever at escape while you are paroled from your shackles?"

"You said that well, sister," the other whispered.

The first sister smiled at the compliment revealing unusually long sharp white incisors.

The sisters gazed at him expectantly.

"I agree to your terms," answered Perault. Already his mind was working through the details of his departure.

The women clapped with glee.

"Let's release him, then!" The first sister darted to Perault's hands while the other sprang to his feet.

"Oh, no!" The sister near his feet exclaimed. "We have no key! What shall we do?"

The first sister tapped her cheek a moment, then said, "I suppose we'll just have to break them!"

"But won't Naamah be very upset when she returns to find him unrestrained?"

"I suppose she will!"

The sisters giggled and laughed. Perault was crestfallen. There was no way these small women could break the iron shackles. He had tried many times himself to no . . .

The sisters took hold of the iron binding around one wrist and an ankle. There were two sharp cracks simultaneously as the weight of the irons slipped away. Then the process was repeated and Perault was free. He sat up, glancing down at the broken shackles on the floor for confirmation. Indeed, each were sundered as if cracked by a heavy steel mallet. He turned his gaze on the sisters who stood stark naked having already dropped their gauzy shifts. Their unkindly exquisite features manifested identical hungry lustful smiles. All thoughts of escape evaporated in Perault's mind. He was at their mercy.

Perault soon discovered that although Jaria and Daria lacked the sustaining power excited by Naamah, the sisters could do well enough to stimulate his well-exercised cravings to satisfy their appetites. When they finally departed, he was drained of more than the production of his gender, but a good portion of his lifeblood as well, leaving him teetering dangerously at the edge of deaths door.

– – –

Naamah was in a rage.

"Look what those little whores have done!" She nearly shrieked. "You promised him to me, and me alone, and now he is nearly dead! What can be done?"

Perault was barely conscious as he watched through heavy-lidded eyes. Naamah wore a very tight one-piece black leather bodysuit with silver buttons down the front open to expose a large portion of her breasts. Closer stood the brooding figure of Prince Zracul staring down at him with intense angry eyes.

"They are impossible to control!" Zracul replied crossly. "Whatever I tell them not to do, they do anyway just to spite me."

Something swished and snapped behind Naamah that Perault's dull mind at first perceived as a whip until its persistent twitching back and forth played more like the agitated motion of a tail. *A tail?* His bleary eyes strove to focus more fully on Naamah, and had he the smallest reserve of energy he would have instantly recoiled. As it was, he could only stare in disbelief at her beautiful face transformed by long fangs protruding over her plump bottom lip and short black horns curving above her forehead. The rustle of leathery wings tipped by sharp barbs peeking over her shoulders completed his vision of insanity.

"What will you do?" Naamah demanded of Zracul.

The count pondered a moment before turning to face Naamah. "I will place a ward on the door so that only you and I may enter this chamber."

"And what about restoring my knight?"

"The simplest method would be to give him a taste of my blood," Zracul suggested as he coldly scrutinized the marks on Perault's neck.

"No!" Naamah decried with a sharp snap of her tail on the stone floor. "I wish for him to remain pure and clean."

Zracul motioned with his hand as he strode out the doorway. "Come with me," he told her. "I have an elixir that will return his body to the pinnacle of health."

Naamah gently stroked Perault's cheek before she followed Zracul out the door, closing it firmly behind her vellicating tail. The room was thrust into darkness and shortly the knight fell fast asleep.

Perault awoke with a start. He lay unshackled in a comfortable bed rather than the rude plank he expected to die upon. Gazing around the small chamber, he realized it must be the same one as before. Yet now it held not only a bed, but a bath, and a small table with a wash basin and mirror. There were paintings of strange landscapes on the walls, and the scent of lavender weighed heavy in the air from a silver vase filigreed with gold holding freshly pick flowers. A lantern hung idly on a peg illuminating everything by the dim amber of a steady flame.

For a moment, Perault thought it was all part of a hallucination brought on by some new drug given to him whilst unconscious. He dismissed the idea. His head felt unburdened by lethargy or dissociation which until that moment was a constant state of his being from the first night he came to the Agrabuta. Laying clear-eyed and lucid, he wondered how long he had been insensible after Zracul's vile sisters nearly drained him dry. All he could recall were fleeting glints of Naamah holding his head against her soft bared breasts; sometimes dribbling a sickly-sweet liquid between his lips, while other times singing a soft mellow tune that comforted him. The memories couldn't be real. Based on his short history with the seductive Naamah, it would be completely unlike her in every respect. Just like the wings, tail, and horns he dreamt she displayed while conversing with Zracul. It must have all been the delusion of a mind starved of the proper flow of his lifeblood.

Sitting up in bed, Perault looked fixedly at the only door to the chamber. Surely it was locked. He slid out of bed, placing his feet firmly upon the soft fabric of a thick rug covering the cold stone tiles beneath, and strode slowly on unsteady legs to the door. He was unclothed, as before, but that mattered little if the door were locked. His mind dared to hope for escape. He held his breath, reached for the latch, pressed the release, and pulled.

The door swung quietly open!

Perault was astonished. How could they be so foolish to leave the door unlocked? Perhaps no one expected him to awaken so soon, and considered the extra step unnecessary. Whatever the reason, he didn't care. If he could leave the room, then he was that much closer to escape should he evade the foul residents and find a way out. Perault moved to look down the dark hallway and found himself weirdly peering into his own room. Stepping back, he could clearly see the darkened passage extending to his left and right from the doorway; the lamplight over his shoulder reflected dimly off the grey stone walls and thick red runner on the floor. He thrust his hand out the door and suddenly a disembodied hand appeared from the opposite direction! Perault jumped back with a startled croak and the hand disappeared just as he withdrew his own hand from across the threshold. This was madness! Anger and confusion clouded his judgement and without regard to unforeseen consequences he rushed forward and leapt into the corridor.

Perault landed easily, but his stomach dropped like a heavy mallet at the jarring sight before him: he was staring into his own room. *Sorcery*, he thought to himself as he slammed the door shut and made his way back to the bed where he sat dispirited, puzzling through his current predicament. He knew little about the arcane, but if he could keep his mind clear, and pay close attention to anyone coming and going from his room, some revelation on the matter could elucidate a means to his escape.

Just then, the door opened, and framed within stood the beautiful figure of Naamah wearing a short red silken robe and matching heels. Perault could not suppress a quick intake of breath, nor did he notice it. The woman smiled broadly showing bright white teeth with pointed incisors he recalled from his dream. She stepped inside and let the door close behind her.

"You are awake!" she chortled with the barest hint of her usual cruel humor. "And you look as strong as ever."

Naamah untied the loose belt at her waist allowing the silky garment to slide off her pale slender shoulders and onto the floor. Perault was relieved to see no evidence of wings or tail. As she approached, the seductive sway of her naked hips and full round breasts brought a surging heat of desire that completely arrogated every sense of his physical and emotional being, dispelling all thoughts of escape, or for that matter, existing anywhere else but right here, right now.

"I love you."

Those simple words whispered lightly in his ear, and suddenly, Perault understood everything.

Days or weeks had passed. He wasn't sure, nor did he care anymore. Nearly every minute was spent with Naamah. Every minute she was gone he craved to have back, only to repeat those minutes no different than the first when she returned. She left the room rarely, and when she did, she returned with food, wine, or water for bathing. Never did she bring her tools of passion and pain, chains to restrain his limbs, or contrive any method of torture to enhance her pleasure. Naamah was a creature of passions still, and oh, by the gods, what passions she stirred within him! This was a Naamah Perault only began to know. A decidedly improved

Naamah who instigated inconceivable notions that, to entertain as a new reality, would betray everything he was – Temple Knight, a man betrothed, noble of Lyonesse. What was he now, or better to ask: what had he become?

Perault leaned back to look deep into her blue eyes and asked, "Why?"

If she were any other woman, his blasé response to her endearments would have incited a torrent of indignation and reproofs culminating in furious shrieking and possibly violence. Not Naamah. He knew she would understand the question precisely as he intended. There was no immediate reply as the edges of her lips slightly twitched with indecision.

"I have never loved a mortal man," she began hesitantly. "There are too many disadvantages for one of my species . . . and for the man himself, of course."

"Mortal man? Species?" Perault repeated. "The context eludes me."

Naamah looked away, her face flushed with irritation that Perault interpreted as inward-looking rather than directed at him. He had never seen her irritated, let alone angry, aside from the strange dream where she raged over his treatment by Prince Zracul's wicked sisters.

"I am not as you," Naamah spoke in nearly a whisper. "I was summoned from another world to serve an ancient demon who possessed the body of a powerful man. As a Knight of Lyonesse, I'm sure you would recognize his name quite vividly. He was Terril Djago, Count of Cambria."

An icy shock rippled over his flesh. Although Perault heard the stories about how the count's personality had changed substantially in the months leading up to the battle on the Dormonts, he agreed with the consensus of the nobility that, for reasons unknown, he had simply gone insane.

"The demon was released from the body of Count Djago upon his death, but something, or someone, must have interrupted its search for a new host and somehow forced the demon to return to the Infernal Planes." Naamah shrugged, "It worked out well for me as I was no longer tied to a master, and free to do as I pleased."

"Is Prince Zracul not your master?" Perault dared to ask.

She laughed suddenly. "No, my dear knight, he is not my master. Merely a kindred spirit I sought out for safety and guidance in a world I didn't understand very well. I am not like he and his family, although in truth, we are similar in many ways."

Naamah gently placed her hands on the side of his face and kissed his lips. When she withdrew, Perault noted an astounding change in her features – soft, serious, and a whiff of trepidation?

"You asked why I loved you," her face was close, the scent of berries on her breath bade him smother her lips with his. He resisted the urge as he was struck by the rarity of the occasion when she plied no seduction or amorous intent against him.

She continued, "I must make myself plain. It is time you fully understand exactly what, and who, I am. Accept or reject me as you wish. But know this: if you find that your heart reciprocates in kind and you accept my love, I will mark you as mine, and you shall become my mate until the end of your days."

Slowly, ever so slowly, she stepped back until she was satisfied he could take in her full naked form. There was a slight wavering in the air as a metamorphosis occurred that left Perault slack-jawed with wonder. Standing before him was Naamah in all her glorious beauty as he always knew her, but now he beheld impossible alterations he believed subject only to wild dreams. It was all true. From the base of her spine a long serpentine tail uncurled reaching the floor with length to spare, sweeping in long nervous arcs quick and unsettled. Short curved horns ridged by narrow rings like the core of a great oak curled back from her forehead, and leathery black wings capped high and low with sharply curved hooks stretched wide from her back obscuring the entire chamber beyond.

Perault stared with no voice to speak, taking in every detail. Internally, he knew what he saw was a disgusting display loathsome and vile that he should want to kill without mercy or regret. A wicked demoness repellent to the senses, nauseating, repulsive. A foul thing of darkness and evil by anyone's standard, especially that of a Temple Knight dedicated to the purifying light of Sunna! His face must have reflected his inner turmoil, for when his eyes found her face, she bore a sad countenance bleak and hopeless.

"Naamah," Perault barely managed to croak her name. At the vulgar sound, her proud pose withered, and with drooping wings she turned her head to look away expecting the rejection of her lover.

Seeing her thus, Perault's noble heart shattered into a million tears as every conviction he ever held turned topsy-turvy with his fleeting psyche. The irrational became rational, and the impossible possible. The monster had fled. He saw only the woman standing before him. A woman who made him feel alive. A woman who professed her love for him not for his title, position, power, or anything else. Just him.

"I accept you," Perault had found his voice. "I will be your mate. And I will love you until my last breath,"

In a sudden rush she was on him. Legs wrapped tightly around his hips, she pressed her desperate body against his, drinking deeply of his kisses as her wings gently enveloped their passion.

Chapter 5 - Kiltullagh

"By Tivr, if I don't get off this boat soon, I'm going to scream." Reskalin paced at the bow of the *Sprinter*. In the little space that there was, she barely took a half-dozen steps before turning to complete the circle.

Enguer sat with his back against the rail watching her. He looked drowsy as if he might doze off at any moment. "Sit down Reskalin and relax. Tomorrow at this time we will be on land again."

Reskalin shook her head. "Relax? How can I relax? Three days ago, we were ambushed by a singing sea-witch and her fishy-faced warriors . . ."

"Morgen." Enguer interrupted.

"I don't care what they're called," Reskalin kicked his leg as she passed. "And then all the fog. Three days of it on the river!

"Mist, not fog, dear. That's why it's called the River of Mist." Enguer was fully awake grinning at her like a happy idiot.

"Do you want another kick?" Reskalin fumed. "The only reason I'm sure we haven't been standing still the whole time is that the river finally gave way to a lake. But did the fog go away? Nooo."

"It's still Mist; the Lake of Mist, remember, sweet pea?" Enguer's smile was infuriating.

Hearing his flippant words, Reskalin thought her head might explode. "I'm going to throw you over the side!" Face flushed with rage, she grabbed Enguer by his collars and tried to pull him up. He barely moved. She tried again, but he slowly overpowered her, pulling her down on the deck to face him. Reskalin would have punched him if he didn't have hold of her arms, and if he wasn't so much stronger than she was. Yet, for all his strength, he was gentle as he drew her close, still with that stupid smile of his, pressing his lips to hers. Reskalin felt the rage drain out of her as she went limp in his arms. Still, in a final act of defiance, she bit his lip bringing a crimson bead to the surface of the skin before laying her head on his chest.

"Why are you so on edge lately?" He whispered into her hair as he stroked the back of her neck. "It's not like you to be so impatient. Is there something we are in a hurry to get back to in Ys?"

Reskalin closed her eyes, felt the rock of the boat more intently, and immediately opened them again before she became nauseous. She had to tell him. Of course, it would be better to wait until they returned to Ys, but her frequent mood swings were becoming harder to explain away.

"I'm pregnant."

She felt his body tense. Angry warmth flooded through her once again. It was probably a good thing she couldn't see his face with her own pressed against his chest. Still, if the wrong words came out of his mouth, she might just stab him.

"What?"

Despite her rising anger, Reskalin almost laughed. Enguer was no fool. He heard what she said clearly. She knew he was just stalling to let her revelation sink in. Rarely would he speak about anything of import without thinking on it for a moment. Reskalin let his hesitation pass.

"The other day I rode out to the Druid's Enclave and sat with the Master of the Grove for a time. Her name was Elder Sactria. I offered a sizable donation to her circle, and she was kind enough to perform a ritual that bestowed upon her a vision."

"What kind of vision?" Enguer's whispered question sounded hoarse in her ears.

Several seconds passed as Reskalin reconsidered telling him the next part. She finally decided it was best to get it all out at once so not to go through the tension she was feeling from him again. She spoke her next words in a quick, flat tone, "She said that if I continue with the pregnancy, in six turns of the moon I will birth twins. Girls. Your daughters." There, it was all out in the open now.

Enguer tensed up again. More than the first time. And said nothing! Reskalin felt furious heat rising to the follicles of every hair on her head. "I've decided to go through with it. I'm going to keep them," the syllables tumbled out more heated and defiant than she intended.

Enguer's body relaxed suddenly as all the tension built up over the last few moments seemed to dissipate entirely. Still, he said nothing! Reskalin's mind was screaming to know why. Was he just giving in, knowing that she wouldn't change her mind? Was he disappointed that the twins weren't boys? Would he not want anything to do with them just like her own real father? She felt the first drops of rain on her head. *Great.* Might as well be cold and wet in her misery. Her building anger and anxiety suddenly gushed into rage. *Enough was enough!* Reskalin fiercely pushed away from Enguer's chest and swiveled her head to face him ready for a fight.

Another thick drop of water landed on her livid cheek. There was not a cloud in the sky.

Lines of moisture ran from her husband's tear-filled eyes. His smile was warm and affectionate. In a voice thick with emotion, he said, "For a moment, I feared you would choose differently."

The simple statement cut through her anger, overwhelming her with deep shame that she could ever doubt this good man who, despite all her flaws and sordid history, happily desired her over anyone else.

– – –

"This must be Kiltullagh," Captain Rusee's sharp-eyed stare scrutinized the mist enshrouded water-logged shore crowded with crumbling ruins. "The great Sea-God Allod as my witness, I am surly glad not to be trapsing around in that soupy mess. Although I must commend your bravery to do so."

Qellel was not inspired by the prospect of slogging through a frigid swamp with almost zero visibility and no certainty as to where they were going. "Please take us further down the coast, Captain. Perhaps we will find a patch of dry land or a serviceable dock."

Qel shuddered as much from the cold as from the eerie nature of this place. There wasn't a single grunt from a frog or warbling whistle of a bird to entertain the ear as might be expected. Not even the buzz of an insect interrupted the gloomy silence. Aside from the soft slap of the oars slowly pulling the *Sprinter* forward, it was dead quiet.

"I wonder if this place was always so dismal." Havacian strode forward wearing his backpack over a heavy navy-blue cloak.

Glancing at his friend, Qel lowered his voice to just above a whisper. "Something about this mist strikes me as very unnatural. Can you feel it?"

"Yes," Havacian nodded. "Should we tell the others?"

"I think we should wait. We don't know them very well yet, and even if they are undaunted, the ship's crew may not take it so well." Qel knew how superstitious sailors could be, especially after barely surviving the Marimorgen a few days earlier. They needed the ship to be here waiting for them when they returned from searching the ruins.

"There!" shouted the captain. He was pointing port-side forward to a stretch of pebbled beach coming into view. "Prepare to anchor!"

Enguer, Reskalin, and Khulani joined Qel and Havacian at the ship's rail. The beach was studded with broken ruins large and small, but at least it was on dry land.

Quickly the crew of the *Sprinter* slowed the ship and retracted their oars. An anchor was dropped fore and aft to steady the ship, and a small rowboat was unlashed and lowered the short distance to the water.

"We can take up to three at a time in two trips." The captain eyed each of them ruefully as if wondering which he was seeing for the last time.

Qel climbed down into the rowboat followed by Havacian, and then called to the ranger, "Enguer, would you join us? Your skills would be well-suited to scouting the area while we wait for the others."

Enguer glanced at Reskalin and touched her hand. A word passed between them, but Qel could not hear what they said, and then Enguer hopped down beside them landing in the rowboat as softly as an agile cat.

The sailor rowed them quickly over the calm slow-moving waters of the placid lake taking only a few minutes to span the fifty yards or so from ship to shore. Enguer was the first to jump over the side, scampering up the beach on silent feet, and disappearing into the thick mist. Qel and Havacian followed only a few steps from the water so as not to get lost. Qel was certain Enguer could find his way back to them with little trouble. Almost immediately, the sailor pushed off to return to this ship for Reskalin and Khulani.

Qel's boots crunched in the gravel fallen from the broken ruins. He was impressed by the ranger's ability to move so quietly over the shifting ground, remarking, "He dove right in, didn't he?"

"Enguer reminds me a lot of Aelrindel," Havacian chuckled as he retrieved a light-globe from a pocket and set it aglow. It illuminated only a few extra feet before the light was reflected back by the heavy mist. "Without the pointy ears, of course."

Quietly chuckling, Qel produced his own light globe and activated the sphere with a word so to scan the surrounding area. "I wish Aelrindel could have joined us."

Havacian nodded. "I think he wanted to, but his priority had to be the mission his father assigned to him. Although I can hardly guess why an unruly princess of a human kingdom would concern the Sylvan."

Qel snickered at the idea. "Perhaps he will say more about it when we return to Ys."

The Atlanteans waited a short while before the splash of oars alerted them to the rowboat returning with Khulani and Reskalin. Their voices carried through the mist as their shadowy figures walked up the slope of the beach to where Qel and Havacian were waiting.

"This damn mist will have me soaked through in minutes," Reskalin complained.

"I do not mind the wet," Khulani replied. "It is the cold that I cannot get used to. Even in the months of the short moon, the winds that bend the grasses of the Ihbr Rrbi are like a comfortable embrace."

"Can you turn yourself into a bird big enough to fly me there?"

Khulani barked a short laugh, "Not yet."

When Reskalin and Khulani entered the circle of illumination cast by the light-globes, Qel smiled in greeting. "We are waiting here for Enguer to return."

"I see you have utilized your time conjuring up a glowy ball to light us all up," Reskalin was smiling sweetly. "Oh wait! My mistake, there are *two* of them. How marvelous."

Qel had the feeling he was being mocked in some way that he didn't quite understand, and responded with the first thought that came to mind, "Would you like one?" he asked uncertainly.

"Why not?" Reskalin was still smiling. "Perhaps we should *all* have one. That way, whatever creature Prince Zracul mentioned was guarding this place will have no trouble pinpointing exactly where we are."

Immediately, the two light-globes winked out. Qel was glad for it so that none of them could see how red his blue-skinned cheeks were blooming.

"You're right, that was stupid of us," Havacian mumbled.

As Qel's eyes adjusted to the strange twilight of the misty beach, he could make out nothing more than the darker outlines of his companions. They looked more like shadows than people of flesh and blood. Except for Khulani. In the place on his shadow where his eyes might have been, there were two dots shining with a the blueish-white glow.

Tearing his eyes away from the druid, Qel looked in the direction of Reskalin's shadowy form. "Enguer should return soon."

"I'm here now," Enguer's voice from behind caused Qel to nearly jump out of his skin. "I never expected Atlanteans to be the jumpy sort." There was amusement in his tone, but at least it didn't sound condescending.

What a pair these two are, Qel thought as Enguer's shadow joined Reskalin's.

"I didn't go far," Enguer began. "Just far enough into the ruins to see that Kiltullagh was no small town in its day."

Reskalin sighed deeply. "How will we ever find this sphere? Captain Rusee said he would wait a week, maybe two if we check in with him, but it could take months to find, assuming it still exists."

"Maybe," Enguer nodded. "However, I did find what appears to be the main boulevard spanning the length of the city. I followed it north where it ended in the remains of what was once an expansive port. If we go south instead, it might lead to a temple or palace or some other location that would be more likely to house such a valuable artifact."

"What about the mist?" Reskalin asked. "We might not even see the buildings unless we are right on top of them. I can barely see ten feet as it is!"

"My vision is clear," Khulani interjected. "So, I can be our eyes."

Enguer's shadow turned toward Qel and Havacian. "Can either of you do anything about the mist that will allow us to see through it?"

"They can make pretty balls of light," Reskalin declared.

Qel imagined that sweet smile painted on her face as his cheeks bloomed red again. "The source of my talent is Elemental Fire. I have not learned much beyond that, yet. Havacian?"

Havacian cleared his throat, "My talent utilizes Elemental Water and since the mist is comprised of many tiny droplets, I should be able to affect an area for a short time when needed."

"That could be helpful," Enguer's shadowy hand scratched at his shadowy chin. "Especially if this so-called guardian Prince Zracul spoke of is real. I have seen no evidence of it yet, though."

"Let's stick close together in any case," Reskalin reasoned, "and rely on Khulani's eyes to tell us what the rest of us are blind to beyond the veil of mist. Havacian, prepare whatever is required to clear the mist in case we are attacked, and Qel, keep the fire at your fingertips white-hot and ready."

As much as Qel wanted to dislike Reskalin for all the teasing, he had to respect her ability to assess a situation, devise a coherent plan, and lead with authority. Qel suspected that if things turned for the worse, it would be because of her leadership that they might survive.

– – –

"This is the boulevard that runs roughly north and south from here." Enguer pointed at the smooth stone pavers that widened beyond their view in the thick mist. Most were broken by roots thrust up between them and other vegetation that disrupted the once linear pattern assembled to provide easy conveyance for wheel, hoof, or foot. "It's about forty feet wide and runs nearly two-hundred yards north to the port. I don't know how far south it extends. What can you see Khulani?"

Khulani was standing very still with his head cocked as if listening for something in the distance. His eyes were rolled back in an unsettling display of white orbs shining with soft luminescence. "It is strange," he paused. "No. Not strange, unnatural. I sense no creatures in this place. No bird, snake, lizard, or even a rat dwell here." His eyes rolled forward to their natural position, although his pupils still glowed through the mist. "And you are correct, Enguer, the boulevard continues south for at least a mile."

"What about the buildings?" Reskalin strode a half step closer to the druid. "Do any standout?"

"Time has taken a toll on every structure here. Trees grow within houses, branches and roots break the walls, vines cover everything – some buildings entirely – and there is crumbling stone everywhere. I see fragments of strange symbols I do not recognize on some of them, and not a single house or trade shop rises above the first floor, although I think most might have been as high as two or three long ago."

Reskalin sighed heavily. "That's not very encouraging. If we must dig through every building to find this sphere, I'm afraid our task will be impossible to complete. Maybe if we go back to Ys and explain to Prince Zracul what we found, he will consider sending a sizable work crew to excavate the city until they find it."

"Maybe we can help with that." Havacian glanced over at Qel who nodded as if he knew what his friend was thinking. "The sphere is magical, right? I mean, it must be if it can do what Prince Zracul claims. Qel and I can detect magic nearby if we concentrate. In fact, we can sense a faint dweomer all around us right now."

Reskalin's features twisted with an array of emotion. This was a dangerous look Enguer knew well as his wife was on the verge of losing her patience.

"How are you going to know where the sphere is if, as you say, everything here is magic?" she nearly shouted.

Havacian to a small step back, clearly startled by her outburst.

Qel came quickly forward and replied in a calm voice, "What Havacian is trying to say, is that the sphere would likely radiate stronger magic than the ambient magic we feel around us. So, rather than dig through random ruins, we can walk the city and investigate only the areas where we sense spikes of magical energy."

Almost instantly, Reskalin's stormy visage softened to a sarcastic smile. "Well, the two of you might just prove your worth after all."

"Let's get going then." Enguer didn't care to spend one more minute than necessary in this blinding mist. He couldn't sense magic like the Atlantean wizards, or see through the mist like Khulani, but he did have a sixth sense for danger honed by years in The Wilds with his father – a legendary ranger and member of an adventuring group called The Five – and the raised hairs on the back of Enguer's neck was telling him that they were being watched by something very dangerous. "We can start by taking the boulevard south and see where it leads us."

Everyone was in agreement with his plan, so Enguer slowly led them south, picking the easiest path along the ruined boulevard as they went. From time to time, Khulani would describe the ruins ahead, beyond their vision. There was very little new to tell other than rubble from collapsed buildings in the street, or trees growing through the pavers appearing like monstrous creatures in the mist before they could be seen for what they really were. Still, the Atlanteans remained frustratingly silent as the group moved on, passing block after block of vague silhouettes cast by crumbling structures that took on unusual shapes hinting at imagined fears.

Their progress was slow, hampered often by ruins they had to climb over, or branches and vines they were forced to hack through. In the days when the boulevard was clear of such obstacles, they would have crossed the same distance in a fraction of the time. Two hours of exhaustive effort passed before Khulani sighted something new.

"The boulevard comes to an end at a large building two-hundred yards ahead. I believe it is mostly intact. Maybe a temple of some kind. I cannot be sure until we get closer." Khulani suddenly stiffened. "Wait, I see something moving."

Havacian sounded a more urgent warning, "I sense it too. It's closing fast!"

Enguer knocked an arrow in an instant, his senses strained to hear, smell, or see anything in the gloom ahead. Reskalin stood frozen next to him with a curved sword in one hand and a long-tooth dagger in the other, while Khulani and the Atlanteans halted a step behind. All of them stared forward utilizing whatever perceptions they possessed to understand what was coming.

A few seconds passed and then a few more.

"What's happening?" Reskalin's harsh whisper cut the silence.

Khulani was the first to respond. "It has stopped not far away. Maybe fifty feet."

Qel nodded his agreement.

Reskalin relaxed a little and turned her head to look at Khulani and the Atlanteans. Her eyes were tight with agitation. "Well, what the hell is it?"

Once again, it was Khulani who answered. "A very unusual creature. It is difficult to see its shape because the form of it blends with the mist. Sometimes the eyes are visible, as they are now. The eyes are very large. I cannot guess its intentions, but I believe it is curious about us."

"It is also a creature of magic," Havacian added. "It must be the guardian we were warned about."

Reskalin slowly slid her blades back into their scabbards. "Okay. Let's all relax and put our weapons away. Maybe it will leave if it doesn't feel threatened."

"I don't think that's how it works with a . . ."

Qel's words were lost in the eruption of a deep-chested voice that must have echoed all the way back to the *Sprinter*. "VRTOG GOHON! CRIP PRIAZ IADANAMAD NOALN EDNAS GIGIPAH. BABALON UNDL – NIISO CORAXO!"

No one moved or spoke for several long moments.

"It is gone," Khulani finally whispered.

Havacian's almond-shaped eyes were stretched wide as he turned to face the others. "That sounded like a warning."

"Or a threat," Qel agreed.

"Stay here while I scout ahead on my own," Enguer slid a ring over his finger and promptly vanished, yet his voice spoke from the space he had occupied. "We may be standing at some unseen threshold that prevents the creature from attacking."

Before Enguer could take half a dozen steps, Reskalin hissed urgently "Wait! The mist moves around you, marking your progress."

He knew she was right. Enguer was invisible, yet she was staring exactly where he stood. Reskalin's sharp eyes had saved the two of them on many occasions and if she could track his movements, he had no doubt the mist creature could as well. Removing his ring, Enguer strode back to the group, and did his best to keep his aggravation at bay when he spoke, "Then we will have to stay together and hope the creature, guardian, or whatever it is finds our numbers intimidating enough to leave us be."

"It knows we are here," Reskalin reasoned. "So, we should run as quickly as we can to the temple where we may find cover, or better yet, get inside and close the door to keep it out if the building is not in ruins. You say about two-hundred yards, Khulani?"

Khulani nodded, "Yes. Maybe a little less."

Reskalin crouched. "Okay, ready? Don't stop no matter what. If anyone gets separated from the group, find a place to hide and we will find you once we have a secure location. GO!"

Chapter 6 – Revelations of Blood

Ahes lay limp and exhausted, draped like a warm blanket on top of Zracul. Their bodies were stained crimson, as were the sheets and the bedding around them. For two days and two nights the pair engaged in explosive passions that would not be satiated. At first it was like a competition between rivals, but as each became familiar with the other's intimacies, they succumbed to a wild hunger that drove their writhing bodies together again and again. Twice someone entered the chamber attempting to playfully join in. The first, Zracul thrust against the far wall with such force that the figure crumpled on the floor never to rise. Ahes made no objection. The second was less timid as he attempted to force his way into the mix. This drew a violent response from Zracul who tore out the man's throat with his bare hands, splashing his innards across the floor and walls. Zracul expected Ahes to react with horror or at least a stern reprisal, but as he turned back from casting the bolt on the door, he found her laying in the slowly expanding crimson pool moving her arms and legs back and forth as if she were making snow angels, all the while giggling at the pleasure of it. They spoke not a word and quickly resumed a frenetic discourse of heightened desires painted red.

Hours later, Ahes rose from the sticky gore and called for her attendants. Zracul sat up admiring her shapely curves discolored as they were with the lifeblood of a dead man. There were cries of shock and surprise when her attendants arrived, but Ahes quieted them with softly spoken words that even Zracul could not perceive. Thereafter, her followers went about the business of preparing baths, removing the bodies, and cleaning the room unmoved by what they saw.

"I have determined that we are compatible," Ahes tone was matter of fact. "You may proceed with courting my affections."

Zracul barked a laugh. They were clean again, soaking side by side in large brass baths of steaming water. "I'm pleased to have passed your test, but won't your father, *the King*, have something to say about it?"

The Princess rose seductively from her bath and stepped into his, lowering herself slowly with her thighs tight against his hips. She gasped with pleasure at his energetic accord, then leaned forward and whispered, "My father will do as I say," her tongue licked the wine from his lips as she spoke, "as will you. Remember my terms."

Little was said after that, and when Zracul finally departed The Black Door, he was content to leave her panting and satisfied, if not begging.

– – –

"All is nearly ready, brother," the sonorous voice was subdued in a conspiratorial tone that clashed oddly with the usual behavior of the speaker. "Once we have the sphere, the rest should become clear to us."

"Relax, Vadim," Zracul replied in an offhand manner as he walked slowly around a heavy oak table set in the center of the room. "No one can hear us. I've taken precautions." He was appraising an unusual construct that took up a goodly proportion of the tabletop, marveling at how his brothers managed to transport the immensely heavy thing to the highest level in the east tower of the Agrabuta. It appeared to be constructed from mainly platinum components fused together where the pieces met. Lambent light from lanterns hanging at intervals between shuttered windows around the room reflected off the polished metal and was nearly blinding at certain angles.

"We built the entire structure within this chamber," Fain offered as if reading Zracul's mind. "Otherwise, it would have required a crew of men and at least two hoists to lift it so high. Not to mention a team of stone masons to break down the wall and rebuild it again after we got it through. No doubt a project of that sort would have been the subject of observation and inquiry with endless speculations by many throughout Ys before it was done."

"Yes, yes. You did well, brothers," Zracul's tone held an edge of exasperation. Of his two brothers, Fain annoyed him the most. He never let an opportunity pass where he might fish for praise or flattery. Still, Fain was also a talented scholar with a mind for grasping what most others could barely conceive. "Assuming it works."

Vadim shifted nervously, directing his gaze at Fain who stood against the grey stone wall where conflicting shadows eerily flited across his stern features.

"It will work," Fain replied blandly. "Assuming we have a sphere to put in it."

Zracul checked his anger, ignoring his brother's insolence. That was the other thing about Fain, he could never allow the smallest slight to go without reply.

"If," Vadim paused. "When we have the sphere, which one of us will test it?"

"I will, of course," Zracul snapped. "And there will be no 'testing.' It will either work or it will not." He glanced at his brothers. Neither showed any emotion one way or another. They knew he was their master, and would never question his authority or challenge his decisions.

"It will be no easy thing to control it," Fain remarked. "In fact, I expect it will be quite dangerous if any of the incantations are off by even the slightest enunciation or . . ."

Fain again! Zracul was at his brother's side in an instant, speaking plainly into his ear with undisguised malice, "You will teach me everything."

Clearly shaken, Fain nodded stiffly, and muttered a hoarse reply, "of course I will."

"Leave me now," Zracul commanded. "I wish to study the tome in peace."

Without a moment's hesitation, the blurred forms of Vadim and Fain disappeared swift and silent down the spiral stairway.

With a great sigh, Zracul strode to one of the windows and opened the shutters looking out upon the city. Ys was no less beautiful at night than it was in daylight. Perhaps more so. Some called it 'the city of a thousand towers.' They would be right in saying so, for that was the dominating feature that stood out even more than the impressive harbor. Everywhere, illuminated towers wide or narrow stretched high above the crenellated walls. Between them arced walkways strung with colorful lanterns swaying over broad avenues, green parks, and whimsical waterworks limned in lamplight or massive braziers of flame lifted high. It was not yet midnight. The streets were crowded with the revelry of citizens and the wonder of foreign travelers that would hardly slacken until the sun peaked over the eastern horizon. Only then did Ys rest for a short while until the business of the day crowded the streets once again.

As was his usual custom lately, he planned to meet Ahes at midnight. She would frolic among her favorite followers dragging her entourage from place to place until she found one that fit her mood. Sometimes they were high in a tower, or low underground, or somewhere in between. Certainly, they all looked different, some had themes, but to Zracul they were all the same. In any case, the night would always end with he and Ahes drained by their passions and drenched in blood. Yes, that was the way of it every night now. Ahes was aroused by the inclusion of blood as a sensual element of their erotica. So far, she preferred he do the killing, although Zracul soon discerned it was not due to any distaste on her part. She seemed to study his methods with curious attentiveness as if her observations would someday define the creature that he was. Maybe it would. He would have to tell her eventually. Perhaps sooner rather than late. Zracul had come to Ys with a purpose. He always planned to "court" Ahes so to compel her to perform a single task. Nothing had changed in that regard. But what had changed, and what he didn't expect, was that he would yearn to keep her.

Ahes lounged on a cushiony divan with a glass of red wine in hand as she secretly scrutinized Zracul from under her long eyelashes. He was just a few feet away sitting casually in a plush chair reciting the history of his homeland, Vradesti. It was her first time in the Agrabuta. An ancient estate that represented the last of 'old-Ys,' from before the high towers and embracing walls that reached out into the harbor and distinguished Ys for the fabled city that it was. Over the centuries the Agrabuta changed hands many times, yet always managed to remain well preserved. As far as she could see, the interior was clean and maintained with furnishings and décor that blended in color and style, if dated. Except for this room. The modern divan where she sat was oddly mismatched with the chairs and tables and not even those matched with each other! This was a room decorated by a man.

Upon arrival, she met Zracul's brothers. One was a big brooding man with a deep voice introduced as Vadim, and a smaller man with intelligent eyes and a piercing gaze called Fain. Almost as an afterthought Zracul gestured to a pair of young women peeking around a corner that he identified as his little sisters, twins by the look of them, Jaria and Daria. They were a strange pair whispering and giggling to each other all the while flashing lurid wicked smiles her way. Of course, Ahes was introduced to them all previously, when they came to the palace to see her father, but she hardly remembered. The mystery of Zracul was deepened further a little while later when a beautiful woman with long blonde hair and deep blue eyes breezed through the room wearing a seductively tight one-piece leather jumpsuit studded with silver buttons that fastened a plethora of flaps in curiously advantageous positions. She waved idly when Zracul introduced her as his daughter Naamah. Or maybe he said sister. Either was irrelevant and untrue, for it was the sentience of the Greater Demon Aesmadaeva that peered through the beautiful brown eyes of Ahes, and it saw right through the farce. Naamah was a summoned creature from the Infernal Planes, the home to all greater and lesser demons, devils, and fiends of every variety. She was a fiend with a special talent for lurid seduction and domineering charm often employing torture and pain as an erotic stimulus to the men, and sometimes women, she controlled. Ahes wondered if Zracul was powerful enough to have summoned this creature. That gave her pause. She, as Aesmadaeva, could not have done so. At least not yet.

"So, that's my homeland in a nutshell," Zracul was saying. He leaned forward, stretching a hand toward her. "Now it's time you discovered who I am."

A thrill shot through Ahes as she gently placed her hand in his. They stood together, and he led her down a dark hallway to his bedchamber. The room was vast with tall windows covered by burgundy curtains trimmed with gold. There was a black iron-cast spiral staircase connected to a balcony running along the wall where hundreds of books were lined in mahogany cases. Heavy oak furnishings adorned the room with ancient tapestries hung from the walls and thick rugs covering the stone floor. A massive candelabra hung from a thick chain that could be lowered to light the dozens of pillar candles it held illuming the vaulted ceiling and all else within. Yet, the most poignant feature was the wide-framed over-sized bed with ruby-toned sheets pulled taunt over a thick mattress.

Zracul released her hand to pour two glasses of wine from a large carafe sitting on a small table between two excessively cushioned chairs. He handed her one of the glasses and gestured toward the nearest chair.

"Sit," he bade her.

She did so with gentle ease not wishing to give away her enthusiastic anticipation of his promised revelation. Hours of contemplation had left her no closer to guessing his true nature, and this from the perspective of a Greater Demon having lived thousands of years, was no small thing. Now, so close to the truth, she was almost giddy.

He kneeled in front of her, leaning in close. "No matter what happens, stay seated until I come to you," he breathed. "And do not be alarmed at anything you see. No harm will come to you."

Ahes looked deep into his soulless eyes and could almost see the flicker of flames burning within. Her body shook with uninhibited nervous energy causing the multitude of gold chains layered around her neck, arms, and ankles to clink almost rhythmically. She wasn't afraid. Almost nothing provoked any semblance of real fear in her. Aesmadaeva was yet a powerful demon, even within the frail flesh of a mortal princess.

Zracul kissed her lips lightly before stepping away toward a narrow door Ahes assumed was a closet. She was desperately trying to be patient, but her desires were nearly driving her wild. All afternoon had been spent in idle conversation and introductions when all she wanted to do was tear off her silken gown and ravish her lover. That, combined with her nervous anticipation of whatever was behind that door, had her cravings pleading for release.

The narrow door creaked with opening. It was dark inside so she could not see what was within. Zracul reached into the darkness as if to take something, and then slowly withdrew, turning to face Ahes as he stepped back, pulling into the light . . . a girl. A pale young woman clothed in a humble unadorned dress like those worn by simple folk in the country outside of Ys.

Ahes was confused and disappointed. Was this their plaything? What did this woman have to do with who he really was?

"Watch," his voice held an ominous tension that focused her attention more fully on the spectacle at hand.

There was a wrench of tearing fabric as Zracul tore the back of the woman's dress and slowly let it fall around her ankles. Something was odd about the girl. She was not terrified and pleading as the others whose blood they bathed in. She was calm, sedate, with unfocused eyes, and the absence of any expression. And older than first glance now that her well-rounded mature breasts and wide childbearing hips were exposed.

Interest piqued once more, Ahes expected Zracul to bring the woman closer or tear out her jugular. Instead, he moved behind the woman with one arm tight around her smooth waist and a hand tilting her head to the side where he gently brushed away the hair from her neck. There was no reaction from the woman. Ahes watched with fascination as Zracul slowly bent his head close over her pliant neck.

The woman jerked with a sudden spasm and opened her mouth wide but did not cry out. Zracul held her tight as his teeth bit down firmly on her neck. It went on for long minutes with little movement except for the occasional convulsive jerking of the woman's naked body in his arms and the progressively ashen tint of her skin. Ahes watched entranced by the spectacle. Whatever was happening, this lecherous performance stirred a primeval lust in her so volatile that it threatened to explode in an irrepressible fury of wild abandon. She found that she was standing, wine spilt upon the priceless rug unheeded, and her dress absently piled around her feet. She was naked save for her chains shivering over the goosebumps on her flesh, with her long blonde hair freed to cascade around her shoulders and down her back.

She took a step forward and stopped, momentarily frozen by the sight of a trickle of blood running down the woman's neck. Zracul twisted his head to look at Ahes without removing his mouth from his captive's artery. She saw dark orbs of the blackest night staring back at her. So dark, they seemed to radiate the absence of light against the flush of his ruddy face revitalized with vigor and life. Zracul opened his mouth wide stretching the skin on the woman's neck until it snapped back with the release of suction produced by long fangs dripping crimson from corresponding angry ruptures weakly throbbing with the last few beats of her blood-starved heart.

– – –

Dim light filtered through the narrow spaces of the curtained windows as Zracul awoke. The sun would be setting soon. Curled under the silky sheets beside him lay Ahes still deep in a fitful sleep. He sat up on his pillow and gazed around the room, his eyes stopping to regard the stiffened corpse of the farm woman he drained the night before. It might have been two nights ago. Everything was a blur after . . .

He recalled that once he finished consuming the lifeblood of the farm woman, he felt the usual exuberance and vitality rush through his veins like liquid fire. That was always the time when he was the most vulnerable as a sort of euphoric paralysis came over him for a few minutes while his body processed the intake of ingested nutrients. Once his vision cleared, he was startled to see Ahes standing only a few feet away completely naked. He recalled his surprise at the expression on her face. Her eyes were wide and mouth agape in shock, astonishment, amazement, disbelief, wonder . . . but lacked any hint of fear, terror, horror, or disgust that anyone else might have betrayed. That was the moment he realized there was something otherworldly or supernatural about her. He had no time to think on it as he was barely able to drop the woman from his arms before she was replaced by the passion enflamed princess bearing him to the floor with lusty kisses as she tore at his clothing. The many hours that followed were consumed with the enterprise of two inexhaustible lovers scaling impossible heights to reach a climax only to discover greater peaks in the distance to conquer. Ahes was fired by an avaricious hunger like never before, and it wasn't until she lay limp and indolent, did she finally admit satisfaction.

"Why do you drink their blood?"

Not realizing Ahes had awakened, Zracul was jarred from his thoughts. She lay deep in her pillows gazing up at him with clear brown eyes and the beginnings of a smirk at the edges of her lips.

"The lifeblood of mortal creatures, man or beast, give me sustenance to live," he watched her expression closely as he replied. There was no change. She appeared genuinely intrigued.

"I have observed you eating and drinking," she countered. "Can you not subsist on food alone?"

Zracul shook his head. "I eat and drink for the pleasure of it, but I take blood to survive. Human lifeblood provides the highest nutritive value, then animals, and finally other humanoids like Dvergr Dwarfs and Hauflins."

He could almost feel her intense scrutiny as her tone shifted to a soft thoughtful timbre, "How did you become this way?"

Zracul could discern no reason to obfuscate his explanation by telling her about his complex relationship with Ornias, a Greater Demon from the Infernal Planes, fused to him, sharing one mind, the source of all his powers. Instead, he said, "I am not entirely certain. It is a mystery I pursue for unknown answers that I may never discover, the source of which is shrouded in ancient magic I was subjected to while exploring the depths of a nameless cavern I stumbled upon when I was younger. All I really know is that my condition is both a gift and a curse."

"Since you have not always been this way, would it be right of me to presume that you consider the consumption of blood as the curse?" Her eyes glimmered with intelligence no one would suspect, and Zracul could sense her guarded skepticism sifting through his words.

"Quite right," he agreed. "But there is more. For example, I have lost the capacity for sympathy altogether, and nearly the same with empathy. And although I am capable of intense lust and desire, as you know, I lack the capacity for true love."

She did not bat an eye at that last part. Zracul could not immediately decide if that was good or bad for him.

"So, what are the benefits?" she prompted.

There were many, he thought. Some were so subtle they almost went unnoticed. He reminded himself to keep it simple and told her thus, "My physical strength and stamina compare to ten strong men. I do not suffer from disease or illness. I can move more swiftly than the eye can follow should I desire, and crawl up walls with the skill of a spider. And I shall never age beyond my prime," he paused. "I am essentially immortal."

He felt Ahes stiffen. It was her first reaction to anything he said thus far. He guessed the wheels were turning fast in her head as her thoughts worked toward the inevitable conclusion. She propped herself up on one elbow so that her gaze was level with his.

"Why did you refer to it as a 'condition' earlier?" There was hope in her eyes, and an expectant shift in her posture. They wanted something from each other, and he was in the unique position to grant her desires.

Zracul turned on his side to face her. He noticed a thin ray of light from the window dancing across her face highlighting her golden locks with the slight sway of the curtain. She was undoubtably the most beautiful creature he had ever seen. "My brother, Fain, has defined it with a name that translates in our language to 'Eater of Life,' or 'Life-Eater,'" Zracul shrugged. "I suppose it's as good as any since we are the only ones who know anything about it. That will change soon enough. Nevertheless, I called it a 'condition' because whomever has the infection can also infect others, with or without their consent."

Ahes could hardly contain her excitement although she tried to hide it. Still, Zracul could hear it in her rapidly beating heart and see it in the blood pulsing through her veins. He almost laughed out loud. They were almost there.

"So, will the one infected by the other be subject to the same 'gifts and curses' as you called them?"

"Indeed," Zracul replied.

Ahes sat up in the bed, her excitement no longer withheld.

"Tell me, what do you call the condition in your language?"

"Vampyr," he replied simply.

She leaned close, placing her hands on the sides of his face, and finally dared to ask the question he had been waiting for, "Zracul, my love, will you make me a Vampyr?"

He had her.

"Yes."

Chapter 7 – Temple of the Frog

Reskalin sprinted into the mist followed immediately by Enguer and Khulani. Although Qel and Havacian were younger and taller than the others, their long strides could not keep pace with their companions. The sound of their running steps was distinct but soon directionless in the mist. If not for the shattered pavers of the boulevard guiding their direction, Qel was sure they would have lost their way.

"The creature is nearly upon us," Havacian spoke between breaths. "The vapor in the air trembles with arcane energies as it gets closer. I can feel it."

Qel tried to expand his focus. It was difficult with the effort of running, and he lacked the ability to commune with water like his friend. He tried to respond and found his lungs heavy as if he were underwater. The icy mist was getting thicker. He couldn't breathe. Qel wanted to stop and cough up the fluid collecting in his lungs. Yet, he knew to do so would mean death. The creature was on them. He could feel it now, twisting and coiling around them like an ethereal serpent trapping its prey. It was all he could do to croak, "Havac . . ."

Havacian was coughing so hard that Qel doubted his friend heard him until he cast back a quick glance as he thrust his arms forward and back again in a wide arc. Teetering at the edge of consciousness, black spots clouded Qel's vision, blotting out the remainder of Havacian's movements. With lungs burning and legs trembling from lack of air, Qel knew he was seconds away from passing out. There was a quick flash, and the air shimmered all around them. He could breathe again! Qel inhaled like a drowning man. The air was so cold that it felt like daggers in his lungs, and nearly stumbled from the unexpected sting accompanied by the onset of life returning to his body. Even so, the air was pure and fresh like a winter night among the vineyards of his youth.

"You okay?" Havacian rasped. He was nearly inaudible from the effort of breathing.

Qel couldn't risk losing his breath, so he simply nodded in response. Looking ahead, he could detect the nearly invisible curved edge of a bubble encompassing them as they ran. He felt dry for the first time in days and reasoned that Havacian must have managed to not only repel the water-laden air around them, but also remove the excess moisture from their bodies. It was an incredibly complex spell invoked in just a few seconds. Qel was more than a little impressed by his friend's progress.

A moment later, the boulevard abruptly split ninety degrees left and right at a wide stone stairway that climbed steeply up the front of a building between stained marble columns rising into the mist. It must be the temple. Without hesitation, Qel and Havacian took ran up the steps to a set of gargantuan copper-plated double doors long since turned green with neglect. One side of the doorway was closed, but the other was open just wide enough to squeeze through. There stood Reskalin urgently waving for them to get inside. When they entered, she slammed the door shut on creaking hinges.

"What happened?" Reskalin demanded. "We thought we lost you."

Qel could not speak. He collapsed on the floor next to Havacian as the two of them struggled to catch their breath from the long run that nearly took their lives. A dim light-globe came to life in Khulani's hand illuminating his companions and not much beyond. The druid crouched next to Havacian, then to Qel and briefly touched each of them on the forehead. When he did, Qel felt all the exhaustion quit his body along with the ache in his lungs and legs leaving only the memory of their ordeal to linger.

With more strength than he would have expected, Qel cautiously regained his feet and pulled his sodden cloak tighter to ward off the cold. At least they were out of the drenching mist. "Thank you," he muttered to Khulani receiving a sincere white-toothed smile and a nod from the druid in return.

Reskalin stood with arms crossed at the edge of the light, her questioning gaze unsympathetic emphasized by shadows darkening the recesses of her face to cast an almost demonic appearance over her features.

Qel sighed, expecting a harsh interrogation. "The creature caught up with us, and we nearly drowned." He was in no mood to entertain Reskalin's biting temper.

"Drowned?" Reskalin's dubious reply set Qel's teeth on edge.

"Yes, drowned, "Qel snapped. "Whatever that thing is out there, it can turn the air to water, and we nearly drowned in it."

"Actually," Havacian spoke in the relaxed tone he always assumed when conveying precise information. "The creature breathed a mist of heavy water that enveloped us. I believe this ability must be deliberate and directional such that it might also be avoidable if we could see it coming."

"That could be useful," Reskalin conceded. "Do you have a better idea what the creature might be?"

Havacian's gaze dropped to the green-tinted floor tiles and brought a hand to his forehead pausing in thought for a minute as he muttered what sounded like calculations of some sort. None of this was new to Qel. His friend was often spontaneous and funny except when it came to computations that mattered. Finally, he looked up. "It moved much faster than we could run. I know that for certain. It's smooth movement gave the impression of one that glided or flew, rather than run through the mist. Perhaps more importantly, just before the heavy vapor began to drown us, it stopped. I'm guessing it had to do so in order to either cast, emit, or breathe the deadly wave of mist over us."

"A very interesting choice of words, Havacian." Khulani's calm voice was like leaves rustled by a soft breeze. His eyes still gleamed with an inner glow that Qel desperately wanted to ask him about at a better time. "Why did you describe it as a 'wave of mist'?"

"Because that's how it felt." Havacian settled into an instructive cadence Qel was far too familiar with, and he almost felt sorry for Reskalin given the avalanche of details about to follow. "It came over us quickly, just short of immediate, and with the overwhelming pressure of vapor suddenly condensed around us, it became impossible to breath. The stress of the moment nearly caused me to miss that particular feature of the experience. You see . . . what's so funny?"

Reskalin chuckled quietly while shaking her head. "Only an Atlantean could manage such an analysis in the face of death. I think I get the picture, thank you, Havacian. Now, let's see where we are exactly."

In the privacy of his own mind, Qel applauded Reskalin's smooth handling of what could have been a lengthy commentary on their near-death experience and decided to adopt the method next time Havacian rambled on further than his attention would allow.

Khulani's light-globe flared to life as it floated out of his hand and above their heads illuminating the expanse of the entry chamber where they stood. It was a large open area with a high domed ceiling held aloft by petrified rafters. Under a thick carpet of dust, the walls and floor were painted green, chipping at the corners. The passage of time was evident in places where small fissures grew to wide cracks that ran the length of the chamber. Hints of faded images shown through the dusty gloom on the walls and ceiling that were too far gone to even guess at what they might have once portrayed, and had there been any furniture it would have surely rotted away. There were no windows and except for the giant copper-plated entry, the only doors that might have fully enclosed the area decayed long ago leaving reddish stains of rusted hinges on the stone opening that now framed a dark hallway.

"It appears there is only one way to go." Khulani gestured toward the hallway.

Qel approached the ominous opening and peered into the void. "I sense lingering hints of arcana that pervade every stone of this place. We should be cautious. This temple is ancient. Additionally, the walls and ceilings may not be stable throughout." He turned to his companions. "There is a passive energy here long dormant. We should proceed with care. The creature outside may not be the only Guardian of Kiltullagh."

– – –

"Enguer and I will take the lead," Reskalin squinted at the Atlanteans with pursed lips, balancing the benefit of keeping them close to warn of magical traps versus the need to move silently in the dark. As with most decisions she made in life, Reskalin chose to side where she was most confident – herself and Enguer. "You two will be clumsy and loud in the dark. Give us a ten-count before you follow and use your light-globe at its dimmest to find your way. If the corridor splits or we encounter a doorway, we will wait for you to catch up before we decide our direction.

Qel and Havacian nodded their agreement, but Reskalin was already looking past them at Khulani. "Would you mind guarding the rear, good druid?"

"Of course," Khulani's eyes still held an unsettling glow that no one seemed to have the courage to question. "Do not be afraid. I will change my form to one better suited to quiet steps, ears to detect the subtlest sounds, and a nose that can sniff out the slightest changes in the air. Oh, and I cannot control my light-globe while in another form, so you may wish to bring out your own."

Khulani stowed his light-globe plunging them all into darkness again. Seconds later, Qel's luminous globe flared to life just as a blurry aura shimmered around the druid. His body widened and bent at striking angles until a wolf the size of a horse was standing passively before them, staring with Khulani's glittering eyes.

"Incredible," Havacian muttered to no one in particular, his own eyes wide with wonder at the transformation.

Reskalin, too, paused to stare at the druid-turned-wolf. Druids were not so rare that almost anyone could claim to have witnessed one change into an animal at least once in their lifetime. They favored birds, deer, and porpoise; whichever offered the most efficient travel form desired to cross land or sea. Or so she had been told. It made sense to her, thus she believed it to be true. However, the massive creature standing before her now was a beast capable of snapping bones and rending flesh. Never had she seen a druid take such a vicious form. Her respect for Khulani grew ten-fold in those few seconds their eyes met, and despite her initial apprehension, was glad to have him on their side.

"Let's go." Reskalin turned on her heal patting Enguer on the back just as the ranger placed the ring on his finger rendering him invisible. The appearance of Reskalin's hand stopping in mid-air where Enguer was standing accompanied by the audible clap of palm on leather might have been a little disconcerting for the others, but not so for her. From the first day they strode stealthing through the dark corridors of the Orks Enclave on the far side of the Asinippi Mountains to the dusky alleyways, sewers, and subterranean byways so often frequented by the crime guilds in Arre, Reskalin's keen hearing could discern Enguer's location even when he wore his magical ring.

Together, the pair moved slowly down the corridor, stopping frequently to listen before continuing forward. Reskalin slid one hand lightly along the wall so not to miss a connecting hall or doorway, and she knew Enguer did the same on the other side. They progressed in total darkness, keeping far enough ahead of the Atlanteans and the druid so that their companions light-globe and untrained footfalls would not spoil their furtive advance. So far, the temple was quiet, except for the occasional drip of water from the ceiling or down a wall. The floor was composed of stone tiles that shifted slightly if cracked or broken, there was a slight descending grade, and sometimes a shallow puddle or small pile of gravel gathered over centuries of neglect. Reskalin and Enguer navigated every peril without a sound to betray them.

Abruptly, Enguer stopped and a half-second later Reskalin knew why as the toe of her supple leather boot encountered the edge of stairs leading down. Slowly, they descended the age-worn stone steps one at a time. The corridor was still wide enough to continue side-by-side allowing Reskalin to brush a hand along Enguer's cloak or trousers from time to time so he knew she was there. His years as a skilled ranger skulking through The Wilds and later under her tutelage prowling urban environs had developed in him a talent for silent movement unmatched by anyone she ever knew. Except, perhaps, the FatMan. And Enguer's senses beyond that of sight were nearly as sharp as her own. Still, she knew the occasional contact kept his anxiety at bay if nothing else, for he always worried about her, no matter how much she protested or assured him that she could take care of herself. Sometimes it infuriated her to think that he thought she needed anyone to look after her! How many times would she have to prove that to him? Her anger never lasted. All Enguer had to do was hold her in his arms and her objections melted away like a summer snow. She would never admit it to him, but she liked the idea that he worried over her, because secretly, she worried over him. And the thought of anything that could take him away from her tore Reskalin's heart to pieces. Soon enough, there would be two more to worry over, and if it wasn't for Enguer . . . she just couldn't imagine doing it on her own.

"A door." The words whispered in her ear nearly made her jump. Sometimes it amazed her how Enguer continued to develop his abilities. It wouldn't be too long before he was talented enough to avoid detection by even her sensitive ears if he chose to. He better never choose to.

Reskalin could feel the door in the darkness. It was stone, felt cold to the touch, and something was chiseled into it. An image, she thought, not symbols or words, and it left a powdery substance on her finger tips. She traced the thin seam between the door and its frame and soon realized that it was massive, far taller than she was. It was a set of double doors with a rusted metal handle and no lock. The doors were closed, but they were balanced so precisely that the stone swayed slightly as their hands carefully explored its surface.

"There is some kind of powder on the door," Reskalin whispered. "It's all over my hands."

"Mine too." Enguer replied. "I think it's from whatever is engraved on the door." There was a short pause before he continued. "It smells like rotten eggs, so I'm guessing it's yellow ochre that was used for color."

"Careful, then!" Reskalin hissed. "Sometimes an amber crystal found in old volcanoes and mines is ground into the yellow ochre to brighten the color of the paint. The crystal is very toxic. It is popular among those who engage in the production of poisons. Keep it away from your face!"

Enguer grunted in the dark next to her. "Okay. Let's wait for the others so we can get a better look at what we've gotten ourselves into."

The minutes passed in silence allowing Reskalin a moment to consider the door and what lay beyond. Thanks to the FatMan's adamant insistence, she grew up with teams of tutors to ensure a proper education in something other than information gathering, smuggling, extortion, and murder. She knew enough about ancient structures to know that any chamber with painted reliefs must be important. Yellow ochre was easy enough to come by these days, and relatively inexpensive, but a few hundred years ago it was less available, very expensive, with the nearest source over a hundred leagues from where they stood. She reasoned that any door painted with yellow ochre must also hint at something important within. Perhaps important enough to protect from anyone foolish enough to violate a sacred temple of a long-dead civilization. That part worried her the most.

The dim glow of a light globe slowly materialized in the corridor followed by the light scuff of leather boots on stone tiles. Reskalin was pleased with the Atlanteans respectable effort to step quietly and keep their mouths shut. She was even further impressed with Khulani in wolf form padding along just behind them in the shadows so quiet that even her perceptive ears could not detect his approach.

Enguer appeared at her side and whispered into her ear, "Do you want me to go in first and scout the area?"

Reskalin shook her head. "No. We will all go in together. I would bet your weight in gold that the object of our search is not far away now. Be wary of the dangers that may accompany it."

Qel and Havacian came to a halt a half-step away. As tall as they were, the massive head of the wolf peered over their shoulders, its glittering eyes unsettling in the darkness. Qel nodded without speaking, but Havacian gazed wide-eyed and mouth agape at the door beyond. Reskalin turned to see what held the wizard's attention, and came face to face with the looming image of a frog-like creature painted dull yellow with a pair of large ambers set in eye sockets higher than she could reach twinkling like lurid flames in the luminescence of Qel's light-globe floating sedately above their heads.

"Vrtog," came Havacian's hoarse utterance.

"You think it's another temple guardian?" Enguer asked.

"Not the guardian," Havacian's eyes remained glued to the image on the door. "A God."

An icy ripple cascaded down Reskalin's spine. She could not have explained why fear gripped her in that moment, nor the feeling of doom that followed.

Reskalin shook Havacian by the shoulder to bring his gaze back to hers, "What do you know of this . . . God? What sort of people worshiped this vile thing?"

Havacian rubbed his hands over his eyes and face as if to clear the fog after a disturbing dream. "In my first year at the Wizards Enclave in Atlantis, I found a book of old fairy tales. Many of the fairy tales were familiar as my mother knew them well and often read stories to me at bedtime. I was young, as are all first-year apprentices, and I missed my mother terribly." Qel placed a comforting hand on Havacian's shoulder when he paused to take a breath. "Anyway, there were several fairy tales I did not know. Most of them were terrifying, but one stood out among the rest. It was the story of the ancient city of Anura, populated by happy and prosperous Anurans thriving on fishing, kelp farming, and oyster harvests."

"So, this frog is a benevolent God?" Reskalin glanced up at the image on the door. The creature did not appear kindly from her perspective. If anything, the amphibian's tense pose, open mouth and strained lines curved around eyes filled by flickering ambers suggested the creature was set to leap forward and devour whomever the artist of the relief imagined stood before it. "Are our fears of what we may find beyond these doors unfounded?"

"Like all fairy tales, this one begins in a favorable light," Havacian was staring up at the Frog-God again. His eyes were dull and introspective, yet focused as if he could see into the past, present, and future at the same time. Maybe he could. He was an Atlantean after all. Reskalin shivered uncontrollably a second time, but did her best not to show it. She reminded herself that Qel and Havacian might be young and inexperienced in the ways of the world, but they would grow into powerful wizards one day if they lived long enough, and it would be better they remember her as one who showed respect rather than scorn.

"You should know that the Anurans were not exactly human. They were essentially humanoids with the features of a frog – webbed hands and feet, a frog-like head, and thick greenish-yellow skin. Yet, they walked upright as we do, fashioned tools, and spoke language like humans." Havacian shrugged. "I'm sure there is more to it. That was just my observations of the pictures in the story book."

Havacian reached over Reskalin's head and ran a hand along the edge of the relief on the door. She immediately moved a pace away to avoid the yellow dust stirred up from the ancient pigment even as she apprehended that she and Enguer were already covered in it from their earlier examination before the Atlanteans arrived with their light-globe.

"The story goes that the Anurans were content until they encountered humans for the first time. Initially their meeting was peaceful, and they traded oysters, coral, smoked fish, and pearls for colorful textiles and iron tools. Soon enough, however, the Anurans recognized how the humans mocked them and their God as inferior, demanding more and more pearls to satisfy their unquenchable greed. This led to misunderstandings, anger, and conflict between the two cultures." Havacian exhaled a long breath. "And then came war. But the Anurans were not a war-like people, so they turned to their God, Vrtog, for protection. According to the story, Vrtog swam to the lowest depths of the Primal Sea where he discovered a reef of oysters that spread hundreds of leagues in every direction. The largest lay proudly on a high mount overlooking their domain, surveying the countless millions of smaller oysters with their shells fused together to form one massive community that crawled up the mount in ageless layers with barnacles and sea anemones to unite with the greatest of them all. This oyster was a muscle of massive proportion so old that its irregular shell looked more like a squat boulder densely encrusted with sessile organisms and swaying tendrils of aquatic plants that it wore like a crown. Vrtog swam to this king of oysters because he knew it held a huge pearl eons in the making, and that the pearl was trapped within the prison of the tightly clamped bivalve. For twenty days and twenty nights Vrtog plead with the oyster to give up its prize. He explained the predicament of his people and rationalizing that the greedy humans would finally be satisfied and leave the Anurans in peace if he were to offer them a gift of the oyster king's pearl. But the oyster remained unmoved by his plight as it basked in the timeless currents embracing it like a soothing shroud. Enraged, Vrtog demanded the pearl, before attempting to force the shell apart by beating it with sharpened rocks. Still, the pearl was beyond his reach no matter what he tried. In frustrated defeat, the Frog-God returned to the surface where he happened upon a giant sea otter rolling on the shore. Vrtog was exhausted and in no mood to parlay with the ridiculous creature until he noticed oyster shells littering the sand where it played. He watched through incredulous eyes as the otter plunged into the water and reemerged only moments later with a huge tightly shut oyster. With it, the otter swam to a jagged prominence near the beach and utilizing its two powerful claws beat the oyster against the rocks until finally the bivalve broke in two. Vrtog's was utterly shocked at what he witnessed and approached the creature with an offer to reveal the location of the endless oyster reef if only the otter would consent to freeing the huge pearl from the oyster king. With an excited flip of his tail the giant otter agreed!" It was obvious to anyone that Havacian was fully engaged in the telling of his story, but Reskalin was getting anxious. They had lingered too long, and if they ever had the advantage of surprise, it was likely long since passed.

"Havacian, I really need you to get to the point of this story so we can decide how best to survive what awaits us on the other side of this door." Reskalin silently congratulated herself on her patience while at the same time wanting to explode with exasperation when Qel quietly chuckled in the background. It was all she could do not to punch the Atlantean in the face.

"Yes, of course." Havacian's blue-tinted cheeks flushed with embarrassment. "As you might guess, Vrtog led the giant otter to the boundless oyster reef, where it wrenched the massive oyster king from its perch and returned to the surface. It took a mighty effort, but eventually the otter broke the oyster king in two, but before Vrtog could intervein, the otter slurped up the entire contents within the shell leaving only the huge gleaming pearl and the two halves of the mighty shell discarded in the sand. Unfortunately for the otter, the meat of the oyster king had long since turned into a foul toxic sludge that quickly worked its fatal revenge upon the giant otter while Vrtog, unmoved and unsympathetic to the otter's final thrashings, swiftly flicked out his sticky tongue to retrieve the precious pearl, swallowing it whole so that he might return unencumbered to his people in Anura!"

Reskalin narrowed her eyes at Havacian in an expression she knew the Atlantean couldn't miss. "So . . ."

Havacian swallowed hard, shifting his weight from one foot to the other nervously as he spoke, "So, it turns out the pearl was not a pearl but a magical orb of great power that had been sealed inside the rotten corpse of an ancient oyster at the bottom of the Primal Sea by none other than the Tuatha De. Not knowing this, Vrtog tried to barter the pearl in his negotiations with the humans as he planned, but their Chief was an elder shaman who recognized the sphere, and it struck such fear in his heart that without a word of explanation he fled with all his warriors. A year of peace followed for the Anurans until one day a dozen Tuatha De arrived. Without parley or warning, they released a terrible serpent of mist upon the city. Vrtog knew his people were doomed as they had no defense against this creature. So, he bade his priests to perform one last ritual to preserve their God for eternity, and deny the Tuatha De their prize."

The Atlantean's eyes met Reskalin's stern gaze boldly for the first time since they met and she might have been impressed if not for the dire pitch twisted with emotion in his voice, "When the Tuatha De burst through that door more than a thousand years before we ever thought to come here, they found dozens of Vrtog's priests dead on the floor with swollen black tongues and contorted postures that bore witness to their agony before the black henbane they had taken freed their souls. Towering over them all stood the stone idol of their Frog-God gazing into eternity through cold hollow eyes devoid of all expression except one – satisfaction."

Chapter 8 - Awakened

If Atlantean druids existed, Khulani knew of none. Yet, he had come to know many Atlanteans over the years, and they were, in his estimation, deserving of their reputation as high-level thinkers with extraordinary intelligence and insight. However, they also earned another not so favorable quality; they tended to laboriously relate in excruciating detail whatever topic they deemed significant or essential in their communication with others. Atlanteans took great strides to ensure that whomever they were conversating understood the 'why' of a matter as equally as 'what' the issue was about.

Standing at the brink of a doorway separating the hallway from the heart of the temple, Havacian finally concluded the story of Vrtog, the Frog-God, and the Anuran people. The story piqued Khulani's natural curiosity, that left him wanting answers to a myriad of questions. Perhaps Havacian would indulge his curiosity on the return to Ys.

Khulani relinquished the guise of the Dire Wolf in favor of his natural human form so that he could more readily communicate with the others. Reskalin was asking the very question at the fore of his mind. "Why haven't you told us this story before now?" she demanded in a heated whisper. "It is not so different than the tale told by Naamah when we all met at the Agrabuta."

Havacian shrugged, casting his gaze to the floor. "Her tale and mine held too many disparities that I doubted the relevance of either. The story I related was based on a fairy tale, and hers came second hand from a hermit. Either could be true or neither. Only after running for my life from a mist-serpent and then discovering this door with the image of Vrtog have I concluded that there may be some truth to both."

Khulani clapped his hand on Havacian's shoulder in a subtle display of support. "Naamah recounted that the mist-serpent swallowed a powerful 'sphere,' and Havacian's story claims this Frog-God swallowed a mysterious 'pearl.' So, we can go back outside and confront the mist-serpent or open this door and see what's inside. It maybe we will find what we are looking for. maybe not." Without hesitation, Khulani pushed open the left slab of the stone double doors revealing a vast chamber shrouded in darkness on the other side.

Taken completely off guard, Enguer drew back on his bow even as Reskalin brought forth her blades, hissing a curse that would make a sailor blush. "Dammit druid! The door might have been trapped, or something waiting on the other side."

Khulani smiled broadly, "But there was not. I will explore ahead." Without waiting for a response, he quickly transformed back into the huge wolf to better see in the dark.

"Enguer," Reskalin whispered. "Don't let me forget to pry those ambers out of the door before we leave."

Moving silent and cautious through the doorway, Khulani's sensitive ears picked up Reskalin's comment. His wolf-lips curved in the semblance of a smile.

The area beyond the doors appeared more cavern than chamber with sections of grey stone, polished smooth, abruptly terminating into an expanse of rough chiseled rock. The partially tiled floor was thick with dust and chippings centuries undisturbed. The high ceiling showed no work at all. As Qel's light-globe slowly drifted inside, arched alcoves twenty feet wide and similarly high were illuminated on the walls to right and left of the entry with three more running up each side of the chamber along the tiles before transitioning to the coarse natural walls of the cavern. Within the alcoves, beautifully painted murals depicted the Frog-God Vrtog towering over crowds of frog-like people indulging in their worship, sitting in benevolent judgement, blessing bountiful harvests of aquatic plants and snails, or proselytizing to a younger generation of frog folk. At least, such was Khulani's interpretation of the scenes peering through the sharp eyes of a Dire Wolf while he silently padded deeper inside the chamber.

"Remarkable," came Enguer's hushed voice from behind. "They seemed to have enjoyed a peaceful life, encouraged by their deity to thrive, love, and worship no different than human societies."

"Yet it was the humans whose greed drove Vrtog to seek out an item of power to protect his people. Ironically, the pearl he discovered, which would ultimately cause their demise, came not at the hands of humans, but rather the Tuatha De." Havacian spoke without malice, and the silence which followed confirmed the unspoken truth that avarice was not a uniquely human flaw.

Khulani gazed again upon the passive scenes. He had to admit that humans were the cause of much of the suffering in this world they called Plethwih. Even the Imaziyen, of whom he still counted as his brothers and sisters, were prone to strife on the endless savannahs of Ibhr Rrbi. Even so, other humanoid races like the Tuatha De, and the Reptilians from the far-off land of Mu were known for atrocities equally horrific. If not for the Atlanteans, he wondered if there would be no peace at all. His thoughts wandered as the light-globe climbed slowly higher and forward. The ceiling was easily sixty feet above their heads and the darkness, pushed back incrementally by the encroaching illumination seemed endless. Khulani crept along with it as the others instinctively stayed back several paces knowing that his wolf-enhanced senses would detect danger far sooner than they. Gliding several more feet ahead, the dim light soon revealed several small mounds spread over an area of about thirty feet. A heavy layer of dust obscured the contents of the mounds until Khulani was less than a span from the closest one. He came to a dead stop.

"Khulani!" Reskalin's hoarse whisper broke the silence. "We are coming forward."

Raising his head to sniff the air, Khulani detected no decay or rot, only the earthy scent typical of a natural cave. Yet, he could see the cold remains of ancient bones forming the vague figure of a small humanoid with an irregularly shaped skull in the mound before him.

"These must be the Anuran priests that Havacian spoke about," Qel observed. He strode to a nearby mound, crouching low, but made no move to disturb them in any way. "I see no injuries. They were not hacked or clawed." He moved to inspect the other mounds. Havacian did the same on the opposite side.

"If they died by ingesting black henbane, as the story suggests, then they would not display physical injuries," Havacian offered.

Reskalin shook her head, "Does this mean the fairytale is true? Did they sacrificed themselves just like you described?"

"For what purpose?" Enguer chimed in. "Havacian's story was not clear about why the Anuran priests sacrificed themselves."

Khulani flickered back to human form. "Havacian, you mentioned that Vrtog required one last ritual from his priests to 'preserve their God for eternity.' What do you think that meant?"

"I found that passage odd as well, but I am confounded by it." Havacian continued to inspect the mounds without looking up.

A moment of silence followed, then Reskalin suddenly uttered, "By the gods . . ." drawing everyone's attention.

The light-globe had continued its forward progress while the group was distracted by the mounds of bone. It revealed another twenty feet of the cavern previously hidden in darkness. There, a black granite base five feet in height and some considerable size in diameter with the edges curving away in the darkness, rose before them. However, it was what the light revealed further that astounded everyone to speechless wonder with every foot of darkness and shadow slowly pushed away.

At first the curves and slopes made little sense to the eye or imagination. Of the stone one thing was clear - it was polished and shined to a perfection that could only be attained by devoted labor over time. Given the incomplete nature of the temple, the statue must have been the singular focus right up until the end.

Slowly the light revealed more. Nearly touching the cavern ceiling, the light-globe laid bare the forward projections of the great statue leaving the lower reliefs in dark shadows. The effect was disconcerting as it gave the impression of a creature emerging from the dark mold rather than a thing uncovered and exposed. Forward grew the light and high almost to the limits of the hollow dome whereunder it sat, a grim line appeared like a mild smile below two narrow cavities easily identified as nostrils on the monstrously broad expanse of a salientian face. Already the lowest curvatures of bulbous eyes graced the retreating shadows even as two angled appendages thicker than the trunk of a hundred-year-old oak broke the plane of gloom led by sharp claws that curved over the edges of the granite base on opposing sides. It was then that the thirty-foot width of the stone creature could be discerned as well as the assumption of nearly fifty feet of dizzying height.

It was no secret then what the light-globe was divulging to those below. It was a great stone statue of Vrtog, the Anuran Frog-God. And yet, before the full revelation of the effigy's entirety, before the shroud of dim gloom fled wholly from the great rounded orbs that shaped amber eyes at the apex of its imposing form, was the weight of its presence felt.

"Give us more light please, Qel." Enguer slowly stepped back and away from the mammoth statue as he spoke.

Khulani followed Reskalin's incredulous gaze to the top of the stone Frog-God where he too was startled to see a pair of huge amber gems the size of prize-winning pumpkins flickering with internal light, life-like in their stone eye sockets. Suddenly the room flooded with bright daylight from Qel's light-globe hovering against the ceiling radiant as a small sun. The abrupt expansion of sight and comprehension of their surroundings was jarring as it seemed there was no corner or cover that was not starkly exposed by the intense illumination. The few dozen feet of dim light surrounded by an expanse of darkness and mystery no longer obscured the gargantuan proportions of the cavern chamber where they so confidently strode. As if in response to the bright light, Vrtog's amber eyes flashed with greater intensity.

"The air is practically alive with magic!" Havacian shouted. His voice echoed eerily off the distant walls. Khulani could sense no magic, but the fine hairs on his arms rose with forewarning as his primal instincts bred through generations of tribal life on the Ibhr Rrbi screamed internally that something wasn't right.

Qel urgently pulled Havacian away from the effigy and called out a warning, "We must have triggered a trap set for anyone approaching the statue! Get back!"

It hardly needed to be said. Slowly at first, they were all stirred to put more distance between themselves and the towering Frog-God. They only managed a few steps before there was a sharp crack of rending stone followed by a shudder that shook the cavern sending a shower of small rocks falling from the ceiling and down the walls. Khulani knew it was no coincidence of an earth tremor that nearly jostled them off their feet. Like the others, his eyes were locked on the statue leaving no doubt about the cause. Vrtog moved!

The Frog-God still held the appearance of stone as it crawled heavily from its granite perch. Each step of its weighty claws and scrape of its belly across the edge of the platform sounded no less like stone. The shuddering ceased, but the creature's steps still caused a terrible vibration in the floor and a skittering of gravel. Khulani absently worried that the thing might bring the whole cavern down on their heads. He had no time to ponder the idea as the monstrous stone God of the Anurans opened its wide mouth and belched a thundering croak. The wave of sound took Khulani off his feet, tossing him like a ragdoll thirty feet across the floor where he rolled through the fallen chips, shards, and sharp-edged rocks another fifteen feet or so. The heavy stench of mold, fungus, and dust hung in the air as he quickly regained his feet. Khulani could feel cuts, abrasions, the metallic taste of blood on his tongue from the violent upheaval. Nearby, his companions were rising to their feet riddled with injuries he observed as minor, if numerous like his own.

Reskalin was crouching with a long dagger in each hand, Enguer rose next to her with his powerful bow drawn taunt, Havacian stood a little further away focused upon a conjured ball of watery luminescence, and further still Qel's hands flared with hot fire illuminating his grave countenance. Khulani was on the verge of transforming into . . . he knew not what. For that matter, what could any of them do to harm this massive creature of stone? And if this thing was a God, could it be killed at all? He had no time to contemplate options when, to his astonishment, the thing spoke:

VOLCAM HOATH, FAFEN, A ANURAN!

The words poured forth like a prolonged croak resonating from deep within the bowels of the Frog-God if not from ancient time itself. It loomed over them as if expecting a reply. The whole of it motionless except for amber eyes flaring through faceted jewels that rolled slowly to shift from one face to another.

"Did either one of you understand that?" Reskalin never looked away from the creature, but it was clear to whom she was speaking.

"Only the last part, 'Anuran,' the people that once worshiped Vrtog. It's strange that the Tower of Tongues is no help with understanding the rest." Qel glanced over at his friend holding the large blue orb roiling between his hands staring into it as if nothing of any urgency transpired around him. "Havacian?"

After what seemed like an unholy eternity, Havacian replied in a distracted manner, never taking his eyes off the orb. "It is the 'Werdhom Enoch,' or more commonly known as the so-called language of angels and demons. Why the Tower of Tongues does not translate the words for our ears is unknown."

The Tower of Tongues. Khulani first heard about this structure when he was a neophyte at the Druid's Enclave near the lands of the Nabta People. It was an enormous tower with balconies thick with hanging ivies and vines that reached all the way down to its wide base. Here, Atlanteans resided amongst the people of Kur-gal in the city of Eridu, a great distance away to the east. Further even than the Eastern Kingdoms. The Atlanteans claimed that it was because of this tower that all creatures capable of speech could understand each other regardless of their native language. It was a remarkable achievement that served to uncomplicate trade, ease tensions between disparate cultures, and avoid conflicts wrought from misunderstandings or errors in translation. Khulani knew not how the Atlanteans accomplished such an arcane feat so powerful to affect the entirety of Plethwih, but he knew it was true, and he admired the blue-skinned people greatly because of it. Unfortunately, it seemed that the miracle of the Tower of Tongues would be of little help to them with the Frog-God Vrtog.

Havacian continued, "My impression is that the Frog-God is asking for his ancient followers. I can only surmise that Vrtog expected the mist-serpent to abandon Kiltullagh after the final ritual mentioned in the fairytale. He must not be aware of the tragic disposition of the Anuran People and the destruction of their city."

At the mention of the Anuran People, the amber eyes of the effigy fixed sharply on Havacian and again emitted a belching croak:

ANURAN

"I think he's getting impatient," Enguer observed nervously. "How can we make him understand what happened to his people?"

"And more importantly," Reskalin cut in, "that we had nothing to do with it?"

Havacian finally tore his gaze away from the watery sphere and said, "I think I have a way to accomplish both and more."

Khulani had no idea what Havacian had in mind, but he knew that no matter the outcome they would have to find a way to destroy the stone monstrosity or return it to its previous unanimated state. For such a creature was a corruption of nature that could not be suffered to exist under any conditions. God, or no.

Tense moments passed standing in the shadow of Vrtog the Anuran Frog-God. Qel watched as Havacian hastily weaved fluid patterns of arcana from the magical orb hovering lightly upon his open palm. The arrangement of the magical spawning quickly became familiar to Qel, and not just because he understood the arcanics of enchanting, but because he had seen iterations of this particular spell many times before. In fact, it was this ability in a far more primitive form that alerted Havacian's family to the potential of his arcane talent when he was a young boy. Even after the two of them graduated from the Imperial Wizards Enclave in Atlantis, trained to control arcane effects of far greater scale and complexity, Havacian often entertained his family, friends, and lately the quiet camps they shared in their travels together on this 'Journey of Discovery,' utilizing this simple spell to...

It suddenly dawned on Qel the modest genius of his friend's intellect. Havacian never ceased to amaze him with not just his breadth of knowledge but also his intuition, sometimes bordering on adolescent innocence, to work through a problem to its logical solution with stunning alacrity. Qel just smiled while Havacian brought the invocation to swift conclusion, and if the others shifting alarmed glances in his direction thought he had lost his sanity, well, he was more amused than bothered by it.

A screen of radiant water manifested above their heads at a height sufficient for Vrtog to take notice. The stone figure's amber eyes quickly rolled to the unexpected display, but it did not shift or flinch at its sudden appearance. Almost immediately, a scene took form in the water. There were many small figures representing the Anuran Frog-People bowing in worship before a much larger figure appearing exactly as the one that stood over them now. Like all the other stories Qel had seen Havacian create in this way, the creatures in the presentation were depicted through a rapid succession of breaks in the screen of water lending the impression of movement in the scene with enough detail that the figures were recognizable, if symbolic. To Qel's imagination, it was akin to shows performed in markets to entertain children with the action played out by puppets that everyone knew who or what they characterized even though they held only vague resemblance.

Qel fervently hoped that Vrtog would see it similarly. Surely Anuran children were once entertained thus? Again, the watery vista changed. This time the Frog-God was shown smaller as if distant with the familiar archway of his temple over his head. In the foreground, the Anurans went about their daily lives as a dark cloud formed above them. The third scene was split in two with the image on Vrtog's right displaying the very room where they currently stood except there were a dozen Anuran priests working desperately to produce a powerful enchantment, while the image on the left revealed the Anuran city in chaos. Vrtog's glittering eyes rotated independently to take in each display separately at the same time. Although the priests were a spectacle to behold, it was events transpiring in the city that commanded Qel's attention. There, a terrible serpent of mist and vapor was tearing through Anuran bodies with tooth and claw that were sometimes substantial and solid, and other times vaporous with its sleek body held aloft by long wispy wings propelling it with unnatural speed through the twisted alleyways. At times, the Anurans would form up in ranks bristling with long serrated spears and mount a desperate defense. The mist-serpent evaded the hazards of the frog-folks resistance by rearing its formidable head, stretching wide its terrible maw, and releasing upon the unsuspecting Anurans an ocean of heavy water within which they all drowned.

Not Qel, or any of those around him, nor even the Frog-God, made a sound. All stared at the tragic fate of the Anurans. With the point made clear, the curtains of water became one again. This time, only the temple chamber was in view. The terrified priests clustered together at the foot of their God. Vrtog sat unmoving on his platform - the same one from which he descended moments earlier. Something was different. Whereas the figures of the priests appeared to shift and move, Vrtog, now bearing a dark grey pallor, did not. The Frog-God sat still as stone. There was a flash of light that white-washed the scene, and when the watery display reformed an image, it was that of the temple door bearing the image of Vrtog, sealing away the Frog-God forever. The curtain of water where the last image was shown fell to the floor of the cavern splashing a wave over everyone with a surprising volume of water. Havacian was soaked through and through with his blond hair matted against his face. Droplets of water hung precariously from his pointy ears and nose as he stood quietly gazing up at Vrtog.

For long terrible minutes the Frog-God stared silently at the empty space where the last scene hung before it fell to the ground. No one made a sound. And just when Qel dared to hope Vrtog might have reverted back to inanimate stone, those great amber eyes slowly rolled to stare down at Havacian. For his part, Havacian appeared calm, and without a word simply pointed toward the open doorway adorned with the likeness of Vrtog.

The Frog-God effortlessly shifted its huge stone frame to face the door sending Qel and his companions scattering out of the way. And in a deep croaking voice that rumbled with barely contained fury Vrtog bellowed frightful words with enough force to shake the entirely of the cavern.

"Ol torzvl od iolci babalon vovim baltim vonpho, teloah, fargt piadph ioiad!"

Qel and the others were violently thrown to the ground just as Vrtog leaped over them, plunging through the far smaller doorway.

"Run to the wall!" Enguer shouted as he half-dragged Reskalin struggling to regain her feet while growling a tide of colorful curses.

Qel turned to run for Havacian, but Khulani was there first, already transformed into the great Dire Wolf. With shocking ease, he snapped up a wad of Havacian's robes and bound toward the nearest wall arriving at the edge of the chamber a good half-dozen steps ahead of Qel. The cavern continued to shake and rumble sending rocks large and small cascading from the ceiling high above. Only a few times were any of them forced to sidestep falling debris where they stood flattened against the wall. Qel vowed to himself right there and then to always follow Enguer's advice, especially where caverns were concerned. When the quaking finally ceased, the floor of Vrtog's chamber was cluttered with jagged stones of every size and although the air was filled with a heavy cloud of dust, the illumination from above assured Qel that his light-globe somehow survived.

"Is everyone okay?" Enguer and Reskalin appeared out of the dusty gloom. Their faces, hair, and clothing, previously sodden from Havacian's watery presentation, were completely covered by a grey plaster from the dust of pulverized stone.

"Khulani and I are fine!" Havacian called from somewhere nearby. "Qel? Can you hear me?"

Qel, coughing to clear his lungs of the dust he inhaled shouted in return, "I'm here, Havacian!" he hacked out the words. "Just got a frog in my throat!"

If Qel hadn't been in the throes of a coughing fit, he might have appreciated the laughter his joke produced in the others before they too began to hack and spit to rid themselves of the airborne particulates. It was a welcome break in the tension they all felt up to that moment. As the companions stumbled their way toward the doorway, a cool breeze from without forced the dust to the back of the cavern clearing the air around the doorway, revealing an awe-inspiring sight. Where once stood the pair of stout wooden doors now gaped a hole that continued as a crumbling tunnel at least four times the size of the original opening.

Even brave and resolute Reskalin shivered as she said, "The power of that thing is incomprehensible. Thanks to Havacian, we didn't have to test our resolve against it."

"If the sphere is inside the Frog-God as Havacian's story claims, we may yet." Enguer's sober words were chilling.

Khulani stepped forward again in his human form. "Unless any of you need healing for your injuries, we should get above ground quickly. It might also be possible for us to tip the scales one way or another if the frog and the serpent engage in conflict."

A wan smile flickered over Havacian's exhausted face, and he managed a faint shrug. Qel almost laughed. His friend was a mess of dirt and mud that might require more than one bath to remedy, but he understood the message Havacian was sending. They conveyed it back and forth many times in their travels. This was the Journey they were meant to follow, and it mattered not to the Journey if those on it lived or died.

"We all bear cuts and bruises," Reskalin scanned each of them with quick brown eyes. "But those can wait until we get out of here."

No one objected, so Qel and the others followed her through the newly expanded corridor taking care not to stumble over the jagged shards, shifting gravel, and ponderous boulders left in the wake of Vrtog's passage. They furtively travelled through the darkness led by Enguer's instincts and the illumination of the light-globe Qel continued to maintain. The sounds of shifting and sliding rocks echoed with nearly every step. If he could have sprinted ahead and out of the temple, he would have, but Qel could see the debris was too hazardous to navigate without care. He would have to keep his panic in check despite the feeling that they were merely one loose stone away from a catastrophic collapse that would turn temple to tomb for them all. Even Khulani, trotting behind them in Dire Wolf form, gazed ahead with wide fearful eyes as if he were contemplating the same thoughts.

"That was a neat trick you pulled off back there," Reskalin caught Havacian by the arm as he stumbled over a pile of loose rocks. "There is no doubt in my mind that you saved all our lives."

Havacian kept his eyes on the ground as they walked. "Thank you, Reskalin. I felt it was the best option considering our odds of defeating it otherwise."

Reskalin laughed a genuine, feminine chortle and ruffled his blond locks with her hand. "You have good instincts, Havacian, and I respect that. Now, if we could just get your friend in line, we might survive long enough to get back to Ys!"

Qel's cheeks reddened. He was walking on the other side of Havacian and not technically part of the conversation. Still, he thought to reply as it was obvious that he was the butt of her joke. To his surprise, Havacian's wit beat him to it as he whispered a not-so-quiet reply to Reskalin, "Don't worry, he'll come along. He's just slow for an Atlantean."

Reskalin's laughter echoed off Qel's ego as surely as it did the rocks all around them until their brief moment of levity was abruptly interrupted by a distant thud, followed by a rigorous vibration in the floor. Rocks jarred loose slid recklessly down the walls as everyone stopped to stare silently ahead through a renewed haze of dust.

"Let's get going," Reskalin's stricken features had lost all joy in an instant. "Quickly! The way out can't be far now."

No one objected.

The group doubled their effort as they moved through the treacherous debris. The Atlanteans were the slowest, holding fast to each other to avoid an injurious fall. Qel was thankful for Khulani's patience as he brought up the rear in wolf form. Those great paws could have easily skipped over the fallen rocks and left them behind. Although time passed with agonizing leisure and the corridor rocked with vibrations that threatened to bring the walls down around them, Qel finally caught sight of daylight through the increasingly humid mix of dust and water vapor.

Enguer and Reskalin were standing astride the gaping hole that previously supported the set of copper-bound doors they passed through on their way into the temple. Of the doors themselves, there was no sign, nor the hinges they were once fastened, or the frame that held them. Enguer urgently motioned for Qel and the others to position themselves next to Reskalin and away from standing directly in line with the opening. The Atlanteans barely moved to the side when there was another boom, much louder than before, a violent shaking and a spray of small rocks that shot through the doorless gap and ricocheted into the darkness. Khulani, the last one to move, cut short a yelp when a few of the pellets penetrated his backside as he leapt out of the way.

"Khulani!" Qel shouted over the racket. "Are you injured?"

The massive wolf wavered into the form of Khulani. There was blood soaking the robes covering his right hip. "Mostly my pride," the druid replied. "I will be fine."

There was no time for further concern as Enguer called out, "Follow me!" and rushed outside. They all made a quick exit and soon crouched behind the cover of an ancient wall that must have once formed the corner of a grand structure.

Qel squinted over the top of the wall. Even with the heavy shroud of mist that obscured the sun and turned the remains of Kiltullagh into featureless shadows between darkness and light, his eyes still needed a moment to adjust from the dank black of the temple's interior. A heavy thud shook the ground from somewhere in the mist. Although several loose stones clattered from broken walls here and there, the effects were felt far less above ground than below.

"The Frog-God is moving north through the city," Khulani informed them.

Reskalin crouched between Enguer and the druid, looking in the same direction as if there were something to see. "We will follow, but not to close."

Taking care to watch their steps, the companions strode into the street. Qel recalled his light-globe hovering near the hole that led into the temple and stowed it away. He fervently hoped he wouldn't need it again anytime soon. Slowly at first, the group crept through the remains of Kiltullagh following a line of ruins pulverized by the passing of a massive body and the thunderous thuds that resounded frequently in the distance. Presently, they drew closer to the source. The ground shuddered with increasing violence and there were other, strange sounds unrecognizable, that soon filled the relative silence between earth-shaking thumps. First came a high-pitched shrieking like that of metal scraping stone followed by a sharp hiss. Least recurrent came what Qel would describe as a gurgling sigh, although he had no reference by which to name it so. Fortunately, Havacian was quite certain about what it meant.

"That's the sound I heard when the mist-serpent tried to drown us with its breath," he announced to the others.

"Then Vrtog and the serpent must be battling with one another as you anticipated," Khulani remarked. Qel was relieved to see the blood on the druid's cloak was dry and that he no longer limped when he walked. It was comforting to have a druid among them with some measure of healing talent should it be needed.

"There are fewer ruins ahead," Enguer observed, "and I believe we have been gaining elevation, although the slope is very slight. I wonder why the creatures have moved to the outskirts of the city?"

Reskalin's brows furrowed as she voiced her thoughts. "Perhaps Vrtog knows something of his home that the serpent doesn't and leads him to a place where he has some advantage."

"It does appear that the mist is becoming less substantial as we near the edge of Kiltullagh," Khulani pointed toward an earthen rise where no ruins were evident, and the air was less obscured by vaporous moisture.

A breathy roar echoed from beyond the hill followed by the sharp splintering of stone by an inexorable force. Then the rear side of the Frog-God's smoothed rounded head briefly appeared above the crest of the incline as the creature effected a loping hop that ended with a tremendous ground shaking concussion.

"There!" shouted Reskalin. "I'm going to climb to the top of the mound to get a better look. If you follow, take a care on the treacherous incline!"

Before her words were out Enguer was already groping his way up the rise with Khulani scrambling up beside him. Reskalin was quick on their heels. Qel looked at Havacian, noting his dubious expression as he watched the others dexterous ascent.

"I'm not much of a climber," his friend muttered.

"Neither am I," Qel agreed. "But we must try and get up there. They may need our help and guidance to get through this. Think of it as . . ."

Qel's words were cut short as the end of a rope *thunked* down at his feet. The other end was tied in tandem between Khulani and Enguer lying on their bellies at the top of the hill. There was another sharp *crack* of stone simultaneous to the powerful *thud* of another earth-pounding hop that might have sent the three sliding back down had they not anticipated the possibility and drove their daggers deep into the dirt to use as stable handholds.

"Come quickly!" Khulani called down. "Before he jumps again!"

Havacian picked up the rope and awkwardly edged up the rise hand-over-hand slipping and kicking sprays of pebbles as he went. He arrived at the top just as the next hop landed, but Khulani's strong grip kept him from sliding back down. Qel ascended next with no more competence than his friend, if at least a little faster, and situated himself next to Havacian to gaze upon the fantastic scene playing out before their astonished eyes.

With the vaporous haze no longer clouding his vision, the sun high overhead floating through the expanse of a clear blue sky, and the distant thrum of waves beating a languid rhythm against a rocky shore, Qel might have thought it was a beautiful day. From where he and the others lay upon the crest of the high hill overlooking a broad swath of tall green grass beaten down and pocked by massive divots, waged a war between two nightmarish creatures. Until this moment, the mist serpent was a creature of mystery unseen within the vaporous mists of Kiltullagh. Now, yet wraithlike and wispy in appearance, it was clearly of draconic form and feature with a long twisting body shielded by vague scales, long flowing wings trailing nearly to its whip-like tail, sharp-taloned claws extending from bulky appendages front and back, and a gargantuan head mounted by a pair of horns curved back toward heavily muscled shoulders with a broad snout snarling through pointed gnashing teeth, and piercing red eyes below a thick scaled brow. The creature's gurgling roar echoed as much from its stone adversary as from the hills as it swept in swift arcs around the plodding Frog-God raking angry claws and lashing tail across granite skin impervious to such futile harassment.

Even so, Vrtog did not have the appearance of a creature untouched. Whether due to its flight through the narrow corridors of the temple or the supernatural assault by the mist dragon, its stone carapace was now riddled with fractures radiating from jagged divots attesting to hefty chunks of its stoney mass torn away by terrific force. And only when the mist dragon slowed for a fleeting moment could Qel detect the ruinous state of its tattered wings and shattered scales. One of these creatures would not survive the meeting, but which one it might be, Qel surely did not know.

The Frog-God sprang twice the height of a tall man and fell with the weight of a mountain that made the ground quake and tremble. It twisted as it landed, extending two short appendages capped by sharp-nailed claws that raked through the semi-incorporeal flank of the dragon briefly exposed as it circled too close to avoid the cutting blows. A gargling roar of angry pain escaped the breast of the serpent as a stream of thick vapor exploded from wide lacerations ripped through cloudy scales and indistinct tissue of the nearly gaseous creature. As for Vrtog, its drab features betrayed no satisfaction at what must have been a devastating strike, but even had it transpired, the elation would have been short-lived for the mist dragon lent forth a scalding steam from its widened maw directly into its adversary's smooth chest. In an instant, the jet of hot spray swelled and widened the web of exposed fissures crisscrossing the Frog-God's torso. Presently, a piercing *CLAP* numbed every ear as Vrtog's chest exploded in a shower of stone shrapnel that burst forth, tearing through the mist dragon at immeasurable velocity and on toward Qel and the others watching from atop the nearby hill.

"Look out!" Reskalin shouted.

Qel, being the last to climb the hill was the least exposed when the scalding shards tore into the hillside. Even so, one shard cut a line across his scalp as he desperately ducked for cover. Others cried out in pain as the fierce wave of blistering fragments impaled the earth around them leaving hundreds of steaming holes. It lasted but a second, and when Qel opened his eyes, to his horror, Havacian slouched over the crest of the hill, his body convulsing from dozens of sizzling tears in his robes that were just beginning to stain with crimson.

Blood suddenly poured down the front of Qel's face from the single wound that left a gash from his forehead through the center of his pointed ear, but it was deep, and the shock of his friend so suddenly pin-cushioned dead or dying was too much. Darkness took him, and in his fading vision he saw, as if in slow motion, Khulani crawling through the dirt toward him, covered in his own blood, shouting Qel's name from far away.

Chapter 9 – A New Hunger

The metallic clink of the final steel manacle was locked into place around Ahes's wrist. It felt cold against her skin and too heavy to lift for more than short periods at a time. It wouldn't matter since the manacles that bound her wrists and ankles were all attached to thick steel chains that hung from the wall restricting her movement, stretching her legs and arms wide apart. She sat on a bed of fresh straw with her back against the dank wall of the cell wearing no more than the day she was born watching Zracul complete all the preparations for her transition. As he checked and double-checked her bonds he explained for at least the dozenth time what she should expect.

"The process will start within minutes of the Blood Ritual. Once it is in you it cannot be reversed. Only death prior to completion can end the transition. For most, it lasts three days, some as long as four. Rarely has it ended earlier. In the first hours expect to become violently ill as your body cleanses itself of all foreign matter. Don't worry, I will wash the awful away. After that, the hallucinations will start. They will seem real to you in every way. Thus, I have taken precautions to ensure that no one may enter the cellar except for me while you are here. When that ends, the pain begins. You will feel like every bone in your body is breaking, every organ rupturing. Your skin will be on fire and your head will want to explode. There will be blood. Lots of blood. You will scream for the mercy of death. This too shall pass, and you will sleep for many hours, maybe days. When you awaken, your first sensation will be the need to feed. I will have fresh sustenance on hand. After that, you will bask in the pleasures of your new endowments. We will hunt together, feed together, and play together. Plus, much more you will learn later."

Zracul completed his inspections and sat down beside her. "Oh, and try not to struggle against the chains, it will only make it worse. My brother, Fain, has enchanted the metal to make them far stronger than they appear."

If a Greater Demon Lord of the Infernal Planes could ever be described as 'giddy,' Aesmadaeva well fit the description this day. The demon took great pleasure in the thought that it would inhabit Ahes's perfect immortal form, never aging, never getting sick, and never dying for ages to come. The Blood Ritual and the painful process that her body would undertake to complete the transition bothered it not at all. However, it had one question left unanswered in the off-chance the demon necessitated abandoning its host. Under normal circumstances, it was hardly an issue considering the frailty of mortal life. That would change after the transition, and since the death of one's host was the only way a demon could willfully extricate itself from a body it possessed, Aesmadaeva had to know if there was a way Vampyr could die.

"Are your brothers and sisters also Vampyr?" Ahes asked.

"They are," Zracul nodded, "and soon there will be more."

"Are you planning a world of immortals then?" she smiled in jest.

He laughed with her saying, "That would be ambitious of me, wouldn't it?"

"I wonder," Ahes reached out impulsively to touch the dark curls at his collar, but the chains restrained her movement. "When I am immortal, does that mean I can never die?"

"Strictly speaking, there are ways we can die or be killed," Zracul shifted so his face was close enough for her to finger his tresses. "Should we be decapitated, dismembered, devoured, or burned to ashes there is no coming back. All are easily avoidable. Conversely, if we fall from a great height our bones will mend, suffer the most vicious cuts, stabs or gouges our flesh will heal, no matter how deep the wound. We can even drown and life will soon stir within us again when exposed to air once more."

Aesmadaeva was satisfied.

Ahes touched her forehead to his, breathing her last words as a mortal woman, "I am content. Let it begin."

Zracul grinned broadly. The long incisors that drew lifeblood from so many victims were no longer extended and wanting, they were back in line with the rest of his gleaming white teeth in perfect order. He pulled back the sleeve from his arm, and drew the edge of a sharp blade across his broad wrist. A thick darkly crimson fluid ebbed from the cut, but flowed no further as if anticipating its role.

Zracul brought his wrist close to her lips and whispered, "Place your mouth over the cut and draw deeply. Once it begins to flow freely take as much as you are able." He pressed his wrist hard against her lips and settled himself comfortably beside her.

Aesmadaeva had tasted blood through the lips of many hosts and always marveled at how its flavor, tang, and viscosity was distinctly varied from person to person and most especially person to animal. Zracul's lifeblood was immediately startling on the tongue. If any imaginative comparison could be made, Aesmadaeva likened it to a kind of liquid metal with the consistency of molasses.

Ahes drew with all her effort at the reluctant fluid seeping from Zracul's wrist. Abruptly, as if the Vampyr willed its release, his blood flowed freely across her palate and down her throat in great gasping gulps. Within minutes her gut felt heavy and extended, yet she drew more. Aesmadaeva pushed her on an on to drain what she could from Zracul despite her distaste of it and the nausea rising in her gut. The demon expertly manipulated the levers in her mind that controlled her physical responses to calm her body, and induced cravings to draw more. Zracul slumped on her shoulder. She could feel convulsions wracking his body. Her teeth bit down hard on his wrist to keep it in place and drew all the more until his lifeblood slowed to a trickle and he sagged like a lifeless doll. When she finally released him, the weight of his body pulled him down beside her where he lay motionless. If he yet breathed, she could not discern, nor did she have long to speculate as her own physical response to imbibing so much blood produced a gag reflex that caused her to heave a terrific crimson geyser between her legs, nearly reaching the door of the cell several feet away.

The sickness would not end there. It continued in torturous waves evacuating bile, mucus, sweat, and waste with a vengeful aggression that left every orifice a swollen burning cavity of throbbing misery. Hours passed slowly for the wretched body of Ahes, but not so for Aesmadaeva. The demon could easily disconnect from the pain and suffering of its host and maintain full awareness of Ahes's physical condition in case it was moved to mitigate any incident leading to permanent harm or disfigurement deemed undesirable. Aesmadaeva took this time to ponder the circumstances of recent events and scour eons of memories for any creature remotely similar to Zracul's eponymic 'Vampyr.'

Aside from a few insignificant animals and insects, the demon could point to no specific source in the history of Plethwih, natural or supernatural, as the origin of Vampyr. Aesmadaeva further considered its home dimension. The Infernal Planes were, more precisely, seven hellish planes connected as one. Each was ruled by a Greater Demon who lorded over hosts of lesser demons under its absolute command. The Greater Demons spent their immortal lives constantly at war with each other, forming and betraying alliances, and generally existing for the sole purpose of subjugating one or more of its fellows. In this place, among a myriad of lesser fiends of every conceivable horror, there was not one Aesmadaeva could consider a parallel to Vampyr. Even if there were, only the seven Greater Demons and thirteen Chaos Demons managed to escape the Infernal Planes when one faction of the Tuatha De, who were at the time embroiled in a Civil War, inadvertently opened a rift between the Infernal Planes and Plethwih. History would record it as '*The Breaking*.' However, once the surviving Tuatha De realized their blunder, they used all the power at their command to seal the rift with what is now known as the 'Sea of Glass.'

The next two-thousand years was a golden age for Aesmadaeva and the six Greater Demons. They had a new world to subjugate and there was none to stand against them. Before long, Plethwih was carved into seven great kingdoms ruled by a Greater Demon in a near replica of the Infernal Planes. Except that their subjects were humans enslaved to serve them. The thirteen Chaos Demons, having no ambition other than to create the chaos on which they thrived, were mostly an annoyance. In those days, the Greater Demons inhabited monstrous physical forms they knew from the very beginning of their existence on the Infernal Planes. Inevitably, the demons made war on each other, using humans and beasts alike as no more than fodder, paying little heed to the machinations of the Tuatha De hiding in the frozen north.

After centuries of brutal warfare, the demons were weak and exhausted. Their downfall came swiftly when the Tuatha De rallied humanity and other races of Plethwih against them. Yet even at their weakest, Aesmadaeva and the others were still powerful and they controlled terrible hordes of hybrid-demons spawned over generations of mating with human populations. In the end, the arrogance of the Greater Demons allowed them all to be trapped by the Tuatha De within the prison of an enchanted pithos. They were stripped of their physical bodies, leaving only the essence of their consciousness to writhe and rage in darkness. The Chaos Demons quickly followed in similar fashion and the hybrid-demons were slaughtered.

Aesmadaeva languished in the maddening existence of the pithos for fourteen-hundred years, until, by an extraordinary turn of events, a young Tuatha De woman named Anesidora lured a Fire-Priest of Kronus to the Temple of Metis where the pithos was to be stored untouched for eternity. She was unaware of what dangers the pithos held and her youthful curiosity got the better of her. At Anesidora's bidding, the Fire-Priest melted the wax seal with divine flames, and the demons were set loose on Plethwih once again. Yet, to their extreme displeasure, the demons having no physical form, were forced to quickly find a living creature to possess or their essence would wither away. In the absence of a suitable host, Aesmadaeva found itself in the humiliating position of inhabiting frogs, snakes, dogs, and common folk with no power or influence. To make matters worse, it learned through rare contact with other demons that there were a pair of powerful arcanists, perhaps Tuatha De, who had discovered a method of returning the demons to the Infernal Planes; something no demon desired now that they lacked the advantage of their physical forms. Rumors intimated that already several Chaos Demons and even a few Greater Demons were gone from this world.

In Ahes, Aesmadaeva found the perfect host as long as it could stay quietly unknown within her, and the immortality of a Vampyr would provide easy continuity to serve its purposes. Still, through all the demon's history, the Vampyr emerged as an enigma unsolved that left Aesmadaeva disquieted.

A sudden chill exploded over Ahes, alerting the demon to a new stimulus. Through the Princess's hazy vision, clouded by fever and swelling, it observed Zracul dowsing her with buckets of cold water to relieve her boiling temperature and clear away the awful. Apparently, the Count survived the severe depletion of his lifeblood and recovered enough to perform the tedious labor in only a dozen hours or so. Ahes shrieked with sudden fury. She was not conscious; the hallucinations were upon her now. Aesmadaeva partitioned off her memories and silenced the mindless outbursts to lessen the effect of them. The demon desired peace and quiet for a span to think matters through.

– – –

The hallucinations dragged on for more than a day. Zracul came to check on Ahes periodically, sometimes sitting next to her for hours just watching, or perhaps consumed by his own thoughts. Aesmadaeva did not need her eyes to "see" Zracul and the emotions that played over his face. The count most often regarded the princess with a vague unreadable countenance as she twitched from time to time barely rustling the chains holding her upright. The cause finally dawned on Aesmadaeva – Zracul probably expected more histrionics during this phase of the transition, so the demon set her to thrashing and wailing whenever he came by.

On a night near to dawn, when Ahes rested placidly between bouts of deliriums, Aesmadaeva sensed the smallest turbulence in the air as two shadows flickered close. The demon instantly prepared to launch a devastating psionic attack to defend its prized host, but stayed the onslaught when the shades resolved into the solid forms of Jaria and Daria wearing nothing but their wicked smiles. Aesmadaeva admired their beautiful lean bodies endowed with supple curves and pretty faces that would have rivaled the exquisite perfection of Ahes's visage if it wasn't for the perpetually impious smirks that despoiled their charm. The nearly identical twins carried a small bucket from which they drew a pair of sponges dripping with water. They knelt on either side of the princess, and gently worked the sponges over her skin. Aesmadaeva watched them closely, unsure of their true motives as it seemed unlikely that Zracul would send his sisters, known only for their cruelty, to bathe Ahes. The ablutions continued for only a short while before the sponges lay forgotten on the floor and the sisters explored deviant pleasures touching and kissing Ahes even as they pleasured each other. If this was all it was about, Aesmadaeva could care less. It was apparent the sisters Vampyr were obsessed with control and no doubt took mischievous delight in spurning their brother's will. If Ahes was in possession of her own mind, she would never know the perversities played upon her this night. But it was Aesmadaeva who observed every detail with great interest, for the demon was Ahes, and a time would come when it would use this knowledge against the sisters to best advantage. *So carry on Sisters,* Aesmadaeva's laugh echoed hollowly within the blighted consciousness of the princess, *the stranglehold about your throats is my grip slowly tightening!*

– – –

On almost any other occasion Aesmadaeva would delight in the sufferings of a mortal creature whose screams, shrieks, and wails reverberated through a dank cold cellar. This was not the case as, once again, circumstances necessitated a moving performance on the part of Ahes that assured Zracul she was transitioning according to his expectations. Still, the demon could not assuage qualms the count must have felt on the instances when he used his own psionic energies to probe her mind only to be smoothly rebuffed. It was no different than when Aesmadaeva attempted to examine Zracul's mind days earlier. The demon was startled that the count possessed psionic ability at all, let alone the knowledge to use it so expertly. This prompted Aesmadaeva to reconsider the derivation of Vampyr as not a natural or supernatural condition, but instead arcane. Prior to '*The Breaking*,' the Tuatha De were highly proficient at manipulating a creature's physical form and fusing it with powerful abilities designed to serve a specific function. They did this with dragons, trolls, orks, giants, and many other monstrosities that stalked the darkest forests and remote climates of Plethwih today. Still, Aesmadaeva was unaware of any creature other than the most powerful demons, and a smattering of humanoids owning the highest intellect capable of psionics. It was an enigma both Zracul and the demon, through Ahes, shared regarding each other that held no easy answer, so it would seem.

Fortunately, these visits were far shorter in duration as the spectacle of Ahes straining wildly at her chains in frequent convulsions of unrelenting pain caused Zracul no less irritation than Aesmadaeva, if somewhat more sympathetic. And soon upon his departure would the demon bring palliative restraint to her mind again restoring the blessed relief of silence and only resume the torturous commotion on the count's return. Another day and night passed thus, with no other visitors except for Zracul.

By the morning of the third day, the spasms of pain receded. Ahes slipped into a restless slumber with rapid breathing that was more like the panting of a dog. Aside from the weariness on her face, and the bruises, cuts, and gashes where the manacles touched her wrists and ankles, she looked no different than before. Inwardly, however, Aesmadaeva monitored a multitude of astounding changes. Everything in her physiology, from the cells in her blood to the way her organs functioned, was regenerative. The subtle decay of aging had ceased altogether. The tinsel strength of sinew, hardness of bone, and cellular immunity increased exponentially. More could be determined once she awakened. The demon wondered at the changes affecting her physical capabilities considering the profound biological alterations that transpired. With the transition nearly complete, Aesmadaeva was eager to explore the new wonders of his host. To that end, the demon set about accelerating the process where it could by integrating its consciousness more fully with her body, adopting her internal resources, fusing itself as a more permanent resident with the expectation of an eternal amalgamation between its mind and her body.

As evening approached, Ahes began to breath in a normal rhythm, her bruises were gone, and the cuts and gashes had disappeared leaving no scars. Her body was ready to awaken, thus Aesmadaeva reconnected through her vacant consciousness and opened her eyes. Almost instantly Ahes was overwhelmed by a cacophony of sight, sound, and scent beyond that of any normal human. The demon quickly adjusted her sensory input to control the chaos of new sensations. Everything from the distant scratching of a mouse behind the wall, the stench of awful washed down the drain in her cell the day before, to the sudden acuity of every tiny detail that leapt out encumbering her vision. Aesmadaeva supposed she would have naturally adjusted over time, but the demon had little patience to wait. The constraints of the current environment in no way impeded the demon's comprehension of the extraordinary evolution her basic senses were improved. Her vision approximated that of an Antilles Sea Eagle. Her audible range was comparable to the sensitivity and location origin determination of the great Dire Wolf. Her olfactory prowess was equivalent to the pheromone finding honey bee. These were creatures Aesmadaeva knew well as each once served as its host. Impressive as all this might be, there was an immediate need greater than all others demanding urgent satisfaction, and that was her body's desperate hunger for one thing: blood.

– – –

Long before he entered her cell, Zracul knew something was off. There she was, bright eyed and beautiful with a smile stretched across her lips. Her flawless naked figure, though gaunt, displayed not a single mark. But the connection he normally sensed with one transitioned by his own blood was entirely absent. It was an unbreakable bond that tied his creatures to him, and him alone. Through it, he could assess their condition, always know in which direction they could be found, and summon them to him no matter the distance. Most important, they were compelled to do as he willed.

"So, I survived," her smile broadened. "Are you surprised?"

He collapsed to his knees and kissed her savagely. She responded with like enthusiasm. When he finally relented, he stared deep into eyes sparkling with life and vitality, and replied, "Of course not. You are the strongest, most intelligent woman I have ever known."

"I am also the most ravenous," she teased. "Did you bring me something to assuage my hunger?"

Zracul laughed, "I have, indeed." He immediately set to releasing her by touching a heavy gilded ring he wore on his index finger to each of the manacles, whereby they immediately opened and fell loose from her arms and ankles. "A meal you will favor above all others!"

He stood, holding her hands as she easily rose from the floor where she had sat the last several days. Ahes showed no grimace of pain, stiffness, or aches from the long confinement. He didn't expect that she would.

Turning to the hallway outside the open door to the cell, Zracul called out, "Julienne! Join us, if you will."

A man in his twenties, bearing a stocky muscular build and a handsome face framed by short brown curls obediently strode from around the corner and into the cell. He said no words, nor did he display any hesitancy or fear. His green eyes stared dully from an expressionless continence. His skin smelled of lilac from recent washing, and he wore no garments.

Zracul stepped aside, and just in time as Ahes practically bowled him over in her rush to get to the throbbing arteries pulsing seductively in Julienne's neck.

"I thought a pretty one would add a nice garnish to your first meal," Zracul dragged a stool from the corner and sat down. "Although I expected it would be a few more hours before you recovered from the initial disorientation of all your new senses."

Ahes sat cross-legged bent over the man's head in her lap, his neck arched back staring with vacant eyes at the ceiling. Except for the occasional tremors in his limbs, his body was still as she drew out his lifeblood. With great reluctance, Ahes briefly looked up and grinned through crimson teeth and said something to the effect of, "I'm adaptable."

Zracul chuckled as she returned to her meal with gusto, noting the smattering of blood that covered her face and dribbled down her chin. "Looks like someone's going to require a bit of table etiquette rather than wearing their food like a three-year-old," he jested.

Not bothering to look up, Ahes snorted loudly in reply, then immediately began to cough violently. Zracul laughed all the more. He enjoyed watching new Vampyr struggling to master their abilities. "Take it easy," he cautioned. "Draw too much and you will feel bloated for the rest of the day."

Ahes unceremoniously released the young man's head and rolled him off her lap. "I feel reborn," she marveled, "and energized."

Zracul rose from his stool intending to retrieve a bucket of water from the corridor when, in a blur of motion, Ahes was practically wrapped around him, with lips pressed firmly against his, tearing at his clothing, ripping away long shredded strips of fine fabric. Zracul did not protest. She would find him a more than willing partner in their couplings. Especially now that there was little concern for the fragility of her mortal flesh. She was like he; indomitable, unrepentant, irrepressible. Immortal.

Two days and a night followed before Ahes finally relented. They lay sprawled upon the floor of the cell panting to regain their breath. Zracul was sure she could have continued for far longer if their bodies were not starved for energy. It was time to feed.

"Let us wash," he suggested, "and then I will teach how to hunt."

Ahes sat up, breathless, with arms atop her knees, nodding in agreement. After a minute to regain her air, she gestured to the far corner, "What about that one?"

Zracul glanced at the pallid lifeless corpse of the young man he brought for her first meal slumped in rigid repose against the stone wall. "He will be taken away presently," he waved dismissively. "One of the best features of the Agrabuta is the ample space for internments at the back of the property. It was a huge selling point when we were looking for a new home in Ys. I also liked that it was situated at the top of a hill, and somewhat remote from the bustle of the city."

"That's all well and nice," she replied with disinterest, "but right now I am famished, and all I can think about is sinking my teeth into a warm artery. Feed me!"

With a laugh, Zracul sat up next to her. "Off to the baths!" he announced. "Then we will find you a plump young sack of blood that will return the exuberant glow to your lovely cheeks."

"Just so." Ahes smiled with enthusiasm.

They rose from the floor together, and in a blur of motion the pair departed, leaving the silent lonely cell to the ministrations of the poor departed Julienne, whose clouded eyes stared forever into oblivion.

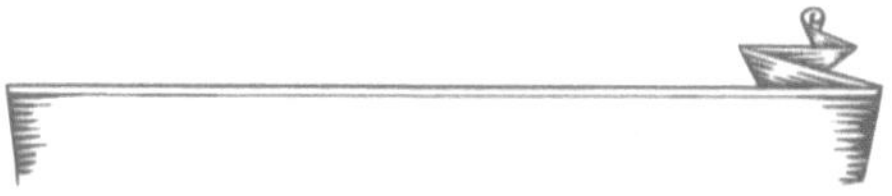

Chapter 10 – No Easy Return

Enguer shook his head fiercely to clear the intense ringing in his ears. All he accomplished was to cast a spray of blood from his shoulder-length curled brown locks. It was then that he realized his scalp was matted wet from several stinging abrasions. So too, the exposed skin on his arms showed crimson streaks, some trailing from the mail shirt he wore where it failed to fully prevent the super-heated shards from penetrating through the links.

"Enguer," the sound of Reskalin's shaky voice called to him nearby. He closed his eyes tight, then opened them again to steady his vision. When he lifted his gaze, he found Reskalin resting prone next to him below the rim of the hill with a look of horror on her face.

Enguer wished he could laugh. He must appear the image of death covered so in blood. No doubt he was afflicted by a thousand small puncture wounds stinging or burning under his flesh, but so far as he could tell none of his injuries were life-threatening. Still, Reskalin could not know this as she urgently wriggled toward him on the slope with a fold of bandages in hand she must have pulled from behind her leather corset.

"Where is the worst of it?" Her breath was heavy with fearful concern, and her eyes glistening with moisture betrayed her emotion. It was an unusual departure from her habitually stoic nature.

The numbing disorientation weighing heavy on Enguer's vision lifted enough for him to gently grasp Reskalin's hand already coursing over his face ceaselessly blotting away the blood with the dampened cloth. "I will be fine," he lightly squeezed her fingers to emphasize his assurance. "What of the others?"

"The druid is tending to the Atlanteans," Reskalin replied in a somber tone. "I fear Havacian," her voice cracked with feeling, "may be beyond his power."

Silence hung between them as Enguer studied Reskalin's face. Somehow, she had avoided even the slightest injury from the spray of stone shards. Perhaps Enguer was not so surprised. His wife had reflexes to rival a wary panther. Unfortunately, he and the others fell far short.

From beyond the safety of the hill, behind whose slope they cowered, came the screech of stone against stone followed by a bemoaned roar. Enguer stretched his arms up the incline and blindly dug his fingers deep into the smoldering clumps of grass-covered soil, painfully pulling himself far enough to peek over the edge of the hill, dreading what his clearing sight might reveal. Next to him, he could feel more than see Reskalin crawling with him to peer over the summit. Suddenly her body tensed, and she released a startled gasp, even as Enguer's eyes struggled to make sense of the scene before them.

Moments earlier, the hill where they lay was carpeted by lush grass flowing down the opposite side to a roughly level field of vibrant green dotted with pale flowers extending half a furlong wide to a bluff overlooking the Lake of Mists. Now, the ground was mostly bare earth scared by shallow craters twice the width of an ox cart. Long furrows of frayed soil stretched from a common point near the cliff, and widened in a cone shape toward the hill. Everywhere in between, stone shards large and small littered the ground. On the far side of the field, a heavy pall of thick vapory mist hung in the air obscuring all but a pair of dimly illuminated amber orbs set high in the shadowy silhouette of the Frog-God crouched at the edge of the precipice. All was quiet and still, save for the drubbing beat of the surf some distance below the overhang.

"Is it over?" Enguer whispered without turning his head. His bleary eyes searched for any hint of movement.

After a long pause, Reskalin replied, "Maybe." A longer pause followed and then, "Wait. Look!"

The mist slowly shifted and compressed, quickly picking up speed as it narrowed into a twisting vaporous ribbon that suddenly shot off over their heads. Enguer ducked reflexively as it passed and watched it disappear into the murky mangle of overgrown ruins behind them.

"The mist serpent, or whatever it was, may yet be a problem if we don't find our way out of this place soon." Enguer stole a quick glance back down the hill where Khulani feverishly working his arts over Qel's prone body. Havacian lay unmoving next to him. "And from the looks of the Atlanteans, it will be slow going."

Reskalin stared ahead unblinking. "I see the sphere." She pointed to the imposing figure of Vrtog clearly visible with the fast-dissolving mist.

Enguer studied the titanic stone creature. The mass that once formed Vrtog's chest, belly, and lower half of its jaw was vacant. Fractures riddled what remained of the Frog-God's exterior like an unending spiderweb with small chunks of broken stone falling loose, crumbling where they landed. And there, deep within the cavity that was its throat, Enguer caught a glimpse of something reflective. The rounded edge of a glass-like sphere. It was about the diameter of a small shield. Enguer could see grey cloud-like swirling patterns moving within, like a raging maelstrom. His gaze widened with amazement as the creature haltingly shifted its bulk. Subtle flexing movements in its colossal stone frog legs suggested Vrtog was preparing to leap forward.

"Oh damn." Reskalin jumped up and sprinted down the hill toward the Frog-God.

Startled by her unexpected movement forward rather than back, Enguer leapt up and rushed after her, calling, "Reskalin wait!"

Stone cracked and grated as the Frog-God attempted to set itself to jump, but the heavy wobble of unbalanced movement displaced enough of the loose earth under its wide feet to make its perch on the edge of the precipice unstable as the edge rapidly crumbled away.

Enguer immediately recognized the danger as he closed the gap with Reskalin. "Dammit, wait! You won't make it in time!"

Her pace did not slow, nor did she reply. Vrtog must have also realized the peril under its footing and struggled to find a foothold on the fast-deteriorating edge, but with the loss of so much mass on the front of its body, all its weight was working against it. Amber eyes flared with desperate intensity as it belched a final rumbling croak – and fell backward over the edge.

Reskalin jumped.

Arms stretched forward, Reskalin's fingertips brushed the edge of the sphere as the Frog-God tumbled over the disintegrating bluff. Enguer desperately reached for her legs, his grasp barely closing around her ankles in time to jerk her back from the precipice and onto the rock-strewn ledge where she landed roughly on her face. Her cry of pain was drowned out by the tremendous crash of stone impacting the rocky shore one hundred feet below. Heedless of the blood running from her nose, Reskalin scrambled to the edge and looked over. The shattered pale stone held no resemblance to the original form of Vrtog, the Frog-God. Even the huge amber eyes were crushed to dust. Remarkably, the sphere remained intact. It gleamed in the bright sunlight of the day even as a storm of dark clouds roiled like a tempest inside.

"I almost had it," Reskalin's frustration was muffled by the cloth held over her broken nose.

Enguer grunted surprise at her words as he did his best to dampen his fury at his wife's poor judgment, "Almost! You would be cradling it in your dead arms down there if I hadn't grabbed hold of you. Have you lost all your senses?"

"You're right, I don't know what I was thinking," her tone was shockingly conciliatory. "Now help me up. I need you to reset my nose."

– – –

"Can you walk?" Reskalin forced her tone to stay soft and even in the face of her impatience to get back to the ship. Despite her vehement objections, Enguer insisted on climbing down the sheer cliff overlooking the rocky shore to secure the orb from among the broken remains of the Frog-God. He was all alone. What if the mist serpent returned? Or something worse drawn by the thunderous crash that could probably be heard as far away as the City of Atlantis across the Primal Sea! She was being ridiculous, and she knew it, but Enguer was no longer simply her husband. He was the father of their unborn children and somehow that counted for something more.

"Yes," the Atlantean's reply brought Reskalin back to the present. "I am tired, but so are we all, and that's nothing compared to . . ." Qel's voice trailed away.

Reskalin nodded silently. She could see the loss in his eyes. It was a feeling she knew well, until the day she learned how to push away such feelings of attachment and numb her mind to it. The exception in her life was the FatMan, and more recently Enguer, and now two baby girls she had never even met.

"Are you comfortable with the travois, Khulani? You can move well enough?" Reskalin bent to check the knots and buckles that secured Havacian's body to the improvised A-frame lashed to the back of the great wolf. The beast twisted his head around to look back at her with large clear eyes and nodded. She still wasn't used to seeing Khulani's baleful gaze peering back at her in one of his many animal forms. "Alright, let's go."

Reskalin led them back the way they came, sometimes moving fast, other times at a slow crawl, depending on the volume of ancient rubble they were forced to traverse. She marveled at the size of Kiltullagh now that it was no longer concealed by mist. The strange, pitted coral-like architecture was faded and crumbling from centuries of deterioration. Thousands must have walked these dusty streets on their way to market, temple, or trade, she mused. Families too, with little fish-people running and laughing under sunny skies. Gods, she was getting sentimental.

Captain Rusee and his crew were anxiously waiting on the *Sprinter* just as instructed. Although initially alarmed when Reskalin appeared from the ruins covered in grey dust and blood, with a massive wolf in tow, they relaxed considerably once Khulani shifted back to human form. The captain had a lot of questions that Reskalin begged off in her haste to get Havacian carried aboard, promising to fill him in once they found Enguer a league or so to the north and east down one of the many inlets along the coast. It pained her to think how long it might take to search them one by one while he waited alone and vulnerable on the rocky shore. Qel and Khulani paced the deck with nearly as much angst as she did, which for some reason gave her comfort.

"Well, that explains the thunderous sound we heard coming from the city," offered the captain after hearing Reskalin's tale.

The *Sprinter* was crawling along the shore as close as safely prudent, pausing only when passing an inlet that might take them to the cliffside where Enguer was stranded. The sailors strained at their oars in the ebb just after hightide making slow progress, but Reskalin knew enough about sailing that this was a fortunate thing, for lowtide would be perilous so close to shore and more so within the inlets. If they could only find a way to locate the right inlet, they could sail further out without stopping at each one. Captain Rusee made it plain that should they not find the inlet with enough time to get in and out before lowtide, they would be forced to linger on the Lake of Mists until the next morning. That gave them five to seven hours to retrieve Enguer, and although the hours passed with plodding exasperation, Reskalin's skin crawled as if time was passing with fleeting haste.

She stood at the rail with the captain scrutinizing the coast as they slowly passed. The land rose from the water in easy gradients of green grass, sometimes interrupted by steep cliffs as high as fifty feet, shallow coves, or river-like inlets that caused them pause. Trees covered the higher elevations with no further evidence of ruins or habitation once Kiltullagh was out of sight. Still, life was abundant on the Lake of Mists. Vigilant deer stared with nervous flicking tails from the tree line, a fox slunk through tall grass stalking a plump rabbit casually munching on sour wild berries, a sleek hawk or majestic eagle seemed to float in place as they rode wind currents above the cliffs awaiting the opportunity to snatch a quick meal out of the rocks where any number of creatures burrowed and nested.

"You know," the captain broke the silence between them, "seems to me that no other animal can compare to the freedom of a bird. Look at them!" He pointed to a small flock of black birds flitting over the tops of the trees. "Flying high over land and sea, they go where they wish without any . . ."

"By the Gods!" Reskalin exploded, startling the captain. "That's it!" She turned and scanned the deck of the Sprinter until her gaze landed on the druid who slumped wearily next to Qel and the covered body of Havacian. He was dozing in the warmth of the sun after the exertions of the day. Reskalin nearly paused, but time was running short. "Khulani! Join us please."

The bleary-eyed druid hoisted himself from the deck and smoothly strode forward. "Is someone unwell?" he asked as he arrived.

"I know you're very tired," Reskalin could see the exhaustion in the lines of the druid's features, "but I must ask if you have enough strength to assume a form that can fly?"

At first. Khulani's brows furrowed with confusion, then his dark eyes seemed to clear with understanding. "Of course!" Khulani nearly shouted. "Fatigue has clouded my mind. What better way to find the inlet that will take us to Enguer."

Reskalin was overjoyed, but kept the emotion suppressed for the moment. "You have the energy for the task?"

"I believe I have the reserve," Khulani nodded. "It took a great deal of effort to place Havacian in a state of stasis to stave off decay until we return to Ys. Qel is hopeful we can find a priest who can return life to his body. I'm not so sure, but we must try. In any case, I will fly back to Kiltullagh and trace the inlet where Enguer awaits back to the lake."

Overwhelmed by sudden emotion, Reskalin hugged Khulani fiercely whispering a simple, "thank you," before realizing that this open display of sentiment was not at all like her, and she awkwardly pulled away.

To Reskalin's embarrassed relief, Khulani was smiling but said nothing. Then he took a step back and his human figure shimmered and shifted into the form of a giant eagle. Gasps and startled cries arose from the crew, but quickly settled into excited murmurs as the great eagle hopped up on the rail and spread its wings. The breeze ruffled the small feathers on its face and breast, powerful claws flexed with anticipation, a high-pitched, prolonged, gull-like cry burst forth twice in rapid succession shocking the crew again, and then it took to the sky in an explosive leap followed by a graceful beat of sail-sized wings.

"Well, that was something," Captain Rusee muttered as they watched the eagle circle high into the sky before turning southward.

Reskalin's cheeks reddened at the comment unsure if the captain was referring to the eagle or her unusual display of emotion. The truth was, ever since she left Enguer at the bottom of the cliff in Kiltullagh, all she wanted to do was cry. And it was really pissing her off.

The cold wind rushed over Khulani's broad wings as he soared higher on the rising thermals. This was his nirvana. From the moment he gained flight form as a young neophyte, Khulani felt no greater joy than when he was on the wing, high aloft, under the bright stars or cold moon. Even the blazing desert sun or frosty wind did not deter his delight of skimming the clouds. Yet today, Khulani had more on his mind – foremost being the recovery of Enguer Rand.

Rising higher still, Khulani's eagle vision could clearly plot the way back to Kiltullagh, and without the constraints of land or sea, it would take a third of the time to reach the cliffside where their friend was waiting. Khulani's mind wandered back to the ship where Havacian lifeless body was stretched out on the deck. He had grown to like the Atlantean in the short time they travelled together, and he felt great remorse, even a little shame, that his druidic skills were not enough to save him. Fortunately, Khulani possessed a small sprig from the Tree of Life that grew at the center of the Enclave in the Matu Forest, and it was through the divine blessings imbued within the branch that he was able to preserve Havacian's body until they returned to Ys. This thought weighed heavily on Khulani's mind. The other Atlantean, Qel, was optimistic that they would find a priest or healer with the power to bring Havacian back to life. Khulani wasn't so sure. Of all the druids he had ever known, only the ArchDruids possessed this arcane knowledge, and they were loath to use it except in the most extreme situations. A price was exacted from the caster with each use, although he didn't know what that cost might be, it must be significant. Even the magical sprig from the Tree of Life was consumed in the effort to sustain Havacian let alone return his life. Khulani feared that Havacian's death was inevitable, but how could he convince Qel of this when there was even the smallest chance? The two Atlanteans were best friends since their first days as acolytes in the Wizards Enclave in Atlantis. They graduated in the same class and began their ritual 'Journey of Discovery' together. To look at them, the pair seemed to be opposites. Qel was dark-haired with a cheeky sense of humor. He was a student of the Red Hall, elemental fire, commonly known as a Red Wizard. Conversely, Havacian exhibited voluminous blond hair, and the typical personality of an academic. He was a graduate of the Blue Hall, elemental water. Strange indeed that they should be such fast friends.

Khulani's attention was drawn to the ground where the ruins of Kiltullagh rapidly passed beneath him. The mist was beginning to slowly return as it crept over the ruins from a dark hole in the center of the city. Already the mist dragon must be recovering from its wounds. Khulani steered away from the hole not wishing to encounter the serpent a second time even if it was in a weakened state.

Seconds later, the battered field appeared. He suppress a shudder soaring over this place he never hoped to lay eyes again. He angled lower, swept over the field without slowing, and across the bluff at the top of the cliff. Below, Khulani could see the shattered remains of the Frog-God strewn over the jagged boulders forming a narrow semicircle at the end of the inlet. The lower tide revealed a bit of sand and more rocks, but his eyes were glued on the solitary figure sitting on a boulder with one arm propped atop a cloudy sphere the size of a large pumpkin. Enguer peered upward as soon as Khulani glided into view. Although his eagle form was much larger than any natural creature of the same kind, he coasted silently high above Enguer and cast no forward shadow. It was an impressive measure of the Ranger's awareness of his surroundings that he noticed Khulani's approach immediately.

The druid screeched a greeting as he banked into a slow spiral. Enguer waved in reply, indicating he recognized the eagle for who it was. Khulani would have liked to land and transform back into human form to speak with Enguer, but that was not an option since he would need hours of rest before he could summon enough energy to perform the transformation again. That would not please Reskalin at all. As it was, she was nearly wild with desperation to have Enguer back. Khulani was aware the two lovers had been together for some time and laughed with the others when they told tales of their adventures which were often dangerously reckless. That was when their group first set sail on the *Sprinter* and were still getting to know one another. Recently he noticed that something had changed between Enguer and Reskalin. They seemed closer, cautious, and more protective of one another.

Khulani dipped his wings to either side, screeched once more, and then dove out of his spiral to only a few feet above the water as he glided away from Enguer following the curve of the inlet. The Ranger waved again and sat back down with the strange globe. It was a good sign he understood, thought Khulani, before he tucked in his legs and beat his wings in sweeping arcs to gain elevation. Once he gained the desired altitude, he realized the difficulty with locating the correct inlet from the lakeside. Several inlets cut into the land from the Lake of Mists. Some led to coves and shallow bays while others were longer and interconnected almost like a fjord. To follow one randomly would baffle the most capable captain as to which connection to take and what direction it might eventually go as many changed their route unexpectedly or twisted back on themselves. The inlet that led to Enguer was actually quite straight and easy to follow compared to the others, if they were lucky enough to choose it over the dozen or so plausible routes in sight.

It took Khulani less than half an hour to navigate the inlet back to the lake. Ironically, the *Sprinter* was anchored just to the north in deeper water; this inlet was the last one they passed. Khulani heard someone on the distant ship call out. He had been sighted, and his eagle eyes watched the crew scramble to bring up the anchor and man the oars in anticipation of the news he carried. When he landed, Reskalin rushed over clearly expecting him to transform. Instead, Khulani did his best to indicate that the *Sprinter* should follow his flight. It was an exercise in frustration to the point that he almost gave up, but after several long minutes Captain Rusee seemed to understand Khulani's intent comparing the giant eagle to an albatross that sailors often followed for luck or land when lost.

"Let's get underway then!" Reskalin practically shrieked before angrily stomping away.

Khulani took off and circled overhead while the Sprinter slowly tacked to the south heeling sharply from the strong portside winds. He understood Reskalin's impatience, but he was also sure it would be exponentially worse if he changed back to human form and then missed a turn guiding them from the deck of the ship. He learned a long time ago how different the world looked from above and how easy mistakes could be made traversing the surface in unfamiliar terrain.

The Lake of Mists was relatively calm except for the frequent white caps produced by the down drafts that felt a little stronger than they had experienced thus far on their journey from Ys. Khulani knew little about sailing or the fickle nature of large bodies of water sailors often feared, but he knew the smell of a storm approaching and wondered what calculations Captain Rusee mind must be churning over in addition to the dangers of piloting the *Sprinter* through the inlet at low tide if they didn't make it out in time. Khulani brushed away such thoughts to focus on the route back to Enguer. Captain Rusee was a good sailor, and he would do what was best for the safety of his crew and passengers no matter how much Reskalin badgered him to take chances to speed their progress. At least Khulani hoped so.

By the time the *Sprinter* arrived at the base of the cliff where Enguer patiently waited with the unusual sphere, the swell was only an hour or two away from peak low tide. Khulani circled over the area as Captain Rusee anchored and dispatched a pair of sailors in a rowboat more efficient at navigating the submerged rocks close to shore. He watched as Enguer eagerly jumped in the small vessel, the slow return to the ship, and the welcome embrace the Ranger received from Reskalin almost before his feet hit the deck. Khulani might have enjoyed the moment with them except that he was needed in his current form to safely guide them all back to the Lake of Mists. Below, the *Sprinter* was already pulling up anchor and preparing oars to turn the ship back the way they had come.

The return was an excruciating exercise for both the *Sprinter* and Khulani. Rowing against the tide and the wind slowed their movement by half. Sometimes Khulani was not sure they moved at all as he glided ahead of the ship with barely a beat of his mighty wings. If it wasn't for his concern for those aboard the ship below, Khulani might have enjoyed the cool winds and spectacular array of orange and yellow bands highlighting the clouds edges with the slow retreat of Sunna toward the distant horizon. With one eye on the *Sprinter*, he watched with appreciation other winged predators taking flight in the hope of finding an evening meal. Hawks and eagles spiraled high over clusters of rocks and grass expanses keeping sharp eyes peeled for the slightest movements. It reminded him how hungry he was. And tired. Not far ahead he could already see the outlet to the lake and the calm waters beyond. Mist was rising further out where warm winds from the south passed over the cold waters to rapidly cool the air. It was a peculiarity with this body of water that lent its name to an unusual weather pattern rather than an effect caused by the mist dragon in Kiltullagh, although no better environment could such a creature ask.

Khulani peered through eagle eyes down at the *Sprinter*. The excited gestures of the crew indicated that they, too, had spied the outlet. A bellow from the captain sent everyone scurrying across the deck, the timing drum picked up the beat, and the oarsmen pulled a little harder without complaint anticipating the open expanse of the lake where they could safely rest a while and enjoy a warm meal already in the making by their talented cook. Khulani smiled inside, looking forward to joining them. He cast his gaze back to where the birds of prey circled a moment before. Apparently, the little raptors had been victorious in their hunt as they were gone. All of them. In fact, everywhere he looked was eerily devoid of the natural stirring of nature in the hours before sundown. Something wasn't right. A feeling of dread came over him as he realized that only the presence of a much greater predator could so completely send the lesser beasts into hiding. Khulani barely finished the thought when he felt a jarring impact of a heavy body. The piercing agony of sharp claws driven deep through his feathered back, grasp at flesh between his wings. A startled screech escaped his curved beak followed by the remote cries of surprise from below. Unable to maintain lift, Khulani plunged toward the water with the thing on his back holding fast. The creature shrieked a high-pitched roar and sank a viscous bite to the side of Khulani's feathered neck. It retracted, spitting feathers, and bit down hard again, this time with less force as Khulani anticipating the strike, and sharply twisting his head to the side in an effort to avoid the worst of it.

The slow swells of the lake below were rapidly approaching. Khulani banked his wings in a last-ditch effort to reverse position on his foe. They were going to hit the water hard, and the collision might be marginally survivable if the other creature absorbed the main force of the impact. But no matter how he turned and twisted, the power of the larger creature was immoveable. It was in complete control, allowing the swift decent that they both knew would kill its prey and leave it relatively unharmed to swoop away and devour the carcass at its leisure comfortably perched on some nearby rock or jut in the surfside cliff. This creature was a proficient killer adapted to the environment where it lived, intelligent and clever, practiced in the art of rendering its quarry lifeless with minimal danger to injury itself. This was a fierce beast Khulani knew well from books and study if not from practical experience.

Until now.

A thrill of excitement shot through his feathered breast knowing that for the first time he was in the presence of a creature he had admired for so long. If he were not just seconds away from becoming its evening meal, he would have appreciated the moment far more. The monstrosity shrieked in a fashion easily mistaken for a young dragon, and although it certainly belonged to the draconic family, even the eldest of these creatures would never come close to the enormity of their draconic cousins. This was what many in the Western Kingdoms named Wyvern. Yet, no matter what they were called in lands of desert, snow, or any environment in between, Wyvern's were among the most adaptable, ferocious hunters the Tuatha De ever created. And now that Khulani was intimately familiar with the fabled beast, he could soon learn to become one in flight form, similar to the way he could assume the form of the giant eagle he currently sported. Of course, he would have to survive this encounter if he ever hoped to enjoy the benefit of their meeting.

Had Khulani been an actual giant eagle, the surprise attack by the cunning Wyvern would have surely spelled his doom. However, as a druid in the flight form of a gigantic eagle, he had a surprise up his sleeve, and it was a big one. It required only a second of concentration, and that's all he had, as the mass of the great eagle abruptly shifted into the much smaller man-sized figure of Khulani. The Wyvern reacted by groping at the air with its claws in disbelief before flaring out its leather wings to slow its fall. It was a futile effort so close to the surface of the water and without the eagle as a giant shock-absorber the collision was going to hurt.

"Now!" Someone shouted from the deck of the *Sprinter* bobbing only a few dozen yards away. Suddenly the Wyvern had another problem as a score of well-aimed bolts and a jet of searing flames slammed into the creature's body shredding the leathery wing on its left side. The Wyvern lost all lift, spun around, and crashed into the waves on its back, killing it instantly. Khulani made a much smaller splash only a few feet away, but he had entered the water in a rigid dive that stung but did not injure. By the time he got his head above water, the remains of the battered Wyvern trailing whisps of smoke and a flow of crimson, slowly sank to a watery grave. The *Sprinter* arrived an instant later and Khulani was hauled from the lake to the cheers of everyone aboard. Although relieved, a wave of sadness for the demise of the Wyvern weighed like a stone in Khulani's gut. It was one of the few monsters created by the Tuatha De that had a chance of assimilating into the natural order of Plethwih. Even the druids accepted it as the only unnatural beast allowed to thrive rather than hunted to extinction.

"I've never thought of druids as more than a bunch of horny tree-hugging nature fanatics with skinny legs chasing around unclad dryads and whatnot," Reskalin strode up to Khulani, who was practically hanging between Enguer and a burly seaman. "But today you have earned my respect," she took hold of the strange circular stone hanging from a leather thong around Khulani's neck, bent close, and kissed it. The stone flashed with scintillating light, drawing gasps from those gathered around. Reskalin released the stone, glanced curiously at Enguer then back to Khulani, "and my gratitude."

Khulani was flooded with emotions. He wanted to laugh, he wanted to cry, but mostly, he was exhausted, and if it wasn't for Enguer and the sailor holding him up he doubted he could remain standing. The best he could offer was a smile under eyes awash with tears. She had kissed his druid stone! It was said that doing so gave the druid insight into that person's soul. Did Reskalin know this to do as she did? As for anything else, perhaps he would find out. For now, he had to rest.

Chapter 11 – Plans Revealed

"How about that one?"

Zracul shook his head. "You see the greyish-blue bags under the fellow's eyes? And notice his skin looks thin and shiny? He has a disease that makes his lifeblood unpalatable."

"Fine," Ahes sighed with frustration. "Let's find another. I'm starving!"

"Be patient," he smoothly chided. "It's important that you learn how to identify a healthy subject. Bad lifeblood can leave a Vampyr sick and miserable for days!"

"You know patience is not one of my redeeming qualities," she shot a playfully dark look in his direction, "but I will be a good student for as long as I can bear it."

Zracul barked a short laugh, saying "Then, we shall both be tested!" He spent the next few minutes pointing out a few more undesirable persons walking in the lamplight of the street below. They both wore all black standing on the balcony of one of Ahes's frequent haunts. From the chamber behind them, music played, and people laughed oblivious to the dangerous predators that so often walked among them, weighing their worth to use for pleasure or hunger. There was a certain power in this knowledge that Zracul found particularly gratifying.

"That one there looks young, healthy, and appetizing," Ahes remarked with a quick gesture toward a pudgy woman clad in garments typical of a chambermaid. She walked with a quick step carrying an empty basket that suggested she was headed to the night market on her way home after a long day at work.

"Adjust your hearing to focus on her, and her alone, shutting out everything else, and tell me what you hear," Zracul instructed.

He watched Ahes staring hard at the woman. Her eyes narrowed, then relaxed as she focused inward.

"She has a strong heartbeat, and the flow of her lifeblood is unrestricted," Ahes recited. "Her gait is strong and unwavering."

"Very good," Zracul was impressed. She was a quick study. "Now that you know which one you want, how should we take her? Remember, we cannot leave bodies drained of their lifeblood all over Ys. That would only invite trouble that might eventually involve the Atlanteans, which is the last thing we want."

She snapped her gaze on him, surprise painting her features. "Why should we fear the Atlanteans more than anyone else?"

"Well, aside from the true-blood Tuatha De, of whom very few remain, and the Sylvan, who rarely involve themselves in the affairs of humans, the Atlanteans have substantial arcane resources and an inexplicable commitment to the success of humanity. That makes them extraordinarily dangerous to our kind." Zracul idly watched the chambermaid continue down the street.

"What about humans who are trained in the arcane arts?" she pressed. "Wouldn't they be just as much a threat to us?"

Zracul shrugged, "Most humans are self-absorbed with fragmented loyalties, and any of them powerful enough to cause us trouble would be hard pressed to abandon their arcane studies to involve themselves in an investigation that held little interest for them."

The chambermaid was out of sight having turned down one of the many cross streets. Ahes seemed to have forgotten all about her when she said, "Enough about wizards and Atlanteans. Let's go get that plumb chambermaid before I wither away!"

"She gone now," Zracul waved a hand toward the street. "How might you find her?"

"I have her scent," was her clever reply.

Zracul allowed a wolfish grin to spread across his face. Impressed he was. Impressed he was, indeed!

The pair quickly dashed over the edge of the balustrade and disappeared among the shadows of the night.

Ahes kicked off her sandals and stretched her long pale legs languorously over the soft sheep-skin leather divan with her head propped under one hand. Her short strapless silky red gown and sallow complexion contrasted starkly against the black leather as she eyed Jaria and Daria sitting hip-to-hip on a short burgundy couch on the opposite side of the room. Each was garbed in frocks composed mainly of layers of black gauzy silk with a deep neckline that shifted seductively when they moved revealing narrow strips of their porcelain skin beneath, and ankle-high laced black leather boots lifted like stilts on thick six-inch heels. From under long eyelashes darkened by kohl, the twins glanced uncertainly at Ahes from time to time drawing a roguish smile from the Princess that only served to heighten their apprehension. Thus far, Ahes had little interaction with the sisters since her transition to Vampyr, but whenever the girls would pass by, their acerbic giggling was pointedly pitched to get her attention.

Vadim and Fain sat in oak framed high-backed chairs paneled with burgundy cushions further along the curved wall of the chamber with an open window between them. They too, were dressed nearly in all black except for their fitted tunics of pure white with silvered buttons and high collars that peeked above their coats in the high fashion of the day. They were handsome men a few years apart in age. Vadim was the larger with long black hair tied in the back, heavy dark brows, and dark eyes over a strong straight nose and squared jaw. Fain was smaller, exhibiting delicate features, short hair parted to one side, and intelligent deep brown eyes that shifted often to Ahes with long covetous intensity. Like the twins, she had little opportunity to interact with the brothers, but thus far they had been polite and appeared genuinely pleased at her addition to the 'family.' Ahes idly wondered if Zracul would mind if she played with them from time to time.

It was a bright clear night. Even the colorful glow above Ys could not pollute the sky of all the brilliant points of light twinkling in blues, reds, and whites. The distant murmur of crowds and frequent high pealing laughter resonated within the princesses' sensitive ears giving rise to her impatience to get on with the impromptu meeting so she and Zracul could go out and join the fun. Occasionally, a strong cool breeze blew through the open window provoking flames within the lanterns to flicker, and furling the pages of a large tome Zracul stood over like a vulture with keen, searching eyes. Ahes wondered for the hundredth time why he summoned them all here to sit in the silence of the east tower watching him read a damn book for the better part of an hour.

Finally, he slowly closed the book with great care and cast his gaze around the room. "Where are Naamah and Perault?" he asked no one in particular.

He was answered by universal shrugs.

Zracul's eyes focused on Vadim, "Brother, retrieve them in all haste, if you please."

"Of course, brother," Vadim replied and disappeared down the stairs in a blur.

"Who is Perault?" Ahes asked. She was somewhat taken aback since the name was unfamiliar to her. Aside from the servants and grounds keepers, she thought she knew everyone of import residing in the Agrabuta.

"A knight. A Temple Knight. Naamah's latest plaything," he replied with indifference.

Ahes lifted an eyebrow and spoke in a tone of mocking amusement, "Strange to invite a Temple Knight to your super-secret meeting, isn't it?"

Zracul laughed heartily, obliterating the repressive intensity in the room. He never took offence when she poked fun at him, even in front of other people. It was one of the characteristics that made them so compatible, among other things.

"She made him her mate," he said with an obvious tinge of incredulity. "Perhaps he will be useful in our endeavor."

"I look forward to hearing all about it," she smiled, then turned her attention to the twins. "Jaria, or Daria, whichever one you are," Ahes gazed pointedly at the one on the left. "Would you fetch me a glass of Mekali red?"

Daria glared at her, showing the whites of her teeth in a dangerous snarl, unmoved to comply. Jaria's dark, defiant stare was a perfect reflection of her sister's. Ahes pretended not to notice, an insolent smile pasted like a mask over her face.

"Daria," Zracul's tone was stern and commanding. "Your new sister has asked you for a favor."

Daggers of hatred flared in Daria's eyes, she growled, and without so much as a word sped like an angry shadow down the stairs. Jaria quickly followed.

"Stirring up a hornet's nest would have been a safer bet than instigating the twin's ire," Zracul chuckled.

Ahes shrugged one slender shoulder. "It's what women do. We have to establish a pecking order in the home for proper balance. I can handle them, and I don't need you coming to my rescue."

Zracul looked very pleased at that, and turning, simply shrugged at Fain who sat quietly unable to suppress a smile.

There was a distortion in the air as a glass of red wine filled to the rim appeared on a small table next to Ahes. When she looked up, Daria was sitting in her place on the couch followed almost immediately by Jaria. Both glared venomously at the princess as they watched her pick up the glass and lift it to her lips without spilling a drop. Ahes drank deeply of the wine, slowly set the glass down, and produced a thin needle from between her lips.

"Nice try ladies," she spoke through teeth clutching the needle. "But cheap. You can do better."

The twin's faces colored red as the burgundy wine, darting quick fearful glances at Zracul. He was watching Ahes, pointedly ignoring them. She drew the needle back into her mouth, and her tongue went to work, jaw moving weirdly from side to side. A few seconds later, Ahes produced the needle again. This time it was tied in a tight double-knot.

The room was silent with awe. Then another blur swept into the room and Vadim appeared in his chair.

"Naamah is on her way," he announced. Looking about the room, he must have comprehended the awkward silence and asked, "Did I miss something?"

Fain burst out laughing. The twins sunk deep into the plush couch glowering. Ahes was pleased to note the fresh flush of desire that colored Zracul's neck and cheeks. Then the quick snap of whip-like tail and brush of leathery wings heralded the arrival of Naamah at the top of the stairway.

Ahes regard the woman coolly. She was wickedly beautiful. Even with horns protruding from her forehead, leathery wings retracting smoothly on her back, and the long-pointed tail constantly swaying like a writhing serpent, she was a stunning beauty. As usual, Naamah was clad in an all-black slinky leather bodysuit. The version she wore on this occasion was sleeveless with open leather laces running at a gradient along both sides of her torso and down her legs exposing milky white skin beneath, ending in over-the-ankle black leather boots flared at the top with a moderate heel.

"Good of you to join us," Zracul greeted her evenly. "Where is your knight? We were all looking forward to seeing him."

From the corner of her eye, Ahes caught subtle movement. The twins shifted uncomfortably and somehow managed to glower even more darkly than before. With some surprise, she realized Naamah might be an unexpected ally in the house.

"I was just about to go out and procure a proper wardrobe for him to wear," Naamah stated simply. "Otherwise, he would be standing here unadorned and free as the day he was born. I'm sure he wouldn't mind. I just thought the rest of you would find it uncomfortable considering his generous . . ."

"We get the point, Naamah," Zracul interrupted. "Please have a seat."

Naamah strode toward the divan where Ahes lounged with her glass of wine. When the princess made no effort to make room, Naamah sniffed loudly and altered her course to a wooden bench set against the wall. Ahes noticed the twins brighten a little at the subtle exchange, and dared to wonder if they might become the better allies in the future once they submitted to her dominance. Ahes loved the prospect of family intrigue.

"I have called you all here so you may finally discover why I have brought our family to Ys," Zracul stood near the center of the room pacing back and forth while he spoke. "I will keep it brief and uncomplicated as we have little time to prepare. Not too long ago, our brothers and I discovered a tome that represented a future for Vampyr as more than just a race of supernatural creatures hiding in shadows, living in the darkness at the fringes of civilization. This tome could be our deliverance into the light of day where we could openly rule kingdoms and empires. And eventually all Plethwih. The tome, this tome," Zracul placed his hand over the large open book sitting on the table, "describes an orb it names as the Sphere of Elements. According to the tome, when used with the guidance of the author and certain enchantments written therein, the Sphere of Elements is capable of controlling vast areas of atmospheric weather to devastating effect. All we needed where three things; One, the Sphere of Elements; two, a precisely constructed setting to place it in; and three, this tome."

Zracul's gaze circled the room, alighting briefly on Ahes, and then he said, "A few weeks ago, Fain discovered the location of the sphere. It was purported to be located in the ruins of an ancient city once called Kiltullagh on the northern shores of the Lake of Mists. Thus, we came to Ys as a logical hub to recruit a talented group of explorers, adventurers, swashbucklers, however they be named to retrieve the sphere, and test its powers. The former we accomplished with the help of Naamah and her charms," Zracul bowed with appreciation in her direction. She smiled brightly in return, and he continued. "I sent them on their way with the promise of a chest of gold upon their return with the sphere."

"Why didn't you just send your brothers, or even your sisters, to retrieve the sphere? Surely, you would have it in hand that much sooner." Ahes asked. The twins were glowering at her again.

"That would have been the preferred choice," Zracul acknowledged. "But the tome describes a guardian that yet prowls the dead streets of Kiltullagh. An ancient creature of the mists with the ability to rend the flesh and drown trespassers with its vaporous breath. As a recent transitioner to Vampyr, you may not yet understand how dangerous that is to our kind. Although drowning by itself will not permanently kill us, it can incapacitate until air is available once more. In the meantime, we would be completely helpless. I value our small family in much higher esteem than to take such risks."

"What about this group you hired to find the sphere?" Ahes was almost certain Zracul would have thought of every possible hitch in his plan, but she wanted to understand a few of the more important details. "If they are smart enough to avoid or defeat this guardian, wouldn't they be more than a little concerned about handing over an artefact with the power you described?"

"Most certainly they would!" Zracul wore a crafty smile. "Except, they believe the sphere is an artefact imbued with long forgotten magic capable of healing the Creeping Disease, which they believe I am currently at threat of dying from."

"Well done," approved Ahes. "And what about this stand, or setting, you mentioned?"

Zracul bowed to her compliment. "That, yes, has been painfully reconstructed to the smallest exacting detail by our brothers, Vadim and Fain. It is on the floor above us if you would care to have a look later."

"I would, yes!" Ahes replied eagerly.

"And as far as the will to use the Sphere of Elements," Zracul smiled broadly spreading his hands wide in dramatic fashion. "That task belongs to me, of course."

"So, what is the purpose, brother?" Jaria asked mildly.

"Yes. Tell us brother, how will the sphere make us masters of Plethwih?" added a cynical Daria.

Zracul placed a thoughtful hand over his chin and started to pace again. "Good questions, both," he praised. "We will test the sphere on Ys, so we are confident we know how to use it to full affect. But the real target, and the one that must be obliterated if we are to realize our dreams of conquest and dominance, is the destruction of Atlantis." The chamber was dead silent.

Zracul continued, "Once the City of Atlantis is drowned under the waves, the few who survive will have little thought for anything else but rebuilding their society, and by the time they can organize any modicum of structure or defense, it will be too late." He leaned against the table whereon the great tome lay and sighed. "To speak truth, we run a great risk by testing the sphere on Ys. If the Atlanteans suspect a whiff of arcane influence propelling the maelstrom, they may seek out the origin and destroy us before we can advance our plans further. Still, it must be this way, for without a test, we risk failure simply because we lacked the practical knowledge and experience to control the sphere effectively."

Fain cleared his voice drawing everyone's attention. "You have spoken with great passion about what needs to be done, but what happens when it *is* done? What do we do then?"

Zracul's wolfish grin presaged a monumental disclosure to all in the room. "When Ys lays in ruin, and the people cry out for release from their misery, you will go out and give them what they crave. Feed as you must, but your primary objective will be to build an army of our kind that will swarm over our enemies led by you, their masters. All will fear the silence of our marching, day and night, the strongest will become one of us, and the weak will be cast upon altars screaming and writhing in their own blood, sacrificed to a new hedonistic deity that all will know as Zracul, Father of Vampyr!"

The famed poet Vyvian was known to have observed in verse, '*The darkest hours of the night come just before the first light of dawn*.' Ahes thought perhaps the line should be amended to include at the end, '*when one awaits their lover*.'

After the gathering earlier that night, Zracul remained in the tower with his brothers working over the tome, while Naamah and the twins departed the Agrabuta to do whatever they do. As for Ahes, she returned to the chamber she shared with the count and sprawled across the bed expecting him to join her presently. Allowing the princess's body to rest, Aesmadaeva took the opportunity to contemplate the implications of Zracul's plans. On the surface, it was a bold and exciting endeavor with exceptional risks with equally exceptional rewards. Yet, it was unclear how the count regarded Ahes any different than his brothers and sisters in the plan. Aesmadaeva would have to take steps to ensure that Ahes was lifted above the other Vampyrs in equal status to Zracul. As his mate, it stood to reason that if he ascended himself a God, then she must then be considered a Goddess. And should he view her role as subordinate to him, then he would soon find her a dangerous adversary. That would not be Aesmadaeva's preference, of course, as it found Zracul the perfect companion, and one that together they could accomplish almost anything. Even divine ascension. Because of its very nature, Aesmadaeva held an advantage that no other Vampyr could ever claim: It/Ahes could not be compelled by the will of Zracul. What's more, Aesmadaeva was aware that Zracul already realized that, which made Ahes particularly dangerous to him. Yet, he seemed inexplicably unconcerned about it thus far. Maybe it was the *need* they felt to be with one another. No real love could ever exist between them, but avarice, lust, and the unique compatibility of their companionship must be a bond equally powerful. Aesmadaeva meditated on the subject for a while.

Hours later, Aesmadaeva felt a presence enter the room. It wasn't Zracul.

Ahes's eyes popped open to discover the malevolent figures of Jaria and Daria looming over her. "Why have you invaded my chambers uninvited?" Ahes asked calmly.

"*You're* chambers?" Jaria laughed sardonically.

"You mean to say our brother's chambers, yes?" Daria followed.

"Do you think you're the only one to share his bed?" Jaria flashed a wicked smile.

Daria sniffed at the air, "I can still smell the tang from our bodies mixed with his on the sheets you lay upon so easily."

Ahes was very still as she stared up at the twins mocking her. There was a demons fury building inside her. Not because of what they said about their intimacies with their own brother, or the slight about who the chambers belonged to, but the audacity of these two little fools to try and intimidate her. "Is that all you came to say?" Ahes yawned to demonstrate her boredom with the conversation. "If so, you have my leave to depart by the way you came."

The twin's faces flushed with anger.

"We came to give you a warning," Daria growled.

And in a heated voice Jaria added, "Your position is temporary. Long after he's bored with you, we will be at his side."

"Who will you turn to then?" Daria snapped angrily.

"You had better learn your place quickly, *Princess*, or we will . . ." Jaria never finished what she was going to say.

In silent rage, Ahes erupted from the prone position on the bed where she lay so calmly a second before, and slammed the twins into the vaulted ceiling of the two-story chamber. She held each of them by the neck with her taloned hands, their bodies hanging limp from psionic paralysis while her bare feet curled over the edges of a wooden buttress keeping them aloft in an impossible display of supernatural strength. Their expressions turned to horror, shock, disbelief in the grip of the woman who they thought to control.

"Let me give *you* a warning," Ahes snarled. She could barely hold back the temptation to snap their heads off and toss them into the hearth. "I will always be above you. If Zracul becomes a King; I will be Queen. When he is a God; I will be a Goddess. In all things we are equal, your brother and I. Is that understood?"

Neither woman could reply with more than tears of rage and frustration trailing down their ashen cheeks.

"One more thing," Ahes smile was pleasant if limned in acerbic venom. "I know well your tang. I can still smell it on the intimates of my body. Do you suppose your brother can smell it too?"

The twin's eyes grew wide with fear.

"Yes, I know what you did in that vulgar cell. Every lewd detail." Extending her long tongue, Ahes gently licked the tears off their faces in slow lingering strokes while the women helplessly sobbed in humiliated silence. "Your tears taste sweet upon my tongue."

Scowling, Ahes shook the pair in violent reproach like helpless ragdolls, then released their minds and bodies, despite wanting nothing more than to tear them limb from limb.

The twins fell toward the floor flailing their arms in desperate circles, but just before the bone-breaking impact, their forms altered into distorted shadows that streaked with haste borne of terror out the door. Ahes laughter chased them down the gloomy corridor like vengeful spirits.

"You must feel terribly neglected," Zracul teased.

Ahes sniffed with mock indignation, and swiftly turned her back on him causing the short train of her blue seafoam gown to follow with a dramatic swish across the floor. "Of course I do."

In an instant his chest was pressed against her luminous pale skin exposed by the open-back design of ethereal fabric that tapered from her smooth lean-muscled shoulders to a sharp point betwixt her compactly rounded buttocks. Ever so slowly, he planted gentle kisses up the curve of her neck as he slid his arms around her waist pulling her tighter against his body. "I have much to make up for."

She spun in his arms too fast for the eye to follow and pressed her lips against his drawing a vigorous series of deep forceful osculates that fired his passions to the exclusion of all other thoughts as they slowly sank to the floor. "I forgive you," she gasped as they tore at the fabric of each other's attire with little heed for the mending that would be required if they were ever to be worn again. Zracul had arrived in the chamber just after dawn, but there would be no further semblance of coherent words between them until late in the afternoon.

Hours later, an open window facing seaward drew in a cool salty breeze over languid bodies hot with sweat. Zracul was staring up at the vaulted ceiling as he recovered his breath. Next to him, with one slender leg thrown over his, lay Ahes. Her heaving breasts were beginning to relax after the feverish activity that had consumed most of their day. His keen eyes spotted a pair of deep gashes in one of the buttresses that he never noticed before. He stored the information in his mind for another time as there was a matter of far more import he needed to discuss with Ahes and time was running short.

"I need a favor," Zracul rotated his head on his pillow to face Ahes nearly nose to nose. Her sultry brown eyes were staring back at him.

"You have something new in mind?" a cheeky smile played over her lips.

Zracul laughed. "Yes, but that must wait a while."

She propped herself up on one arm and cocked her head in a gesture of curiosity that allowed her golden curls to fall around her face. "What can I do?"

"As I understand it, the sea gates are closed one hour after dark every night and reopened at dawn," he looked at her for confirmation.

"So they are," she agreed.

"But is it true that they are only locked when Ys is under threat from extreme weather or invasion?"

"That is the way of it," she shrugged.

Zracul pondered a moment, unsure of Ahes's relationship with her father since they had never spoken of it. That the king viewed the princess as a petulant child beyond his control was well known, but how did she feel about him? He chided himself for not taking this into account earlier.

There was no more time to delay, he would have to press on and trust that she was with him. Afterall, she made no complaint the night before when he announced that Ys would be the first test of the destructive power of the Sphere of Elements, assuming she did not underestimate the magnitude of the devastation that it brought. He was sure her reaction to his next words would expose her feelings entirely. "And is it also true that your father, King Gradlon, bears the only key upon his person at all times?"

She stared long at him without expression or emotion. Zracul could almost see the wheels churning behind her eyes, calculating her response. He took it as a good sign that she did not immediately react with outrage.

"I have a question for you, almighty Zracul, Father of Vampyr," Her tone was blunt rather than derisive but it took him by surprise all the same. "Last night, when you proclaimed your imminent ascension to divinity, exactly what role did you see me playing in this fanciful future of your making? Am I to be one of the 'Masters' leading armies of Vampyr over the ramparts of obstinate kingdoms?"

Zracul immediately understood his error. In his exuberance to reveal his plans for the future of their family, he had not taken into account their personal ambitions. In reality, it mattered little what they wanted since he could compel them to his will. Not so for Ahes. By some miracle beyond his understanding, she retained her free will. And if he was honest with himself, he had to admit that he preferred it that way. It was a strange thing. Although he and Ornias were of one mind, somehow the demon could, on occasion, separate itself briefly as it did now – laughing at him.

He lifted himself up on one elbow to meet her unwavering gaze. There was no doubt in his mind that this was the moment when Ahes would be his lover forever, or his greatest enemy. He chose the former. "My culpability has been laid bare. I know it does not matter that it was not my intent to demean you by exclusion or explicit implication. I should have, by unambiguous elucidation, made apparent my intentions much sooner."

"And that is?" she lifted one eyebrow expressing expectation.

"That you are equal to me in all things, now and forever, side by side, as lovers, rulers, masters, Vampyr, Gods, and whatever else we might be. And I vow to announce to all who will hear me those words when we gather again as a family after the fall of Ys." He spoke the vow as sincerely as he knew how and earnestly hoped he could keep it.

Ahes leaned forward and kissed his lips. "Our bond is sealed. I accept your apology, and your vow." She leaned back smiling comfortably again. "Now, what would you like me to do with the key once I retrieve it from my father?"

Zracul felt a flood of relief. He could have no greater ally than Ahes. "Throw it in the sea for all I care," he made a waving motion with his hand. "All that matters is for the Seagate to remain unlocked from tonight onward."

"So soon?" Ahes showed surprise.

"If possible, yes" Zracul nodded. "Everything is in place. All we need is the sphere, which I expect to have this very evening."

Ahes sat up in the bed showing off the fine curves of her full breasts. "And then what?"

Somewhat distracted, Zracul replied, "Two days hence, Ys will be in ruins. Then while our family carries out my instructions in Ys, you and I will commandeer a large ship, load the sphere and apparatus, then cross the Primal Sea where together we shall lay waste to the City of Atlantis. We shall bring about the downfall of the Atlantean Empire, and from the dust shall be born the Age of Vampyr!"

Chapter 12 – Hope

Near to evening, the thrice tintinnabulation signaled Ys was in sight. Captain Rusee called for a slight adjustment to the forward sail practically lifting the *Sprinter* bearing off the northern winds in a direct line toward the distant harbor. Not soon enough, the colossal black doors of the sea gate set within the titanic embrace of the high seawalls came into view with the shadows of the tallest towers silhouetted just beyond. The seawalls were a miracle of engineering designed to protect the huge harbor of Ys sheltering not only ships, but the populace within from the worst of any storm surges which threatened to flood the city. In daylight and good weather, the doors stood open, inviting mariners from all parts of Plethwih to engage in free trade or find rest in a safe port. Tall towers bristling with ballistae and archers rose like grim guardians astride the doors while two large warships bearing light blue banners lingered nearby, reinforcing the fierce independence of the storied city.

Qel was both relieved to finally return to Ys, and devastated that Havacian was not returning by his side. These emotions he suppressed in favor of a singular determination to find someone, anyone, with the power to bring his friend back to the world of the living. Through druidcraft, Khulani managed to preserve Havacian's body in the days it took to sail back to the city, despite the exhaustion he endured guiding the *Sprinter* to Enguer followed by the Wyvern attack that nearly turned fatal. All for the strange sphere. It was this unusual orb swirling with storm clouds, flashing with lightning from within that gave Qel hope. The prince claimed that it held the key to curing the Creeping Death – a disease that not even magic could cure. If indeed that was true, then maybe it could bring Havacian back as well. At his insistence, Reskalin and the others agreed to go directly to the Agrabuta as soon as they docked. And if the orb held no hope for Havacian, Qel would immediately seek out every high priest and conveyor of powerful magics that he could find. Time was growing short. According to Khulani the preservation spell would expire at sundown on the next day, and another could not be applied. Thus, if Qel did not find a way to return Havacian to life within two days, his friend would be lost forever.

Swarms of seabirds hovered over ships passing through the gates, especially fishing vessels where a lucky gul might steal an errant fish head or morsel of bait from an unattended bucket. Sailors on the larger crafts sent volleys of arrows into the clouds of birds causing momentary havoc as they dodged and darted to avoid the deadly shafts. By Qel's estimation, what few were brought down thinned the feathered population imperceptibly as they hovered together once again. He idly wondered if the sailors pursuit of their avian foes was for deterrence or sport.

Looking ahead to the docks, Qel was dismayed at the crowd of ships large and small maneuvering for position in line to one of the many piers jutting out into the harbor. Each group of piers was controlled by a small craft bearing a port official accompanied by a half-dozen Ysian marines. The official assigned the specific pier, or wharf with a level quayside if they carried cargo, or a suitable berth commiserate with the size of the ship. The port of Ys was said to boast over a hundred moorings, and with the sun not long for the horizon, Qel was sure it would be full by the time the sea gates closed for the night. Fortunately, the harbor officials proved to be extraordinarily proficient, and Captain Rusee had the *Sprinter* securely tied to the dock in less than an hour.

"It's been my pleasure serving as your captain during this difficult voyage," Captain Rusee proudly addressed Qel and his companions as they prepared to disembark. He glanced over to where several of his crew had carefully strapped Havacian's body to a gurney now lifted on each end by two burly sailors. His voice lowered, his eyes clouded with sympathy as he took a step toward Qel, "May the gods favor your quest to find a way to bring back your friend. Some say when an Enlightened One is taken from the world, a new star appears in the sky. Well, I have no need for another star to navigate my way."

Even though Qel was more than a head taller than the captain, he felt small next to the charismatic man. "Thank you, captain," Qel managed a thin smile. "Perhaps our paths will cross again one day."

After saying their farewells to captain and crew, Reskalin led their group onto the busy dock toward the main processional that cut through the city in the direction of the Agrabuta. As a final demonstration of his charity, Captain Rusee ordered six of his biggest sailors to carry the gurney and clear their way through the crowded streets. Qel could not have been more appreciative. With every hour that passed, his anxiety grew more and more acute. In his mind, the clear *tick, tick* of a countdown was ever-present, overriding every other sense except for reason. But already, he was feeling the irrational tug of panic.

When they arrived at the grey-stone two-story manor, darkness had overtaken the sky. Yet, the abundance of brightly shining lanterns that lined every street, poured colorful illumination from doors and windows, pushing the shadows from beneath every awning and overhang to lessen the feel of night versus day. Ys always came alive after sundown. The people emerged cheerful and fun-loving wearing colorful flowing silks, tight gossamers, or something in-between. Most notably, the style was almost always proudly risqué leaving little to the imagination. There was excitement in the air, like the feeling of static electricity that left goosebumps on one's skin and a heady feeling of anticipation. Someone new to the city might wonder about the occasion of the merriment. A holiday? A royal's birthday? No, any citizen might laugh – every night in Ys was a celebration!

Qel noticed almost none of it. The Agrabuta stood at the edge of the city elevated atop a hill like a dark stain on a white dress. Only the portico was illuminated, and light lanced through a few curtained windows, but unlike the other estates, the grounds remained dark. The door opened almost as soon as Reskalin rapt upon it, and there stood the well-dressed elderly doorman slightly hunched and pale of skin.

"Please come in, Lord Zracul is eager to see you." Stepping back, the doorman pulled the door wide. "May I have your fallen comrade taken to the oratory?"

Reskalin turned to look back at Qel. One of her eyebrows was cocked higher than the other. Qel nodded in return.

"The oratory, you say?" Reskalin stepped close to the doorman. "Please make sure our friend is carefully looked after." She discreetly passed the man a few coins, but the clink of the metal gave the transaction away.

The doorman appeared unbothered. "Of course, My Lady. Have your servants stay here with your friend on the gurney. I will take you and the others to Lord Zracul, and then return to guide them to the oratory where I assure you, he will be safe and sound."

Reskalin looked back at Qel again. He was reluctant to leave Havacian's side. Should some accident occur, the stasis might be interrupted, and his friend would be lost. Before he could reply, Khulani spoke up, "I will stay with Havacian. You do not need my presence to relate the details of our journey to our host."

Qel breathed a long sigh of relief clasping the druid's shoulder warmly, "Thank you, Khulani," then nodded his confirmation to Reskalin.

"Very well," she smiled at the doorman. "Take us to Lord Zracul."

The sitting room was exactly as Qel remembered. The light was dim and easy on the eyes, unlike the luminous glare radiated by the overly abundant lanterns in the city. Lord Zracul sat in his chair just as before, but this time he was alone without his stunning daughter Naamah lingering in the background.

Zracul nearly pounced from his chair when they entered, smiling and gesturing for them to find comfortable seats, "Sit, sit! It is so good to see you have returned!" His eyes immediately latched on the bulging satchel carried over Enguer's shoulder which clearly held a large spherical object. His gaze shifted to Qel as servants appeared from the shadows bearing trays of steaming mugs meant to warm his guests on this chilly evening. "I understand you suffered the tragic loss of a dear friend. The Atlantean called Havacian, yes?" Qel nodded. "My deepest sympathies to you Qel. To all of you!"

One servant placed a glass of amber liquid on the small table next to Lord Zracul's chair before exiting the room.

"Thank you for your words, Lord Zracul," Qel studied their host's suddenly calm demeanor. This was a man who knew how to exercise control. This was a man who knew something of arcane arts. "Your good doorman was kind enough to allow the use of your oratory as a temporary resting place for Havacian. His body is closely tended by Khulani, the Imaziyen Druid whom you met previously. After we have concluded our business, I would have a word with you regarding my friend's status."

Zracul leaned forward in his chair and raised his glass in the air, "I am so pleased that you have brought our friend to my home. Your home, I should say, as you are all welcome to come and go as you please, stay a night or ten, and dine without invitation at your pleasure. If you have brought what I believe must be in the younger Rand's satchel there, then my life is saved and a man's saviors are, at the very least, his family." Lord Zracul stood with his glass still raised. "I look forward to speaking with you later this evening Qellel of House Mekali, standing shoulder to shoulder within the holy consecration of the oratory, where I shall pay my humble respects for his great sacrifice on my behalf. To Havacian!"

"To Havacian!" Qel and the others repeated, then resumed their seats.

As if on que, servants entered again with platters of cheeses, meats, and sweet pastries they placed on low tables within easy reach. Next, large glass goblets filled with a lesser known, extraordinarily expensive mellow red wine from the Mekali Vineyard, touted for its smoke-like sweetness reminiscent of sweet tobacco on the finish. Qel was impressed.

Once the servants cleared the room, Lord Zracul sat back, took a sip of his wine, then set his gaze squarely upon Enguer. "Unmask my salvation and earn your fortune, son of Gauren."

Enguer stood and unbuckled the satchel holding the sphere. A slight smile played over his features that Qel interpreted as immense pride or satisfaction at so frequent comparison with his legendary father by their host.

When the orb was free, Enguer held it up for Lord Zracul to see clearly. As always, a maelstrom of storm clouds coursing with jagged arcs of lightning silently raged within the globe. For a moment, Lord Zracul appeared taken aback by the sight of it. His dark eyes glistened with moisture, his hands shook as he very nearly dropped the wine glass he was holding before he managed the small miracle of setting it on the side table without ever taking his gaze from the orb. He reached out for it, expecting

Enguer to bring it forth. The ranger complied, but before he crossed half the distance to the transfixed lord, the door burst open and two young women marched into the room.

"Hello Brother," one spoke. "Are we interrupting?"

The two women looked identical except for what they wore, as slight as it was. Qel knew right away they must be Lord Zracul's younger sisters by their pallor complexions, full lips, jet hair and eyes, similar sulky facial features, and confident manner. Their choice of dress, or undress, consisted mainly of well-placed fragments of jewelry, ribbons of transparent fabric, and a profusion of erotic piercings. If it wasn't for their long jet hair, there would be no mystery at all concerning their physical perfection. Qel couldn't wrap his mind around all the piercings.

"Yes," Zracul's countenance darkened considerably as he looked the pair up and down. "Going out?"

"Of course," one of the women replied, tossing her hair back to reveal what small regions of her anatomy that remained unseen. She walked over to where Enguer was standing awkwardly holding out the raging sphere. "Is this the Sphere of Elements you've been going on about, Brother? It's very pretty."

Her twin was close behind, but her eyes were on Enguer. "This one is pretty, too. Can he come with us, Brother? Please?" She ran a finger down the side of Enguer's face while pressing her body close against him.

Qel watched Reskalin's complexion shift through tones of reds and purples as she slowly stood from her chair with murder in her eyes. It was a curious reflection of the look on Lord Zracul as he too stood up.

"Enough!" Zracul commanded in a booming voice startling everyone in the room. "Be on your way to whatever debauchery you have planned for the night. I have business to conclude!"

The woman pressing against Enguer slowly slid around him until she was forced to separate because of the large orb he held in his arms and joined her twin strutting casually toward the door from which they entered. Neither appeared perturbed in the least.

"We're off then, Brother," one called as she reached the door. The other stopped and spun on her heel to rake the furious Reskalin up and down with her intense gaze.

"Relax, sister," the twin spoke in a soothing tone. "We will not seduce your man this night. Besides, we hear two hearts beating within your belly, how could we deprive your children of a father?"

Reskalin's eyes widened nearly the size of saucers. Qel had never seen her in such a state in the short time he had known her, and he wasn't sure if violence was about to follow.

Apparently, Lord Zracul held the same concerns as he thrust his hands forward and shouted "Out!"

Invisible force sent the twins flying though the open door, slamming it behind them. The sickening thud of bodies impacting the opposite wall in the hallway was left hanging in the silence that followed.

"I am truly sorry," Lord Zracul held his head in his hands. "Jaria and Daria are young and foolish, and I have been far too generous with their independence in a city that holds little moral values. Please forgive their insult."

Qel didn't know what to say, but to his surprise, Reskalin did. "There is no offense, Lord Zracul. We were all young once. How many times do you suppose our actions mortified those responsible for looking out for us?"

"You are more kindhearted than I deserve, Reskalin," Zracul appeared to calm considerably. "I thank you all. Shall we pretend the discourteous interruption never occurred?"

"Of course we can," Enguer realized he was sweating and quickly moved forward to transfer the tempestuous globe into the eagerly waiting arms of Lord Zracul.

Over the next hour, Reskalin and Enguer related the particulars of their journey to recover the sphere. For most of that time, Lord Zracul stared into the orb as if communing with the strange artefact. He must have been listening to every word as he spent almost another hour asking questions or mined the details for further clarification on one aspect of their adventure or another. Meanwhile, Qel remained mostly silent, contemplating what the woman meant by Reskalin having "two heartbeats inside her belly" or pondering why the other woman referred to the orb as the 'Sphere of Elements.' He could only surmise that Reskalin was pregnant, which filled him with joy, but the sphere . . .

"Thank you for indulging my curious mind. I'm sure you are tired and eager to rest after a so trying an expedition." Zracul stood, incredibly, the orb floated next to him like a docile pet. "I will have rooms prepared for you . . ."

"That is not necessary," Reskalin interjected quickly. "We have rooms at an Inn nearby, and it would not be polite to impose."

"It is no imposition," Zracul assured them. "However, I completely understand your need to separate from this whole ordeal that has brought far more loss and distress than any of us could have anticipated.

Zracul pointed to a nondescript chest sitting against the wall. "There is your reward. I feel like it is meager compared to what you have given me. I hope you will find it satisfactory."

Enguer and Reskalin sauntered over to the chest and lifted it off the floor with no little strain.

"I would be happy to have it delivered to your rooms at the Inn where you are staying if you like," Zracul offered with a mild smile twisting over his lips.

"No, no. We can manage." Reskalin assured their host.

Qel was not so sure. He didn't know much about women and pregnancy, but he sure Reskalin should not be lifting heavy weight for long periods of time. "Wait a moment," he called out as he traced luminous patterns in the air.

A few seconds later a grey disk the size of a small cartwheel appeared out of nothing, floating waist-high in the air. Qel motioned forward and down, and the disk lowered to the ground next to the chest.

"Set the chest on the disk," Qel beckoned to Reskalin and Enguer who were more than happy to comply. Once settled, he gestured for the disk to rise, and it lifted the heavy chest effortlessly to a level height above the knee. Finally, Qel spun an incorporeal rope barely visible to the eye, connected one end to the disk, and handed the other to Enguer. "You're all set."

Enguer pulled on the rope and the disk moved forward easily. "This is incredible," Enguer marveled.

"It's only good for an hour. So don't dally getting back to the Inn." Qel had no idea where they were going since they didn't take the time to rent rooms at any Inn between the docks and the Agrabuta.

Reskalin kissed him on the cheek and announced, "We'll see you at the Silver Horseshoe Inn later tonight?"

"Certainly," Qel smiled as he watched the pair pull the floating disk holding the chest out the door.

Alone with Lord Zracul at last, Qel was eager to address the subject of his fallen friend.

"That was quite impressive," Zracul complemented. "Perhaps you wouldn't mind teaching me that spell on a better occasion?"

"Of course," Qel readily agreed. "It's one of the first spells all new acolytes learn at the Wizards Enclave, with so many heavy tomes to lug about."

Zracul laughed hardily at that.

Qel was feeling anxious again. When the laughter faded to silence, he said, "I would like to discuss why I brought Havacian here tonight."

Zracul placed his empty glass on the table strode toward the door. "Let us go to the oratory and pay homage to the fallen Child of Atlan."

Moments later, they found Khulani sitting on the floor next to a stout table where Havacian was consigned to repose until determined otherwise. The druid's eyes snapped open as soon as they entered.

"Well met," Khulani stood and bent a slight bow of respect to Lord Zracul.

"It's good to see you too," Zracul returned the greeting. "You're exploits in Kiltullagh, and in particular over the Lake of Mists battling the Wyvern, is stuff of legends."

"I cannot speak for legendary," Khulani chuckled, "but it was certainly unforgettable."

Zracul offered a nod of deference to the druid, "However it shall be remembered, you have my everlasting gratitude."

Khulani stepped back and addressed Qel as Lord Zracul turned his gaze on Havacian's body lying cold and still atop the sturdy oaken table. "Our friend endures as expected. I know you have important matters to discuss with Lord Zracul, take whatever time you need. I will be waiting outside."

Qel thanked the druid as he departed and presently joined Lord Zracul next to the table. For a long moment they stood together in silence.

Shadows cast by candles set in the wall behind the table danced across Havacian's features producing the impression of movement. It was a disquieting illusion Qel endured with stoic resolve as he contemplated the words he hoped would convince Lord Zracul to help him recover the life of his friend from the cold clutches of death.

"The druid has preserved Havacian's body well," Zracul spoke with quiet reverence. "How much time remains before the spell expires?"

Taken aback by Lord Zracul's words, Qel immediately recalculated his estimation of his host's depth of knowledge concerning the arcane arts. It gave him hope that the solution to Havacian's dilemma might be found here, and at the same time heightened his trepidation.

"Tomorrow at sundown," Qel replied. He prepared to go on. This was the moment he had thought about every waking second since they departed Kiltullagh. Each word was practiced and committed to memory to be repeated now with perfect articulation, emphasis, and emotion designed to maximize the prospect of persuading Lord Zracul to his cause.

Qel opened his mouth to speak.

"I know why you brought him to me," Zracul spoke first. "You anticipated that the sphere may have the power to return life to Havacian, just as it brings hope to cure my affliction."

"I cannot deny it," Qel admitted. He suddenly felt foolish and embarrassed. "I am on a desperate quest with very little time to persuade, cajole or compel one with the power to accomplish this task."

Zracul faced Qel, placing a gentle hand upon his shoulder. "I require no convincing, my friend. From the moment Havacian was carried off the *Sprinter*, I was aware of his circumstance. I knew what you would ask, and already resolved to agree."

Qel could hardly contain the thrill of joy that raced through him, manifesting in a broad smile that could not be restrained. His reply was thick with emotion, "I will forever be in your debt."

Zracul's brows furrowed as he shook his head. "No, you will not. Havacian died obtaining the key that will save my life. So, by returning the favor, I believe that makes us even."

"Do you know the process? Is there something I or Khulani can do to help?" Qel asked hopefully. He wanted to get underway as soon as possible so he would have time to find another option in case the sphere did not work as intended.

"The sphere is beyond my knowledge to use properly as my brothers have done the research required to understand the complex workings of the artefact. Remember, it was always intended to be used on me rather than by me." Zracul's eyes drifted back to the table, gazing down at Havacian. "Our friend here has far less time than I do, thus, we must give him priority. I have already summoned Vadim and Fain back to the Agrabuta. They should arrive presently, and so will begin our preparations. When you return, Havacian will stand before you as alive as he ever was. You have my word."

"Return?" Qel was crestfallen. "Can I not stay and be of some assistance?"

"My brothers are not as worldly as I am," Zracul shrugged apologetically. "They would likely be intimidated by the presence of an 'Enlightened One' at a time when all their attention must be focused on the task at hand. I fear any distraction, even a small one, could be tragic. It is not worth the risk. Wouldn't you agree?"

"I suppose I must," Qel reluctantly agreed. He hated the idea of leaving Havacian here alone, blindly trusting a man he hardly knew, betting his friend's life on an untested artefact operated by strangers. What choice did he have? None as far as he could see. This was Havacian's best chance. His only chance.

Qel spent a quiet moment by Havacian's side before Lord Zracul escorted him to the front door of the Agrabuta. Khulani was sitting on the front steps watching and waving to scantily clad passersby on their way to some nocturnal adventure or another.

Zracul patted Qel on the back as he walked out the door. "Return at midnight. Not a minute earlier, please. And prepare to greet your friend. Trust us."

Qel was in no mood to talk as he and Khulani strode down the main processional. There was no doubt in his mind that Lord Zracul was an eccentric, and he couldn't help but worry over the authenticity of his assurances. For all Qel knew, using the sphere to revive Havacian might be nothing more than a test run before they turned its power on Lord Zracul!

"Where are we going?" Khulani asked after they had walked nearly back to the harbor.

"The Silver Horseshoe Inn," replied Qel.

Khulani appeared confused. "You know where to find this place?"

Qel had no idea. "I suppose we should ask for directions."

"Just one more thing." Khulani pulled him to the side of the street so they could stop without the risk of being trampled by the revelers. "Why are we going to this Inn?"

Qel couldn't understand Khulani's concern. "Because that's where we will meet up with Reskalin and Enguer."

Khulani cocked his head as a big toothy grin stretched across his face. "So, we are going to a place to meet two thieves who possess all the riches we earned from our journey to the Lake of Mists?"

Momentarily stunned by the implications of Khulani's words, Qel abruptly burst into a fit of laughter that verged on hysterical, releasing all his pent-up anxiety and worry, drawing incredulous stares from everyone close enough to witness an Atlantean dancing on the edge of insanity. It was exactly what he needed.

– – –

No sooner was the front door shut behind him did two figures appear in the darkened hallway.

"Animate the Atlantean," Zracul instructed his brothers. "When you are done call me and I will do the rest."

Without a word, Vadim and Fain glided through the open doorway of the oratory.

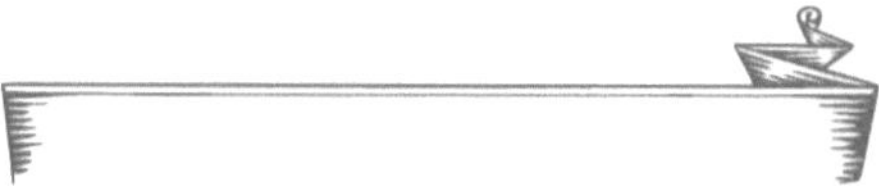

Chapter 13 – An Awful Reckoning

Ahes wrapped herself in a long-hooded cloak and descended the front steps of the Agrabuta just as the sun fell below the western horizon. For once, she was going to traverse the city streets in a clandestine manner unknown to all she passed. Her precautions were inconsequential for the most part as she raced through the streets and byways at speed too quick for the most discerning eye to follow. Passing the road leading to the harbor, she paused to observe an odd assortment of folk jostling quickly in her direction. The most obvious was a tall blue-skinned Atlantean wearing red robes jogging beside a covered gurney carried by four sailors. Keeping time behind them followed two humans wearing black leather armor and an ebony man dressed in the trappings of a druid. She watched with discrete curiosity as they hurried by, briefly pondering if these were the adventurers hired by Zracul to obtain his so called 'Sphere of Elements.' Banishing all further thoughts on the manner, Ahes turned up the broad avenue that led directly to the palace. To right and left, grand estates lined the way where the most affluent and influential claimed residence within close proximity to the center of power in Ys. During the day, the avenue was busy with servants, tradesfolk, and carts laden with barrels of the best ale or wines, baskets of produce, crates stuffed with salted meats, bolts of colorful fabric, and a multitude of various supplies mundane and exotic to boggle the mind. It was all in service of the night, when the avenue blossomed with bright colorful lights, music, and entertainers. Here to, the traffic of nobles and high society enroute to fancy balls or extravagant parties arrived at the great houses in lacquered carriages where they would vie for position and advantage in the high-stakes game of political maneuverings. It was all very tedious and boring, so she thought. When Ahes arrived at the gates, the startled guards were struck by her sudden appearance, until they recognized her as the princess, and quickly ushered her inside.

Ahes casually strode down the wide driveway carpeted by pea stones to where paved walkways were illuminated by hanging lanterns. Intersecting pathways meandered away to small enclaves where on could sit in quiet meditation among gardens, fishponds, and fountains. The scent of honeysuckle was heavy in the air at this time of year prompting a strange nostalgia tied to memories that Ahes, as Aesmadaeva, regarded with little emotional relevance. Ignoring the unwanted feeling, she continued along the walkway to a side entrance to the palace closest to her chambers.

The residential wing, which included her rooms, were almost always quiet day or night with no children dwelling within. A fact her father was quick to point out whenever the subject of finding a proper match for her came up. She wondered if he would approve of Count Zracul knowing him only as the Primogeniture of a faraway land with strong implications for profitable trade. The irony of it, was that he probably would.

When she entered the reception chamber to her rooms, she found it warm with the glow of embers in the hearth and brightly lit by lanterns hung high in every corner. A bowl of her favorite fruits sat on the table next to a carafe of red wine. Although she had been gone from the palace for some time, everything was exactly as she expected.

The door to her sleeping chamber suddenly burst open as her chambermaid, Tipa, rushed in. "Oh, thank the Gods!" She hurried over to take Ahes's cloak. "The king has been in a mad rage at Your Highness's long absence. He even sent out the guard to scour the city."

"And they returned with no word of me?" Ahes flung herself into a plush lounge chair and gestured toward the carafe.

"They certainly did. It seems all of Ys had observed Your Highness's comings and goings to one place or another," Tipa filled a goblet with the red wine from the carafe and handed it to the princess. "But the king was no less troubled. In fact, the nature of the places Your Highness was purported to frequent sent him into an even greater fury!"

"Well, that's just lovely," Ahes sighed. "I would imagine the guards at the gate have already informed him of my return. Do you know where he is at the moment?"

"Yes, Your Highness, he is in the Great Hall hosting a banquet for visiting nobles from Eriu," Tipa replied nervously.

Ahes took a long draught of her wine, then held out the glass for Tipa to refill. "Go tell the guard my father has already dispatched to summon me that I will be along soon. And when you return dress me in one of my older dresses. You know, the tedious ones with long sleeves and frilly pleats. Perhaps I can dull the edge of his wrath by presenting a more 'virtuous' façade."

"Yes, Your Highness." Tipa quickly refilled the goblet, then darted out the door to intercept the guard. Ahes could already hear the man's stomping stride and rustling chainmail far down the hallway making his way toward her rooms.

Tipa returned just in time to fill Ahes's goblet from the dwindling carafe of red wine once more before hurrying off to ready a trio of dresses for the princess to choose from. In the meantime, Ahes considered the problem of taking possession of the key to the Sea Gate. Her father always wore it around his neck day and night. He never took it off. Not when he bathed, took a woman to his bed, nor even to lock or unlock the Sea Gate itself. Drugs or drink would not work since the key was enchanted so that it could only be transferred to another if the King gave it over freely or upon his death. A simple Psionic compulsion would have been the best option. Not so for the king! His will was inordinately strong. And not only must he give her the key, but it must be done in such a way that none would be the wiser to its absence during the time when it was needed the most! Otherwise, alarms would be raised and everywhere and everyone would be subject to search. Yet, once Ahes had the key all she had to do was throw it in the sea or down a hole where it could not be retrieved in time to save the city no matter what spells or incantations were used to find it. Without exception, the key to the Sea Gate was the most important and protected treasure in Ys, more so than the horde of riches piled in the palace vaults, any land title, estate, or the life of a wayward princess. The more Ahes contemplated the problem, the more it seemed the king would have to die.

An hour later, Ahes was clomping angrily down the quiet corridors of the residential wing followed by a weepy sobbing Tipa.

"Enough, Tipa," Ahes commanded when they stormed through the doors to her chambers.

"Yes, Your Highness," Tipa sniveled as she poured wine for the princess with shaking hands.

Ahes thrust a second glass toward Tipa. "Fill one for yourself and keep them filled until we are both blind drunk!"

With soppy eyes glistening with tears, Tipa did as she was instructed.

"The nerve of that man!" Ahes raged to no one in particular. "To berate me in front of his guests. How humiliating!"

Tipa stood in the center of the room weeping into her wine, shaking her head as if to dislodge the memory.

"And this stupid dress!" Ahes tore at her dark blue gown, ripping long strips of fabric away, tossing them into the air. "It did nothing to curb his tongue. Not in the least!"

The chambermaid sank to the floor with furious sobs as she pulled the shredded material into a neat pile.

"And what did I do?" Ahes shouted. "I stood there like a simpering toddler taking it until he dismissed me to my rooms!" She slammed her fist on the table, shattering it with one blow, sending fruit flying into the air. "He dismissed me like a child!

An awful wail rose from Tipa slouched in misery among the tattered blue fabric, frills, and lace.

Ahes flung herself onto the divan free of the clothing she so despised and stared down at Tipa sobbing on the floor. With no little effort, she composed herself with a long draught of wine, refilled the glass herself, and thought how desperately she wanted to be with her lover right then. She looked again at Tipa whimpering quietly in her fine green dress. Such a pretty girl. Soft brown hair, wide doe-like eyes, naturally tanned skin smooth to the touch with the tight rounded proportions of youth.

"Tipa," Ahes called to her sweetly. "Come sit with me. Let us take consolation that we have each other."

Brushing away her tears, Tipa crawled up on the divan and lay her head upon Ahes's exposed breast. In a staggering sniveling voice she said, "I-I'm s-so sorry, Y-Your Highness. I wish I-I could h-have done something." Tears ran down her face dripping over her nose and along the curves of the princess's bare chest.

"Poor Tipa," Ahes spoke in a soothing motherly tone. "It must be terrible to witness your princess scolded so bitterly, and naught to do but stand helpless." She lifted Tipa's chin to look into her innocent brown eyes. "It will never happen again. I promise." Ahes kissed the young woman gently on the mouth, and then more passionately as she skillfully removed the dress from her quivering body. It was not their first time together. Tipa knew well how to please her. Tonight, would be different. Tonight, Tipa's suffering as a palace servant would come to an end. It was the least Ahes could do for the girl, so loyal and willing in her service.

– – –

A naked woman sprawled unconscious in the corner of the room. She was a screamer. The kind that just wouldn't stop. Zracul couldn't stand the high-pitched shrieks that barely paused for proper sobbing. The woman started screaming before he ever touched her, and never let up until he finally punched her in the side of the head. In his frustration he nearly killed her, and he would not have cared except that he needed a live one this morning. Normally he would have sent Naamah to retrieve a suitable humanoid to feed upon. She always brought him the highest quality fare – clean individuals with lean muscular frames free from abnormalities and usually very attractive, although that last part was hardly a requirement. Her victims were always quiet, probably charmed by Naamah's unusual allure. Zracul appreciated how very particular and thorough she was in all her duties. Unfortunately, Naamah was still preoccupied with the knight, and his brothers were fatigued from the effort of raising Havacian from the dead. Thus, he was forced to rely on his younger sisters, Jaria and Daria, to handle the undertaking. Of course, they were very reluctant to interrupt their late-night revelry to accept the chore, but at his insistence and threats of grave punishments, the twins immediately returned with the howling woman. The poor strumpet was probably one of the depraved whores attending whatever wanton festivity his sisters so often attended. The woman reeked of cheap perfume and a dozen other rancid stenches Zracul cared not to think much about, so he ordered his sisters to wash her thoroughly and burn her clothes. To his amusement, they were quite vexed by that and returned the whimpering woman a short time later beaten and bruised, arms tied behind her back with a gag in her mouth, but clean nonetheless. Zracul was sure her blood was likely spoiled by exceptional degrees of alcohol, drugs, and disease, but that was no matter for her purpose today. He dismissed Jaria and Daria with a laconic wave and considered for a moment why it was that Naamah was so diligent in her service whereas his own sisters always seemed to deliberately make choices designed to annoy him!

Zracul sighed. The woman was never part of his plans. At least not so soon. After Vadim and Fain brought life back to Havacian, Zracul forced the disoriented Atlantean to take his blood, thus beginning the transition to Vampyr. It was the first Atlantean Zracul ever turned, so perhaps he should not have been completely astonished when Havacian completed the entire cycle of transitioning in hours rather than days. Whether it was due transitioning so soon after death, the Atlantean's alien blood, or both, Zracul did not know. He expected to heavily sedate Havacian before Qel returned so that he would be assured his friend lived again before sending him away until the transition was complete. Maybe it was better this way. When Havacian awoke, Zracul would compel the Atlantean to send Qel away while he recovered at the Agrabuta. After that, it wouldn't matter. Ys would be a disaster, and Havacian would join his family building a race of Vampyr.

A stirring of sheets interrupted his ruminations. He turned away from the woman to find Havacian on the verge of waking. In a blur of motion, Zracul shackled the woman's feet to chains attached to the floor, covered her fully with a blanket and returned to the Atlantean's bedside within the blink of an eye. There he waited until Havacian's large almond-shaped eyes flickered open.

"Where am I?" he asked as he studied the man stranding over him.

Zracul seated himself on the edge of the bed, smiling broadly. "Welcome back, Child of Atlan. You are in my home – the Agrabuta – in Ys. How are you feeling?"

"You . . . you are Lord Zracul," Havacian spoke in a slow, groggy tone. "I feel strange. Where are Qellel and the others?"

"Qel, will return in a short while. He is very eager to see you." Zracul replied in a calm soothing voice. "As for the others, I would imagine that they are already spending the proceeds of the reward I paid them for returning with the artifact you and your fellows were commissioned to obtain for me."

Havacian's eyes lit with joy, "They are all alive? And they found the sphere?"

"Yes, and yes," Zracul nodded. "And your reward is the fact that we are speaking together right now."

"What do you mean?" Confusion replaced the brief flash of joy in Havacian's eyes.

Zracul lay a comforting hand atop the Atlantean's, knowing what he was about to say would come as a shock. "You have been dead from the day your party departed Kiltullagh. At Qel's insistence, the Imaziyen Druid, Khulani, placed your body in a kind of stasis, or state of preservation to prevent your decay. When they returned to Ys, Qel was verging on panic, willing to do anything to return your mind and body to life. As it happens, my brothers Vadim and Fain excel at such things, so I agreed to have them raise you from the dead. That was Qel's reward."

"What you say is absurd, but for some reason I believe your words." Havacian brought a hand to his face to wipe away the rivulets of tears that wet his cheeks. "Qel saved me. As did you and your brothers. Thank you."

Zracul stood from the bed. "Let's reserve your gratitude until I tell you the rest. Both you and Qel share the reward of returning your life, but there is also a price. A price that you must bear alone and never reveal to another living soul."

Havacian attempted to sit up in bed, but he was too weak, falling back on his pillows, breathless, exhausted. "What price?" There was an unmistakable tone of suspicion in the question.

"Close your eyes a moment and listen to the sounds in the room." Zracul instructed.

The Atlantean hesitated. His continence reflected unease at the suggestion, but presently he complied.

Zracul continued, "What do you hear?"

Havacian opened his eyes, annoyance painted across his furrowed brows. "I hear my own breathing, that's it."

"Try again," Zracul urged. "This time, listen carefully."

Havacian sighed and closed his eyes again. After a few moments, his breathing slowed, and finally with some trepidation, he spoke. "I hear my heartbeat. No, two heartbeats. Three..."

"That's right, Havacian, you hear three heartbeats in this room – yours, mine and – what is different about the third heartbeat? What does it make you think of? How does it make you feel?" Zracul took a silent step away from the bed toward the blanket that cover the woman.

"I don't know, its . . . It . . . I can hear the flow of blood pumping fast through arteries and veins. It is not the same as ours. This one flows smooth and fluid, whereas ours sounds thicker, stronger, powerful. Suddenly it's hard not to hear the third heartbeat and the flow of blood. Somehow it calls to me. Somehow, I yearn for it. Why can I think of nothing else, now!" Havacian's eyes remained closed, but he was sweating profusely and tossing his head from side to side as if engaged in a terrible struggle like one experiences in a dream. "I feel a craving! I want to go near. Wait! I know now it's the heart of a woman. A living woman! She is afraid, no, terrified. For some reason that excites me, and I crave . . . Why do I crave?" Havacian's eyes shot open, "Why do I HUNGER?"

Zracul slowly pulled the blanket off the naked woman shackled to the floor. She was consciousness, immediately pressing herself further back against the wall staring with wild eyes, and sputtering unintelligible words through the wad of cloth in her mouth.

In near panic, Havacian found the strength to sit up. His horror-filled eyes instantly shifted to the trembling woman. "No . . ."

"That is the price for your life, my dear Havacian." Zracul no longer smiled. "If you feed upon her, you will live. Your body will experience many astonishing changes. I won't ruin the surprise for you, but it's inconceivable until it happens." Zracul was unmoved by the tears flowing down Havacian's face frozen in horror-struck disbelief. "Yet, you have a choice, my friend, as awful as it may seem. You may also choose to resist the hunger. Refuse to feed. You should know that today is the only day that you will have the chance to make this choice. For once you feed, drawing the succor of another's life to satisfy this craving, never again will you have the will to resist." The shackles rattled sharply against the stone floor as the woman at his feet struggled desperately against the bonds around her wrists while her tongue pressed against the gag in her mouth. Unheeding, Zracul took another step toward the door. "If you feed, you will live long and grow powerful. The hunger will return from time to time compelling you to feed again, and again, and again. And seeing as it is my blood that is the source of your life, you will be under my influence, compelled to come to me at my call. If you feed, you can lead a normal life, or at least make it appear as though you do if you are careful, and Qel will be reunited with his friend, never knowing the difference. If you resist, you will die."

All was suddenly silent in the room. The naked and bound woman kneeled in her shackles staring wide-eyed at Havacian, her thin lips quivering, cheeks streaked with tears. Her mouth was clear of the gag and a moist clump of cloth lay between her knees. Zracul quietly departed. There was no point in waiting for a response from the Atlantean as none would be forthcoming. He slammed the door in place, but did not lock it. For a long while Zracul waited in the corridor on the other side of the door listing to the pair breathing in the other room. They made no other sound. Finally, a knowing smile touched the edges of his red lips, and he turned away. Before Zracul reached the end of the dark hallway, a desperate shriek broke the quiet of the night, then ended just as quickly. Another moment passed, before a piteous wail rose with such sadness and sorrow that it gave the Lord of the Agrabuta pause to shudder.

Chapter 14 – Blessings and Betrayal

It was a busy evening at the Silver Horseshoe Inn. The city was in joyful spirits replete with festivals in every market and crowded tavern, Throngs of people representing nearly every race in Plethwih strutted hither and thither along the streets scantily clad in vibrant silks and foamy gossamers. It seemed to Enguer that in the short time they were away from the city, the trends of fashion underwent a new metamorphosis. If he thought the evening wear was risqué before, now it was downright scandalous! For once, he was glad that Reskalin was not around to sharply criticize the beautiful Ysian women who confidently sashayed in seductive outfits in a suggestive display of their finest assets. He toyed with the idea of buying Reskalin such a guise to wear for his enjoyment, but it was more likely she would make him eat it. Perhaps an edible version, he chuckled internally.

"You are in a good mood this evening," Khulani's bright smile lit up his ebony features and brown pastoral eyes.

Enguer liked the young druid. He often wondered how a man of such few years gained the depth of wisdom that had earned the respect of all their companions over the course of their most recent adventure. Companions, Enguer scoffed to himself. They more than that after everything they had been through together. This group would be friends for life. He was sure of it.

"I am!" Enguer agreed most heartily. Then he signaled to the server to bring two tankards of the tavern's stout ale as Khulani sat down on the bench next to him.

The druid leaned back gathering his earth-toned robes around him prompting the score of bones and feathers hanging by leather thongs to sway erratically. "I am surprised to see you here without your second half."

Enguer laughed, “Indeed! Reskalin has business with certain associates, and specifically a woman, who she would rather not expose me to more than necessary.”

“Oh? Does this woman cause you trouble?” Khulani Asked.

“In a sense, I suppose,” Enguer chuckled. “She is extremely flirtatious, even in the presence of Reskalin, and so the trouble would likely be hers since my wife is just as inclined to stick a knife in the woman’s eye than suffer the disrespect.”

“Reskalin is a jealous one,” Khulani grinned lifting a mug offered by a pretty server. “But do not worry, when she has your babies, her protective nature will shift to them, and you will find jealousy the least of your worries.”

“I will miss it, I think.” Enguer sipped the foam off the newly filled mug. Changing the subject, he asked, “Qel is returning to the Agrabuta tonight?”

“Yes,” Khulani confirmed with a nod. “I offered to join him, but he is determined to go on his own.”

Enguer eyed the druid for a moment as he took a big swig of ale. “Do you really think Prince Zracul and his brothers can revive Havacian from the dead?”

“It is possible,” Khulani paused as if considering his response. When he spoke again, there was a quizzical look on his face, “I cannot guess what method they may use to accomplish this miracle. Powerful priests and druids have the means to return life under certain conditions, through prayers and blessings from the Gods. Only the highest among our order and the clergy have the standing to accomplish this. Prince Zracul and his brothers strike me as neither priests nor druids, so their process is unknown to me.”

“I hope it’s true, and Havacian is returned to us,” Enguer said solemnly. “For Qel’s sake.”

“For all our sake,” Khulani added. Enguer nodded his agreement.

“Are you a druid?” A beautiful young woman with long auburn hair falling in curls over silky pale shoulders was abruptly standing in front of them. As was the style, her long bare legs extended from the thin silky folds of a sheer light blue gown.

Khulani blinked in surprise, sitting up straight on the bench to address her, "Yes, I am a druid. How can I be of service?"

With a quick inhalation she turned to a group of young men and women about her same age and enthusiastically mouthed something while gesturing toward Khulani. The group reacted with similar excitement, then she turned back and asked in a pleading voice, "Would you grant me blessings? I am betrothed and expect to take vows of marriage in a few days. It would bode well for my future if I received blessings from a real druid!"

Khulani's broad smile appeared on his face. "I would be happy to bless your marriage! However, it would be more seemly to offer blessings surrounded by nature rather than a crowded inn smelling of ale. Is there a convenient garden nearby with less noise?"

"Oh yes!" the woman clapped happily. "I'll show you."

She latched on to Khulani's arm as soon as he stood up and pulled him toward the door as he called back to Enguer, "I be right back."

Enguer heard the woman chatter excitedly to Khulani as they walked away, "Don't worry about the marriage, the blessings are for me. Oh, look! Here are my friends . . ." Then the gaggle of young people practically carried Khulani out the door.

A little over an hour later, Enguer realized Khulani should have returned. He might have noticed sooner, but he was deep into the ale by then and engrossed in various conversations with other patrons in a similar state. Excusing himself with promises to shortly return, he stumbled out the front door of the inn and gazed through bleary eyes up and down the street. Before him stretched a line of people a goodly distance to some event taking place far up the long boulevard where flashes of light regularly illuminated the sky. Forgetting Khulani for the moment, Enguer strode up the road with mug in hand toward the brightly lit area. The crowded line wound down the side of the street before abruptly turning through a stone archway heavily laden with ivy, and into a community park enclosed by a tall iron fence.

Rather than push through the crowd, and risk spilling any ale, Enguer made his way around to the side where the lights were brightest and peered through the fence. Inside, lush gardens, fishponds, and tranquil waterfalls formed the usually serene landscape around a meandering pathway. Not so this night! Scores of people stood quietly in a line following the winding path that led to a patch of grass surrounded by improvised poll torches. In the center of the grass mound was a stone bench, and there sat Khulani! Standing close to the side and just behind the druid was the proud semblance of the woman that first asked for his blessing at the inn. She appeared to bask in the glory of her association with the impromptu event as if she was solely responsible for its making. Perhaps she was, Enguer thought with great amusement. And her friends were on hand, diligently guiding one person after the next before Khulani to receive the Blessing of Sunna culminating with a flash of daylight each time.

Enguer turned his gaze to follow the thick line of people down the street. There were hundreds waiting. Khulani would be blessing people all night! Maybe it was the drink, or the circumstances that led to this impossible situation, or a combination of the two, but somehow Enguer found the totality of the druid's predicament absolutely hilarious.

With a roar, Enguer raised his mug, and shouted drunkenly to Khulani through the gate, "Ho Khulani! Don't you know druids don't belong in the city? Next time shed your costume, apply a pair of good breeches, and walk among the common folk devoid of constant adulations!"

The miserable druid directed a dark look at Enguer which only heightened the ale-fueled hilarity of the moment. The ranger laughed all the way back to the inn.

– – –

Qel stood in the open doorway where he expected to find Havacian. If not for the small lantern provided by the elderly doorman, the corridor he had travelled to come to this door, and the small room beyond, would be cast in complete darkness. Inside, the lantern first cast its warm glow upon a pair of empty shackles attached to the floor against the wall, and a wadded-up cloth seemingly cast to the side. Qel started to reach for the cloth as the light illuminated the bed. He froze, staring at the form of Havacian laying in a serene slumber, his chest slowly rising and falling with each deep breath. Qel forgot about the cloth and moved with haste to Havacian's side. His eyes welled with tears at the sight of his friend. Blue-tinted skin shown with the warmth of life, no sign of injury remained, not even scars from the deep lacerations suffered from the explosion of shards cast by the dying Frog-God. He looked as healthy and unaffected as before that terrible moment. As if sensing another presence in the room, Havacian's eyes slowly opened. There was a brief smile on his face as he stared up at Qel in those first few moments of awakening. Then shadows seemed to darken his eyes, and his smile faded to a grim line that held no warmth.

"You are here," he said, raising a hand to touch Qel's face.

Qel could not abandon his smile so soon. Just hours ago, he believed his friend was lost forever. Yet, here he was, restored to life as if everything that happened before was nothing more than a terrible dream. "Of course I'm here," he hung the lantern on a hook in the wall and took Havacian's hand in his own, squeezing tight. "Where else could I be while my best friend in the world was lying here . . . recovering?"

Havacian's eyes suddenly showed fear, his hand twitched with a quick spasm as he looked beyond Qel searching the shadows in the room. "Have you seen Zracul?"

"No," Qel replied. "The doorman let me in. Is there something that you need? Should I call for him?"

"No!" Havacian whispered hoarsely, tightening his grip on Qel's hand with shocking force.

Qel winced, and gingerly removed his hand from Havacian's loosening grip, wondering where this unusual strength came from. He had never known his friend to possess such a grip!

Havacian did not seem to notice Qel's discomfort. He rose swiftly to a sitting position, swung his legs over the side of the bed, and grabbed Qel by the shoulders. "You must leave here now."

Qel was taken aback by his friend's unexpected motion, but it was the fear and pleading in his eyes that was truly jarring. "Havacian, are you still unwell? What is the urgent matter? Perhaps I should call for Prince Zracul after all."

"*NO!*" There was rage in Havacian's low roar, and the lines on his face twisted in anger. "Not him, not his brothers, not those . . . things . . . he calls his sisters. None of them must get their teeth into you!"

"Havacian, I . . ."

"Listen!" Havacian shook Qel by the shoulders like a ragdoll. "We are like brothers you and I. And I know you will not do as I say unless you are convinced that I have told you everything. So, despite warnings to the contrary, I tell you now that the Havacian you see before you is not the brother, friend, comrade that you knew before. That Havacian died in Kiltullagh, and he is never coming back."

It was true. The man before him, to all appearances, displayed the face of Havacian, yet failed to demonstrate the light-hearted mannerisms of his old friend. He seemed serious and direct with an intensity like . . . like . . . a mature Atlantean. While studying at the Imperial Order of Wizards Enclave in Atlantis, Qel heard stories about young happy-go-lucky graduates like himself and Havacian who departed on their 'Journey of Discovery' only to return transformed with an almost humorless, introspective, pensiveness that all Atlanteans underwent as their minds developed to maturity. Except that it usually occurred slowly over time, not from one day to the next. Could his friend's death and revival have accelerated the process? Was there something degenerative that . . .

"Stop." Havacian shook him again, gently this time.

"Stop What?" Qel was always a little annoyed when his thoughts were interrupted.

"You're thinking along the wrong lines."

Qel peered closely at his friend. "Can you read my mind now?" It was a serious question.

"No," Havacian responded grimly. "But I can see it in your face. Already you are contemplating the errors of the process that brought me back to life, and what corruptions might have altered the result. I know you, Qel, and I can offer every assurance that the forces that returned life to mind and body were both deliberate and precise. Now put that aside and listen. Please. We don't have much time."

Slowly, Qel nodded his assent. He would listen, surely, but he would not immediately discard the other possibilities until he knew more. Ha! This was exactly what Havacian was predicting. It was more than a little unsettling how intuitive this new Havacian appeared to be!

Havacian took a deep breath and sighed, "Zracul is not as he seems. He is possessed of some ancient dark force or entity, I am not sure exactly in all truth, but I felt it stirring within him as I awakened from oblivion. Whatever the consequence of its existence, I am sure that it is irrevocably a part of Zracul. They are one. No less than a heart can be separated from one's physical body and remain living."

Qel studied his friend's face closely, listening to the words he spoke, detecting the slight quiver of fear, awe, and anger. If nothing else, Qel held no doubts that Havacian believed with all his heart that the words he spoke were true and correct.

"Zracul used his powers to give me life," Havacian continued, "and in a conventional sense he has succeeded, but that is not all. Through a co-mingling of his blood with mine he not only revived life in my veins; he gave a small piece of himself. A piece corrupted by that inseparable dark entity. Like the illnesses the priests speak of which spreads throughout the body contaminating every vessel and organ, so it is with this infection."

"How was Zracul's blood transferred into you?" Qel needed more facts. "Was it a magical process that we could study and dissect like we used to do at the Enclave?"

Shaking his head slowly, Havacian replied, "No. It was the basest of methods. There was no magic involved that I could sense when I awoke."

"We need to find a priest." Qel took hold of Havacian's arms. "Do you need help standing? Can you walk?"

"Stop." With gentle hands, Havacian firmly detached himself from Qel's grip. "The priests can do nothing for what ails me. I'm not sure if there is anything that can remove this dark infection. It saturates every part of me to the smallest particle."

Heat rose to Qel's cheeks as sudden fury consumed him. "Then we must find Zracul and force him to reverse this 'dark infection' or at the very least describe the method to cleanse it from your body!" Qel started to jerk toward the door, but with alarming strength Havacian held him in place.

"You agreed to listen," said he. "Now listen as there is more you should know."

With an exaggerated sigh, Qel relaxed enough to stand impatient with arms crossed and foot tapping. Once Havacian would have laughed at such a pose. He wasn't laughing today.

"Not even Zracul can undo what was done," Havacian began again. The anger that twisted his face relaxed, his eyes took on a doleful light, his breath came easy smelling vaguely metallic. "There is nothing that can be done. At least for the moment. I must leave here alone tonight and make my way to some distant place where I can study my strange case and explore whatever options avail themselves. I cannot predict how long I will be gone. Perhaps forever."

"That sounds reasonable enough," agreed Qel, "but why not return to the Wizards Enclave in Atlantis where centuries of knowledge have been collected? Certainly, the Masters will take special notice of your case and offer invaluable wisdom and guidance in our search for a remedy."

"That will not work . . ."

"Fine," Qel interrupted. "How about the Demesne in Avalon? The Sylvan will surely be helpful, and their knowledge goes back thousands of years!"

"Listen," Havacian hissed angrily. "None of these places would be safe. I must go somewhere isolated from civilized populations. Not even in close proximity to the smallest village or lone settlement will do. I cannot be anywhere near any people of any race. It would be unsafe."

"Is Zracul's reach so long that he could discover your whereabouts so easily?" Something wasn't quite right. He could see pain in Havacian's watery eyes now. There was something his friend was reluctant to say. "I will go with you," Qel resolved fervently. "I will help you find the remedy and keep you safe from Zracul and anyone else for as long as it takes. Even if the search consumes our entire lives!"

For the first time Havacian lowered his gaze allowing a few heavy teardrops to fall upon the loose robes gathered in his lap. When he finally looked up again, the moisture was gone from his eyes replaced by steely resolve. "I do not fear for myself. It is the people who would not be safe from me," he practically growled. "So, I must go alone without anyone. Especially you."

This evening was one shock after another! Qel stood dumbfounded. How could his greatest friend cast him away so easily?

Havacian's face softened and his voice took on a low consoling timbre, "Let me explain. This Dark Infection, as we have come to call it, has changed me in many ways. I no longer crave or desire food as we have come to think of it. Although I believe I am still capable of eating and drinking in the usual fashion if I chose to do so."

"So, what do you desire?" Qel asked with trepidation. He knew there could be no good answer.

"When I awoke from my fatal sleep, Zracul was not the only one in the room," Havacian spoke with in a matter-of-fact cadence that he often used when explaining complex incantations or enchantments. Qel knew his friend was detached from the subject, imparting detail and fact, all emotion repressed, and given the subject matter, Havacian's low monotone had a chilling effect on Qel.

"There was a woman in the room. She was bound naked to those shackles on the floor." The way he waved so casually to the chains a few feet away, made Qel shudder. He went on, "I could smell her hastily washed body, the lingering remnants of perfume mixed with sweat, salty tears, the bile rising in her throat, and . . . her fear." Qel felt the hair rising along his elongated skull as Havacian continued. "It was revolting and exciting all at once. I wanted to have my way with her then and there, but there was more! So much more. I could hear her pounding heart, the flow of blood through her veins, just like I can hear yours now," the look in Havacian's eyes was feral and wild. Qel considered fleeing right then! Still, he paused. Never could he think that Havacian would do him harm. He wasn't so sure anymore, yet he waited fearfully to hear the rest.

"The sound of her blood coursing so easily through her body was maddening! Yet I did not understand. I craved her in ways that did not seem compatible. I wasn't even ashamed." Qel detected a small quaver in Havacian's voice for a moment despite his own terror and revulsion that had him paralyzed and unable to turn away from the sickening words that flowed indifferently from his friend's mouth.

"Among other things, Zracul advised me that human blood was the most desirable to satiate my hunger, although any blood would due as a matter of survival. Then he walked out the door leaving me alone with the woman." Qel stayed quiet listening to every word, but his mind was screaming, *what were the other things*?

"For a while I thought to resist the urges growing in me. Her smell filled my senses, and the sound of her blood raged like a waterfall in my ears! I was so hungry. Still, I kept the cravings at bay, refusing to allow Zracul to control my desires. It was a weird stalemate inside this little room, but not the one you might expect. It was betwixt the woman and me. She sat so still just staring. She was terrified of course, but she barely shook as if her movement would set her fate in motion. And I stared back at her, fearful as well, resentful, desirous, growing more ravenous by the minute." Havacian paused. Perhaps he was reflecting on the moment. Qel waited like the woman. Terrified of what turn the story might take next. He wished he could have left the room right then and never heard a word more of it. He'd make up in his mind a happier end . . .

"The woman and I might be deadlocked in this room even now had it not been for her nervously chewing on her bottom lip. I first became aware that she bit through the soft texture of the supple skin by the sweet metallic tang that suddenly drove my senses to a feverous eruption. I didn't even know what it was until the thinnest line of crimson slowly crept from the edge of her mouth and down her chin. Looking back now, I doubt she ever realized that she drew blood. The sight of it, in addition to everything else drove the hunger in me to heights of fury I was powerless to stop. She knew it then too, shrieking for all she was worth. The awful sound stunned me for a second or so, but then all the pent-up energy exploded inside me, hunger overcame desire, and within another second the screaming stopped as I ripped out her throat and feasted on her gushing artery. I must have been near starvation since there wasn't much left of the poor woman when I finally climbed back into the bed desperate for sleep. Someone must have taken her away and cleaned up the mess before you arrived as hardly a trace of her remains."

Havacian stared curiously at Qel and asked, "Are you Okay?"

Qel wanted to scream in terror at what he just heard. He knew in his soul that it was all true. In a quavering voice asked, "Are you hungry now?"

A wan smile curved the edges of Havacian's lips, "Not like before, but I will be again soon. That is why you cannot come with me. Every second would be a temptation that would wear upon me until. . . you know the rest."

"So, what now?" Qel wanted nothing more than to be somewhere else. Yet, he still held out hope for the tiniest nugget of information that could help him help his friend.

Havacian removed the leather thong from around his neck holding the orichalcum crystal he received upon graduating from the Wizard's Enclave in Atlantis and handed it to Qel. "Keep this safe. Maybe I'll need it again one day," he smiled.

Qel knew it was Havacian's most prized possession. "Won't you need it when you are beyond the towers?"

"I can no longer sense the power in the orichalcum," he responded sadly. "Any power I can contrive will now come through the darkness inside of me."

Qel fastened the thong around his own neck. "I'll keep it here next to mine until the time comes for you to take it back."

Havacian gazed long at Qel as if memorizing his features, before rousing himself to remark, "Before you go, I need to tell you a few things. After the woman . . ." he let the thought dangle a second before continuing, "I told you I slept. I also dreamed, but not in the usual fashion. Instead, I was able to manipulate my consciousness in a sort of out-of-body experience. I don't know if this is usual for my recent condition or something else. But I was able to move through walls and investigate the interior of the Agrabuta. You need to know that Zracul, his brothers, sisters, and Namaah are truly evil creatures. And they are powerful. The other thing you should know, and I am reluctant to tell you this knowing how you will probably react, is that Sir Perault is here. I think he's been here for some time. Maybe from the first night we met Zracul."

Qel was stunned. Again! "Is he alive?" he asked hesitantly.

"He is," Havacian nodded. "However, Sir Perault has been in the hands of Namaah for a long time. I don't know how much of his mind remains intact." His friend clutched at Qel's cloak with one hand and jerked on it as if to give emphasis to what he said next, "Beware of Namaah, she is not what she appears to be."

"How do you mean?"

There was fear in Havacian's eyes. Not for himself, but for Qel. "She is a fiend summoned from the Infernal Planes. Stay away from her, or kill her on sight if you must. Her words can sway a man to her bidding."

"A fiend!" Qel knew Havacian well enough that it was no exaggeration. "Are the others like her, as well?"

Havacian released Qel's cloak shaking his head. "Something like her, but not fiends. More dangerous. I am certain of that. I don't know what they are." He cocked his head as if listening for something. "You have to go."

"When will you leave?" Qel asked trying to keep the despondency he felt from his voice.

"Not long after you." His smile was reminiscent of the old Havacian. "I wish I could stay with you, but because Zracul's blood flows in my veins now, he claims he can compel me to turn against anyone. Even my closest friend."

Qel hugged Havacian tightly, and said, "When you find the remedy . . ."

"You'll be the first to know," Havacian finished.

And for the briefest moment in time, the two were young companions on the cusp of a grand adventure once again.

Chapter 15 - Preparations

Dim light filtered through unshuttered windows streaked with heavy raindrops falling from dark clouds rolling in from the north. Breezy gusts whistled over the gables of the palace setting the blue pinions of Ys fluttering one way then another. Ahes didn't want to open her eyes. Even the dim light was harsh and bright. The chamber was cold. She lay upon wet sheets that made her shiver all the more. Tipa must have left the window open when they moved to the bedroom. She remembered it was hot, the sweat from their bodies salty on her tongue as they smoothly writhed with pleasures given and taken freely during the night. Until . . .

Ahes opened her eyes, rotating her head on the soft fabric of the pillow to take sad measure of Tipa's beautiful brown orbs gazing back at her. The princess sighed, wondering what her chambermaid saw with her eyes fixed beyond the present reality, as it was her head, and only her head, which lay on the pillow next to her. The remains of Tipa's body were scattered all over the chamber. Her blood covered the light blue sheets with crimson stains spread from sticky pools, while her arms, legs, and torso were broken and distorted beyond any semblance of recognition. Only her pretty face and hair were left untouched. It was a shame to end her service this way, but Ahes would no longer need her after today. And if anything, she saved her chambermaid from the terror of dying in the maelstrom that would soon engulf the city. Nor would she subject the lovely girl to the depravities Jaria and Daria would visit upon her sooner or later if Ahes removed her to the Agrabuta. Instead, Tipa received the mercy of a quick and unexpected death with no fear as she lay in the arms of her princess. What happened after that was simply fury taken out on flesh no longer living. She would miss Tipa.

Ahes rolled out of bed and peered out the window. It was time to get cleaned up and make ready for the approaching storm. The Sea Gate would stay open all day to grant safe harbor to any ship in harm's way. Later that night, when her father gaged the strength of the storm too great a risk, he would leave the palace to lock the Sea Gate until the tempest passed. That's when she would strike, leaving in her wake a dead king to rule over a dead city. And may hell have them both.

It was a pleasant time of day to sit outside and break the night's fast. The morning breeze brought the salty tang of the sea unspoiled by the stench of fish that would mark the return of the fishermen in the afternoon. Seagulls squawked and quibbled at the slim pickings at the docks while the citizenry of Ys slowly began to start their day. Looking east down the great boulevard, Reskalin casually glanced at the golden rays of the sun breaking through distant clouds like great glittering bands of majesty highlighting wide swaths of the sea wall and clusters of ships at dock, as she tapped rapidly on Enguer's thigh under the table out of sight. He tapped back in similar fashion, although with more hesitancy, since his fluency in thieves cant was a skill not yet entirely mastered.

"*Siione asked about you, of course*," Reskalin tapped.

"*Oh?*" Enguer's reply was suitably neutral.

"*I told her to advise the FatMan that I am with twins.*"

His hand stayed silent on her thigh. Appropriate, but guarded, she noted with satisfaction.

"*You know what she said?*" Reskalin kept the pace of her tapping slow and even so Enguer would not miss anything, nor did she pause for a response. "*She said I should return to Arre for the term of my pregnancy and pack you off to Courth as men are little help, and more often than not an additional burden for the expectant mother. She said it with smile! You know that snarky little half-sneer that I hate but somehow men find appealing? Then she had the gall to assure me how well you would be taken care of in Courth and that she would see to all your needs personally!*"

A moment passed before Enguer replied, once again, "*Oh?*"

Reskalin felt heat rise to her cheeks. Perhaps applying a trifle more pressure than intended, she dug her recently sharpened nails into his thigh drawing a swift intake of breath and a slight bulging of his eyes. After he recovered from his shock, Enguer gently placed his warm hand over hers and squeezed it tight. Those small gestures always had the effect of deflating her anger, making her feel guilty for lashing out at him. It was one of the reasons she loved him, she supposed. But it was not fair that he had the power to diffuse her anger so readily.

She wondered if Siione was just jealous her. Unlike Reskalin, Siione was not an adopted child, but the result of a brief dalliance between the FatMan and a tavern wench he seduced in Courth thirty years ago. As Enguer was fond of pointing out, that made Siione her older sister. Apparently, the relationship didn't last long; however, the FatMan was loath to simply abandon his daughter to an uncertain future, so instead set them up in a fine house on an estate he owned outside of Port Francik with a monthly stipend for expenses and a grant for Siione's education. Of course, no one, including Siione was ever to know that the FatMan was her father. Fortunately, or unfortunately, depending on one's perspective, Siione's mother professed the truth on her deathbed after suffering the Creeping Sickness for some months. Thus, Siione took ship to Arre and in a nearly fatal encounter that instead turned embarrassing and awkward, reunited with her father. Siione stayed with the FatMan as an "Apprentice" with the strict understanding that their true relationship must be kept secret. Remarkably, Siione thrived in the dangerous environment of the underworld and, like her father, proved to have a shrewd talent for the business of organized crime. This was at least one area where she and Siione were much alike, and despite Siione's pedigree, the FatMan had never shown partiality to one or the other.

Reskalin's ruminations were interrupted by the arrival of the Atlantean, Qel at their table. He asked in a somber voice, "May I join you?"

"Of course!" Enguer answered cheerfully, pushing a chair out from the table with his foot. "We were uncertain if we would see you again, so we left your share of the gold paid by Count Zracul in care of an official-looking Atlantean at the tower. Reskalin insisted that we stuff the satchel with wool so it wouldn't be obvious what was inside." Enguer paused. "We left a bag for Havacian as well. How is . . ." his words trailed off awkwardly.

"He's dead. Havacian is dead." Qel, normally clear-eyed and steady of gaze, dropped his eyes to the table as he spoke. "Prince Zracul was unable to return life to his body for reasons beyond my understanding. I had his remains removed to the tower so he could be transported back to his family in Atlantis for proper burial."

Reskalin watched Qel carefully. She sensed something very odd in his behavior. His sepulchral tone and downcast eyes seemed calculated. And that statement 'for reasons beyond my understanding'? Since when did this Atlantean, or any Atlantean for that matter, ever believe anything was beyond their understanding? She reached across the table and took Qel's hand, saying, "We're so sorry. Havacian was a fine man. We liked him very much for the short time we knew him." At the same time, she silently tapped out a message to Enguer under the table, "*Something is off with him. He is concealing something.*"

Enguer's reply, "*He is mourning. Leave him be.*"

"Thank you," Qel smiled wanly looking up at her. Deep pockets of moisture glistened at the edges of his large almond-shaped eyes. The Atlantean was suffering the loss of his friend, that much was real.

Reskalin pulled back her hand as Khulani strode up dressed at odds with his usual fashion. He sported a long leather dust jacket well-oiled to repel rain and snow under which he wore a tailored yellow silk tunic with the front open to reveal a muscular chest thick with fine black curls where hung a leather thong from his neck bearing bones and small feathers. Then there were the tight brown pants accenting every curve of his slender legs, a broad black belt, and knee-high boots of supple leather.

Reskalin could barely suppress a bark of laughter. She glanced at Enguer whose face was alight with a mischievous smile. There was much more to this story she would have to pry out of him later.

"Is that Khulani?" Enguer grinned. "No one will mistake you for a druid today!"

Even Qel's mood shifted favorably as his eyes brightened at the sight of the druid. He smiled curiously when Khulani sat down heavily beside him.

"It is clear to me now why druids stay away from the cities," Khulani huffed. "I did not realize how strong was the devotion to Sunna in the Western Kingdoms. There was still a long line waiting for blessings at sunrise! My new friends wish for me to build a grove right here in the city! They would speak of nothing else!"

"So how did you manage to sneak away? Shouldn't you still be bestowing blessings in the park?" Enguer grinned with unconcealed mirth.

Khulani spread his hands wide. "I became very dramatic, and spoke loudly telling the gathered people that I must attend Sunna at sunrise. So, I transformed into an eagle and flew away. What else could I do? My followers are relentless in their devotion."

"Followers?" Enguer laughed. "Be careful, Khulani. This is Ys, and in Ys, devotion can be as fleeting as the latest trends. And what about Sunna. Wont she look unkindly upon a druid abandoning his duties to the people?"

"First, it is the duty of a priest to serve the 'people,' not a druid." Khulani shifted uncomfortably in his chair, pulling at the fabric of his pants. "Second, I flew to the beach and prayed as Sunna rose above the horizon bringing the world another glorious day. Her gladness shown down upon me. And third, these pants are very tight in sensitive areas."

Everyone laughed at that. Then Enguer said, "Tight as those pants may be, your disguise becomes you!"

"It is not a disguise," Khulani grumbled as he shifted to stretch the seat of his pants.

Reskalin cleared her throat loudly to gain their attention. "Qel has sad news about Havacian."

Qel repeated what he had stated earlier, his voice thick with emotion. Khulani appeared stricken by the news, offering his condolences and promising prayers at the next sunrise. Then they sat in silence at the table for a while, each one absorbed in their own thoughts.

Suddenly, Qel straightened in his chair and exclaimed, "I have been so consumed by grief that I neglected to tell you something important." He paused for a long moment, and when he next spoke, the words he chose were careful and deliberate. "There is one thing I left out about Havacian because it was very distressing; however, I believe it is too important not to mention." The Atlantean glanced around the table but would not meet Reskalin's gaze.

Another long pause, and then Qel took a deep breath, and said, "When I arrived at the Agrabuta, Havacian was alive. Barely."

Reskalin observed shock on the faces of Khulani and Enguer.

"He was suffering convulsions and conscious for only brief spates," Qel continued. "Zracul left the two of us alone for a few minutes while he rushed to his study where he thought to find some solution among his many tomes, so he said."

Qel was looking down again. He was clearly uncomfortable telling half-truths and outright lies, Reskalin surmised. But she was unsure which part of it was truth and which not.

"In that time, Havacian became abruptly lucid," Qel went on. "He told me he was shifting through the veil of life and death uncertainly with no anchor to one or the other. In this strange existence he revealed how he could see beyond the walls of the room where he lay and perceive truths about people that were hidden to mortal eyes."

Qel looked up then with unsettling intensity, "He said Sir Perault was in the Agrabuta under torture by the creature Naamah, and that he had probably been there since the night we first met Prince Zracul."

Enguer leaned toward Qel, tightly clutching the edges of the table. "We must tell the guard," He started angrily. "They will extract him. Even if it must be by force!"

"No," Qel shook his head emphatically. "They won't. Before Havacian died, he told me that Zracul, his brothers and sisters, and Naamah were not as they seemed. He begged me to leave the Agrabuta safely and find what help I could but not, under any circumstances, attempt to exact revenge upon Zracul alone. It was his last request and I honored it, although it took every fiber of my being to leave that place without burning it to the ground with all of them in it!"

"The city must have stronger powers to call upon than the Guard," Khulani insisted. "If not, we could go to the palace and claim that a noble from Lyonesse, which Sir Perault would seem to be, has been taken against his will, and locked inside the Agrabuta."

"There's more," Qel sighed. "A friend of ours from Avalon joined us on the voyage from the Emerald Isle to Ys a few weeks ago. Whereas Havacian and I came here with no particular objective in mind other than to experience the world outside of Atlantis, Aelrindel, our Sylvan Elf friend, was sent for a purpose."

"Mysterious," Reskalin commented raising one eyebrow high. "Although not surprising. Let me guess, something to do with Princess Ahes?"

Qel jolted as if struck by lightning. "I promised not to speak about his business in Ys, only that which pertains to the current predicament."

"You don't have to say a word about it, Qel," Reskalin scoffed. "It's written all over your face."

"*Go easy,*" Enguer tapped under the table.

"*Fine,*" she replied with a final point that made Enguer jump, drawing everyone's attention.

"Look," Reskalin drew all eyes back to her. "We have been through a lot together, and earned each other's trust. I don't expect you to break your promise to your friend, but I can't have you holding back any information that might be relevant to whatever we decide here today. Perault's life hangs in the balance. So, can you trust us?"

Qel's blue-tinted cheeks grew progressively red with shame as she spoke. He began to reply, then abruptly stopped.

"The question is, can you trust me?" a soft masculine voice with lilting accent spoke from over Reskalin's shoulder sending her into the air like a nervous cat. She was on her feet, spinning around with daggers in both hands like claws.

"Who are you?" Reskalin growled dangerously.

A tall lean man with long silvery hair and sharp angular features doffed his hat revealing the sharp points of his ears. "Aelrindel, at your service," he greeted them all as one.

"Damned Elf," Reskalin was shaken to the core. It was a rare thing for her to be caught off guard to such a degree. If the elf had been an assassin, she, and possibly Enguer as well would be dead, so light was his tread to get so close unnoticed.

"I've been called worse," Aelrindel smiled. He offered his hand to help Reskalin climb down from the table. "And you must be the famous, or infamous, as you like, Reskalin of Arre, aka 'The Raven,' so I hear."

Reskalin ignored his extended hand and slid off the table on her own. "Why don't you sit down so we can end the spectacle." Her voice was pure ice. She didn't like attention. Especially when she appeared the fool.

Aelrindel pulled a chair from another table and sat between Qel and Khulani. Well attired, the elf wore breeches, tunic, and boots similar to that of Khulani, except the colors were a blend of warm earthtones and far more stylish. He also favored jewelry in the form of rings encrusted with small gems, and necklaces of gold and platinum that slid against each other noiselessly as he moved somehow immune to the harsh clink of metal against metal. Trailing behind was a long-hooded cloak cinched at the neck that draped over his longbow and quiver of arrows fletched with emerald green feathers. At his waist hung a pair of curved scimitars; one on each side. Reskalin thought he looked like a dandy outfitted for war, but not unlike most elves she had seen.

"So, this is Aelrindel of Avalon," Reskalin stated flatly. "I have heard much of your skulking around Ys observing the activities of Princess Ahes. Have you seen everything you came to see?"

Qel groaned and seemed to shrink a little in his chair. The young Atlantean was not a man of intrigue, Reskalin noted. He was honest and forthright, much like Enguer. Maybe that's why she liked him so much. The elf on the other hand . . .

"Relax Qel," Aelrindel smiled at his friend. "I know you kept your word. Reskalin has extensive sources and contacts who doubtlessly keep her well informed." He turned his attentions back to Reskalin. "I must admit that I am taken aback by your lugubrious beauty. It's a wonder you managed to disguise yourself as a man for so long so convincingly." The elf's gaze flickered over to Enguer. "And this must be the renowned Enguer Rand, son of the legendary Gaurin Rand. I salute your success in Courth against those rabid . . . what were they called?"

"Lukánthropos," Enguer provided cheerlessly.

"Lukánthropos! Yes, that's it!" Aelrindel exclaimed. "It was a remarkable feat how you escaped their clutches and then guided an army back to their lair to end their corruptive existence."

"I was one of many to defeat the beasts," Enguer replied with typical modesty.

"Ah, but the only one of many capable of tracking the beasts to their stinking hovel." Aelrindel's features could not hide the scorn he felt for the creatures. Reskalin knew the Sylvan hated anything that corrupted or abused nature. To them, nature flowed from their Goddess Niamh, and was the source and semblance of what might be called religion.

Aelrindel sat back and looked curiously at Khulani. "You are a mystery to me," he spoke quietly as if the thought were only meant for himself. "From your ebon skin, dark eyes, and lean build I would say you hail from the lands south of the Great Sea. Caspian perhaps. No. Not Ta Shemau or Ta Mehu, either. Hmmm. Your clothing appears incongruous of the people, but maybe Mouillian?"

Khulani's wide smile displayed white teeth prominent against the background of his dark complexion. "My name is Khulani and I am a druid. The first from the Imaziyen tribes. I do not normally dress in this fashion, but I have learned that I stand out too much in the city wearing the traditional garments of my faith. So, I clothe myself this way to avoid attention. Or, as Enguer says, 'in disguise.'"

Aelrindel laughed. "It is my honor to know you, friend druid." The elf continued to smile as he took in the entire table with his gaze. "All of you for that matter."

Enguer glanced at Reskalin before he said, "Qel was about to tell us something important you told him before you arrived. What is it?"

Aelrindel leaned forward, smile fading, his voice took on a more serious tone. "Let me tell you about Princess Ahes."

For the better part of the next hour, Aelrindel lay bare the true vice in stark lustful detail of everything he witnessed involving Princess Ahes and Zracul, who by this time had taken to the honorific 'Count' rather than 'Prince.' Absent was the Sylvan elf's casual demeanor. Rather, his tone was bland, tinged with raw disgust at the debauchery he described with lurid displeasure.

Khulani felt his hair rise and his cheeks burn at much of what he heard. Almost none of it could he ever have imagined people of any race to willfully engage. Yet here, in this beautiful city, flowed an undercurrent of licentious degradation displayed openly by the daughter of the king and her foreign lover that the people of the night freely participated in and emulated with wanton abandon. And how was their behavior regarded by the populace? As nothing more than the latest trend of which they could shamelessly boast and bray to one another as if it earned them honors or accolades. Maybe it did in this rotten city. It only hardened Khulani's conviction that all civilized people with their great kingdoms and shining towers were doomed to eventually fall under the crushing weight of their own degenerate corruption back to their origins of tribalism and barbary.

"This is why the guard, the palace, nor any official or noble of Ys short of the king, would be a helpful ally against Count Zracul," Aelrindel sat back in his chair having fully conveyed his account.

The table was silent for a while as everyone considered the implications. Khulani agreed with the elf; any public plea for assistance on their part would be quickly swatted down by Princess Ahes and likely attract her wrath for bringing such accusations against her lover. He was about to speak when Enguer said the words all of them must have been thinking, "If Sir Perault is to be saved, then it is up to us to do it."

There were grunts and nods of agreement around the table, but Enguer appeared unconvinced by the muted response. "Shall we go once more into the breach, my friends? Speak now your assent or walk away. The choice is yours."

"I will go," Qel announced fervently, the first to reply.

Khulani quickly added his agreement, "I too, will come."

Reskalin nodded curtly.

"What about you, elf?" Enguer directed his hard gaze across the table. Khulani could see a hint of animosity in the ranger's eyes with little expectation.

For his part, Aelrindel sat calm and contemplative, with eyes cast down and inward. He was the pensive thoughtful elf now, judged Khulani, typical of Sylvan he had known in the past, especially if they happened to be druids. It seemed to him that all elves naturally possessed a quiet wisdom inherent to their race.

Finally, with eyes still fixed on the table, Aelrindel spoke in a soft timber, "I do not know Sir Perault, nor much about him save what little Qel could impart." He slowly lifted his gaze to meet Enguer's intense stare and continued in a rising voice that brooked no uncertainty, "But, Havaciante of House Talika is my friend as is Qellel of House Mekali sitting next to me, and mine friend's enemy, is thus mine enemy. I am with you."

Enguer bowed his head showing the elf respect, and addressed them as a group, "Then we are all of one mind and one goal. We will rescue Sir Perault from the Agrabuta and destroy any creature that gets in our way."

"This will require some planning," Aelrindel cautioned.

"Agreed," piped in Reskalin. "We should plan to do what must be done under cover of darkness. Shall we say midnight?"

Everyone muttered tentative agreement.

"Good. While you all discuss the details, I'm going to see an associate who may prove helpful to our endeavor. I expect to be back soon after dark." Reskalin kissed Enguer on the cheek as she rose from her seat. Before stepping away, she cast a parting comment to the group, "I suggest going with whatever our new friend here recommends." Then she strode into the street and quickly disappeared in the crowd.

Khulani was sincerely impressed with Reskalin. She reminded him of the Amazigh women he and his best friend Rebiku met in the mountains one night long ago on their way to the land of the Nabta peoples. The women were fierce and beautiful warriors from a matriarchal tribe living isolated from the Imaziyen. Rebiku died a few months later, never returning home. But the Amazigh woman he lay with that night bore him a son that would continue his father's bloodline. Khulani missed Rebiku and still harbored deep regrets over the loss of his best friend.

Aelrindel was speaking about the Agrabuta as Khulani abandoned his reflections to rejoin the conversation. The group hunched over the table making their plans for the better part of the morning. It was sound strategy, thought Khulani, but he worried about a change he sensed in the air. A storm was coming. And not just a passing of rain and thunder, something more, like a tempest. Except it was fueled by the darkest most vile evil that felt oddly familiar. Khulani shivered, but kept the strange sensations to himself.

Chapter 16 – Garden of the Dead

Perault scrutinized his likeness in the tall mirror Naamah rolled into his room that morning. It seemed like ages since he last regarded his reflection, and he was not unsatisfied with what he saw. Curiously, the image before him was a more clear-eyed youthful version of himself, if a trifle gaunt in the cheeks. All lines of tension and worry were gone, and with them fled the strains of living up to the tenets of the Temple Knights, the pressures associated with his betrothal to Lady Melisende Brigham, and the responsibilities of a noble of Lyonesse. None of these applied to him now. He felt unburdened and free for the first time in his life. It was liberating.

In a further departure from his usual mode of dress, he was donned in all black. The silk tunic he wore was tailored to fit, as were his light cotton breeches, and soft leather boots. The garments felt light and airy except where the silk grazed his chest. There, he still suffered the sting of a tattoo, or many connected tattoos, of archaic script and arcane symbols. They were inked in faintly phosphorescent crimson lines, arcs, and geometric designs extending from just below his collar bone down to his waist. It was Naamah's mark that claimed him as her mate. There was a bare glimpse of it through his open collar. Perault needed no reminding of the significance of this mark. Naamah was very clear about what it meant before she applied them, and only after he agreed to it of his own free will. Verily, it was something like a marriage contract, if mostly one-sided. Perault would be free to go and do as he wished in his life, but should she summon him, he would be compelled to go to her at once. Further, he understood that should he engaged in carnal relations with another being ,natural or no, without Naamah's consent, she would know of it, and the life of that being would be subject to her whim. Of course, Naamah could not be constrained by the same condition. Yet, she agreed that any time she spent with Perault was strictly for pleasure, whereas her engagements with other men were simply to satiate her hunger as her sustenance derived not from traditional fare, but the seed of man. Perault accepted all of it with no remorse.

A lithe figure glided into view, standing close at his side so that the two appeared together in the mirror. Until that moment, Perault never realized how much shorter than he she was. Naamah barely reach the height of his shoulders. She was dressed in a long black gown of sheer gossamer silk slit down both sides from her waist with a neckline that plunged to a point past her navel. Wings, tail, and horns were no longer visible, but she would have looked beautiful either way. They were supposed to go out that night, which would have marked Perault's first occasion to leave the Agrabuta since he arrived there, but their plans were thwarted by the fierce winds and rains that had suddenly come over Ys that evening. Regardless, he and Naamah decided to dress up anyway, drink lots of Zracul's expensive Mekali wine, and enjoy an intimate evening together.

"You look beautiful as always," Perault smiled at her reflection.

She slid her hand up his back and caressed the hair at the base of his neck with long sharpened fingernails and returned his smile. "I almost forgot what my knight looked like wearing clothes," she purred seductively. "You look dashing. I look forward to tearing them off later."

"Such a waste of a fine tunic!" Perault protested.

Naamah shrugged, "I will have the tailors bring stacks of them weekly."

"Then I will become the pariah of fashion in Ys," he said in mock despair. "For there will be no silk shirts available for anyone else, and they will be forced to wear wool!"

"It would serve those pretentious fools right!" Naamah laughed, and then cocked her head in a gesture of curiosity. "Now that you are free to do as you please, my dear, where will you take up residence? Of course, you may remain here if you like."

Perault's expression turned serious as he gazed back at her through the mirror. "I am your mate for life, and you are mine. My residence from now on shall be your chambers, and where you go, so shall I"

Naamah's widening smile was most pleased.

Qel crouched with the others at the base of the hill where stood the Agrabuta, the oldest estate still standing in Ys. He noted the misery on every face streaked wet from the pouring rain and the swamp of slick grass and thick mud that clung with annoying tenacity to boots, sandals, hems of cloaks, and anything else passing through it. Glancing up, he could see swirling dark clouds blotting out the stars, casting long diaphanous fingers to the horizons. Strangely, the circulating winds betrayed no inclination to follow the natural air currents further inland, rather, they seemed to deliberately linger over Ys as if by some malicious design. Just walking, then running the short distance from the tavern to the hill turned out to be a tricky affair as they contended with frequent gusts that sent framed canopies tumbling down the vacant streets from the markets or trees ripped from their roots and other foliage hurtling from lush gardens, ornamental shrubberies, and parks along the avenues. Already every corner and recessed doorway was piled with debris.

Flashes of lightning illuminating the sky near to daylight prompted the hardiest of them to flinch and jerk, followed quick by the intense deafening boom of thunder lasting a few seconds at a time. Closest to him squatted Aelrindel, his pointed ears twitching from the rain or nerves, he couldn't tell. Beyond the elf, Qel could see the whites of Khulani's eyes reflected in the dark recesses of his hood held tightly in both hands to keep the wind from thrusting it back. Further still were the dark shapes of Enguer and Reskalin huddled together against the hill as they all rested a few minutes to catch their breath.

Soon enough, Enguer was up and running at a crouch along the muddy switchback pathway that climbed the hill to the back gate of the property near the stables. Reskalin followed a few feet behind Enguer, and the rest of them went forward in suit ascending toward an opening in the high stone wall that surrounded the rear of the estate. When they were all gathered at the gate, Reskalin motioned for everyone to huddle close so that she could be heard above the noise of the storm.

"As soon as I get the gate unlocked," she shouted, "run to the stables. If we find anyone there, we'll truss them up so they can't raise an alarm. Then we'll plot our course to the servant's entrance of the Agrabuta."

Reskalin didn't wait for their nods of agreement. She knelt before the gate, unrolled a small leather pack holding strangely shaped metal implements in tight slots, removed two of the tools, and set to work at the lock. It didn't take long. The gate creaked open on rusted hinges and they all filed through following Reskalin toward a large structure with a high brooding gable. Having only seen the Agrabuta from the front, Qel was surprised by how expansive the open space was in the back. Through the rain he could make out the shapes of two small structures that were probably tool sheds and a larger single-story cottage that was likely the residence of the groundskeeper. No light shown from within. There were also several plots of freshly turned soil that Qel guessed was a garden, although it was hard to tell if anything was growing from it. About a hundred feet from the stable, the manor house was by far the largest building in sight, boasting of two floors with a series of eight high windows across the top and six along the bottom. A vaulted roof of dark grey slate tiles slanted boldly between two crenelated towers that rose to a third level with an open parapet at the top. All the windows were shuttered; however, narrow slivers of light shined through many of them including those on the upper most level of the east tower.

Arriving at the front of the stables, a commotion of nervous stomps and breathy whickers were audible beyond the weathered timber walls. The large double doors were blocked tight from within, but the normal-sized caretakers' door beside it was unlocked. Reskalin opened the door and held it so, as Enguer and Aelrindel rushed into the darkened interior. Not even the smallest light shown from within. Only a few seconds passed before Reskalin motioned to the rest of them to follow her inside.

As soon as the door closed, Aelrindel activated a small light globe dimly illuminating the immediate interior. At least a dozen stalls lined each side of the well-maintained stables enclosed by split doors open at the top. Shiney black nostrils puffing from broad muzzles poked out curiously from several of the dark interiors. The strong scent of fresh straw underfoot and horse dung permeated the air. At the far end of the stables the light reflected off the silver filigree and shiny black lacquer of an elaborate carriage with curtains pulled back from the windows revealing a red upholstered interior.

Aside from the huff and jostle of horses, and the muffled noise of the storm raging outside, it was remarkably quiet within the thickly timbered walls of the stables allowing the group to speak at a normal level, although no one deigned to do so as Aelrindel conferred quietly with Reskalin. The pair were debating the best way to gain entry to the Agrabuta since they had little foreknowledge regarding the number of doors in the back of the manor house or whether the windows were barred. In their planning earlier that morning, they agreed to take a stealthy approach rather than forced entry so to come upon the inhabitants unawares. On their two previous visits to the Agrabuta they saw no evidence of guards inside or out, but Havacian's warning about the unusual nature of the family, conveyed by Qel, gave them pause against rushing in blindly.

Finally, Reskalin and Aelrindel seemed to come to agreement. The dim illumination of the light globe held low by the elf cast Reskalin's features in striking contrasts of shadows as she explained their next steps. "Aelrindel and I agree that the best way to quietly enter the Agrabuta will be through the closest window on the ground floor that shows no light behind it. Once inside, we will go quietly as possible using only the hand signals I demonstrated earlier to communicate until we find a secure location. Remember, we know there is an elderly doorman, one or two servants, maybe a cook or two, Count Zracul, his two brothers and two sisters, Naamah, and perhaps even the Princess Ahes inside the house. And they could be anywhere. Our objective is to find Perault and get him out, not a pitched battle in the dining room. We are outnumbered, and we have no idea what their capabilities are. So, we will try to avoid the residents if at all possible. However, in the event that. . ."

Reskalin suddenly went silent and the light globe winked out leaving them in darkness at the sound of the latch turning on the caretaker's door. Slowly it creaked open. The dark hulk of a heavy-set man wearing a wide brimmed hat dripping with rain was silhouetted in the doorway. Behind him, the storm raged worse than ever, and the wind that rushed by him into the stables carried the very distinct stench of rot and decay.

Qel and the others stood about fifteen feet within the interior facing the man. It was impossible to see his features or the expression on his face in the darkness. Behind them, the horses caused a sudden ruckus kicking at the doors to their stalls, snorting, and whistling through flared nostrils. Everyone was frozen for long seconds unsure of what the man would do.

"Hello?" Enguer called loudly over the storm.

Not expecting anyone to speak, Qel nearly jumped out of his robes. But the greeting seemed to fall on deaf ears until Aelrindel took a step forward.

"Tress-pass-erss," the man lisped the single word more like the hiss of a serpent than a word spoken like a man. It sent chills up Qel's spine. Without another word, the caretaker slowly backed out of the doorway into the storm.

Aelrindel leapt forward stopping the door before it closed. He was poised to continue out to confront the dark figure, instead, he froze in his tracks. Enguer, close on his heels, nearly collided with the elf but at the last moment veered to the side and skidded to a stop right beside him. Qel and the rest crowded behind looking out through the spaces between them to where the shadowy man stood less than two paces away obscured by the driving rain. Yet, it wasn't he who held Aelrindel's attention. It was the garden several more paces beyond, or more accurately, the writhing figures straining to pull themselves out of the muddy soil with disjointed arms and contorted legs attached to malshaped torsos topped by lolling unsteady heads wobbling upon feeble necks. No, not a garden, Qel realized with trepidation. It was a graveyard. And it regurgitated at least half-a-dozen of the revolting creatures each conveying the prodigious stench of rot and decay.

"Close the door," Aelrindel instructed Enguer. His tone was calm with not a hint of fear or panic, as if he could not see or accept the veracity of his own eyes. Enguer did so without question.

Once again, the light globe came to life in the elf's hand. All around, Qel observed haunted anxious looks on his friends faces and surmised his shown the same. Enguer found a short heavy plank propped up in the corner and set it within large iron hooks bolted to the back of the door to secure the entry. Then he turned to the group and shrugged.

Let's get away from the door," Reskalin called over the clamor of the horses.

They backed away a few feet, except Khulani who was going from horse to horse, lightly touching each between the ears, whispering words that soothed the animals. They soon ceased their kicks, stomps, and snorts. Aelrindel commanded his light globe to rise above their heads where it hovered freely while he attached a dry flax string to his longbow. Everyone was tense with the anticipation of a fight.

"I'm going to see if I can find another way out of here," Enguer set out in a run toward the back of the stable where the exotic carriage was parked.

Reskalin peered at Qel through thick eyelashes as her nimble hands deftly checked the array of knives sheathed all over her armor. "Are you ready, Qel?" she asked. "We might have to make a run for the Agrabuta. I don't know how hard it is to kill a thing that is already dead – or even if they can be killed."

"Fire will destroy them, and I can help with that," Qel tried to smile but he doubted it was very convincing. "Otherwise, take out their limbs, especially their legs. That will slow them."

Khulani returned during the last part of Qel's recommendation and added, "The eyes and head are vulnerable as well, but do not be too surprised if a creature's body flails around blindly without them."

"Khulani," Aelrindel eyed the druid up and down. "Can you shapeshift into a beast that has both bulk and speed?"

The druid considered for a few seconds before answering, "Yes. What did you have in mind?"

"If, as Reskalin suggests, we must run for it, would it not be expedient if the way ahead was cleared for us by a beast of great strength?" Aelrindel asked.

"Ah, it is a good notion," Khulani agreed. "I will be ready if it comes to that."

Qel was about to comment when Enguer appeared out of the darkness shaking his head in frustration. "If there's another way out of here, I can't find it," he slammed hist fist into his palm irritably. "If we only had more time. . ."

Something slammed hard against the caretaker's door, followed by a series of heavy banging against the stables larger double doors. Each time the force grew stronger until the wooden beams holding the doors shut splintered, and the hinges shrieked as the nails securing them to the door frame pulled free.

"They will be through in seconds," Reskalin cried. "Make ready!"

Qel and the others moved back a few more paces and spread out. Aelrindel stood with Khulani at the center of the arc they formed to face the rush. Reskalin and Enguer were crouched on their left, while Qel stood a span to the elf's right.

"When Khulani deems there is space enough in the door, he will transform into a great beast and clear the way to the Agrabuta," Reskalin shouted so they could hear above the loud battering at the doors. "I will find the best way inside, and there we will barricade our entry as best we can."

"So much for a quiet entry," Qel called back. "Everyone in the Agrabuta will hear the ruckus!"

"If you have a better plan, speak now!" Reskalin barked.

Qel didn't have a better plan, but he knew the one Reskalin suggested was not good either. At best they would be trapped between the creatures outside and the creatures inside with few options to escape, let alone find Perault. If there were only six or seven of the creatures, maybe they could destroy them all and return to the original plan of entering the Agrabuta by stealth. Qel settled his mind to make ready evocations of fire he anticipated would destroy them the quickest.

The stable doors were about to fall. Already large jagged gaps made visible the heavy downpour and flash of lightning without, letting in the noise of the storm, and the shrieking winds. As one body the creatures came a final time against the doors breaking their last will to stand, sending them flying in great chunks of timber to the sides on warped hinges. There was a brief pause as the ragged assailants stood frozen in the wide opening glaring from sunken eyes in bloodless faces at the five living souls standing defiantly in a halo of soft light cast from Aelrindel's light globe hovering above. Qel saw hunger in the eyes of the walking corpses and jealous hatred suffered of beings flush with the life that should be so brutally stolen from them. It was a strange exchange of sentiment that held both groups enthralled for what must have been mere seconds, yet seemed an eternity, until the horses caught the pungent stink of death in the air rousing a wild panic that brought time shrieking back to the present.

The creatures lurched forward with a lunging burst of speed. Feathered shafts flew unerringly from bent yew in the skilled hands of Enguer and Aelrindel, the flash of a dagger sped straight and true from Reskalin's practiced arm, a mighty roar burst from the ferocious muzzle of a huge brown bear with claws extended in rampant pose where Khulani had stood, and Qel released a jet of searing flame rivaling the heat of the sun. Where came seven, then came only three.

Heavy thumping of hooves and cracking wood, alerted Qel and the others of danger bearing down on them from behind. Qel leaped to one side as Enguer and Reskalin sprang the opposite way. They were just missed by the sharp hooves of a dozen black steeds with long flowing manes and elegant tails charging in full panic toward the demolished opening of the stable. Aelrindel rolled under the bear who roared menacingly in defiance shocking the horses enough to split around the beast left and right. No fear instinct would save the three rotting creatures in their path as they were trampled to fleshy hulks before the exquisite steeds disappeared in the obscuring darkness and downpour of rain. The pounding of their hooves was still loud in Qel's ears when awful shrieks and screams from the animals rent the air, but just as quickly ended.

Qel regained his feet, as did the others, watching the rain come down in unrelenting sheets. It was otherwise quiet.

"Psst," Reskalin hissed to Aelrindel. "Can you hear anything?"

The elf's ears twitched as he cocked his head to listen. He held his hand up, "Something . . ."

He needn't say more, they all saw it then. Plodding figures slowly emerged from the darkness. There was a score of them. No, two score at least. Qel's heart dropped to his stomach, these were not good odds. He made ready his fire, the bear squared up on all fours growling with muted rage, Enguer and Aelrindel held shafts to ears, and Reskalin drew a long knife in one hand and a curved sword in the others. *This was how heroes died,* thought Qel. He didn't feel like a hero. He felt terrified.

The dead lumbered into the stable in jagged ranks, but this time there was no pause. They spotted their prey and mindlessly staggered onward brandishing skeletal claws and slavering maws craving living flesh; and the unremorseful need to extinguish life forever.

Chapter 17 – The Reavers

Shaft after shaft sunk to their fletching in putrid flesh unheeded by the Dead-Walkers. While most of the deadly missiles found their marks; blinding eyes, crippling legs, the creatures came on undaunted, even to the point of dragging their disfigured bodies forward with taloned claws. A great roar reverberated through the stable with the power of thunder as Khulani's enormous bear form charged into the mass stomping, biting, and rending with great swipes of its massive claws. Fire erupting from the Atlantean's open palms lit the interior in streams and arcs burning through dead flesh like kindling and introduced a new stench that made Reskalin want to retch out her own guts.

"Qel, watch your flank!" Reskalin yelled at the top of her lungs.

The blue-skinned wizard turned on the advancing corpse, and with a quick hand motion it combusted with a force that sent it reeling into the nearest stall. Then Qel was urgently whirling again to engulf two more Dead-Walkers in searing flames.

Reskalin could not keep further vigilance on the Atlantean as she had her own lifeless monstrosities to deal with. She surged forward with scimitar in hand delivering a crushing blow to the knee of the closest creature dropping it to the ground, she spun away leading with her long knife angled upward cleaving cleanly through the skull of the next walking corpse leaving only its lower jaw intact. She kicked the creature in the chest propelling the blindly flailing torso into a Dead-Walker immediately behind it. Arrows sailed by her head, sometimes so close they brushed her raven black hair, drilling deep into the next line of animated flesh. Reskalin backed up two paces and nearly tripped when a claw gripped the heel of her boot. With a quick slashing motion, she severed hand from wrist, yet it still clung tenaciously while the body propelled itself slowly toward her with one useful arm and a jerking leg. Side stepping its slow progress, Reskalin severed the creatures remaining arm, but it would not relent as it squirmed to reach her with snapping jaws.

Aelrindel bound by her suddenly with whirling blades and hacked mercilessly at a pair of Dead-Walkers simultaneously. Then Enguer too relinquished his bow and set about chopping at any dead thing that moved. Wave after wave of the corpses marched into the grist mill of blades heedless of the slaughter as Reskalin, Enguer and Aelrindel stood shoulder to shoulder against the stinking press of bodies. The three went not unscathed. Each bore terrible gashes in their armor, flesh wounds streamed bloody lines down faces, legs, and arms. Several teeth were embedded in Enguer's right arm where he had hacked through the skull of an unrelenting Dead-Walker determined to chew through his limb.

Reskalin felt the weight of her arms as they grew tired. The finesse was gone from her swordplay as she resorted to the brutal tactics of hacking and slashing at the creatures swarming around them. She glanced ahead at the massive bulk of Khulani's bear form isolated and alone. It was a bloody mass of matted fur stumbling from fatigue as it twisted and turned to disengage Dead-Walkers stubbornly clinging to its back and hindquarters. Qel, separated from them by a few feet, might as well have been miles away. The tall Atlantean managed to keep the creatures at bay with fans of flame, but several of the stalls behind him were alight with fire that would soon reach the roof, and he had no more room to give to keep the Dead-Walkers from overwhelming him.

"Reskalin!" Qel shouted urgently. He desperately pointed toward the opening.

She glanced out between sword strokes, seeing the windswept rain in the dark night, nothing more. A flash of lightning instantly turned night to day and she looked out again. Heads bobbing in slow formation. Two, three dozen of them. Her heart sank, and for a moment she despaired for her tiny unborn twins riding safe in the protection of her womb. They would die today with their mother. The thought drove a mad rage through Reskalin that found quick outlet in the stokes of her sword. It was fury that dispelled the weariness in her limbs and lent reckless energy to her cause. She swore that when they found her body there would be a pile of death around her of a likeness never seen before. Ballads would be sung to honor her, poets would praise her spirit in verse, and in taverns where her tale was told, mugs would be raised in her memory.

A woman's sharp cry called out from the rain in a foreboding chant:

"Rise and away, my shadows of night!
In darkest hours we render bitter bite!
For in Ys are we true Reavers of Death,
Anon steel and fire fiends starved of breath!"

Siione.

Reskalin couldn't believe her ears. Her sister had come! Joy replaced rage as she staved off a Dead-Walker and removed the head of another. Reskalin's curved blade flashed in the light dealing a butchery of slaughter and carnage with every stroke fighting by savage instinct alone. She never expected Siione would relent after the way they parted earlier in the day. Reskalin went seeking aid, but Siione rebuffed her plea, chastised her for endangering herself and her friends to rescue a man she barely knew. And a Temple Knight at that! Even Siione knew something of the dangers within the abode of the Agrabuta and had declared it off-limits to every thief, scoundrel, and rogue in Ys weeks ago. Siione would hear none of it, and even turned her back in a semblance of finality. Infuriated, Reskalin cursed Siione with vulgar words as she departed, expecting never to see her sister again. Yet, there she was, long raven hair wet against her face leading three dozen of the most feared, brutal, savage, uncompromising, cream of the thieves guild in Ys, to their rescue. They called themselves, 'The Reavers.'

On silent feet the Reavers charged like ghosts, disappearing into shadows, reappearing in the light. They did not flinch at the sight of their foe, to these lowest of the low dancing with death was a familiar, comforting shroud they eagerly rejoined. The Dead-Walkers showed no fear even as they turned to face their destruction. Even as the blades carried by the shadows erupted with flames. Even as those shadows leapt high and fell among them like the reavers of death they promised to be.

Only yards away, Reskalin's eyes locked with Siione's, and in them she found acknowledgement and forgiveness. Her sister shouted above the fray, "Go! Your business is in the Agrabuta. I claim this fight as mine!"

Reskalin needed no further inspiration, and so quickly called to Qel and Khulani to disengage with haste. Siione's reavers drew off the Dead-Walkers encircling Qel relieving him to join Enguer and Aelrindel, but Khulani needed no such assistance as the giant bear abruptly vanished and out from the knot of clutching claws and gnashing teeth shot a Goshawk at speed that would rival a bolt from a crossbow. It swept in low to avoid the smoke roiling across the ceiling, and fanned its wings wide as it prepared to land, but in that instant another transformation occurred and Khulani stumbled the last few feet to join his comrades.

"Siione has claimed the fight so we can go on," Reskalin shouted above the din of battle, crackling of fire, snapping of timber, cries of pain, falling rain, raging winds, and thunder that shook the ground, "Are any of you too injured to run?"

They all shook their heads. Nothing else needed saying in that moment so they ran. Out of the burning stable, where the living died and the dead did not rise, and into the rain. It was a shock at first, cold as it was, but it was equally refreshing as it cooled Reskalin's body washing away the stain of blood. She led them straight toward the vague outline of the Agrabuta, passing a scene of grotesque carnage along the way of unrecognizable remains, until Reskalin spotted a long tuft of black hair that had been ripped from a horse's tail. She was saddened by the sight, but kept on running.

When they arrived at the Agrabuta, Reskalin was closest to a dark shuttered window on her left and a servant's door on her right. Keeping with the plan, she set to work searching for a way to unlock or unhinge the shutters from the outside. Only a few seconds passed when Enguer tapped her on the shoulder and pointed further down the wall. Annoyed at the interruption, with the wind whipping at her hair, her gaze followed to where he was pointing. There was Aelrindel, holding the latch on the servant's door so that it stood open only an inch or two spilling lambent light through the narrow crack. The elf looked at her and shrugged, opened the door wider and went in. The others were fast to follow to get out of the rain. With a heavy sigh, Reskalin joined them at last.

Inside, Reskalin peered around the small unadorned room. There were pegs on the wall to hang wet cloaks and cubbies on the floor where servants could doff their muddy boots before entering the manor proper through a door on the opposite wall. Closing the heavy oak door behind her muted a good majority the noise from the storm allowing her to speak quietly rather than shout, "As we *planned*," she stressed the last word, "Enguer and I will lead, based on the floorplan Qel drew this morning; However," she fixed Qel with her gaze, "if we err in direction or you remember something new, make sure you speak up."

"Of course," Qel replied.

"Any questions?" Reskalin looked around at the weary faces and wondered if she would be looking for Siione and her Reavers to bash in the doors and windows of the Agrabuta to save them a second time tonight.

"As a reminder," Khulani stepped forward. "I can provide a temporary respite from weariness that will restore all our strength and vitality. This may be a good time for such a blessing."

"Thank you, Khulani," Reskalin smiled with appreciation, "I must be very tired since that slipped my mind. Please proceed. There is no better time as we are all in desperate need of it."

Khulani strode to a spot in the small room where he could face everyone. He closed his eyes and lifted his hands in the air while he quietly muttered a few words. A shimmering light appeared in the space between his hands that rose like the sun on a new dawn. It quickly grew bright, radiating warmth over them like a summer day, and in those few seconds Reskalin could feel the weariness in her bones drain away. When the light winked out, it was as if she awakened from a good night's rest, fully energized and eager to face the day ahead. Glancing around, it was obvious they all felt the same.

"Let's do this," Enguer brushed wet hair away from her face and smiled encouragingly.

Reskalin returned his smile and squeezed his hand before looking at the others. They all appeared ready for whatever might come next. With great care, she slowly pressed the latch and pushed the door open.

– – –

"I would like to leave this place once the storm has passed," Naamah was saying as she idly twisted Perault's blond locks around her fingers.

It was after midnight, and the frequent shudder of thunder and howl of turbulent winds rushing with ferocious intensity could be plainly heard even through the thick grey stone walls of the Agrabuta that had stood stalwart against the fiercest elements for hundreds of years.

Perault studied her face, gazing up from her lap where his head lay, and mused how beautiful she was from every angle. "Leave the Agrabuta? Would the Count allow it?"

She looked down at him and laughed, "I am not his creature, like the others. I may come and go as I please."

"What do you mean, 'like the others'," he thought it an odd statement for her to make.

"Count Zracul, and his brothers, sisters, and even Princess Ahes, call themselves Vampyr, altered or transformed from the blood of Count Zracul himself," she began.

"Princess Ahes of Ys?" Perault started up, but she pressed him firmly back down in her lap.

"You are no longer a Knight of the Temple to go running about saving Princesses," Naamah scolded. "You are *my* knight now, and mine alone, remember? Just as I am yours."

"Just as I am yours," he repeated.

"In any case," she continued, "it's his blood that gives over control to compel their behavior to his whims. And they must drain the blood of others to survive, just like his wicked sisters that nearly drained the life from you! It gives them powers as well, like exceptional strength and speed, enhanced senses of perception, and immortality. Zracul offered his blood to me once, but I declined finding little benefit to my kind in trade for a tedious existence."

"So, if I were a Vampyr," Perault reasoned, "I too would be immortal, just like you, and we could be together forever."

Naamah's eyes darkened sadly. "You would become a monster just like them. No, I would rather have the limited time of your mortal life as you are, than immortality with a monster at the beck and call of a master."

"Am I not at your beck and call?" he countered.

She smiled and lifted one eyebrow, "Very clever, my dear. But you already know the difference. When *I* call, you can only guess at the pleasures I have in store for you."

"Then I think I shall remain close to you at all times," he brought her hand to his lips and kissed it. "So, where shall we go?"

"Away from here," she gestured with a wave. "Perhaps south to Tarre, or further to the mysterious lands of Ta Mehu and Ta Shemau. We shall wander for a while, travel to distant parts of Plethwih, and live and love lavishly as we go. And then we shall settle somewhere quiet when you are old to live out your remaining years in peace, until I must greave your passing, and spend the next few centuries wondering about our time together, as I collect generations of cats as my only companions."

Perault nearly rolled of the divan laughing, "You have it all worked out!"

"Not really," she laughed with him. "But I'm sure it will go something like that!"

Naamah shifted her slight frame to sit on top of him, lifted her gown over her head, and tossed it on the floor. Delicate links of thin silver chains crisscrossed her naked form connecting to various piercings through her intimacies enlivening fierce desires within him. Presently, his own clothes crowded the floor with her gown and she adjusted to straddle him with her thighs tight over his hips. Their energetic passions culminated in such an ardent pinnacle of paroxysm that she lost control over the guise of her form. Perault was not alarmed. He knew that her arousal was at its height when this happened and this knowledge served to provoke a renewed awakening of his own desires that drove them both toward an escalating, frenzied climax. And at the apex of their passions, with horns visible on her forehead, tail thrashing wildly, and wings stretched to their limits quaking with final ecstasy, the door to the chamber burst open with a sharp cracking boom like thunder.

– – –

Enguer crept side-by-side with Reskalin down a dimly lit high-ceilinged corridor sheathed in wood paneling. The thickly carpeted runner on the floor allowed for a silent stride that was almost effortless. Aelrindel padded close behind with Khulani and Qel bringing up the rear.

So far, they had discovered a small library, and an immaculately clean kitchen with a well-stocked pantry containing mostly dry goods. They had not encountered a single servant thus far, but that wasn't surprising since it was already well after midnight. The route they followed would take them to the corridor outside the room where Qel last saw Havacian. However, that room was not their destination. Earlier that day, when the group was deep in planning for this undertaking, Qel surmised that going in the opposite direction down that corridor should bring them to the general vicinity of the chamber that held Perault. This information was based on Havacian's 'visions,' but it was all they had to go by, and so agreed it was a good a place as any to start.

The corridor ended at an oak door carved with beveled edges and horizontal furrows forming three equal-sized panels with an untarnished brass door latch gleaming in the lamplight. Enguer tested the latch, and finding it unlocked, pulled the door open a scant inch to peek through unobtrusively. A single lamp illuminated the corridor beyond with enough light for him to recognize it as one used primarily for service as it lacked the opulence of the hall where they stood. He strained to listen for any sound that might give away the presence of anyone nearby. There was none. All the while his fingers moved in the rapid shorthand of the guild cant relaying everything he observed to Reskalin. Convinced the hallway was empty, he pushed the door further and let his gaze follow the cold grey stone walls left and right, each ending at a plain wooden door several yards away. Qel said going left would take them through a door to another corridor that ran past the room where he last saw Havacian and then eventually into the receiving room near the front door of the Agrabuta. If that were true, then their course lay to the right.

Enguer entered the corridor and waved for the group to follow. As he skulked toward the door at the end of the hallway on the right, Aelrindel shuffled to the door in the opposite direction to ensure they were not surprised by anyone walking through inopportunely.

"I hear laughter beyond the door, but not close by," Enguer whispered loud enough for them all to hear. "Maybe in a connecting room or hallway." He checked the door and found it unlocked.

The elf sprinted back to the group on silent feet and crowded behind Enguer with the rest of them in case he called for them to charge in. Again, Enguer slowly opened the door and discovered a similar hallway to the one they were in, except instead of ending at another door, it ran about thirty feet then turned sharply to the left. An unadorned oak doorway stood on the left side about midway down the corridor where muffled laughter filtered through indicating someone in residence.

Using basic hand signals that they were all instructed on earlier in the day, Enguer directed Reskalin to keep watch where the corridor slanted left, and motioned for Aelrindel to join him in front of the door, while Qel and Khulani took positions behind them. With slow deliberate movements, he unstrapped the bow from his back and with simple gestures outlined his plan for entry. Aelrindel follow suit, and when they were both ready with bows in hand, arrows notched, he mouthed a silent three count and forcefully kicked in the door.

A grand bedchamber of substantial proportion decorated in lavish feminine excess that the wealthiest noble woman of Ys would envy, opened before them. There was a sumptuousness quality of indulgence reflected in everything from tapestries depicting shocking intimacies, to lewd sculptures and paintings, devices on the walls, straps attached to the enormous bed, and strangely customized furniture that only the most lascivious of minds could have imagined. All of it among a sea of pillows, candles, and wine glasses teetering on small tables.

In the center of this hoard of salacious extravagance was a cushy divan where a starkly pale nude woman with long blonde hair falling about her face panted expressively atop an unseen man laying beneath her as implied by his limp well-muscled forearm thrown over the back of the couch. Her posture was tense, with arms rigidly pressing or griping her companion. Startled by the sound of Enguer kicking the door open, she jerked her head in his direction, immediately recognized the threat of the situation, and screeched like an enraged demon. And demon she might have been with devilish horns curling above her forehead, a long lashing tail thrashing wildly with agitation, and leathery bat-like wings flung wide in the semblance of a nightmare of doom straight out of the Infernal Planes.

Naamah jerked her head toward the sound and shrieked with rage. Suddenly, a crimson bloom appeared on her chest surrounding the fletching of an arrow, and then another. Blood erupted from her mouth falling over Perault like a crimson rain. Her eyes sought his own. They were filled with sorrow and regret, and then nothing as she pitched forward on top of him convulsing once, twice, then still.

Perault began to shake uncontrollably, his hands barely managed to lift her head from his chest only to find the vacant stare of his lover. His voice quavered with shock and disbelief calling again and again, "Naamah? Naamah?" There came no response.

Then faces appeared over the back of the divan. One was tanned, one blue, and one black. Had he gone mad? No, they looked familiar.

"Sir Perault!" exclaimed the black one. "Are you okay?"

"He's in shock," the blue face spoke in a calm measured tone.

"Let's roll that thing off him and get him up in case he's injured," said the man with the weathered face.

All three started around the divan.

Realization of what just happened set in like a hammer. Perault bolted up clutching Naamah's limp carcass unwilling to relinquish any part of her. "No!" he shouted, "Why have you done this!"

They all stopped, and the black one, Perault remembered his name now, Khulani, knelt next to him and said in a gentle compassionate voice, "The devil is gone now. She no longer controls you, my friend. You can let her go. You are safe."

"You have taken everything from me," Perault kissed the top of Naamah's head. The scent of lilac and the brush of her soft hair against his lips made his heart ache to the point of erupting out of his chest. "She was no devil. Not to me." he wailed.

The tanned one, Enguer, and the blue one, Qel the Atlantean, Perault recalled, traded glances. Then Enguer bent toward him with a hand extended. "Sir Perault, let us take you away from here. Take my hand. Leave the monster behind."

A voice hissed urgently from the doorway, "Hurry up! Someone is coming!"

Enguer attempted to slowly pull Naamah's body away. Anger built hotly inside Perault. He slapped the Ranger's hands away shouting, "Don't touch her! She is no monster!" With great care, he gently slid from under her and lay her head lightly on the divan, taking a moment to brush the hair from her beautiful face. Then he stood facing her murderers baring his nakedness before them.

"You see this?" Perault seethed, indicating the blue shimmering tattoos that covered his entire torso. "This mark was our bond. She loved me! She took me as her mate!"

"Sir Perault, please listen," Qel tried to sooth him. "She only made you think . . ."

"No!" Perault howled. "She was not a monster! See?" he slapped the markings on his chest. "And yet by killing her you have made me the monster!"

Whirling on his heels, Perault leapt over the divan and shot through the door roughly pushing aside an elf with white hair standing in his way. He heard them calling his name as he sprinted down the hall, through a door, and dashed down a long corridor crashing heedless through two doors after. He didn't know where he was going, all he knew was that he had to get out. The front door loomed ahead and without slowing he barreled through it into the arms of the maelstrom churning with elemental savagery and mind-numbing chaos.

Chapter 18 - Locusts

Khulani was shocked at Sir Perault's vehement reaction to his liberation from the fiend that was Naamah. He could only conclude that the temptress must have dominated his mind through insidious seduction and torture or some other deviltry unknown to him. The druids had ways of controlling animals to carry out certain tasks or impress a bond that compelled companionship for a time. Perhaps this was something similar. The arcane symbols tattooed on Sir Perault's chest would suggest just such a bond ritual.

"Perault! Wait!" Enguer raced in pursuit when Sir Perault bounded from Naamah's chamber. Out the door the knight had run on swift bare feet, his thickly muscled figure unfettered by the hinderance of garments of any kind, thrusting the elf aside like a ragdoll and disappearing through the door at the end of the hallway.

Khulani sprang forward like a panther a step behind Enguer. They would have continued to pursue Perault, but Reskalin brought them up short with a shout. "It was the doorman!" She exclaimed. "He was coming this way when he heard the racket and hobbled through a side door before I could get a dagger in him. If no alarm was raised before, I'm sure he will do so now!"

"It's time for us to leave," Enguer beckoned for her to follow. "We found Perault, so our work here is done."

Khulani wasn't so sure. It was very strange the way Sir Perault was acting, but he had to agree that they accomplished what they had set out to do. "I believe Sir Perault is heading for the front door to this place. We should follow and try to find him if we can."

"Agreed," chimed in Aelrindel, re-adjusting the leather pauldrons on his shoulders after the rough handling he received on the knight's exit.

Enguer looked back toward the bedchamber and called out, "Reskalin! What are you doing? We must go now!"

From inside the room Reskalin replied, "One second, it's time for the Agrabuta to join the ash pit of history!"

The sounds of metal clanging on the floor and tearing fabric was a curiosity none of them could resist. Khulani strode with the others to the door and stared as Reskalin put the final touches on her plan to burn down the Agrabuta starting with this room. There was a wide grin on her face when she strode out of the bedchamber. The flicker of light accompanied by the crackle of delicate combustibles she left in her wake would soon become a raging inferno.

"What are you waiting for?" Reskalin asked with her usual flippant manner. "Let's go!"

The group quickly resumed their order and ran down the passages that led toward the front door with little regard for the noise they made or who might hear it, such was their haste. All that mattered was getting out of the Agrabuta, finding Sir Perault if they could, and shelter from the storm raging outside.

Turning down a long corridor illuminated by a lantern on both ends, Khulani detected a sudden chill in the air that he sensed more than felt. Evil had found them, and it meant to exact a price with their blood. "Stop!" he cried out.

His comrades skidded to a halt. Reskalin spun around, her quick eyes seemed to look in every direction at once anticipating an attack. "What is it Khulani?" her voice wavered with nervous energy.

"Something is here," Khulani warned. "Waiting for us."

Enguer and Aelrindel pulled the bows off their backs. Qel moved closer to Khulani. He was gripping the crimson stone that hung from his neck with one hand while casting his gaze down the far end of the hallway. The Atlantean suddenly tensed and pointed in the same direction, "I see him."

"What do you see?" Aelrindel demanded.

"I believe he is one of Count Zracul's brothers, but I don't know which." Qel's eyes glittered with arcane red light that was unsettling to behold. Khulani was fascinated by the enchantment as much as he was fearful of what it revealed to the Atlantean.

Hands clapped applause from the shadows of the corridor behind them. "Very good, my blue friend!" The provocative adulation was delivered in a smoothly sibilant tone. "I admire your shadow sight, although I am equally dismayed that we have not been formally introduced!"

A lean man of medium height and a pallid complexion appeared to materialize out of the shadows. His jet hair was parted to the side and short in the back with strands falling over his forehead. He wore all-black attire consisting of tailored breeches tucked into low boots, silk tunic laced with silver at the collars, and a wide belt around his waist holding a long poniard with a silvered pommel. His unwavering black eyes seemed to take in every detail as they passed over the group, before settling again on the Atlantean. "My name is Fain, second Prince of Vradesti and brother to the Primogeniture, Zracul, who has of late taken the honorific of 'Count' in deference to our new sister, Princess Ahes."

"And I," a voice called out in a rich baritone resonating from the opposite end of the hallway, "am called, Vadim, Third Prince of Vradesti, the youngest brother of three." This man bore an impressive physique much larger than the first as he, too, apparated from the shadows. Similar in complexion and wardrobe as his brother, Vadim's jet hair was long, pulled tight over his forehead and tied in the back, while his intense soulless eyes weighed and measured each of them in turn with obvious contempt.

At Reskalin's silent prompting Khulani took position between Qel and Aelrindel in the defensive ring they formed at the center of the hallway. The air was tense with anticipation, although he knew not what to expect from the two brothers. He could sense evil radiating from them like a rank stench under the façade of gentile manners and brusque disregard. Of one thing he was certain, they were not here to trade pleasantries.

"Are you in a rush to find someone?" Fain addressed his question to the Atlantean. "Your friend, I believe his name was Havacian? He departed some time ago, but you know that already, don't you? Perhaps you're looking for some *thing*? You seem to be in a very big hurry. Why is that?"

Qel appeared discomfited for a moment before he responded to Fain. Khulani could see in the Atlantean's face that he knew he'd been caught in a lie and wondered why he told them Havacian was dead when he surely knew he was not. Khulani also surmised that Qel did not expect his friend to be here now, so he also must have known of Havacian's imminent departure. It was plain on the faces of his comrades that they had also come to the same conclusions.

"We were here to find Sir Perault," Qel admitted. "We found him with the creature called Naamah, and killed her. But his mind was in turmoil, and in his madness, ran off in this direction. We have pursued him, anticipating that his intent was to escape the Agrabuta."

"A clever story, my friend," Fain's features were painted with skepticism. "When all you had to do was knock on the front door and ask for him as most are wont to do in polite society. Instead, you and your friends invade our home armed to the teeth. Which makes me conclude that you are, indeed, here for something else. Like a certain sphere, maybe? Did you discover the real power of the orb and think to take it back?"

Fain thought he was cunning, Khulani reasoned, but his surprising declaration was bewildering. What powers might the orb have that they would risk invading the Agrabuta to recover it after so willingly giving it over the day before?

Qel showed no surprise. "Is that why Zracul gave his blood to Havacian? Did he think an elemental wizard trained at the Imperial Wizards Enclave of Atlantis would help him unlock the sphere's true secrets?"

Fain's widening eyes betrayed his surprise. He looked beyond them toward the brooding figure of Vadim and exclaimed, "You see brother? Zracul fails to inform us of important facts! He should have allowed us to leverage the Atlantean's arcane intellect. Imagine how much more devastating the storm might have grown, and in much shorter time!"

"How fortunate to have another Atlantean so soon at hand to correct our good brother's oversight," came Vadim's humorless reply.

"Yes, brother," Fain smiled. "It is."

"Now!" Reskalin hissed.

Simultaneous shafts whistled in opposite directions impacting the walls behind Vadim and Fain. The brothers had vanished instantly, but Khulani still sensed their presence in the room. "They are here," he whispered.

There was a sudden rush of air over their heads. Reskalin shrieked with rage as blood rose from lines on her face like the rake of taloned claws. Subtle laughter followed. Eyes still glittering like the red crystal hanging from his neck, Qel thrust his hand outward sending a stream of fire into the darkened corner above the far door. The explosion of flames illuminated Vadim for an instant before he leapt away bellowing a deep throated screech of pain. Another rush of air brought a cry from Aelrindel who, anticipating the attack, turned in the last second taking the blow intended for his neck which instead ripped across his arm spraying blood over the black chainmail shirt he wore.

Arrows flew with great speed and accuracy, but could never find their mark. Reskalin's whirling blades slashed through air, and Qel's initial success with fire failed the second time as Vadim and Fain shifted tactics by constantly moving from one place to another with speed that not even the Atlantean's ensorcelled vision could follow. In the meantime, rending claws indiscriminately slashed through the companions clothing and exposed flesh drawing blood with every pass.

Khulani hastily brought forth ash from a small pouch on his belt and scrawled a druidic symbol representing the sacred oak tree on the back of one hand. Uttering a word of power, the symbol flared briefly with a greenish hue radiating dark textures of furrows and grooves that instantly altered the appearance of his skin to the likeness of bark from a great oak. It was not stiff or rigid as the bark on a tree, but it provided the protective qualities to resist the deep injurious gashes the brothers were so effortlessly inflicting on the others.

"Give yourselves to us!" Fain's words swarmed around them. "Become one of us! Live the immortal life of a Vampyr! All Plethwih will soon be ours to rule! Your resistance will come to naught!"

"Tighten up!" Reskalin cried out, so the group moved close together, back-to-back with steel raise like the spines on a porcupine.

Qel, having no blade of effective use under the circumstances, called forth a ring of arcane fire to encircle them all. The fire was a useful defense at ground level, but did little to protect them from attacks from above and would eventually cause the hallway to become a sweltering oven if kept up for long. Yet, for the moment, the ring of fire provided some small relief to the group who were all bleeding from multiple injuries requiring attention.

Khulani recognized their dire state. So, spreading his hands wide, he evoked the name of the Sun Goddess, Sunna, *"Isin Sunna, aswe tifawt, amz s-saht!"* A warm wave of illumination flowed from his arms over his companions washing away their injuries, reinvigorating their spirits in the Holy Light.

"Once again," Aelrindel cheered, "Khulani has rescued us from the brink!"

"Just so!" Reskalin agreed, whilst keeping up her vigilance. "Can you do anything about the heat?"

Khulani shrugged. He had nothing to remedy that. They were all sweating profusely. It wouldn't be long before the heat became unbearable.

Qel shot a glance back to Reskalin, "When you say the word, I will banish the fire."

Laughter echoed from around the room. Vadim and Fain clearly recognized the companions predicament as well. Khulani knew that once Qel relinquished the fire ring they would be right back where they started. Their options were few, and he realized their predicament would quickly turn fatal once the brothers tired of toying with them.

"It is too late to save Ys!" Fain continued to taunt. "Zracul sent Princess Ahes to take the king's key. The key that activates the enchantment on the Sea Gate that locks out the storm surge. Yes, the daughter of King Gradlon is one of us now! Do you think she will fail?" The laughter rose to maniacal levels. "How ironic it must be!" Fain continued. "That you will burn while the rest of Ys drowns! Think of them as you die, friends, for even now our brother calls forth a great deluge from the Primal Sea!"

A thought came to Khulani. It was a desperate thought, one he had little confidence would work. Even so, he could think of no better idea to offer. "Keep the fire up until the very last second," he whispered to Reskalin. "I'm going to try something, but it might take a moment or two. If it works, call for Qel to drop the flames and run with all haste to the door. You must stop Count Zracul before he can destroy Ys!"

"What are you going to do?" Reskalin demanded.

"No time to explain. Just trust it will work, and keep up the fire as long as can be tolerated."

Reskalin clasped him on the shoulder and nodded. There was hope in her eyes, and something else . . .

Khulani closed his eyes and calmed his mind, searching deep within his memories, back to a time when he was a neophyte at the Druid's Enclave in Nabta. His mentor, Elder Munatas, had taken he and a few other neophytes on a training mission to the TaShemau city of Nekhen where he met Master Ycae, an Atlantean sorceress, for the first time. They were there to destroy a terrible monster terrorizing the city at night, summoned by a dark cult of priests dedicated to Apep.

After the mission in Nekhen, Master Ycae returned to the Enclave with the druids and stayed for a time. Khulani learned many things from her about how Atlanteans and humans harnessed arcane power from the Orichalcum Crystals in contrast to the way druids converted energies from nature to power evocations and enchantments. She was clear that there were no crossovers between the systems arcane and there was never an instance where one could be conjoined with the other. Except that there was.

The last time he saw Master Ycae, Khulani was preparing to go to Nabta City where he would spend the next few years honing his skills as a healer. She came to his room and they sat on his cot speaking for a while about the wonders and beauty of the City of Atlantis. It was a place Khulani longed to see with his own eyes one day. Just before saying goodbye, Master Ycae pressed a small object into his hand. It was a tiny golden locust.

"This is an artifact from the earliest days when TaShemau and TaMehu were one," he recalled her words as if she had just spoken them. "The dark magics of this ancient time are an enigma to us. I place in your care an inexplicable paradigm of an age when the magic derived from all sources; nature, faith, orichalcum, and others, were one. I deliver the relic to you because fate demands it. A day will come when the destiny of Plethwih rests in your hands, though you may not know it at the time, and you will remember the relic."

She said nothing more. Khulani placed the effigy in a special pouch he always carried with other items dear to him and thought nothing more about it until this moment.

As his attention returned to the present, he realized the hallway was sweltering with heat. Sweat poured over Reskalin's red face with desperate eyes following his every move. Her stare was intense as she resolutely held back the command to terminate the ring of fire. Khulani reached into his pouch of keepsakes, his fingers searching for the tiny object. Once found, he pulled it out, realizing he had no idea how to use it. The gold shined bright, untarnished on the small figure, and it was perfectly smooth with no angles or edges. The only resemblance to a locust were the lines engraved on the outside of the object symbolizing the insect more so than appearing as one. It had been so long since he handled the item that Khulani forgot how small and smooth it was. And with his hands wet with sweat, he had to take care not to drop it as slick as it became on contact with the moisture.

Khulani abruptly understood what he must do. He locked eyes with Reskalin and gave a nod. The relief on her face spoke volumes, and even as she called for Qel to banish the ring of fire surrounding them, Khulani popped the golden locust in his mouth, and swallowed it.

Sweat streamed in thick rivulets down Qel's elongated skull drenching his lengthy sable hair before cascading over the angular features of his blue-tinted face. The red robes he wore felt sticky against his skin, itching from the sweltering heat and humidity trapped within the layers.

The ring of fire he invoked to protect he and his companions was not ideal for an enclosed environment like the hallway where they huddled. Although the heat was projected away from them, it still warmed the air like any natural fire, and with no way for the heat to escape, the hallway quickly became an oven. It was not ideal, but it kept the brothers Vampyr at bay for the time being.

Qel would have to terminate the fire soon. Already the intense heat was taking its toll, weakening their resolve, sapping their strength. He waited for Reskalin to give the signal and knew that as soon as she did, Vadim and Fain would be upon them, rending and tearing their flesh as before. Still, in the face of their misery Khulani gave them hope. Qel watched through his large long eyes stinging with perspiration as the druid fumbled in a small pouch attached to his belt. He soon brought out a very small bead, or marble that glinted gold in the firelight. He was further astonished when Khulani placed the gold object in his mouth and swallowed it whole!

"Now, Qel," Reskalin spoke with remarkable calm that was jarring in its simple resignation to whatever happened next.

With the wave on his hand, the ring of fire winked out, although the heat remained, if tolerably diminished.

"Ah ha!" Fain shouted from his perch near the ceiling in the far corner of the corridor. "Surrender at last! It pleases me greatly as I prefer my prey raw rather than cooked. Wouldn't you agree, Vadim?"

From the opposite corner the larger brother replied with impatience, "I weary of the game, Fain. Let us finish them so we can rejoin our brother in the east tower to watch Ys crumble into the sea."

Mock disappointment clouded Fain's features. "You always take everything so seriously brother," he scolded. "We have a little time. You must learn to loosen up! Marinate your prey in their fear a while before supping on their lifeblood. Their terror adds unique flavor!"

Qel sent a stream of fire at the Vampyr followed by arrows readied by Enguer and Aelrindel. Fain's reactions were lightning fast, but the arrows just nicked him in the leg as he sprang away while the fire singed his hair and scorched a line down the back of his fine tailored jacked.

Fain growled in anger more than pain, calling out to his brother, "Enough! It's time to feed."

Qel felt as much as saw from the corner of his eye his companions unconsciously shuffle closer together to make ready for the deadly assault. All except Khulani. He was standing very still and alone. Qel could not see the druid's face clearly from his position and feared turning to look with the Vampyr upon them.

A rush of hot wind announced the brothers swooping in. Aelrindel barely fended off Vadim talons with his duel curved blades raised with perfect timing to deflect the attack. At the same time Enguer dropped with Reskalin to the floor leaving Fain with a handful of her jet locks and Reskalin with a patch of bloody scalp and eyes burning with rage.

The brothers paused at the end of the hallway, then bound toward them again. Khulani was coughing or choaking, Qel wasn't sure.

"Khulani!" Reskalin cried out fearfully

The druid took on a rigid posture, and his mouth opened wide, stretching beyond what should seem possible, as his eyes rolled back displaying only the whites. Qel expected a scream to follow, instead what came out was far more shocking, if only a little less so than the jarring realization that the druid was somehow channeling power from the pair of orichalcum crystals flaring brightly from the thongs around his own neck! It shouldn't be possible! Qel knew the druids drew power from nature and since orichalcum was not of this world, it was useless to them.

All thoughts of druids and orichalcum and anything else were wiped from Qel mind as he watched in horrified fascination an outpouring of locusts erupt from Khulani's distended mouth in an unending torrent of thousands surging down the corridor to meet the onrushing Vampyr.

"Run!" Reskalin shrieked with all her voice above the deafening buzz of the insects.

Qel ran. From behind, he heard the brothers' angry curses as the locust swarmed over them, followed shortly by cries of irritation, then pain. By the time Qel and the others were through the door, closing it firmly behind them, Vadim and Fain were screaming in agony, powerless in the writhing swarm slowly consuming their flesh in torturous tiny chunks bit by bloody bit.

Qel put his back against the other side of the door gasping in the cool air of another dimly lit hallway. Reskalin pressed a cloth against her scalp where Fain had torn a clump of her hair away. Enguer was beside her applying an ointment to small blistery marks on their exposed arms while Aelrindel swatted away one of the few locusts that escaped with them through the doorway.

"What will become of Khulani," the elf wondered aloud as he squished a locust on the floor with the heel of his boot.

Enguer grunted. "We can't go back in there with all the locusts swarming around. They'll chew us up the same as the Vampyr." He raised an arm exhibiting a half-dozen small bite-marks raised with tiny plumes of crimson.

"He knows what he's doing," Reskalin added hotly. "Now we must do as he bid and find that blood-sucking bastard Zracul before he wipes Ys off the map with his orb. If Khulani sacrificed himself for this cause, I will not let it go wasted."

Qel shot his hand up to the orichalcum crystals hanging from his neck. Both his and Havacian's were cool and dim as always. He shuddered at the memory of Khulani drawing from them. Never in his life had he felt so much power channeled at once. And not only from the crystals. He could feel the drawing through them and their connection to their surroundings as their power was *added* in at least equal measure pulled from the stone of the Agrabuta and the earth below it. His heart sank as he realized that no one would have found the enigma more intriguing than Havacian.

"Qel?" Aelrindel called. "Are you coming?"

The elf was waiting a few paces down the hallway with Enguer and Reskalin several strides further on.

"Of course," he replied, jogging forward to catch up.

They hurried down an unembellished hallway of grey stone that Qel thought must run parallel to the front of the Agrabuta. If they had gone the opposite direction, it would have taken them to the foyer where guests were greeted upon entry to the manor house. As close as they were to the external walls, he could hear the muted roar of winds and boom of thunder; the storm raged on.

Moving as quietly as possible along the stone-tiled corridor, Reskalin urgently thrust her hand in the air indicating they must stop and stay quiet. Lanterns placed at long intervals along the way left swaths of dark space between dim circles of light. In one of these dark spaces another corridor intersected the one they were in and the distant tap of footsteps could be heard approaching at a steady pace. Crouching against the wall, they waited. Soon, a soft bobbing glow slowly illuminated the intersection as the steps grew louder. Enguer and Aelrindel knelt on one knee with bows drawn at the ready with Reskalin and Qel stooped a step behind them.

Finally, the lantern appeared in the hand of an elderly man dressed in house livery who strode casually out of the intersecting corridor and turned to his right away from where the group waited. He only took a few strides when he stopped, slowly turning with his lantern thrust high to see better down the hallway. His dark sparkling eyes registered no surprise when he saw them, but rather than turn and run, he opened his mouth wide to shout and instead found himself choaking on the shafts of two arrows penetrating the back of his palate. He sank slowly to the ground letting the lantern fall with a clatter from a hand clutching uselessly at his throat.

"The doorman," Aelrindel noted, setting right the lantern.

Reskalin strode forward saying, "He's the one that was coming down the hallway when we found Perault and must have alerted Vadim and Fain to our presence."

Qel looked down at the old man. His body jerking with subtle twitches as the blood pooled around his head. "He doesn't look like the Dead-Walkers. Do you suppose he's a Vampyr like the others?"

"He appears to have died like any man shot through the face with arrows," Enguer knelt to inspect the old man closer and quipped, "should we tie him up now?" He was referring to their original plan to truss-up any servants they came across rather than kill them.

Reskalin rolled her eyes. "Let's go."

Qel glanced back as they continued down the hall. The old man's staring eyes still glittered ominously in the lanternlight, and he wondered if maybe they should have tied him up after all. Just to be safe.

Chapter 19 – End of a Reign

"That must be the door to the east tower," Reskalin whispered.

Up ahead, the corridor turned sharply to the right, where a heavy oak door stood on the angle. A lantern hung over the doorway emitting a soft ring of light, but aside from the muffled sounds of the storm outside, it was quiet. Approaching the tower door, Reskalin recalled that the east tower appeared quite large, at least from the outside, including three enclosed levels with windows and a fourth at the top encircled by crenelations. Unless there was access to the tower from below, she reasoned that this was the only entry since the corridor continued south another twenty paces or so before it ended at another door.

"Assuming we haven't been deliberately misled, Count Zracul is somewhere in this tower controlling the storm with the sphere," Reskalin spoke in a low timbre. Her voice was steady, but inside, her nerves were on a knife's edge. "We know the fate of his brothers, and Princess Ahes is back at the palace if Fain spoke the truth, leaving only the twin sisters unaccounted. Whether he is alone or not, we must destroy the sphere."

"Perhaps your sister, Siione, could aide us?" Aelrindel suggested.

Reskalin shook her head, "There's no time. And remember, before we found out what Zracul was up to, I set Naamah's chamber on fire."

Enguer barked a low laugh, "Right, so now we are doubly motivated to finish this before we drown in the deluge or burn with the Agrabuta, just as the Vampyr brothers suggested."

Reskalin was turning back to the tower door when Qel placed a hand lightly on her shoulder, "Wait," he said, pulling a small pouch from his robes. He held it up. "Since we can anticipate how these Vampyr fight, I can place a charm on each of you that will enhance our visual spectrum. It will only take a moment." Reskalin nodded uncertainly, glancing briefly at Enguer, who returned a shrug. Aelrindel stood by passively unconcerned.

The two red crystals hanging from Qel's neck glowed softly crimson in the dark corridor as he blew a sparkling dust into each of their faces. Aside from a brief tingling sensation in her eyes lasting for only a second or two, Reskalin felt normal.

"I'm ready," the Atlantean spoke with resolve as he returned the pouch to a pocket in his robes.

"Very well, let's find out what fate holds in store for us." Reskalin slowly opened the tower door.

The rush of warm damp air combined with the loud roar of wind and rain buffeting the tower, frequent cracks of lightning, rumble of thunder, and the constant bellowing boom of waves crashing against the distant seawall surrounding the harbor greeted the group with ill temperament when Reskalin heaved upon the thick oaken door. Inside, the bottom level of the tower's large open interior stood devoid of any furnishings with only the heavy stone stairway spiraling up to the next level. Four firmly shuttered windows clacking wildly against iron braces held steady against the tempest allowing a bare trickle of precipitation to push through the cracks and pool on the floor. It seemed the windows on the second level had not fared so well considering the noise originating from above and the wash of rainwater down the steps dampening the floor around the base of the stairs. Reskalin led them inside, motioning for Qel to shut the door thus closing off the draft-way that pulled the gusts down the stairs whipping their hair and cloaks so fiercely. Still the noise was nearly deafening, and they were forced to stand close to be heard.

"When we find Zracul," Reskalin paused for a loud boom of thunder to recede. "Spread out and keep him and anyone else busy from range while I go for the sphere."

"Take this," Enguer pulled a woodsman's axe from his belt and handed it to her. "Use the back side of the hatchet to shatter the thing if you can."

Reskalin stowed the axe and turned to Qel, "If Zracul jumps around as his brothers did, cast your flames where you *think* he will go next rather than where he is."

Qel returned a sedate nod.

"It will be louder up there. Keep your eyes sharp and use the hand signals," she glanced over the three men, fearful of their fate as much as her own. "Is everyone ready?"

Aelrindel coolly bobbed his head as he tested the string on his bow. The elf appeared calm and serene as if he were preparing to take a walk in a garden rather than face a powerful creature capable of killing them all. Qel, on the other hand, almost seemed distracted. He nodded his readiness then returned to rooting through a wide pocket sewn on the inside of his red robes. Reskalin could not even begin to wonder what went through the mind of a wizard preparing for battle, let alone an Atlantean. Lastly, she looked to Enguer. His intense brown eyes stared back at her. She saw worry and fear. Not for himself, but for her. She drew him aside from the others and placed her hand on his cheek. She wanted to tell him everything would be alright. *She* would be alright, that he needn't worry. It would be a lie. None of them could know what they faced in the tower above.

Enguer's fingers moved in the silent language of guild cant, '*I need your promise – not to any God or Goddess, and not to me, or even yourself.*'

Reskalin hugged him, placing her mouth next to his ear. This moment was too important, and if it was to be their last, she wanted to feel him close, and know the strength of his embrace. "What promise?"

He held her tight. His breath was warm and gentle on her ear, and his reply carried depths of barely restrained emotion. "No matter what happens to me or anyone else, if we fail, you must promise to escape this place. Make this promise to our children."

Reskalin tensed. He was asking her to make a choice between dying with him, potentially saving him, and the lives of children not yet four months inside her. How could she make such a promise!

"Promise," Enguer repeated when she did not answer.

"Enguer, it's . . ." she began.

"Promise, or we leave now, and Ys be damned!" he interrupted.

Reskalin knew well Enguer's determination when he believed in something so strongly, and thus relented, "I promise." She desperately hoped she would not have to keep it, or even if she could.

Enguer held fast, kissing her cheek, neck, and lips before releasing her. She looked deep into his eyes once more, but soon looked away on the brink of bursting into tears. *What was wrong with her?* She chided herself. *When had she turned into such a weepy milkmaid? On the day she met Enguer.* Was her only answer. Reskalin took a deep breath, cleared her head, and renewed her resolve.

"Let's go!" her shout was punctuated by a crack of lightning that shook the floor and raised the hair on her arms. She darted up the stairs with Enguer and the others close behind.

The second floor of the east tower was a cluster of chaos illuminated by frequent flashes of lightning. All four windows were open. The wind swept through, pressing large sheets of paper against the walls, before abruptly shifting to send them flying around the room. Rain entered the chamber freely on the north side leaving the entire floor a sopping ruin of overturned tables and chairs, coverless books, broken tools, and shiny lengths of shiny platinum bars scattered all over.

Reskalin dared to step into the room, looking beyond the clutter, beyond the window in the north wall, and through the rain. From its high perch on a hill on the west side of Ys, the Agrabuta looked over the streets of Ys, if not the towers, as far as the harbor. Ys was dark. Darker than she had ever seen any city or town. Not a single light played from tower window or street lamp. In the harbor, hundreds of ships bobbed unsteady at their moorings. A few had broken free jamming their great bulks into nearby vessels with every swell. Tall sprays plumed high above the seawall with each crashing wave, the white stone reflected the scant luminosity in the thin breaks between swirling clouds which extended like the arms of a kraken far out into the Primal Sea where . . . she paused to stare.

"Enguer," Reskalin pointed out to sea. "See the darker line of the horizon against the sky? Does it appear to have a slight . . .wavering?"

Enguer stared hard, wiping away the rain driven by the wind into the room, and shook his head uncertainly. Aelrindel looked out as well, but could offer no explanation.

"It's not the horizon," Qel's shaky voice sounded ominous between the eerie, high-pitched howling gusts battering the room. "It's a wall of water."

A chill rushed down Reskalin's spine. They were out of time. "We have to hurry!" she cried out, running for the stairway.

She started up the stairs to the third floor. As the steps twisted around, a dull blue light shown from the room above, and the deep tenor of a man singing at the top of his voice wafted over the wall of noise generated by the maelstrom as she climbed onward.

Lonely shepherd dost not bewail,
When the ewe lamb thus spoke true,
Wenst ye come down to yonder vale,
Jealous murder shall quick find you.
Sayeth the shepherd to the ewe,
Tell the ones that craft my doom,
Bury me near a sheepfold ado,
And place mine pipes upon the tomb.

There stood the creature, Zracul, standing on a wooden ladder attached to a huge apparatus sitting atop a heavy oak table. The construct was built almost entirely of shining platinum angular rods like the ones discarded on the second floor below. The Sphere sat at the apex of the apparatus, held by it, so it seemed, where it glowed with a dull blue light that cast a ghastly pallor over Zracul's pale complexion. *For when the wind blows in the sere,*
The pipes of beech and bone shall play,
And draw the sheep to gather near,
To mourn mine passing all the day.
Then go and tell mine mother dear,
A fair Princess I have gone to Wed,
So she shall live a life of cheer,
And never know her son is dead!

Despite the open windows and no lessening of the storm, the chamber was less chaotic with wind and rain, and not so loud as the floor below. There was a divan, a small couch, and several plush chairs pushed against the walls around the room as if set there for spectators. With some relief, Reskalin saw none as she stood at the top of the stairway with Enguer, Aelrindel, and Qel crowded behind her. When she stepped further into the chamber along the wall, Zracul's gaze shifted to the stairway as if her subtle movement caught his attention. He smiled, with blue fires burning brightly in his eyes, outwardly pleased at their arrival.

"Welcome!" he announced cheerfully. "Have you come to witness the fall of Ys? There are no better seats to be found!" His eyebrows furrowed menacingly, although his smile remained. "Or have you come to die?"

"I believe the time is nigh for a decision, Your Majesty."

King Gradlon peered through the large thick-paned storm window overlooking the harbor from a high tower in the palace everyone knew as 'Storm Watch.' It was nearly midnight, and all day the weather had grown progressively worse. Thirty-foot waves battered the seawall sending a spray of seafoam high into the air as fierce gusts of wind roared around the tower, and hard pelting driven rain forced everyone to cover. Torch light flickering through the windows of the thickly walled guard towers shown bright on each side of the massive sea gate that had been ordered closed hours earlier, but not yet locked. Even from this distance the king could see the sea gate shudder under the weight of water thrust against it time and time again like a battering ram carried by titans of the Primal Sea. Engaging the lock would trigger enchantments long ago imbued by Atlantean wizards as a gesture of good-will between their peoples to harmlessly redirect energies from assault by storms or enemies into the bedrock of the ocean floor rendering the sea gate all but indestructible. But there was a secret Gradlon and only a few of his most trusted ministers knew: the lock only lasted 24hours before the enchantments subsided and could not be reengaged until another day passed. Thus, the king always waited until the last moment to lock the sea gate, thereby granting Ys the most time possible under the worst conditions. Seeing how quickly the storm was gaining strength, he deliberated how much longer he should wait. Gradlon fingered the heavy key laying cold against his skin under his thick ermine-lined vest. If the waves grew much higher, they would crest the seawall making it near to impossible to traverse from the palace to the north gate where he must go to activate the lock.

"Quite so," murmured the King, but said nothing more as he continued to stare through the rain-streaked glass pane.

Ahes watched unobtrusively from a darkened niche at the back of the room adjacent the stone spiral stairway that led to the ground floor of the palace one-hundred and fifty paces below. She had been there with the others for hours awaiting the king's command to sally forth, but so far, he was resigned to wait and watch. In all that time, Ahes and her father had shared no words. Only a respectful nod her way after the look of surprise faded from his face that she was there at all. She could care less.

Long minutes passed until King Gradlon finally turned away from the window. The set of his chin and the intensity of his eyes as much as told Ahes that he had come to a decision. "Are your men ready, Marshal Dounair?"

"Sir Blusant, and Sir Raucier stand ready with Morvarc'h in the courtyard, Your Majesty." The Marshal replied with a short bow.

"Good men," the King acknowledged. He turned to face the half-dozen gathered ministers. "As per the established protocols of our constitution, Marshal Dounair, as my Second, will stay within the safety of the palace while I sally forth to perform this sacred duty only the King of Ys, ordained by the Gods, is granted in so doing if he is of sound body and mind. So, say you all, 'Yea' or 'Nay'?" Everyone in the chamber answered with 'Yea.' Ahes maintained her silence.

"Very well," King Gradlon nodded his approval. He turned to directly address the Marshal, "Dounair, I leave the Kingdom of Ys, comprising all Lands and Territories of this goodly domain in your care until I return."

"So shall I guard and protect this realm with blood and body," Marshal Dounair replied in stately fashion.

Formalities complete, the King pulled on his long leather riding gloves while two servants brought forth his heavy rain cloak and fastened it about his shoulders. When all was ready, he strode with purpose through his parted ministers toward the stairway.

Ahes was already in motion, dashing down the winding steps to the covered breezeway where the two assigned knights waited with the horses. They only saw her when she casually exited the stairway where she turned to await her father. The pounding rain punctuated by the blinding flash of lightning and rolling rumble of thunder was loud in her ears, while the wind whipped her blonde tresses about her face forcing her to pull up the cowl of the oiled cloak she wore over her leather girded riding dress and knee-high boots. Presently, the King arrived at the base of the stairway, stopping short when he came face-to-face with his daughter.

"Is there a matter?" he demanded, fairly shouting with the noise of the storm.

"Yes!" Ahes cried, tightly holding the edge of her cowl to keep it from falling back from the wind gusting under the breezeway. "I'm going with you!"

Her father shook his head, and moved to push by her, "It's too dangerous!" he growled angrily.

With her new strength, it was a simple task to take hold of the front of his cloak to stop his progress. He looked at her with eyes wide with surprise. "Let me pass!" he demanded.

"You told me to take my life more seriously! To be responsible! To grow up!" Ahes shouted over the wind. "Well, here I am. All grown up and ready to be the strong, resilient daughter you can be proud of!"

Her father searched her face as if expecting some trick or jest. Finally, his eyes softened a little and a hint of pride worked over his continence. "Very well! You ride with me!"

Ahes released her father's cloak, and he strode forward waving for the knights to mount up as did he when the stableboy ran forward with Morvarc'h, his famed mighty warhorse. Before he could lean down to help the princess mount, she vaulted up behind him with little effort, and with her arms securely around his waist, the king jammed his spurs into the flanks of the powerful jet stallion. The king steered Morvarc'h toward the broad walkway of the crenellated seawall where it connected to the palace followed closely by his brave knights.

Even with her rain cloak, Ahes was soaked in seconds. More so from the waves that nearly crested the seawall than the rain. Enclosed lanterns set apart every few feet at the base of the walkway illuminated their path, but not all remained lit with the deluge of water that found its way through unmended cracks to douse the fragile flames. The wind rushed horizontal from the sea with sharp gusts that might have flung less weighty steeds into the harbor, while wet stone pavers slick with inches of churning water threatened to cause an errant hoof to slip. Yet, these were fine sure-footed horses bred for such environs that needed no coaxing to run at speed over water.

Nearly halfway across the long curving seawall, Ahes decided it was time. She withdrew her arms from around her father's waist. Alarmed, he turned his head and shouted as she slid off the back of his horse, but his words were lost to the wind and her attentions were elsewhere. Before she hit the ground, her hands gripped and snapped one of Morvarc'h's hind legs with speed and precision only a Vampyr could achieve. The warhorse screamed with pain and fell hard on the walkway skidding a fair distance. She vaguely hoped her father broke his neck in the fall. She was nearly trampled by the oncoming knights pounding close behind their king. They lost control of their horses as they tried desperately to avoid her. One of them, Sir Blusant she believed, went over the edge of the sea wall where he would drown peacefully beneath the waves, never realizing the terror and confusion of Sir Raucier's last moments of life when she ripped out his throat leaving him to gurgle out his last breath on the wet stone pavers.

Looking back to where her father's horse lay convulsively kicking with the last of its storied life slipping away, Ahes felt a fleeting pang of regret. Morvarc'h was an extraordinary beast known throughout the Western Kingdoms. A unique horse boasting of hooves once blessed by the famed 'Blind Druid of Eriu,' Mogh Roith, so that it could pass over water no different than land. Never would it gallop the waves again. Next to the dying horse, a shadowy bulk crouched in the gloom. Her father rose to his feet and stalked forward. There was a gash in his forehead above eyes blazing with fury, and his teeth were clenched in a viscous grimace. Ahes took a step forward and waited. Her taloned hands dripped with the blood of the dead knight even as the downpour of rain and spray of crashing waves washed the walkway clean. She showed no emotion. There was none to give. He stopped a handsbreadth away and grabbed her roughly by the shoulders to look deep into her eyes.

"You are not my daughter!" he roared. "What demon now occupies her flesh?"

He knew! An evil smile curled up her lips revealing unnaturally long incisors, her brown eyes grew dark as pitch blacking out the white around them, and she replied, "Aesmadaeva."

Terror filled the king's wide eyes, bulging nearly out of their sockets when her hand thrust through cloak, tunic, skin, sinew, and bone to claim his still beating heart. She pulled the organ from his chest with such speed that he watched its last beat in her hand before his grip relaxed, and he collapsed onto the walkway, his face forever frozen in horror. She reached down and snatched the key that hung around his neck and held it up marveling at the shiny faceted surfaces that had fascinated her when she was a little girl. Mirror-like, the key reflected images at odd angles: portions of the walkway, her father's cloak, a flame from one of the lanterns, the dark outline of Sir Raucier's dead horse, a blur of motion. . .

Ahes was thrust with force through the air. She lost her grip on the key in the violent shock, watching it tumble away from her as she fell. The walkway was suddenly above her drawing further and further distant. She didn't understand what was happening at first until her eyes caught the dwindling shapes of two pale ovals staring down from the top of the seawall. They were identical, with pretty faces that would have rivaled her own exquisite perfection if it wasn't for the perpetual wicked smirks that despoiled their charm. The night, and all it held, disappeared as Ahes plunged beneath the bone crushing waves.

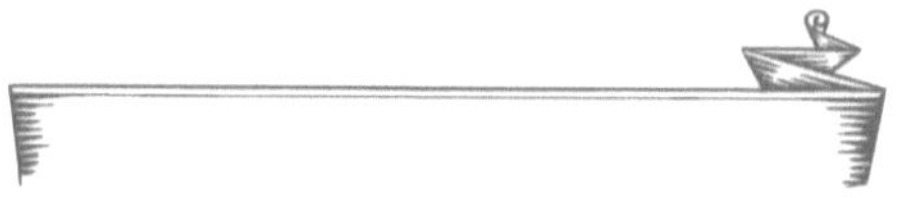

Chapter 20 - Confrontation

"Go, go," Enguer hissed to Qel and Aelrindel as he eased closer to Reskalin.

The elf split left at a run and took up a position behind the divan, even as Qel broke right along the curved tower wall almost directly behind Zracul. Reskalin glided past Aelrindel until the sphere was between her and the count, opposite the Atlantean. Meanwhile, Zracul watched their antics with a cool indifference that was almost unnerving.

"There is nothing you can do to stop what's coming," his tone was calm and dispassionate. "Even if you drove me away somehow, there would not be enough time for you to learn how to control the sphere." He glanced backward at Qel. "Not even you could learn in time, Atlantean. Oh, and by the by, I was sorry to see Havacian go. Although I'm sure you already know I can call him back at any time."

Fire leapt from Qel's extended palms sending forth a ball of roiling magma. It exploded over Zracul's back burning away everything it touched. Simultaneously, two arrows drove deep into the left side of his unarmored chest up to the fletching. The count jumped away as two more arrows impacted the apparatus through the space where he vacated.

Rapidly casting his gaze around the chamber, Enguer discerned a vaguely anthropoidal figure glowing with shifting hues of red within the dark recesses of the high ceiling. The way it moved was consistent with arms, legs, and torso as if he was seeing the heat given off by Zracul's body. An arrow shot straight for it, but the thing moved with blinding speed to another dark location in the rafters long before the projectile could find its mark. It was the elf's arrow, and the accuracy of the shot meant Aelrindel could see the figure as well as he. They had Qel to thank for that.

Two shattered arrow shafts fell clattering on the floor. "You cannot kill me," Zracul called down from above. "Ys is doomed. Do you believe anyone would think you less culpable than I? Who was it that so faithfully delivered the Sphere of Elements into my hands?"

Another magma ball exploded against the rafter where Zracul perched a second before. A loud crack echoed through the chamber from the broken timber. The molten residual caused small ignitions to flare where it clung even as it cooled. "We were deceived!" countered Qel. "How could we know it was this so called 'Sphere of Elements' for which we risked our lives?" The Atlantean seethed with anger. "Havacian lost everything because of your deceit!"

Arrows flew straight and true in a rapid cadence. Many pelted the ceiling, but some found Zracul's flesh as Enguer and Aelrindel anticipated his movements. Enguer glanced at Qel. Fury colored the Atlantean's blue-tinted features darkly red, starkly enhanced by the lurid glow cast by the crimson crystals hanging from his neck This was the first instance Enguer had witnessed anger displayed so openly by Qel who, like all his Atlantean brethren, otherwise projected cool-headed confidence, and control over their emotions.

Cruel laughter, interrupted by a crash of thunder reverberated through the chamber. "You plead ignorance for ignorance's sake!" Zracul cackled. "If anyone in Ys were to survive, would they place less blame upon you because of ignorance? I think not!"

The creature was bounding from place to place to avoid the arrows and molten fire cast his way all the while taunting those below. Enguer got the impression Zracul was enjoying the contest of words with the Atlantean, unconcerned with the arrows he carelessly ripped from his flesh or the numerous small blazes slowly expanding over the rafters all around him.

"Fear not, my friends!" Zracul shouted mirthlessly. "For tomorrow there will be no one left in Ys for you to answer to! Any soul fortunate to survive drowning will discover they were not so lucky after all. Those strong enough will become the slaves of my brothers and sisters who will transform them into an army of unstoppable Vampyr ready to march on my command. And as for the weak? My thorny garden blooms with a horde of living dead eager to consume their flesh!"

A sharp pinging interrupted the Vampyr Lord's verbal sparring, drawing all their attentions to the center of the room. Reskalin was clinging to the side of the platinum apparatus, her boots lodged in the spaces between the glistening rods while holding on with one hand and swinging the hunter's axe with all her might. The sphere flared bright blue with each blow, yet showed not the slightest marring to its smooth luminous surface.

"So, you see!" Zracul chortled. "The sphere cannot be harmed! Look nigh!" He pointed toward the open window facing northward to the sea. "Hither comes the end anon!"

Enguer knew how strong Reskalin was, despite her lean frame, and if she couldn't shatter the sphere with the hand axe, then none of them could. His gaze followed Zracul's gesture toward the north window and realized with a sinking heart that the creature was probably right. There was nothing they could do to save Ys from the onrushing deluge. But there was still a chance to change the final outcome. Zracul would not have his Vampyr army, not as long as Enguer was alive to stop it.

The pinging ceased. Reskalin changed her tactic and began to chop at the platinum rods supporting the orb. The change in pitch from the glass-like pinging to the ringing clang of metal against metal drew the creature's attention. Enguer needed to draw his focus away from Reskalin quickly.

"Your horde of walking-dead have been plucked from the garden," he shouted. "Even now their bodies burn to ash within your stables."

Zracul snapped his head around glaring sharply at Enguer. "That cannot be true!" In a blur he shot through the window, returning a few seconds later, growling like a fierce beast, "I see you brought your own little army. It matters not! They were mere fodder in the wind. I will replace their number one-hundred-fold in due time."

"Sadly for you, not with the help of Naamah," Enguer taunted between bow shots. "She's dead now too."

"No matter!" Zracul bellowed. "She was not like us. She was a tool, nothing more."

The ceiling was fully ablaze backlighting Zracul's silhouette no matter where he paused between quick bursts of speed, yet his agility was impressive, combined with an unnatural ability to cling like a spider to the wall. As it was, Enguer had spent his last arrow. He dropped the bow, drawing his longsword and poniard in anticipation of the creature's rush he was sure would come with the rage incited with his next words.

"Your brothers will be of no use as well," Enguer yelled above the wind, thunder, and Reskalin's clanging. "They too, are dead."

Zracul laughed piteously in reply, "Poor son of a farmer, you know nothing of Vampyr. We are immortal! Drive a dagger through our hearts and we pluck it out! Feather us with your arrows and we cast them down at your feet!" He indicated the splintered shafts and broken fletching scattered on the floor. "Burn our flesh and it will heal before the next day!"

The last of Aelrindel's arrows streaked forth. One caught the creature in the shoulder and the other disappeared in the burning rafters when Zracul fled to a position on the opposite wall almost directly above them. The elf lay his fanciful bow engraved with Sylvan ruins atop the divan and stepped from behind it with duel curved swords drawn.

"Astonishing," it was Enguer's turn to laugh. "How long do you suppose it would take to extract their remains from the frass of a thousand locusts. Is that even possible, I wonder?"

Zracul reacted as if struck. "You lie!"

"Then where are they now?" Enguer pressed. "Do you see our friend Khulani among us? Is it really a stretch to conceive that a druid might harness the simple power to summon insects?"

Enguer barely dropped forward the points of his blades when Zracul almost instantly appeared in front of him with a firm grip around his neck. The creature's face was livid in the shadow of blue light and he seemed unaware that with his arrival he had impaled himself on Enguer's blades. In the periphery of his eye, Enguer saw the elf sprinting to his aid, and Qel's hands weaving an incantation. Neither of them could stop Zracul from snapping his neck. His eyes shifted over the creature's shoulder to where Reskalin was working to free the sphere from the apparatus. She had her back to him, bent entirely upon the task. Enguer was grateful that she would not see him die.

Zracul's grip tightened. The pressure forced a tear from Enguer's eye as he waited for the final violent twist he knew would come. Instead, the grip relaxed, and inches from his face Zracul's lips stretched with a cruel smile.

"Not you," his smile widened to reveal sharp incisors growing long and his brown eyes took on the hollow horror of black voids. "Not yet."

He was gone with the flash of lightning, followed immediately by an angry shout. As Enguer's eyes refocused, a desperate terror replaced relief. Zracul stood next to the apparatus, and in his arms, facing Enguer with her back pressed against the creature's chest, was Reskalin. One taloned hand was at her neck and the other tight around her waist. She struggled to break free, but he held her firm with effortless ease.

"She's a pretty one," Zracul pulled back Reskalin's jet hair and ran his tongue along the curve of her neck even as she kicked and bucked to no avail, "and strong. She will make a fine concubine."

Enguer slowly edged forward. "Don't hurt her. Take me," he implored.

Zracul paid him no heed. "Her heartbeat is strong, and," he paused. The smile widened on his lips once more as his empty eyes settled on Enguer. "I am mistaken," the creature was jubilant. "Three strong heartbeats."

With her arms trapped against her body, Reskalin thrashed desperately gaining nothing for her effort but torment and grief. At the same time Enguer rushed forward unsure what he would do, when Zracul cried "Halt!"

The creature pressed his taloned hand against Reskalin's abdomen forcing a cry of agony from her lips. Enguer stopped only three paces away. "Unless you want to watch me pull the unborn from her belly and feed them to her, I suggest you accept that she is mine now. Her life in trade for Vadim and Fain. It's a good bargain for you as my cost was high."

"Take me instead!" Enguer begged. "I will serve you willingly! My life for hers."

"Enguer, No!" Reskalin shouted. "Do not give this thing the satisfaction. Kill me now!"

Zracul slapped his hand over her mouth and moved swiftly to the closest window. "She will serve very willingly, I assure you." His lecherous laugh was lost in the howling wind bending around the stone tower. Then weirdly, in mid-laugh, he froze as if time abruptly stopped for him alone.

"Take her now!" Qel shouted between gritted teeth, his large almond-shaped eyes fixed resolutely on the creature. Sweat poured down the sides of his face, his body trembled with internal efforts only he could comprehend.

Enguer did not hesitate. He bound forward, tearing Reskalin from Zracul's stiff limbs. Before he backed away, he thrust his poniard through the creature's right eye up to the hilt far into its brain. Aelrindel charged up as Enguer retreated a few paces with Reskalin. The elf leapt into the air holding the scimitar in his right hand in such a way that Enguer judged his intent was to strike Zracul's head from his body.

"Demon . . ." Qel gave out a withering cry, and stumbled forward.

Zracul's features instantly contorted with fury. In a movement too fast for the eye to follow, he backhanded Aelrindel just when the edge of his scimitar was on the verge of cutting through the creature's neck. The blow sent the elf careening into the sphere, dislodging it from the supporting rods atop the apparatus already weakened by Reskalin's labors. It fell with a 'thud' onto the stone floor next to Aelrindel's crumpled form. Enguer's ears popped from a jarring change in pressure when the orb, now murky and devoid of light, fell from the apparatus. The ambient noise from the storm increased tenfold, rain pelted through the windows in horizontal waves, and thunder shook the tower to its foundations. The slow burning oxygen-starved fires in the rafters flared with intensity as unconstrained winds granted them new life that nearly knocked Enguer and Reskalin off their feet.

Zracul wasn't done. He pulled the poniard from his eye socket, tossed it aside, and rushed at Qel. As he had done with Enguer, he grabbed the Atlantean by the neck, and turned toward the window meaning to throw him through it when something from outside hurtled within. There was a bluish blur that knocked Zracul off his feet, and altered the course of Qel's flight out the window to instead crash hard against the wall. Standing above the creature with tattered blue robes billowing wildly stood a tall, lean, blue-skinned Atlantean with wind-swept blond locks glaring with unrestrained hatred.

"Havacian." Dazed from the impact, Qel wobbled to his feet.

"All of you get out!" Havacian shouted. "Now!"

"You," Zracul glowered, "are bound to me."

"I am still the creature made by your blood," Havacian sneered, "but I am not *yours* to command."

Zracul glowered at the Atlantean. "That's not possible. All my creatures are compelled to obey. There is no choice, no cure, no remedy."

Havacian grunted with contempt. "Yet here I stand against you. My alien blood rejects your control no different than one of your kind."

"My kind?" Zracul spat. "I am Vampyr, as you are now."

"You are more than that. More than the man whose body you share now." Havacian's eyes turned black, long fangs parted the sides of his lips. "Demon."

Zracul's black orbs widened with unmistakable surprise. And a glint of understanding. Then rage. "I am the Father of Vampire! My blood will populate an empire destined to rule Plethwih, and worship me as a God! Do you think to stop me?"

As one, the blur of blue robes clashing with black erupted in a chaos of violence within the east tower for which the maelstrom over Ys paled by comparison.

Ivory bones stained a pale crimson articulated the recent affliction of horror that left two skeletal figures reposed in contorted positions against the east wall picked clean of the smallest fleck of tissue. The dried husks of thousands of locusts carpeted the floor except for a tight circle around Khulani revealing a hint of the stone tile below where he lay. The final screams of the Vampyr still echoed in his head as the he struggled to force his exhausted frame to stand upright, coughing from the smoke slowly filling the room through gaps around the door that led back to Naamah's bedchamber. His head swam with a dizzying miasma as if he were waking from a dream, or a nightmare, when the clarity of real and not was still uncertain. Khulani's bleary eyes scanned the hallway. The nightmare was real. He settled his gaze on the stark remains of Vadim and Fain. Their end was long and torturous; a demise the druid would not have wished on so evil a creature as even this malicious duo. It had to be so, to save his friends. To save Ys. To save Plethwih, if they got to Zracul in time.

Khulani felt the cold grip of panic as the memories flooded back. The east tower. The brothers claimed Zracul was controlling the maelstrom with the Sphere of Elements in the east tower. And the Agrabuta was burning. His sandaled feet crunched over piles of withered locusts as he stumbled to the door at the far end of the hallway, exiting into another corridor that ran right and left. Somewhat disoriented, he had a vague recollection of Qel's detailed description of the ways inside the Agrabuta as he knew it. Khulani wished he had paid more attention. The Atlantean had even drawn up a map! He tried to calm himself and think, but succeeded in only conjuring in his mind the vague impression that he should go right. And so, he followed that shadowy corridor with dim lanterns spaced at long intervals until he came to an intersection where he found the body of the elderly doorman lying in a pool of congealing blood next to a broken oil lamp. Khulani recognized the fletching jutting from the corpses mouth; one from Aelrindel and the other Enguer's. Despite the macabre scene, the druid was relieved that he chose the correct course, and continued to the door set in the angled wall that he surmised must be the east tower.

As soon as he pressed the latched and pulled, a rush of air pushed the door violently against the wall flinging Khulani backward several paces. The full force of the maelstrom seemed to occupy the tower. A sustained wind carried rain and bits of paper down the spiral staircase like a howling demon. It whipped his cloak around his body, soaking it at the same time while a cacophony of noise accentuated by the deafening roar of thunder assaulted his ears.

Khulani gathered his resolve and took to the steps keeping flat against the wall so not to get blown over by a sudden gust. On the second floor he found the source of the paper swirling in the wind. At least a dozen badly tattered books were piled against the wall among broken furniture and strange shiny platinum rods. He gave it all little attention, as from above, he could hear the shouts and screams of his companions, and thus galvanized, made hasty work of the steps to the third floor where he witnessed an almost incomprehensible vista of pandemonium.

Sheets of rain rode the wind through shutterless windows and rotated around the room in a swirling vortex encumbered by ash and embers falling from an inferno of flames engulfing timber rafters protected within the high ceiling while superheated stone shrieked and cracked with sharp percussions. Within this diabolic environment two figures, only briefly visible between wild accelerations ending with impacts that shook the walls, were locked in a deadly embrace of wills as much as strength. And among it all, were his companions struggling to survive.

Standing at the top of the stairway, Khulani tried to shout to them, but his voice could not penetrate the terrible wall of noise. There, not far away, Reskalin backed toward the stairs with the gloomy sphere in her arms. Further, Enguer and Aelrindel dragged Qel between them, trying to avoid flying debris and especially the two persons, one attired in black and the other in blue, hurtling from one end of the tower to the other. Khulani stared at the combatants in disbelief. One was surely Zracul. The other . . . Could it be Havacian?

A blazing timber fell from the roof diverting Khulani's attention. It crashed upon an apparatus made from those same odd platinum rods he glimpsed on the second floor. Dozens of the shiny metal pieces scattered across the floor, and as many were picked up by the whirlwind, converting them into deadly projectiles. He had to get his friends out of the Agrabuta before it became their tomb.

Khulani ducked to avoid a broken window shutter flying by and in a few steps reached Reskalin. Even so close his shouts would not reach her ears. He placed his hand on her shoulder, she spun around, dagger in one hand, bracing the sphere with the other. The fierce expression on her face turned to shock and quickly melted into relief. Her lips moved, but he could not hear her above the commotion and resorted to motioning for her to let him take the sphere. She relinquished it without complaint and turned to join Enguer and Aelrindel fast approaching with Qel in tow. They both beamed with smiles when they saw him standing with Reskalin. Before she could step away, Khulani, holding the sphere tightly under one arm, reached out and grabbed her hand. Initially she balked, until Enguer furiously motioned for her to go to the stairwell, and she finally relented.

Still holding her hand firmly in his, Khulani turned back to the stairway. It was only a few steps away. They would be safer there, and hopefully everyone would agree it was time to flee this deathtrap. Reaching the stairs, he pulled Reskalin forward intending for her to go down first. A metallic clattering caught his attention and he looked up just in time to avoid a metal rod skipping along the wall carried by the swirling winds within the tower. He cast a relieved smile at Reskalin when he was suddenly jarred by multiple impacts to his chest and abdomen. He looked down and saw with disbelieving eyes three platinum rods protruding from his torso. Strength left his body, his vision darkened, and he felt the sphere roll out of his arms and clink down the steps. Reskalin tried to grasp him as he fell, but darkness took his consciousness leaving the final impression of her hand holding his in a tight embrace.

Chapter 21 – Agrabuta Burning

Qel was just regaining his wits when he saw Khulani fall. Reskalin, a stricken look upon her face, turned him over and pressed her hands between glistening rods impaled in his chest. She looked back and screamed incomprehensible words they could not hear, but the implication was clear: "*Hurry!*"

Debris was flying dangerously around the walls of the tower, including more of the deadly rods. Enguer and Aelrindel released him as soon as they realized he could walk on his own and they all crouched around Khulani, keeping their heads low. Qel glanced back at Zracul and Havacian. The two had separated. Both looked swollen and battered with terrible rents and gashes that left their clothing in crimson shreds. Zracul splayed his fingers apart conducting blue arcs of lightning against his foe. Havacian reacted by forming a watery barrier from the rainfall that dispersed the electrical charges around him. The hair raised on Qel's arm from the static discharge. The others noticed as well, and it didn't take much prompting with shouts and gestures toward the stairs to get them moving. Hoisting Khulani between them, Enguer and Aelrindel once again took charge of one of their companions. They paused at the second floor, where Qel retrieved the sphere, as the others quickly agreed to keep going until they were once again huddled in the hallway outside the tower. The noise was muted with the closing of the door.

Khulani was in bad shape. Two of the platinum rods were driven into his ribcage and one all the way through his lower abdomen with a short section of it sticking out his back. Blood soaked the clothing around the wounds, but given the druid's injuries Qel might have expected far more.

"Let's cut these robes off," Enguer shouted as he shifted Khulani onto his side while Aelrindel and Reskalin proceeded to remove the heavy layers. "Careful now, I'll cut the fabric around the wounds."

The druid groaned from the movements, and his body shook with tremors. Presently he opened pain-filled eyes. Qel thought Khulani must be in shock. Enguer worried the druid might expire at any moment as he finished cutting away his tunic. Khulani's bared chest was a black palette of blue tattoos displaying geometric shapes and animal figures reminiscent of the marks they glimpsed on Perault. Sadly, a few of the beautiful designs were tragically despoiled by his traumatic injuries.

"H-help m-m-me see-e," Khulani tried to sit up to view the damage to his torso.

Enguer was reluctant at first, and instead he tried to calm the druid. "Be still Khulani, let us stop the bleeding."

"T-t-the bleeding i-is inside," he gasped. "I m-m-must t-try t-t-o save m-myself."

Qel handed the spere to Aelrindel and knelt beside the druid grasping his hand. "Tell me what you need. I will be your eyes."

"W-what is t-t-the color of-f the b-blood?"

"Red around the wounds in your chest," Qel studied the injury in his abdomen where the rod entered and crouched low to view the druids lower back where the rod exited. "Slightly darker red on your stomach and very dark, almost purple from your back."

Khulani closed his brown eyes for a long moment. The tremors wracking his body subsided, and when he opened them again, he licked his dried dark lips, and asked in a rasping voice, "May I have water?"

Enguer complied, helping Khulani drink a little from his waterskin. Then he put it aside. There was deep concern in the ranger's eyes. "Your injuries need attention, Khulani," he said hesitantly. "If you can tolerate the movement, we will try and carry you to the closest temple."

"There is no time," Khulani shook his head causing beads of sweat to run down his face. "The wave will soon be on us. I have only one choice for a chance to live, but I must leave you."

Reskalin dropped to her knees, and with tears in her eyes said, "You have already saved us, Khulani. Do what you must to save yourself."

He nodded. "Thank you Reskalin, I will try."

Aelrindel, standing above them holding the sphere, was sniffing at the air. "I smell smoke. The fires in Naamah's chamber must have spread to the other rooms. It won't be long before the entire manor house is engulfed in flames."

"Yes!" Khulani agreed. "The corridor where we found Vadim and Fain was burning when I left it."

"Will the brothers Vampyr be a problem for us again?" Qel was unsure how to phrase the question regarding the death of immortals.

"They are gone forever," the druid assured them. "Now listen. When I say, pull the rods from my body as swiftly as you can." Evidently, Khulani noticed the doubt in Qel's and the others expressions. "Do not fear! The pain will give me the vigor I need to shape-change. Then, Sunna willing, I will make it through the storm to the Druids Enclave south of Ys. But we must hurry."

"Khulani . . ." Reskalin began. Tears glistened in her eyes and strove down the sides of her face.

"Shhh, mother," he interrupted with a clever smile. "We save our words for a better time. Now, get ready."

Reskalin smiled sadly, and joined Qel and Enguer, each grasping the end of one of the platinum rods impaled in the druid.

"Now!" Khulani's hoarse shout merged into an agonizing scream that became a long mournful howl as his damaged body abruptly wavered, shifted, and enlarged into the massive form of a Dire Wolf.

The beast's insightful grey eyes played over Qel and his companions. It stepped toward Reskalin on silent paws larger than a man's face and gently nudged its great forehead against her abdomen. She gently stroked the long coarse fur atop the wolf's head, before it twisted away with a swift jerk, and loped down the dark corridor in long hurried strides.

"Let's get out of here and find a safe place to shelter until the storm passes," Enguer threw the platinum rod he pulled out of Khulani onto the floor where it clanged with a sharp metallic ringing.

"Go ahead," Qel urged. "I will find you later. But first, I have to know what has become of Havacian."

Reskalin touched his arm. "He defied Zracul to save us. To save you. Havacian would want you away from here and safe."

"I agree," Aelrindel held up the orb. "And without this, Zracul's plans will come to naught, even if he lives."

"Everything you say is correct, but still, I must know." Qel smiled at them. "Call it an Atlantean character flaw."

"Then we will wait," Enguer acquiesced, nervously glancing at the smoke slowly crawling across the ceiling of the corridor that led to the front entry of the Agrabuta.

Qel would not endanger his companions over his folly. "Take the sphere away from here as fast as you can. I will be quick up the stairs, then meet you out front."

Reskalin and Enguer immediately objected citing a liturgy of reasons not to leave him behind. To Qel's relief, Aelrindel spoke up, although himself seeming decidedly unfavorable over his own words. "We must go. I know Qel well, and he will debate us until the Agrabuta is burning around our ears." He clutched Qel's shoulder with his free hand and squeezed tight. "Go with haste, my friend."

At first, he thought Enguer and Reskalin would argue further, but the arguments died on their tongues after a silent exchange of wiggling fingers at each other that Qel found curious. He made a mental note to ask them about it later. With great reluctance, Enguer clasped his hand and Reskalin hugged him tight, before the trio followed the corridor in the steps of the Dire Wolf.

Qel did not wait a second longer. He pulled open the tower door, pushed through the burst of air that rushed behind it, and took to the steps two at a time. The noise was no less deafening, but now there was the additional crash of falling timbers and sharp cracks of heat-stressed stone. Gusts from above brought the heavy smell of smoke and burning wood and the lambent light from fire grew brighter with his ascent.

The second floor was littered with timber embers and ash blown from the floor above. What was left of the books struggled to ignite from the hot materiel, but the powerful winds kept the flames at bay. Qel gained the third floor to an infernal scene. The ceiling was a roiling conflagration dripping fire and embers caught up by the swirling winds in the room until they chanced to be flung from a window, down the stairs, or collide with one of a half-dozen massive timber buttresses hot with glowing cinders strewn at odd angles where they fell.

Qel peered through the haze of whirling debris searching for Havacian. He first found Zracul. The creature was crouched low, chest heaving with his back to Qel, staring across the hellish chamber at the vague form of Havacian stooped near the far window. His friend made a pushing motion redirecting the torrent of rain pouring in from outside into a horizontal mass of frozen projectiles which he flung forward with great speed, piercing Zracul like thousands of tiny daggers. He leapt away roaring with agony, and reappeared near the center of the room sending a blast of force that thrust Havacian into the wall with such power that large chunks of stone blew out the other side leaving a jagged hole behind. Qel suddenly realized there were many such holes all around the room. To his relief, Havacian slowly extricated himself from the wall and regained his feet if somewhat unsteady.

Havacian was always a quick study when it came to academics and arcana, more so than Qel at any rate; however, the Havacian he saw before him was exponentially more powerful, and not just due to the new abilities he attained as a Vampyr. Qel almost choaked on the word in reference to his friend. Havacian had grown substantially in the strength and breath of his capabilities with the arcane literally overnight. In the few minutes elapsed since Havacian first burst into the tower, he had stood his ground and singlehandedly fought Count Zracul to a stalemate. Qel looked for a way he might shift the scales.

He glanced back to Zracul, and was startled to see the monster's black glare from hollow eyes staring back at him. The creature smiled and thrust his hand forward sending crackling arcs of lightning his way. Qel threw up his arms in a vain attempt to fend off the attack when a rush of water, like a horizontal waterfall, deflected the deadly bolts. A cry of malignant glee rose from Zracul's throat followed by the pop and crackle of electrical discharge as jagged branches of lighting enveloped Havacian in a writhing cocoon of blue electricity that scorched his flesh and caused his muscles to spasm. Qel despaired. Havacian had fallen into Zracul's trap saving him! He had to do something. Even if his friend couldn't die from the lightning coursing around his body, it might incapacitate him leaving Zracul to do with them both as he wished.

Qel looked at the ceiling and focused his arcane energy on the fires above. He was a wizard of the Red Hall, Elemental Fire was his domain, and he would use it to his advantage. Qel willed the fires to flare with heat, build pressure in the stone above the burning rafters, raise their internal temperatures to the breaking point. Enclosed withing the high shelter of the ceiling little affected by the wind, the fires drew volumes of oxygen from the churning whirlwind below. Flying debris climbed higher on the hot currents of air; paper and wood combusted, platinum rods turned molten, everything was consumed in the rising inferno. Zracul appeared to take no notice or care. His focus was on the destruction of Havacian, an endeavor he pursued with great delight, roaring with maniacal laughter.

Masterfully, Qel manipulated the balance of heat in the stone ceiling taking care not to allow any portion of it to fail until he was ready. The stone was several feet thick due to the fortified nature of the tower which was also served as the floor for the fourth level above. It was open to the sky with a crenellated wall around the perimeter, an ancient relic of manor houses built for not only comfort, but defense.

Zracul's laughter rioted above the howling winds of the maelstrom, fueling Qel's anger. Havacian made no sound, nor could he with every muscle trapped in desperate convulsions. Higher and higher the temperature rose so that not even the air rushing around him could dispel the heat. Sweat formed heavy on Qel's brow; Zracul was sweating too. The tower's interior took on a bright orange glow from the lowest stones in the ceiling churning with magma. Qel held it all in check until the balance was just right. Zracul's laughter stopped as the creature jerked his gaze urgently to Qel, his black eyes wide with alarm not comprehending the full meaning of the environmental shift in the chamber. Qel smiled. He knew. And released his hold on the ceiling.

A rumble shook the tower. Still confused as to the danger, Zracul released Havacian and jumped straight up with all speed anticipating the floor to fall from under him. Rather, he leapt square into the plummeting magma followed by untold tons of stone as the top of the east tower collapsed in on itself. Qel though he heard a brief shriek before the weight of the falling tower buckled the third floor. Qel was falling. Fear took hold with a savage grip, but he had no regrets. In mid-fall, something hit him hard, knocking the wind out of his chest, and he found himself gasping for breath in tall soggy grass. Through glazed eyes he watched the east tower collapse into a massive pile of rubble flaring with burning timbers and fast cooling magma awash in the rain.

Someone helped him up to his feet. Havacian. His friend was hardly recognizable with so many hideous scorch marks and deep rending slashes crisscrossing his swollen face, darkening his blond locks. It was his eyes, returned to their normal state, that assured Qel it was indeed, the man he knew.

Wordlessly, Havacian grabbed him in a fierce embrace, and whispered, "I will always remember." And then he was gone, leaving Qel standing alone against a maelstrom without, as well as within, for he knew in his heart he would never see Havacian again.

– – –

"Look!" Reskalin cried as they huddled under the eaves projected over the front door of the Agrabuta.

She pointed toward the east tower. Although they could not hear the collapse above the storm, its fall was clearly evident even through the driving rain. Then two figures appeared as if from the air. One standing over another on the ground. It bent to help the other up, they embraced, and suddenly there was only one. Reskalin would know that profile anywhere.

"Qel!" she shouted into the wind.

Reskalin, Enguer, and Aelrindel all raced across the grass hill to their Atlantean friend. Initially startled by their unexpected appearance, they huddled together laughing and hugging, giddy from so long on a razors edge of tension and emotion. Reskalin doubted any of them expected to survive the Agrabuta. Now they must survive the storm.

"It's here," Aelrindel cried out, gazing toward the sea.

They all turned in time to see a wave of titanic proportions crash over the seawall obliterating the Sea Gate, and roll into the massive harbor. The sound of the impact reached them seconds later with a powerful reverberation that shook Reskalin to her soul. Enguer took her hand in his and held it tight. If the sea wall was fifty feet high, she reckoned the wave's run-up close to two-hundred with a shoaling that was already lifting hundreds of ships of every size and shape in its path. The wave rolled over the docks, inundating streets, and boulevards in a fast-rushing wall of water. When the wave front hit, the force of the impact demolished every structure within one-hundred feet of the docks, shattering taverns, shops, and warehouses jammed to the ceiling with crates and barrels. Towers toppled - many collapsing onto others as they tumbled like dried grain stalks under the plow. The whole of Ys was inundated in minutes leaving only the highest elevations untouched. Such was the Agrabuta, burning like a terrible beacon above a drowning city. They were safely above the waterline, with the heat from the fire at their backs.

Reskalin's heart skipped a beat as shadowy forms appeared around them on the hill, then someone gently took hold of her other hand. It was Siione. Her sister looked at her wordlessly with eyes heavy with moisture. Reskalin was sure hers reflected no less. The tragedy of this great and beautiful city was laid out before them in nightmarish reality with an incalculable death toll that even the hardest of men would be moved to lament.

Just before dawn, the rain subsided and the wind died down as the waters receded back into the Primal Sea leaving nothing less than a cataclysmic panorama of wreckage and death in its wake. A few dozen survivors managed to gain the hill during the flooding with the help of Siione's Reavers without any order given to do so. The hard, desperate, cold-hearted men and women at her sister's command acted with uncharacteristic care and empathy toward their fellow citizens that surprised Siione as much as anyone.

If anything good comes of this, Reskalin thought. *Maybe humanity, in the midst of blood and struggle, was as good a start as any.*

Epilogue

The great Dire Wolf loped silently out of the morning fog shrouding the dark forest into the central glade of the Druids Enclave like a ghost emerging just before dawn. Unsurprised by the beast's presence, the druids were making their way to the recumbent stone circle atop a high hill preparing for the first hues of daylight to color the horizon and thus begin the daily 'Rite of Sunna' – a morning dedication to the Goddess of the Sun. All this, the wolf knew well.

Panting from the exertion of running a great distance with no rest, the wolf shook its massive frame to expel the rainwater from its thick coat, then crouched on back haunches with tongue lolling from open snout to cool itself. Inside the mind of the beast, Khulani struggled to hold its form until after the morning dedications to Sunna were complete. Exhaustion coupled with pain from his injuries at the Agrabuta made the task seem almost impossible. He was fully aware that when he shape-changed back into his human form, his condition would be severe, requiring immediate assistance from the most skilled among the druid healers if he were to survive another hour.

Over the last few hours, the rain tapered away and the winds abated leaving behind a combination of earthy flora scents pleasant and invigorating. Overhead, the last of the dark tentacle-like clouds were dissipating into a misty haze as they passed in front of the waning light from Luna that still glistened in the droplets from leaves on tree and bush as well as the shiny reflective pools formed by frequent puddles. And as if to make up time lost to the stormy night, insects, frogs, owls, and other critters of the night joined in a voluminous discourse filling the air with a colloquy known only to a forest at peace.

Khulani worried about his friends. He would not have left their sides if there was any choice other than dying at their feet. The fire in the Agrabuta was spreading quickly through nearby corridors when he made his way out. If those same corridors he tread were impassible by the time his companions departed, surely, they would have found another way to escape.

For the Dire Wolf, leaving the Agrabuta was the easy part. It was avoiding debris tossed by tempestuous winds while searching for a way out though the city walls that proved his first difficulty. With the city gates locked down tight, and the walls too high to jump from without risk of injury, he ended up squeezing through an open sewer grate that passed through dark malodorous tunnels until he found a sloping earthen passage that exited at the edge of the forest. He could only guess it was constructed long ago by thieves and smugglers as a secret entry into the city. It served his purpose as well, otherwise, he might have died there in the sewers below Ys. The concussion of the massive wave impacting the seawall as the Dire Wolf climbed from the tunnel sank Khulani's spirits. And more so, the sight of falling towers and cracking timbers, before the deluge broke through the South and West Gates carrying unidentifiable debris that flooded well into the countryside and nearby forest such that the Dire Wolf was hard-pressed to keep ahead of it at first. It was an arduous flight from Ys; surviving the sewers, the deadly winds, and fast-moving waters in an endless flood, on top of the extreme exertions over so far a distance. Khulani's mind and body paid a terrible toll.

The wolf's large grey eyes witnessed the final devotions to Sunna as the bands of purple and blue hues gave way to lustrous ambers and radiant golds over a horizon of blue sky unmarred by dark clouds. With little effort, Khulani released the aspect of a Dire Wolf, returning to his natural form. The druids descending the hill after the ceremony quickly realized their brother's grave condition and immediately came to his aid. Soon Elder Sactria, the Archdruid, was by his side with the Council of Elders looking on.

The healers desperately worked their magic and medicines, and made no secret that his life hung by a thread. Knowing this, Khulani spoke the tragic tale of Ys between gasping breaths, trembling shock, wrenching pain, dilated vision, and sense of impending doom creeping over his consciousness. When he told all there was, he made a plea to the Archdruid, "Bring our people to Ys. Help them. So many have been lost already. So many innocents. Give them aid. Go to Ys!"

Tears ran down the sad continence of the Archdruid. The shake of her head was barely perceptible when she said, "I want to aid them, Khulani. You know that in your heart. We all do," she gestured to the Elders nodding sorrowfully behind her. "Yet to do so, even now, would put us at odds with the priests. You know this well, and the dangers to our way of life it invites. We cannot go to Ys, but those who come to us will receive relief and comfort."

Khulani despaired at the Archdruid's words. His sight dimmed. He felt his body and soul sinking into darkness.

From far away he heard one healer cry, "We're losing him!"

Khulani sank deeper and deeper into the void.

"Stand back!" The Archdruid bellowed. "Sunna guide me through the darkness . . ."

A luminous glow surrounded Khulani, he felt the embrace of warm radiance, he no longer despaired, his mind was calm, serene, even as he fell into dark oblivion.

Two weeks later, Khulani opened his eyes to the warmth and welcoming light of Sunna.

– – –

Down – down, the struggle was over. A calm descent embraced her, the toil of roiling waves and choaking seafoam forgotten far away. The princess was dead, yet not dead. Her body expelled the ocean from her lungs and took it back in again. Over and over. It was a cycle that would never end until she found air again.

This was precisely what Zracul warned her about when he alluded to the hazards of drowning as one of the few mortal dangers a Vampyr must be wary. For any other Vampyr, were it to occur, was a torturous prospect they could not easily escape on their own. As it was, Ahes was also the Greater Demon Aesmadaeva, and so there were additional options to consider. Thus, bound by her physical body, Aesmadaeva could allow Ahes to linger in the open waters where a predator would eventually consume her flesh thereby releasing the demon to search out another creature to possess or, find a way to shelter the princess until it worked out a way to help her adjust to the new environment. Aesmadaeva liked Ahes. The power in her beauty and charisma was unmatched by any creature ever to host the demon, and it wasn't ready to abandon her quite yet.

In the seconds Ahes was conscious between cycles of drowning, the demon could direct her path by a few feet. It would never be enough to reach the surface, but with luck it could get her to a place where her body might be safe for a while. So further and deeper into the Primal Sea, roughly north and west, did the demon direct her brief struggles to swim, keeping low among the coral and sea grass to avoid notice by anything large enough to make a meal out of her. Days passed below beams of wavering sunlight. The nights were dark, cold, and gloomy, occasionally highlighted by mysterious luminescence of varying shape and color far away. In the early days nothing of significance disturbed the surface high above, until a week passed, and the hull of a ship encrusted with barnacles, muscles, and tube worms cut a line over the sea in the direction of Ys. Aesmadaeva wondered at the success of Zracul's plan. Were his brothers and sisters building the Vampyr army he dreamed of even now? Those wretched sisters! They were the reason the princess was at the bottom of the sea instead of by his side. Ahes should have ripped them to pieces and burned their bodies to ash when they confronted her in Zracul's bedchamber. Perhaps there would be another meeting one day.

Nearly two weeks passed when, during the night something that felt like an arm curled around her waist and swam with haste among a group of similar creatures that bore the semblance of greenish-blue skinned men above the waist and scaley iridescent fish tails below. The princess's memories recalled legends of the fish folk known as Morgan who lived under the sea in a fabulous city men called the 'Rock Garden.' Sailors feared them, sailing wide where the Morgan were known to haunt the shallow reefs that ringed their city. There were stories of those foolish enough to be lured by their sirens to a watery death, and tales of vessels devoid of crew and cargo found adrift not far away. It was said the Morgan consumed those they drowned, but no sailor lived to offer a first-hand account. If this were truly the case, the demon would soon be looking for a new host.

Aesmadaeva suppressed Ahes's drowning response to quell her movements so they would think her dead. Even so, the Morgan quickly realized there was something unusual about the body they discovered and so brought the princess to their king, or so the demon assumed, since it did not understand their language. That changed as Aesmadaeva quickly worked out their strange whale-like dialectology and soon understood their communications. It seemed they thought Ahes to be some equivalency to a witch or sorceress since her body did not react to long periods under water the way other humans always had. She did not breathe, nor did she bloat or decay for reasons that eluded even the wisest of them. They discussed cutting her to pieces, but feared doing so might release a banshee that would haunt their city. Finally, they agreed that the safest solution would be to entomb her within a sea cave under the city, and that's exactly what they did. As far as Aesmadaeva was concerned, it was the perfect resolution. For while she remained isolated and unharmed, the demon slowly worked enchantments upon her, initiating an evolution to the environment that gained her proper function and expression.

A year passed. On the eve of the festival celebrating the return of plentiful migrations for the Wintertide, Princess Ahes opened her eyes. Breath filled her lungs through gills along the curve of her neck on both sides, she saw through special membranes grown over her eyes, long flowing silvery finlets raced down her limbs to webbed hands and feet, and her blonde hair shown like flowing threads of gold. She would be the most beautiful creature among the Morgan, and the most terrible. For once she moved aside the rock that sealed her cavern, much blood would spill before they would accept her as their new monarch: 'Queen Ahes' of the Morgan.

– – –

The smoldering ruin of the Agrabuta was hardly remarkable against the backdrop of devastation that claimed the magnificence of Ys. The rubble of grey stone turned black with ash was still hot to the touch in many places, and if the stately manor house ever boasted of a luxurious interior with fine furnishings, libraries of rare and ancient books, and priceless antiquated art, surely no evidence remained. The Agrabuta burned hot for three days without intervention from anyone in the city since there was no danger that the fire would spread beyond the isolation of the hill where it blazed like a mighty torch leaving nothing of any worth or value to recover.

Zracul knew the heat of those stones well. He was trapped under several tons of them for nearly a week, slowly cooking, and at the same time protected from the flames that would have destroyed his body entirely, forcing Ornias, the Greater Demon sharing his mind, to find another host. He lay under that dark pile for days until Jaria and Daria could finally bear the heat enough to dig him out. It was a sad reunion. They cried bitter tears when he informed them of the fate of their brothers and gave not a single word of protest when he ordered them to return to Vradesti, such was their despondence. Zracul knew it wasn't just for Vadim and Fain they wept, but for the dream they all shared of ruling over Plethwih with an Empire of Vampyr. He had much time to ponder events which led to his near entombment under the rubble of the Agrabuta, and came to the harsh realization that the dream was nothing more than folly.

He gazed over the ash-sundered remains of the Agrabuta for the last time. There was nothing left for him here but hollow memories. Especially his memories of Ahes. For weeks after the deluge he searched for her. Jaria and Daria claimed to have last seen her on the seawall with her father. If she had gone into the sea, she was lost to him forever. He didn't want to believe that was the case, even as the plausibility of her demise in this way was an ending he would have to eventually accept. It was true that a Vampyr had no capacity for love, but it could experience heartache and loss. These emotions ran great within him, often giving over to bouts of wild rages that, if left uncontrolled, would soon gain the attention of the Atlanteans. And there were far too many powerful Atlanteans in Ys these days.

Damned Atlanteans! He pounded a gloved fist in his palm. How could he not have anticipated their response to the deluge? Did he really believe they would just flee back to the Emerald Isle? He underestimated the Atlanteans empathy. How is that surprising since he possessed none? Yet that was the first fact that brought him to understand that even had they succeeded, and rampaged among the population killing, feeding, and transforming them into Vampyr as planned, they were doomed to fail. Once the Atlanteans arrived with their airships full of powerful wizards and priests, a conflict would ensue that the Vampyr could not win.

Secondly, had it not been for that devil Havacian showing up in the tower, Zracul would never have known that every Atlantean they transformed would become an even more powerful adversary they could not control. Just one Atlantean Vampyr was almost more than he, 'the Father of Vampyr,' could deal with, let alone dozens or hundreds. He, his brothers, sisters, Ahes, and maybe even Naamah, were all blinded by the dream.

There would never be an Empire of Vampyr. Such organization would make for an easy target. No. The Vampyr would proliferate in the shadows, dark alleyways, gloomy dungeons, and dim spaces fliting like ghosts silent and unseen in every part of the world feeding, waiting, until one day, if the Vampyr rose again, they would already be among the people.

Zracul turned from the Agrabuta with a dramatic flourish of his black cape and mounted the thickly muscled jet stallion waiting for him. As he pulled on the reigns, the powerful mount reared its front legs puffing a blast of smoke from flared nostrils. The nightmarish steed set off with blazing eyes and fiery hooves carrying Zracul toward the city gates on a route that would end in his distant home of Vradesti, leaving shattered dreams and a broken heart in the ruin of Ys.

Blurred images shifted unsteady to Perault's bleary eyes as he attempted to squint beyond the bright light to gain a sense of his surroundings. His head pounded from a blow he received on the back of the head – when, he didn't know. Reaching up he discovered a bandage wrapped around his skull and winced as his probing fingers found what had to be a deep laceration and possibly a fracture on the right side of his head.

He was in a quiet place. No howling winds rushed down alleyways, no thunder shook the ground. There was no screaming or desperate pleas to uncaring Gods. Just the murmur of soft voices in calm cadences of conversation. The air was tepid with a little humidity, yet he felt himself shiver despite the blanket pulled over his chest. It smelled clean, with strong hints of lavender and alcohol that he recalled as a peculiar feature of Atlantean medicine, so he wasn't surprised when a bluish blur appeared over him.

"You are awake," a kind feminine voice stated. "If you can speak, tell me if your vision is unclear."

Perault's attempt to speak produced a dry croaking noise.

"Take a little water." A cup was pressed against his bottom lip and tipped just enough to allow a small drizzle to moisten his throat. When it was pulled away, the woman said, "Try again."

"I . . . I cannot see well," he managed in a hoarse whisper.

"As I suspected," the blurry face nodded. "It's not an unusual result when one receives a blow to the head as serious as yours. Close your eyes. I'm going to stimulate the nerves between your eyes and brain. You'll feel my hands on your temples and then a spinning sensation. Don't worry, it's nothing unusual. If you feel nauseous, let me know."

Perault closed his eyes. Almost immediately the woman gently lay her soft warm palms over his temples with the light pressure of her long fingers within the tangle of his hair. The warmth on his temples grew, and there was a subtle shift in his perception that lent the impression of floating, followed by a mild rolling sensation which quickly escalated. He wanted to open his eyes to relieve the disorientation and realized the woman had repositioned her palms over his eyes and clustered her fingers on his temples.

"Relax," she said soothingly. "Try to remain calm."

He felt as if the room was about to spin wildly out of control and although logic suggested it was all in his head, he desperately clutched at the side of the narrow cot to avoid getting flung away. It kept getting faster, faster, and faster still. He tried to speak. He wanted to know how long it would last, but only gibberish escaped his tongue.

"Relax," the Atlantean repeated. "Calm your mind." Her assuasive voice helped not in the least!

It was too much. He wanted to grab her arms to pull her hands away from his eyes, but they flailed about like limp ropes as soon as he released the cot. It took all the strength he could muster to hold fast again. He heard himself scream. The screaming went on and on even as the woman's consoling voice spoke, "Relax, we're almost there. Don't fight it."

Then everything stopped. He no longer felt her hands over his eyes, and thus opened them to see a beautiful face looking down at him. A shock like lightning coursed through his body. Naamah! He blinked and she was gone, replaced by another beautiful face. This one was blue-tinted with long almond-shaped eyes, angular nose, and thin reddish lips. Soft brown curls dangled from her elongated skull.

"You see me clearly now, yes?" she smiled warmly.

Perault felt pain in his heart like never before and, without shame or remorse, broke down sobbing, consumed with loss, while the Atlantean woman, knowing nothing of his lost lover, held his hand in compassionate silence.

Later in the afternoon, Perault sat on his cot, back propped against the canvas wall, supping from a steaming bowl of lentil soup. The Atlantean woman, whose name he learned was Schemali of House Droygan, turned out to be a Priestess of Pontus who specialized in the arts of healing and medicine. She was encouraged by his progress, so she said, suggesting he would be fit to resume light activities within a week. To her credit, Schemali never once asked what it was that caused him such raw anguish. Perault was glad he didn't have to contrive an answer.

He glanced left and right at the line of cots next to him under the wide sloping canopy that connected again, and then again like the segments of a twisting centipede, occupying the space of boulevards and avenues around the Atlantean Tower. The tents were filled with survivors of the maelstrom, many with head injuries like his own. None of them spoke, except to Schemali, if even they could. A few simply groaned quietly in the tangent light while shadows played over the canvas walls from figures passing on the road outside.

"You seem to be recovering remarkably well."

Perault was startled from his ruminations, unaware of Schemali's approach, nearly dropping the now empty bowl cupped in one hand.

"Sorry," she grinned, taking the bowl and placing on a small side table. "Let's have a look at the wound on your head. Are you feeling any pain?"

"Just a dull throbbing. I am feeling much better thanks to you," he offered an appreciative smile while she unwrapped the bandages around his head. "Can you tell me where we are and how long I have been here?"

"Certainly," she gingerly probed the areas surrounding the gash on his head with the tips of her fingers. "You were brought to us covered in mud and blood the morning after the flood by a pair of soldiers. They said they recovered you from the rubble of a fallen tower. That was almost a week ago. You were lucky. Aside from the injury to your head, you suffered only a few scratches and bruises. The soldiers thought you might be a wizard with those curious tattoos on your chest."

Perault sagged. The long tunic he was wearing covered the tattoos. He was glad they were covered as he couldn't bear to look at them. "I'm no wizard," he muttered.

She pulled a small covered croc from one of the many pockets of her white flowing apron-like gabardine tied over the front of her priestly robes. "I agree, but those tattoos are quite unusual. Now, hold still. I'm going to apply a bit of ointment to the wound to keep the infection away. It may sting a little." Schemali lightly applied the ointment and almost as an afterthought commented, "I would guess you are a Temple Knight."

Perault's gut constricted. He sat up straight and rigid with a jerk that caused the priestess to step back in surprise.

"Are you unwell?" her large eyes were wide with concern.

"How could you know I am, was, a Temple Knight?"

Schemali resumed dabbing the ointment on his injuries. "You developed a very high fever the day after you arrived and became quite delusional. You spoke the name 'Naamah' many times, and lastly chanted verses; however, all I understood was 'honor my King,' and 'serve with bone and blood' or some such," She shrugged, retrieving a long strip of folded linen from another pocket with which to bandage his head. "I admit that I shouldn't assume so much, but you do have the look of a knight."

The words she uttered had a chilling effect on Perault. He knew well the Oath of the Order, as did all Temple Knights:

I hear the call from darkness, and come into the light.

I am born once again unto Sunna,to live in her sight.

To defend her teaching and follow her faith,

And never reveal the secrets of the order to which body and soul I am endowed,

Ne'er to commit murder, deceit, or lie,

To honor and serve my king and my lord,

Upon pain of death and ruin upon my soul,

In her Grace, I shall serve with bone and blood and spirit,

With every breath within me to the end of days.

"That reminds me," the Priestess stepped back to scrutinize her handiwork with the bandage. "Another man in our care heard your cries and took an interest in your condition. I believe he, too, was a Temple Knight. He was well enough to leave us, but he returns every afternoon to look in on you. I suppose today his patience shall be rewarded. Can I get you anything before I move on to my next patient?"

Deep in thought, Perault merely shook his head.

"Very well, I'll come by again later tonight."

As she walked away, a sudden thought occurred to Perault and he called out, "Schemali, do you recall the man's name?"

The priestess paused in her stride, turning back with knitted brows as she considered, "Lugaid. Yes, that's it. A knightly name, is it not?" she smiled and continued down the row of cots.

Lugaid.

Perault could not recall a Temple Knight or anyone else he ever met by that name. He wasn't particularly surprised. There were hundreds of Temple Knights, and surely, he did not know them all. He supposed a Temple Knight happened to be in Ys during the maelstrom, took an injury, and was looking in on a fellow knight as a courtesy. Regardless of Lugaid's intent, Perault was not prepared to face anyone from his Order. He had renounced his Oath to Naamah, accepted her as his mate knowing what she was, and allowed himself to be marked by her. Perault felt no guilt or regret. He just needed time to come to grips with his current situation. And loss.

The druid, Khulani, said Naamah no longer controlled him after they murdered her. *Had he been controlled?* Perault contemplated the possibility. He knew Naamah charmed men she victimized to feed upon their seed. She had done the same to him in the beginning. Now that she was gone, wouldn't her hold on him have died with her? Yet he felt the pang of bitter loss, a longing for her, love. It had to be real. Real for him and real for her. He couldn't see it any other way, even now. Just admitting such a thing was blasphemy, a desecration of his Oath to Sunna, the Order, and king. Thus, he could no longer name himself a Temple Knight.

It was nearing evening, and if this Lugaid was true to schedule, as most Temple Knights tended to be, the knight should be arriving soon. Perault had no other choice, he had to leave. Searching around the cot, he was relieved to find a short stack of folded clothing and a pair of low boots underneath the side table. The clothes weren't his, but since he arrived wearing nothing but his skin, they must have been placed there so he would have something to wear when he departed. He hastily dressed, taking care not to arouse the attention of Schemali or the other caregivers within sight, and slipped under the canvas that formed the wall behind his cot.

The waning light of late afternoon was bright enough to cause Perault to squint as he peered up and down the street. The chaotic scene of almost apocalyptic destruction took his breath away. Everywhere, rubble crowded the bases of broken towers, buildings, homes, and temples. Among the debris, many items representing daily life were sad reminders that the structures were places people called home, and likely died when they fell. The jagged skyline of Ys still lingered with the dusty haze of obliterated stone and plaster, yet the streets were mostly cleared in the week since the disaster, allowing people to move freely, if dispassionately, about their business under the watchful eyes of soldiers keeping order in the turmoil of madness.

With his eyes slowly adjusting to the light, Perault was able to orient his location in the city by the unblemished Atlantean tower capped by its luminous crimson crystal. The tower served as the center point for the canvas tents twisting down the nearby streets and alleys leaving a narrow space for folk to pass. He had travelled down these ways many times before the flood, but now, nothing looked the same. As his eyes continued to take in the ruined panorama all around, he abruptly stopped and stared into the distance. It was the hill where stood the smoking remains of the Agrabuta. Perault was beset with terrible anguish, and just as he felt his knees about to give way in total despondence, a pair of powerful arms reached forth to hold him steady and a voice called his name.

"Perault? Perault? Is that you?" The man's voice seemed to call from a distance, but something about the familiarity of it drew Perault back from the edge of hopeless abandon. He lifted his head and watery eyes locked on a face he had not seen in some time.

"Drystan," Perault wondered if he was hallucinating. "Is that you, or am I seeing his shade?"

"It is I," Drystan helped him to sit on a chunk of stone from a broken from a fallen tower. "I should ask the same of you. With that bandage on your head and the farm clothes you are wearing, I almost didn't recognize you. Shouldn't you still be in the infirmary? You don't look well."

Perault took a moment to wipe away the moisture from his eyes and collect his thoughts. He was grateful Drystan's wide frame blocked his view of the Agrabuta on the hill. The last time the two had occasion to meet was at the wedding of Drystan's uncle, Duke Maruk of Lyoness to Princess Eselt, youngest daughter of the High King Cadeyrn of Eriu, in Valiant Keep at Tintagel. Their meeting nearly came to blows. At the time, Perault thought little of Drystan. He viewed him with scorn as a matter of fact, and considered him unworthy of wearing the cloak of a Temple Knight. Perault's reasons were uncomplicated. Prior to the nuptials, when Drystan was escorting Princess Eselt's entourage from Teamhrach, in Eriu, to Tintagel, they stopped along the way at Stoddenferry Castle where Earl Fineas Eckert, Perault's father, hosted the wedding party for a night. It was during their stay that Perault accidentally discovered the love affair between Drystan and Eselt. Since Drystan was a fully recognized Knight of the Order with an impeccable reputation, Perault did not expose the scandal, instead, he made it clear that he was aware of it and anticipated Drystan would break it off in disgrace. Some months after the wedding, he learned that Drystan and Eselt ran away together. Duke Maruk was so incensed that he sentenced them both to death after they were captured. However, there would be no executions as Drystan managed to escape and rather than go to war with Eriu over the execution of High King Cadeyrn's daughter, Duchess Eselt was instead exiled to the Vally of Leprechauns. Somehow Drystan rescued Eselt from that terrible fate and as far as Perault knew, they had been on the run ever since. Drystan was a fallen knight who Perault had considered a traitor to his Oath, a man too weak to resist the love of a woman, dishonored, and unredeemable. It was almost comical they should meet here in Ys, face to face, with Perault's betrayals and dishonor no less egregious.

"I was fleeing from a Temple Knight named Lugaid," Perault admitted, "whom I know now must be you."

Drystan's forehead furrowed with confusion, "We both know why I would have cause to disguise my identity, but what reason could you have for fleeing from a brother of the Order?"

"I have not been kind to you, nor would I have reason given your crimes if I was the righteous champion of the Oath that I thought I was," Perault stared down at the dusty road, shoulders sagged in defeat, "but I'm not."

"So, Perault Ekert of Stoddenferry Castle, not yet a full Knight of the Temple, has found humility?" Drystan snorted. "Perhaps it is miracle enough to earn the gold-fringed cloak!"

Heat rose to Perault's cheeks, he glared up at Drystan and growled, "This is not to be made light of." If he had the strength, he would have punched the man in his smug face.

"I'm sorry Perault," Drystan's tone sounded genuine, and his eyes took on a more serious set as he sat down on the block of rubble next to him. "Tell me what has changed."

The two knights sat shoulder to shoulder on a dusty grey block broken from a tumbled tower for the next hour while Perault told his sad tale. He left nothing out, there was no reason to hide anything, averting his gaze from the smoking ruins on the hill that stood as a memorial to Naamah, his lover and mate. Drystan stared in wonder when he showed him the markings tattooed on his chest, and his mouth formed a grim line when Perault explained what they represented. As night fell, Perault spoke with unquieted emotion about how Naamah died, and with her death, his shattered heart. Drystan put an arm around his shoulder and shared Perault's tears. Soon after, Perault allowed Drystan to help him back to his cot in the infirmary where he fell instantly asleep comforted by the release of sharing his story, and more so because it was Drystan to hear it. For there was none other in all of Plethwih that could have understood so well the depth of his loss.

The next morning Perault awakened to the glow of the early sun illuminating the canvas wall at his back. Drystan lay on the next cot over, eyes refocusing from a stare of distant thought when Perault stirred. They both sat up eyeing each other expectantly.

"Good morrow," Drystan spoke first.

Perault replied with a quick nod, he was preoccupied with a burning question that he never had the chance to ask. "Drystan, where is Eselt?"

Drystan dropped his eyes to the floor. "Her father's men found us a day out of Ys and took her back to Teamhrach. I was wounded badly trying to stop them. I should have died."

"The part that confounds me, Drystan, is why you would allow yourself to be drawn to her knowing she was betrothed to your uncle?"

Drystan shrugged, "I can only say this: When the Atlantean Priest healed my wounds, he discovered a geas upon my mind of which I had no knowledge. When he removed it, my feelings for Eselt immediately changed. Although I still loved her, it was not the blind restless infatuation that drove me mad whenever she was away from me." A bitter smile played on his lips. "You see, we didn't have a choice. Now it's gone from me and breaking it likely ended the geas on her. Sometimes I miss it, never have I been driven by love so desperate and needful. Never will I have love like that again."

"I'm sorry," Perault understood well Drystan's plight. "I have been a fool to mock you, judge you. Sons of nobles, citizens of Lyonesse, brother knights, I should have not rushed to your conviction. I think Sunna must have a sense of humor that we have separately fallen, only to land together."

Drystan's mood appeared to brighten as he straightened his back, white teeth flashing behind a smile. "I think we'll finally be friends Perault Eckert. Recently I've decided to seek adventure in the world, forget about oaths, responsibility, tragic loves. Why don't you join me when you are well? We can discover our new selves together without bitter judgment or accusation!"

"My family is aware I came to Ys. When I do not return, they will assume I perished in the deluge," Perault heaved a great sigh as if released from a mantle of heavy chains. "If I am dead, all ties and obligations die with me. Perhaps it is time for me to live anew."

From the throats of more than a score of lizard-headed warriors rose an abrasive rasping hiss, coarse and intense like rocks scraped over a slab of stone. They splashed over the shallow swamp with wide curved swords held high or obsidian-tipped spears thrusting forward hungry for blood.

A plume of brackish water exploded beneath one scaled warrior lifting the creature high into the air until the thrust subsided and it fell from a height sufficient to shatter bones even in the sludge and mire that formed the expanse of this vast swampland. Several such lizard warriors lay crumpled dead or dying in their scale and hide armor which offered scant protection from the watery plumes Havacian erupted like geysers beneath their feet, keeping the small horde of Reptilians at bay. Havacian knew his time was scant. Soon enough, their leader would realize that the Atlantean could only cause so many jets of water to burst forth at one time, and order the warriors to swarm forward together, overwhelming the wizard with their strength of numbers ending the long pursuit. Havacian glanced at the monstrosity that led the band. Its beady black eyes sparkled with unexpected intelligence as it worked through primitive calculations in its scaley head. It was no mystery why this particular creature had risen above its peers to lead the tribe as the presumed chief. For not only was this Reptilian nearly twice the mass of the warriors it commanded, but also a mind quick and clever; at least as far as general battle tactics were concerned.

In the months following the destruction of Ys by Zracul with the Sphere of Elements, Havacian sought to discover a remedy to the unwanted condition that compelled a thirst for blood. Such was the 'infection,' as he called it, that should it not quickly be satisfied, Havacian would lose himself to dark rages he was powerless to control until his hunger was satiated. However, it was not blood that brought him to the Reptilian lands of Mu, it was hope. Hope from an obscure source where he discovered the hint of a legend involving a relic used for rituals in the greatest of their dark temples. If the scrap of lore were true, the ancient relic was used in purification rituals, imbued with divine powers by an unspecified god that might be used to cleanse Havacian's tainted blood. How he would come to possess it, he did not know. So far, he hadn't managed to cross the first few miles of swamp into Mu before being sighted by a patrol.

From atop a small rise in the mire, the Reptilian chieftain called a halt to the probing attacks. A ring of his warriors surrounded Havacian at twenty paces; a distance any of the creatures could easily leap with little effort. The chieftain barked orders that sounded more like a series of grunts, hisses, and tonal growls. Havacian comprehended nothing of their language, but he understood the message as the warriors' postures adjusted for what they all knew would be the final assault. It would be impossible to stop them all. The chieftain held aloft his huge saw-edged battleaxe with one thickly corded arm and glared with joyful triumph at his doomed adversary.

Dropping his gaze, Havacian stood erect to show off the full elegance of his Atlantean form. In contrast to the Reptilian Warriors heavily muscled frames, Atlanteans were a lean people notable by their wide shoulders, narrow waists, elongated skulls, blue-tinted skin, and average height of seven feet. It was an intimidating pose to folk familiar with Atlanteans who often revered them as nearly God-like, "Enlightened Ones." These Reptilians knew little of the Atlanteans and so felt inconsequential fear facing the tall fragile looking blue man wearing tattered robes soaked through with stinking swamp water. Still, as a wizard trained in the School of Elemental Water, known casually as the 'Blue Hall' within the prestigious Enclave of Imperial Wizards situated near the center of the wonderous City of Atlantis, there was much Havacian could do to survive the terrible odds set against him on this pale afternoon. Yet that was the rub; he was now in the unenviable position of fighting for his survival. The darkness inside him knew this and no matter what brilliant plan he might conceive to overcome the assault when it came, Havacian would lose control when his lust for blood was excited to volatile frenzy. This he knew with certainty. This he accepted. He had no choice but to give into the impulse. The only consolation was that he would remember none of it.

The Reptilian chief barked a wild grunt that caused ripples across the waters as he thrust his battleaxe forward to emphasis the fateful command to charge. A tempest of green scaley bodies encased in hide and scale with teeth gnashing and blades flashing in the last light before sunset roared forward unrestrained. Eager maws sought the tang of living flesh, the satisfying crunch of bone and rip of sinew.

What they found instead was death.

To any that might bear witness from afar, the exultant roar of promised victory soon turned to shrieks of terror, wails of pain previously unfamiliar to the dismal swamp or for that matter, the pitched howls of terror, until then, thought beyond the vocal range of any Reptilian.

– – –

"So, the sphere has been left for us to dispose of," Qel muttered as he and Aelrindel rode through the forest north of Ys on great black steeds once belonging to Count Zracul. "The way to the Ouria will not be easy."

Aelrindel pulled up on the reigns stopping his horse at the edge of a small grassy clearing that overlooked the winding curve of a freshwater brook babbling over stones rounded and smoothed by time. "This is a good place to make camp. I will gather what's needed to build a shelter." The elf dismounted, tied his horse to a low hanging branch, and smoothly strode through the trees and out of sight.

Qel never felt more alone. Of course, Aelrindel was a fine companion and friend, but lacking Havacian left Qel sour and embittered. Exhaling a long sigh, he dismounted and went about the task of clearing branch, stone and leaf from the glade that would serve as their home until the port of Ys was open again and they could book passage on a merchant ship to the Emerald Isle.

Although Qel would have preferred to stay in Ys helping where he could to relieve the suffering or assist in the process of rebuilding, he and Aelrindel were the obvious choice to take the Sphere of Elements to the Emerald Isle where they planned to ascend the Atlan Mountains and drop the sphere into the Ourea; a massive active volcano dominating the southern spine of the isle. They all agreed this was the best course of action. If the sphere was not destroyed in so doing, it would at least be impossible for anyone to retrieve. The only debate on the matter concerned how to get the it from here to there. Qel suggested they seek the aid of his fellow Atlanteans at the tower. As one of their own, his words on the matter would hold significant weight and no doubt secure transport on one of the Airships bringing supplies from Atlantis to Ys on a daily schedule. And considering the urgency to dispose of the potent artefact, thus preventing further nefarious exploitation, one such Airship might have taken them directly to the Ourea with haste. However, Reskalin was quick to point out the downside of the plan. Going to the Atlanteans would make the sphere known to many within the hierarchies of influence that might want to study it's powers for a time, with good intentions, before it was destroyed forever. Qel had to concede this possibility. It was decided the sphere should remain unknown, and accompanied by Aelrindel, Qel would quietly chaperone it to a quiet destruction.

Qel glanced at the innocuous burden strapped to the back of his horse. Fortunately, it weighed very little, the only inconvenience being its bulk. The sphere was wrapped in tattered hides to obscure its true nature and dissuade curiosity. For the same reason, they made their camp away from the dreary city to keep it safely out of sight and reach of desperate burglars or lingering Vampyr. Every day, either Qel or Aelrindel returned to Ys to mark the progress clearing the harbor. Despite the supplies brought daily by the Atlantean Airships, it was only a fraction of what was needed for the city to survive. As word of the tragedy spread throughout the Western Kingdoms, the sails of merchant ship big and small appeared on the horizon and set anchor to await a spot to berth. The Ysian marines worked at a remarkable pace and within a week opened enough of the harbor to allow ships temporary moorage where they were directed to quickly unlade their cargo and quit the dock for the next in line.

Another week passed before Aelrindel returned with the news that he found a Mouillian merchant ship departing for the City of Atlantis. They hurried to clear the camp and made it back to the harbor just in time to get aboard, no ship was allowed to linger at the dock for any reason once their cargo was offloaded. The dark-skinned, brightly clad crew proved highly efficient, and the crossing to the ringed Atlantean capital was fair of weather and without incident.

Qel marveled at the sight of his home. Although he lived most of his life there, it was a rare occasion that he viewed the city from the vantage of the sea. It was nearly sunset, and the lingering amber rays caused the surf to sparkle like a sea of diamonds. Just beyond, rose the exterior ring of Atlantis bound by a high wall illumed with fiery gold orichalcum cladding under the shadow of a massive temple lined by towering white columns atop the high elevations of the central island. Higher still, the grandiose temple lifted the colossal effigy of blue-skinned Pontus thrusting his great golden trident toward the sea. It was a sight that drew the breath and gave pause to every soul on the ship.

On any other occasion, when the need for haste and secrecy was not so great, Qel would have liked to call upon his family and stay for a few nights. Instead, they took a series of ferry's which shuttled them through the consecutive land-rings surrounding the central island and onto the far side of Atlantis where the city joined the land. From there, they rode out through the Gates of Atlan, west along the aptly named Atlan road, and into the countryside where they found a place to camp for the night.

The land nearest the City of Atlantis was relatively flat, populated by expansive farm communities and settlements where often grew row upon row of tall green stalks with leafy pod-like husks which at times shown the peak of the cob within surrounded by tightly packed pulpy golden yellow kernels arranged in even rows. It was a popular crop called Maize, borrowed from the Hisat'sinom peoples in the lands across the Primal Sea west of the Emerald Isle. In the near distance, pea pebble driveways led to massive two-story manor houses and surrounding outbuildings that served as the hub for each plantation. Travelling west, the far distance was dominated by the ghostly peaks of the Atlan Mountains, a range of peaks commonly referred to as the spine of the Emerald Isle. Rising above them all, stood the impossibly high white-capped smoking colossus of the Ourea, an active volcano that from time to time shook the foundations of the isle. Left unattended, it would have threatened life on the southern half of the continent. Qel knew that from the earliest days the Ourea was artificially stabilized through the arcane efforts of Atlantean wizards in partnership with the Dvergr Dwarfs who devised a certain expertise when it came to the intimate workings of deep stone and earth. In fact, one of the first lessons Qel learned in the Red Hall was that the Wizards Enclave was originally established for the purpose of controlling the dangerous agitations of the great volcano.

Beyond the arable land grew the westward sprawl of endless trees over rolling hills which marked the slow migrating incline toward the high elevations still two-hundred leagues distant. Many varied creatures called this untamed wilderness home. Most were beasts spawned in the natural course of evolution, yet there were some with a more dubious origin. No few vagabonds from the tumultuous history of the Tuatha De found haven in these lands, and here too would the contrivances of arcane inventions be set loose by creators unable to control their monstrosities or the stomach to destroy them. This was a dangerous wild land that many an explorer wandered in wonder in search of places of natural beauty expansive and breathtaking to behold. Here too were an abundance of legends, some true and some contrived, about treasure and ancient magical artefacts enticing brave adventurers of every ilk deep into the embrace of the forests, caverns, and mountainsides. Few returned to add their tales to the histories, while the ivory remains of those fallen to horrors and perils lay as stark warnings to the next foolish traveler.

It was through this wilderness that Qel and Aelrindel journeyed for many harrowing days and nights as the forest grew thick and dark, and the creatures within more clever and sinister. It was only for the grace of the Sylvan elf's expert skill as a ranger that they avoided dangers and circumvented hazards that otherwise might have permanently arrested their progress. Then came the arduous climb up the steep slopes of the Ourea with packs on their backs and the burden of the Sphere of Elements. Their beautiful black steeds, whose wide hooves plodded efficiently over flat ground could not scale the sharp inclines, and were thus left to roam free and fend for themselves as best they could.

For three days they clambered over sharp crags, vertical spans of rock, ancient flows of rough igneous rock, and treacherous escarpments with arêtes prone to rockslides, most often relying on ropes and pitons to make their way. Qel's experience with rock climbing was practically nil, yet Aelrindel's patience and guidance helped him surmount every obstacle without incident, if slow going. When they finally reached the icy crown of snow and ash, the wind grew bitterly cold and strong gusts threatened to blow them off the side falling to a brutal death far below. Upward, a dimly orange-red glow silhouetted the jagged edges of the craterous maw of the Ourea through the haze of acrid steam. The climb to the edge of the steep-sided opening was easy to navigate, although their lungs struggled for oxygen in the thin air, and they knew they had very little time to linger at such an extreme elevation.

Lying prone on his belly next to Aelrindel, Qel stared with unbelieving eyes over the vast bowl-shaped depression that funneled to a vent wherein the glow of superheated magma bubbled and spit far below. Heat and noxious gas rose with the lethargic plume of an ash cloud which could be seen as far away as the City of Atlantis. How many times had he stared from the safety and comfort of his family home at the very spot where he lay now. Never in a thousand years would he have imagined himself where he was now, or even thought himself capable of getting there. From a distance the white crater at the top of the Ourea appeared small and unthreatening, but closeup it had to be over a thousand spans to the opposite side, and to gaze down the broad vent was dizzying.

It was impossible to speak with the lack of air and abundance of poisonous gas; it was impossible to breath. Aelrindel released the straps on his back holding the sphere and handed it over to Qel. It was still wrapped in the tattered hides made rigid by the extreme cold which peeled off easily to reveal the dull blue-glowing Sphere of Elements with clouds swirling like the maelstroms it was capable of summoning just beneath its glass-like surface. Out of breath, Qel held the Sphere over the edge of the crater and glanced toward Aelrindel. The elf nodded, and Qel released the enigmatic orb, watching as it bounced off the edge of the funnel and disappeared down the long shaft. It was strange how tiny and insignificant such a powerful artefact looked falling into the terrible majesty of the Ourea. Whether or not the sphere was destroyed, Qel would never know, but he was satisfied that no power on Plethwih could ever bring it back.

Nearly a week later, Qel sat opposite Aelrindel with a small campfire between them. They were only a few hours from Atlantis, but the evening was clement with a clear sky that shown bright with stars with few distractions. The next day would find the two travelling separate paths; Qel to Atlantis where he would reunite with his family; and Aelrindel to Avalon City to recite the tragic tale of Ys to his father, a close advisor to the High-King of the Sylvan Kingdom, before returning home in Braetling.

"You have a sad task ahead," Aelrindel stoked the fire with a few small branches. The campfire was more for comfort than warming on this night, with little fear of bandits or beasts so close to the City of Atlantis. "What will you tell Havacian's family?"

"I do not know," Qel sighed. "To say he is dead is not entirely true or false. To say he is in private retreat to pursue arcane research is misleading at best. Nothing I say will be entirely true, accurate, or factual."

Aelrindel pondered quietly for a time, and said, "Why not tell them the truth?"

Qel shook his head, "How can I? If they chose to find him, with the best intentions, their lives would be endangered. If they chose to seek the aid of the Enclave, or the Temple, or the Palace, lives would be endangered. Havacian provided little guidance in this matter other than to warn me to stay away from him while he searched for a way to undo what was done to him. He chose to isolate himself so that I or anyone else would not be exposed to his condition."

"That is wise," Aelrindel Agreed. "Do you plan to keep it a secret from everyone?"

"Regarding Havacian, yes. However, I must inform the Enclave of the existence of Vampyr. They are a threat to all living things with a terrible potential for spreading like a pox." Qel squinted at the elf through the firelight. "What do you intend to tell your father?"

Aelrindel's long narrow brows knitted over steady eyes, "I too, will advise him of the Vampyr among other things," he paused. "But I will honor your decision and reveal nothing about Havacian. Our friend deserves a chance to alter his fate without being hunted."

Qel was relieved. Anything Aelrindel told his father would then be known by the High-King, and soon after the Emperor of Atlantis, the Elders, the High Priest, Archdruids, everyone. He decided to change the subject, "Will you stay long in Avalon City?"

"A few days only," the elf's eyes lit up and his thin-lipped mouth slowly curved into a smile. "I look forward to returning to Braetling. I hope you will come to visit soon."

"I must!" Qel laughed, feeling the tension dissolve around him. "I promised to bring Tolia a few of the games Atlantean children love to play. It would be good to see Tridi and Vnae as well." Qel often thought about how much he enjoyed the last time he was in Braetling. It was only a few weeks before he, Havacian, and Aelrindel arrived in Ys. Vnae was Aelrindel's sister, Tridi her husband, and Tolia their little girl who Qel enjoyed playing games with while he and Havacian were their guests.

Aelrindel laughed with him, "You should hurry, then. It won't be long before Tolia will decide trees inspire more stimulating conversation than any of us!"

Qel recognized the popular joke among the Sylvan. As Tolia grew older, she would develop into a Traetling, like her mother, and her mother's mother. Traetlings, or 'Tree Whisperers' as they were otherwise known, were uniquely Sylvan with the ability to communicate with trees and coax their growth into shapes that could be used for habitation, bridges, and elevated walkways among other things.

Long into the night Qel and Aelrindel recalled stories that made them both laugh, gave them hope for the future, family, and happy times in a world where they witnessed so much hate, cruelty, evil. They and their friends saved Plethwih from untold loss of lives at a high cost to their own. Havacian, Perault, Khulani, the Reavers. So many thousands in Ys died or became forever altered in some way they did not choose. All because of the avarice of one man, demon, Vampyr, or thing called Zracul that held no love for anything or anyone beyond ambition and power. The creature was defeated for now, but Qel feared deep inside that Zracul or something like it would not be long in coming, and he had to do everything in his power to make ready Atlantis.

A loud piercing wail, quickly joined by a second, brought Enguer out of a dead sleep to an immediate state of readied action.

Lying next to him, Reskalin kicked his thigh under the heavy eiderdown. "It's your turn."

He sighed, rubbed his weary eyes, and sat up in bed. "It's a damned cold winter," he complained.

"So why don't you rekindle the hearth before you bring me our lovely caterwaulers," Reskalin's muffled voice called from beneath a mound of bedding.

"Very well," he complied, dragging a blanket over his shoulders before plodding over to the hearth to add a goodly stack of sablewood.

Beleaguered by the continued wailing, Enguer worked as quickly as he could to bring warmth to the room before retrieving the tiresome monsters demanding to be fed at ungodly hours of the night. He had not brothers or sisters growing up, thus his experience with babies was practically nil. Why Reskalin had to go and give birth to two at once he could not fathom, unless it was simply to bring him misery. Enguer immediately regretted the thought. Yes, they made him want to pull his eyeballs out the back of his head, and the lack of sleep often made him disagreeable, but by the Gods his heart nearly burst with joy every time he saw their little faces gazing up at him.

From the next room, the howling duet suddenly stopped. Enguer was impressed. The pair must have synchronized their intake of breath for their next stretch of yowling. It didn't come. His ears perked up to listen. Nothing. Slightly alarmed, he reasoned that the nursemaid, who normally went home for the night, might have stayed over and was changing the children before bringing them out of their nursery. He had to be sure. Just as he turned from the hearth and took a step toward the door, he had his answer. Coming through the open doorway strode the FatMan with a tightly swaddled bundle in each of his massive arms. Only the babes faces shown topped by tufts of jet hair as each sucked loudly on one of the FatMan's thumbs.

Perplexed, Enguer asked, "Is Millie here?"

"Millie?" the FatMan replied with a shrug. "Is that the nursemaid? She goes home for the night, you know."

"Who changed them?"

"Well, I did," the FatMan's tone was indignant.

Enguer was incredulous, "You?"

"I did raise two daughters, so I might know a thing or two," a clever smile grew on his face. "I can give you a few pointers if you like."

Before Enguer could respond, Reskalin called out, "Would one of you two fools bring me my children before they starve to death?"

Enguer took one of the infants from the FatMan. Big brown eyes studied his face and to his delight there was recognition behind them. He reluctantly handed the tiny swaddle over to Reskalin and announced, "Here's Peci."

She took the babe, and removing the swaddle lay her flat against her breast to latch. "This is Sethra, dear. Now bring Peci."

Enguer brought the other one, looking at her closely. "How can you tell the difference?"

Reskalin lay Peci on her chest next to Sethra, and covered the pair with a light blanket. "Isn't it obvious?"

"Not to me," Enguer sat next to them on the bed. "Perhaps we should mark them."

Reskalin flashed him a dangerous look while the FatMan groaned and departed the chamber shaking his head. Enguer was only half in jest. For the life of him he couldn't tell the two apart, and doubted the FatMan or even Reskalin could either. They were born only two weeks ago, and Enguer fervently hoped they would develop some small difference he could recognize as they grew, otherwise he would be known as the addled father who could never get his children's names right.

He drew his feet up on the bed and lay contented next to his little family. Reskalin dozed. Enguer's thoughts wandered in these quite times as they would often do, and he thought again of their last days in Ys. How many times this moment might have never come if things turned out differently. He smiled when he recalled how emotional Reskalin was during that time and, most especially, how foolish she felt about it later. Who would have thought Reskalin would become a doting mother of twins? As a matter of course, there were those who strove to take advantage of what could be perceived as a vulnerability when they returned to Arre. This was a mistake. Only a handful of examples were required to make the point that underestimating Reskalin was a perilous proposition, soon learning the Raven became a viscous tigress when she had something precious to lose. No less so was her father, the FatMan.

Still, the aftermath of the deluge in Ys haunted Enguer dreams. By some estimates, as much as a quarter of the city lay in complete ruin, and if that were so, the remaining three-quarters were only marginally better off. Worse than the destruction was the death toll. Thousands died in that terrible night. Some drown in the flooding, others from falling buildings and towers, and many were washed out to sea with the fast-receding waters after the surge. Rumors circulated that King Gradlon disappeared in a heroic effort to lock the Sea Gate, and tragically his daughter Princess Ahes, was missing as well. Both were presumed swept out to sea as they were last seen riding swiftly along the seawall. Marshal Dounair was the de facto ruler of Ys until the city was sorted out. He was a good choice, Enguer believed, as Marshal Dounair's experience commanding the defenses of Ys lent well to the organized relief efforts and prospects of eventual reconstruction. Remarkably, Siione's Reavers worked incessantly to clear away rubble, seek out survivors, and recover the dead. Reskalin's sister commented that a change came over her elite rogues that night. Not just one or two, but all forty-nine who survived the battle with the dead-walkers and the subsequent flood. She was at a loss for words, but Enguer could see the pride in her eyes. However, the most extraordinary occurrence involved the Atlanteans.

On the day following the deluge, a massive five-masted airship with sails billowing brightly in the late-afternoon sun cast its shadow over Ys as it slowly passed over the city and docked near the apex of the Atlantean tower were glowed radiant the crimson orichalcum crystal that cast its enigmatic glow across the skies of Ys day and night. The ship disgorged hundreds of Atlanteans along with enough food and fresh water to bring relief to the survivors of Ys for at least a few days. Enguer overheard one Atlantean remark that even in the City of Atlantis it was rare to see so many Atlanteans gathered in one place! And they were not just common Atlanteans, if such existed, they were healers from the Temple of Pontus, wizards from the Imperial Enclave, hosts of Atlantean Marines wearing their glass-like Aurinium armor carrying Aurinium swords and pikes, and noble men and women who worked tirelessly to alleviate the peoples suffering as best they could. To their credit, the Atlanteans worked in concert with Marshal Dounair, and not a one of them was too self-important to do the hard and dirty work needed. Over the entirety of the time he was in Ys, Enguer saw no less than one or two Atlantean Airships arriving with food, water, and other supplies daily.

Enguer and Reskalin stayed in Ys for two weeks after the deluge lending their skills where needed, but when Reskalin became unwell, an Atlantean healer advised that the stress was having an ill effect on her pregnancy and prescribed lots of rest until term. Of course, Reskalin was sure she would be fine and wanted to stay in Ys a while longer. She was especially drawn to the children orphaned by the deluge, comforting them during the day, and sobbing in her pillows for them at night. The emotional stress was too much. Enguer finally convinced her that it was time to go back home to Arre and plan for the arrival of their own children. Siione was set to join them. Prior to the deluge, she was sent by the FatMan to Ys for the purpose of overseeing a replacement for the recently deceased Master of the Thieves Guild. This she accomplished; however, a missive arrived from the FatMan the day before they planned to depart. He suggested that she stay a little longer to assist the new GuildMaster with restructuring. She wasn't happy about it, but after a few choice words and shattered ale mugs, she relented. There were tearful goodbyes when they departed Ys. Enguer found it remarkable how Reskalin and Siione, two powerful strong-willed women, broke down in tears in each other's arms with sobbing promises to keep in touch and for Siione to come to Arre when the babies were born. He came close to commenting on the irony of the relationship between the two, but wisely thought better of it as he would likely be hung by his toes from the ship's masts for the return journey.

So here he sat months later, with two beautiful baby girls smiling and cooing at him in joyful wonder. He knew some day the clever pair would contrive ways to twist him around their fingers to get what they wanted with their pretty smiles and innocent pleadings. He was okay with that.

The next afternoon, while lounging in the warmth and comfort of the FatMan's luxuriously furnished sitting room, Enguer took the quiet opportunity to read a book. The twins were napping in their nursery down the hall and Reskalin lay with her head on his lap staring at the flames in the hearth. These were the moments he cherished the most.

A tapestry parted as the FatMan silently entered the chamber. By now, Enguer knew his furtive movements were not a deliberate attempt to act clandestine, rather it was a natural gait born of survival from decades of surreptitiously governing a massive organized crime syndicate that spanned nearly every city in the Western and Southern Kingdoms, otherwise known as Thieves Guilds. Yet there he stood, one of the most powerful figures in Plethwih, appearing as obese as his name implied, wearing what Enguer could only describe as a bathrobe.

"I just received a curious message from Siione, in Ys," he said, holding up a small parchment.

Reskalin sat up. "Good day, father," she sighed.

"Oh yes, good afternoon to the both of you." He glanced around. "Where are my little darlings?"

"Napping for the moment," Enguer replied with a weary smile. He knew that if Sethra and Peci were in the room, the FatMan would have barely taken the time to fling the message at them before giving all his attentions to his 'little darlings,' as he called them. The funny thing was, Enguer could not have stated that the twins brought a change over the great GuildMaster. It was strange how his name was generally invoked out of fear or respect, or that he had a ruthless reputation when it came to guild business. Quite to the contrary, in the time Enguer had known him, he never witnessed the FatMan issue order or action that was unfair or cruel in any way. In fact, his intolerance was primarily for those who committed cruel acts or abused power and influence themselves. The FatMan never allowed his people to prey on the innocent, weak or poor, and woe came to those who defied his directives. Perhaps it was because of those instances that the FatMan was so feared.

"I suppose they need their rest," the disappointment on his face faded away as he returned his attention to the message from Siione. "Anyway, it seems the Reavers have had a sort of spiritual awakening or something. She thinks it was brought about mainly by the trauma they experienced at the Agrabuta and the suffering they witnessed in the aftermath of the deluge. In any case, all forty-nine of them resigned from the guild 'en masse' and formed what they are calling 'The Order of the Broken Hearts.' She wants to know if she should have them all killed."

Reskalin barked a laugh. "Just like Siione," she snickered. "Always choosing the most extreme solution. I miss her."

Enguer was alarmed. "You're not going to allow her to kill them, are you?"

"Well," the FatMan scratched his bald head in thought. "The Reavers were best of the best of the murderers, thieves, and smugglers in Ys trained as an elite fighting force that could strike anywhere and anyone from the shadows. They'll be hard to replace. Plus, it doesn't look good if the guild allows members to come and go as they please. Loyalty is paramount, you know."

"That's true," Reskalin agreed. "Is this 'Order' they formed going to be competition for the guild?"

The FatMan shrugged. "According to Siione, the Reavers, or whatever they are now, have been working with Marshal Dounair and the citizenry to help get Ys back on her feet. Apparently, they are so highly respected that the Marshal is planning to knight them all, and officially recognize their order after he is coronated as the next King of Ys."

"That's ludicrous!" Reskalin laughed again. "Can you imagine these hard-nosed, scar faced, outcasts strutting around Ys wearing the surcoat of a chevalier?"

"Sisters of a like mind, I see," the FatMan held up the message and pointed to a line. "With similar sentiments she referred to them wearing the mantles of Paladins." He smiled broadly and winked at Enguer. "I suppose we can let them be for now, as long as they don't return to their old ways. The people of Ys need as much hope as they can get under the circumstances."

A ruckus of hungry howls arose from the nursery down the hall. Enguer and Reskalin stood up to attend to their children, but the FatMan gestured for them to sit back down.

"I'll see to them," he said cheerfully. And with a spring in his hefty step, he practically skipped down the corridor singing a bawdy tune.

"The last time I heard him sing like that was when I was a little girl," Reskalin mused.

Enguer put his arm around her shoulders, pulling her close. "I didn't think you knew him very well as a child."

Reskalin shook her head as if to dislodge the memories. "It was only a brief time. Right before he ran off with your father, my natural father, Aelrindel, and the others on some mysterious mission after that Myrllin fellow showed up. I spent the next decade in the care of my father's foul-mouthed, rough neck lieutenants learning the business of the guild."

"I recall the story," Enguer sympathized. Then he cocked his ear to listed. The twins were quiet again, but the FatMan's tune had taken a decidedly vulgar turn of verse. "Should we intervene?"

"Why bother," she giggled. "They don't understand his words, and by the time they are old enough I'm sure he'll have them thoroughly corrupted anyway"

Enguer knew it was a jest, but he couldn't imagine those two little seraphs as anything but innocent little girls who would always bring the glint of delight to their father's eyes.

Reskalin jabbed him with her elbow. "Why don't we take advantage of the little time we have and go back to our bedchamber and warm the blankets?'

Enguer was on his feet before she finished her words. "A boy this time maybe?"

"If you get me pregnant again, Enguer Rand," she punched his arm, "I'm going to geld you."

He laughed, opening the door. "By the way, what is the FatMan's real name? Our girls might ask one day."

"I never told you?" there was genuine surprise in her response. "It's quite funny, actually. His real name is. . ." The door closed, muffling the sound as they scurried down the corridor to their rooms.

A few minutes later the FatMan entered the sitting room carrying a happily gurgling infant in each arm.

"Hello?" he peered around. "I guess it's just us, then," he told the girls as he carefully lowered his heavy frame into the oversized lounge chair built just for him.

"Listen here," he said, gazing from one to the other. "Have I ever told you about the grand adventures of a priest, an elf, a ranger, and a mighty wizard led by a wily rogue? Well, they called their group 'The Five,' and what a legendary gaggle of heroes they would so become. Of course, the rogue was the by far the most clever and handsome of his companions, and we shouldn't forget witty, since he was known to. . ."

Thus ends the tale of ***The Broken Pithos Saga***.

Cast of Characters

Note: (m) indicates male and (f) indicates female.

Drystan (m) – Adopted son of Duke Maruk, Temple Knight of Sunna, and Eselt's lover. AKA Sir Lugaid of House Gille Fhaolain, Knight of Eriu.

Enguer Rand (m) – A ranger trained by his legendary father, Gaurin Rand. He grew up in Courth, and for a time was a member of the Royal Order of Rangers who tracked down and killed the Lukánthropos.

Havaciante of House Talika (m) – Atlantean Elemental Water Wizard on a 'Journey of Discovery' with his best friend Qel. He is a recent graduate from the Blue Hall of the Imperial Enclave of Wizards in Atlantis.

Jaria (f) and Daria (f) – Younger twin sisters of Prince Zracul who turned them to Vampyr by his blood.

Khulani (m) – The first druid to come from the Imaziyen tribes.

King Gradlon (m) – Ruler of Ys, Holder of the Seagate Key, and father to Princess Ahes.

Myrddin Wyllt (m) - Myrddin Wyllt, a sorcerer of some repute often spoke prophesies that came true. He likes to drink to excess, and when drunk freely speaks of how he has prophesied his own death, which would happen by falling, stabbing, and drowning.

Myrllin (m) – The Mad Bard, the Prophet, the Sage, the Steward of Hy Brasil. He is a powerful wizard with an obscure past, known by some to possess the ability to foresee the future with varying degrees of clarity. Myrllin lives in a castle-manor on the mystical island of Hy Brasil. When not needed, it is rumored that he hibernates, without aging for hundreds of years, in the dark halls of his home on the mystical island of Hy Brasil. He is the son of the legendary Tuatha Dé hero Dhroghan. His mother is said to be a Nymph Queen, and he is the twin of Wodanaz, whom he is older by exactly one minute.

Naamah (f) – Succubus who fled Cambria after Count Djago was defeated. A fiend herself, she was subsequently drawn to the greater power of Ornias (Zracul) and eagerly entered his service. Until she meets Sir Perault.

Prince Zracul (m) – Primogeniture of Vradesti in the Eastern Kingdoms. He is possessed by Ornias, Greater Demon Lord of Envy and considers himself the 'Father of Vampyr.' Lover of Ahes.

Princess Ahes (f) – Daughter of King Gradlon. She is possessed by Aesmadaeva, Greater Demon Lord of Lust. She and Zracul are lovers.

Qellel of House Mekali (m) – Atlantean Elemental Fire Wizard on a 'Journey of Discovery' with his best friend Havacian. He is a recent graduate from the Red Hall of the Imperial Enclave of Wizards in Atlantis.

Reskalin Rand (f) – Formerly Reskalin Alois, she is married to Enguer Rand. She is a talented rogue who grew up in the world of organized crime in Arre where her adoptive father, the FatMan, is the Guild Master. Her natural father was Tanais Alois, the Archpriest of Sunna in the Kingdom of Courth, deceased.

Schemali of House Droygan (f) – Atlantean Priestess of Pontus specialized in the arts of healing and restoration.

Siione (f) – One of Dyzig (m) and Gigot (m)'s lieutenants from the thieves guild in Courth currently working with the thieves guild in Ys on a secret project. She is also the eldest daughter of the FatMan, although this fact is known to only her mother, the FatMan, Reskalin and Enguer.

Sir Perault Eckert (m) – Provisional Temple Knight from Lyonesse. His father is the Earl of Stoddenferry.

Tipa (f) – The young and beautiful lady-in-waiting to Princess Ahes.

Vadim (m) and Fain (m) – Younger Princes of Vradesti and older brothers of Jaria and Daria. They are Vampyr by the blood of their brother Zracul.

Wodanaz (m) – The Wanderer, Famed Poet, and Minstrel, Seeker of Wisdom, Chronicler of the Fourth Age, Son of legendary Tuatha Dé Dhroghan and a Nymph Queen. He is the younger twin brother of Myrllin.

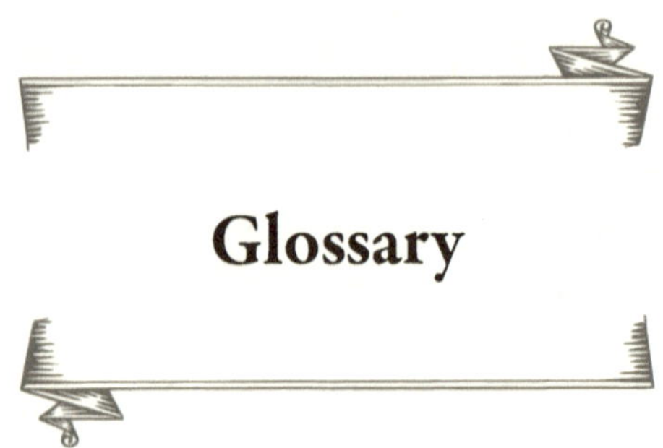

Glossary

Anurans - A long-dead froglike humanoid people who once inhabited Kiltullagh before they were annihilated by the Tuatha De.

Journey of Discovery – A Rite of Passage whereby Atlanteans graduating from the Imperial Enclave of Wizards go out into the world, experience life and new cultures, and hone their skills under real-world conditions for a period of five years.

Kiltullagh – Ancient ruined city once inhabited by the Anuran people.

Marimorgen (f) – Female merfolk residing in the Rock City within the Bay of Morgen. Like Siren, they have the ability to lure sailors to their death by the sound of their song.

Morgen (m) – Vicious mermen residing in the Rock City within the Bay of Morgen.

Morvarc'h - A magical steed with the ability to run on water.

Psionics - The use of psychic or mental powers, such as telepathy and telekinesis. Often employed to control, harm, or compel an individual of lesser intellect.

Tower of Tongues - An enormous tower with balconies thick with hanging ivies and vines that reach all the way down to its wide base. Here, Atlanteans resided amongst the peoples of Kur-gal in the city of Eridu a great distance away in the east. Further even than the Eastern Kingdoms. The Atlanteans claim that it is because of this tower that all creatures capable of speech can understand each other whether or not they speak the others language.

Vampyr – A condition which permanently imbues the affected with supernatural abilities as well as a form of immortality. The condition can only be transferred by ingesting the blood of a current Vampyr. To survive, Vampyr must regularly imbibe the blood of a living creature, preferably human.

Vikja – Barbarians who reside primarily on the Isle of Vikja and Tirnan Yog. They are raiders who also serve as the seafaring trade partners of the Dvergr Dwarfs.

Vrtog – Ancient Frog-God of the Anuran people. His effigy is depicted as a giant carnivorous frog.

Werdhom Enoch - The so-called language of angels and demons. Dark tomes reference it as the first language spoken on Plethwih before mortal folk walked the land or swam in the sea. It is unknown if there are any alive who can speak or understand the language in current times. The Tower of Tongues is ineffectual translating the Werdhom Enoch should it be spoken.

Translations

Werdhom Enoch

Vrtog gohon! Crip priaz iadanamad noaln gigipah. Babalon undl - niiso coraxo! – *Vrtog has spoken! Only those of undefiled knowledge may be receivers of living breath. To the wicked remainder – come forth the thunders of judgement and wrath!*

Volcam hoath, fafen, a Anuran! – *Bring forth my true worshippers, my followers, my Anurans!*

Ol torzvl od iolci babalon vovim baltim vonpho, teloah, fargt piadph ioiad! – *I shall rise and bringeth to the wicked dragon furious justice of wrath, of death, dwelling within the depths of my jaws for eternity!*

Imaziyen

"ISIN SUNNA, ASWE TIFAWT, amz s-saht!" – To Know Sunna, to drink (her) light, to receive health.

About the Author

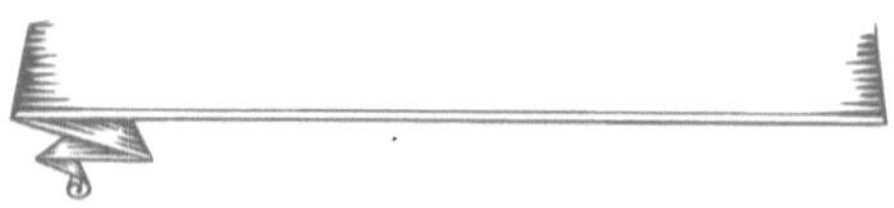

Born in Homestead, Florida, Ravek Hunter grew up in the United States and Belgium. He earned a bachelor's degree in marketing from Florida International University and went on to become a sporting goods executive. He currently serves as a consultant in the same industry and occasionally assists his wife of twenty years at her floral design company. The proud father of two boys, Ravek counts reading, exercising, and family travel among his leisure hobbies.

Over the past four decades, Ravek's passion has been researching ancient civilizations with a focus on the origin stories behind their mythology. His writing style attempts to immerse the reader into the story by bringing to life historically accurate, rich details of the culture and time-period that frame the narrative.

Inspired by classic fantasy authors like Robert Jordan, H.P. Lovecraft, Robert E. Howard, and R. A. Salvatore, Ravek writes to entertain and provoke his readers, who, he hopes, share his fondness for mythology.

Connect with Ravek Hunter

Thank you for reading *Ys: Legend*! If you enjoyed this novel, please consider posting a review!

Friend me on Facebook:

facebook.com/ravek.hunter.50

Follow me on Twitter:

twitter.com/RavekHunter

Subscribe to my blog:

goodreads.com/RavekHunter

Visit my website:

RavekHunter.com

www.ingramcontent.com/pod-product-compliance
Lightning Source LLC
LaVergne TN
LVHW091019080826
845145LV00002B/298

* 9 7 8 1 9 4 8 7 8 2 2 5 8 *